WHEN WATER WAS EVERYWHERE

when water was everywhere

A Novel

Barbara Crane

When Water Was Everywhere
Barbara Crane

Chapter 1 appeared in the Outrider Press Black & White Anthology series, 2011.

ISBN 978-0-9972609-0-8
Library of Congress Control Number: 2016901856

Cover and book design by Ellison | Goodreau
Cover image courtesy of Lee Mothes, Alice Hsieh and the Aquarium of the Pacific.
Author photo by Allison Knight Images

Note to the reader:
This is a work of fiction. It is inspired by the historical John Temple and Rancho Los Cerritos. All names, characters, and events are the products of the author's imagination. Any resemblance to actual persons, living or dead, or actual events is purely coincidental.

Printed in the United States

Lagoon House Press
Long Beach, CA
lagoonhousepress.com

For my husband

PART 1 water

[1]

Henry Scott bent double over his saddle. His eyes were closed, his face nearly hidden by his broad-brimmed hat. His body swayed precariously. The horse he rode looked no sturdier than he, a beast so devoid of flesh, it nearly appeared transparent.

A few people walked by on the road. Scott didn't notice. They glanced sideways at the horse, blinking once, twice, at the man's size, at the animal's withered body. Stilling their usual "buenas tardes," a greeting that came easily to their lips, they looked away. Though Scott could barely keep his seat, he appeared formidable, a tall man engulfed by a long horsehide coat, far too warm for a late September day.

Scott rode on. His horse kicked up small puffs of dust as it moved forward toward the pueblo of Los Angeles, tracking a straight line, as if it knew where it was going. To the north, mountains presided over a wide green basin, a gift of the rivers that ambled along the land in the dry season and thundered from mountain passes during heavy rains. The path stretched before him, dry and dusty—the rainy season wasn't upon them yet. He had risked his life to ride across the continent. He knew little about the weather or the people here. If asked, he would have said, "I know nothing about nothing," a man who gave himself no credit for the things he did know.

The presence of a horse and rider on his left side roused Scott from his stupor. He kept his eyes fixed on his pommel.

"Don Rodrigo Tilman," the man said. "A sus ordenes."

At the sound of the man's voice, the horse stumbled, throwing Scott off balance. He righted himself and looked at

Tilman. He saw a man well over twice his age and half his size. The older man wore a dark suit, like one a judge might wear in St. Louis, the last city that had seen Scott's back. His hat, though, was unfamiliar. Not the tall beaver hat a distinguished St. Louis gentleman would wear. It was, instead, wide-brimmed, made of leather and adorned with silver medallions around its flat crown. Scott couldn't tell whether the man was an American or a Mexican.

"You are going to the pueblo?" Tilman asked in unaccented English.

"Yes." Scott fixed his gaze on the pommel again. His size made his horse appear even more fragile than it was.

"And you are doing...?"

Scott couldn't answer this question. His reasons for traveling so far would take more breath than he had to explain. Night would come upon them soon. He was either going to have to bed down off the road or find a place to sleep in town.

He took a deep breath. "Anyroomsintown?"

Tilman showed no surprise at the man's quick rush of words. "Not many, señor. My man is off buying horses from one of the ranches. You can have his bed in the barn for a night or two."

Scott nodded yes.

"I'm going to ride ahead then. In a mile or so, you'll pass the plaza church. I live in a whitewashed house a little farther on. Go round back to the barn. Think you can find it?"

Another nod.

"Good." Tilman nudged his horse on with his spurs. The horse had barely started off before Tilman turned halfway around to face Scott again.

"I assume you're going to look for work?" Tilman didn't wait for an answer. "Come round to my office in the morning. Down the street from the barn. Above the store. Early." Each word was precise, each thought conveyed with purpose, all lost on Scott. He was thinking of hay—for his horse to eat, for him to lie on.

Tilman turned toward the pueblo once again and this time rode away.

Scott was too tired to be grateful. So tired he wasn't sure he could ride the short distance to Tilman's barn. A fragment of the Catholic Mass repeated itself in his head: "Ave Maria, gratia plena," Hail Mary, full of grace. Because he had heard the chant in a church he rarely entered, he didn't remember any other words, only the sighs of the hundred or so souls who were afraid enough of hell that they woke early on a Sunday morning when they could have used the sleep.

He crossed the Río de Porciúncula, which flowed out of the valley northwest of the pueblo. He passed the Zanja Madre, the Mother Ditch, an aqueduct dug forty years earlier to bring water from the river to the pueblo's small band of settlers. Past grape vines planted by an early French arrival and fields scattered here and there over the landscape.

The pueblo's settlement of humble buildings had looked small from a distance and not much larger as he drew closer. People stopped what they were doing, glanced up at him. Their complexions were darker than his. Mexicans. And darker. Indians. Africans. He had seen all their kind on the trail. In St. Louis, too, where people were more often the pale color of Englishmen. He knew he couldn't converse with any of them. Ignorant of Spanish, he had his mother to thank for schooling him in proper English, though her native tongue was French. He averted his eyes, wishing he could be as invisible as he felt; his hands clutched the reins more tightly than necessary.

By and by, he came to the pueblo's center. Two men pulled a large cart, empty, through the square. Women converged on the church. Dark shawls covered their heads; they looked like shadows in the dusk. A few children played on the steps. Scott made his way past the plaza at the same dogged pace he had kept for two thousand miles. One-story buildings, most of them the color of earth, flanked the road. Dust swirled around him as a wind rose. Warm. September. Evening. Wind. This is how he'd remember his first evening in the pueblo of Los Angeles.

That night Scott slept under a roof for the first time in one hundred eighty days. He fell asleep quickly but awoke sometime in the middle of the night. A dog howled in the distance. Leaves rustled against the roof. The wind blew harder, and the whole barn began to creak and sway. Or maybe it didn't. Maybe he was so unused to sleeping within a structure, he didn't trust the building to last the night. He sneezed twice, then shifted his position on the narrow pallet. At last he fell into a half sleep in which pine forests and deserts, bears and mountain lions moved in and out of view, too far away to touch, too close to ignore.

Scott ran his finger along the back of his shirt collar. The warm wind made his underwear itch. He smelled like a dog. He turned away from the office door, ready to descend the stairs he had just climbed.

"Come in," a voice called.

Scott crossed the threshold and paused, blinded by the sunlight that pierced a shutter slat.

Tilman looked up from his papers and saw Scott squinting. "These hot autumn days," he observed. "Adjust the shutter, will you?" The owner of the first store in the pueblo, he was used to giving orders. Scott did as he was told.

When he turned around again, the man who had talked to him on the trail was standing behind his desk. "Buenos días," he said. "Tilman. Don Rodrigo Tilman."

Scott nodded and shook the man's hand, surprisingly large for a man whose head barely reached Scott's shoulder. "Henry Scott." A cordial greeting and a solid handshake. More than he had expected. More than he ever got in St. Louis. Tilman sat down and turned back to his papers again, leaving Scott to stand in front of him. At last, Tilman looked up.

"So, you'd like a job?" he said. He adjusted the cuff of his full-sleeved white shirt.

"Yes." Silence pressed in on him. If he were home along the banks of the Mississippi at this hour, he'd be assailed by sound: steamboats waiting for cargo to be loaded before heading down river to New Orleans, shouts of a small army of laborers. The whistles and wheezes of a dozen boats made a din that would have disturbed God, if there were one. The country around his father's cabin on the edge of the city would be noisy, too, full of pesky chickens, crying children. Here in the pueblo, a donkey brayed, breaking a silence that spoke not of inactivity but of people, few in number, quietly engaged in work.

"What can you do?" Tilman asked.

Scott didn't know that Tilman had already taken his measure. The man Scott faced had made many good decisions from a single handshake, about animals from a single touch, although he would never admit that his success hung on such fragile knowledge.

"Field work, barn, stable," Scott answered. I can join a group of trappers and walk over the Rocky Mountains, he thought. I can walk twenty miles a day and get up the next day and do it again. I can stay out of the reach of bears and wildcats. I can come into town, appear before you looking more like a beast than a man. He felt his anger rise and then, just as quickly, disappear. Do? I can't do anything. If I could have done something, I would've stayed in Missouri.

"Can you read?"

"Yes," Scott exaggerated. He could sign his name, write a few words, decipher more if given a little time.

"Sums?"

"Yes." This was the truth. He was always good with numbers.

Tilman sat back in his chair. He stroked his clean-shaven

chin as he looked past Scott to the portraits of his wife and daughter above a small table.

"You are from...?" he asked.

"St. Louis."

"And how was your journey?"

Here were questions he could answer.

"Not too bad," he said. It was terrible—the mountains he climbed in uncounted days of rain and snow, the immense desert that nearly took his last breath. Fear of Indians robbed him of sleep and knotted his bowels. A man he befriended fell from his horse, broke his neck. Scott watched him die. Nothing except Scott's determination to put distance between himself and his father kept him going.

Tilman looked at Scott as if sizing him for a coat. His eyes were blue. Scott glanced up, then looked away. Blue as frozen water.

"Ever worked in a store?" Tilman asked.

"For a while," Scott said. "A dry goods store. Sold cloth...and things like that..." He had worked only a week before he was forced to quit. Had to collect his father, who was sleeping off a drinking binge in a widow's vegetable patch. Before climbing the stairs to Tilman's office that morning, Scott had looked in the window of the store below and seen familiar bolts of cloth stacked to the ceiling.

Tilman seemed satisfied. "You're how old, young man?"

"Twenty-one. Almost twenty-two." Scott hung his head. He felt judged, as always, by his father, his would-be employers and, mostly, by himself.

"How quickly can you learn Spanish?"

"Pretty fast, I think." Scott didn't know if he could learn Spanish, but he thought he could get by.

Tilman didn't hesitate. "You can work in my store. Sleep in my storeroom. I'll take a coin out of your pay every week for room and board."

He took up the sheaf of papers on his desk once again. "Oh, one more thing. Did you come past the mission?"

"Yes." The Mission San Gabriel occupied a prominent position along the road between the desert and the pueblo. You couldn't miss it. "See the padre?"

"Saw two. One old, one younger."

"How does he look?"

"Who?"

"The old padre."

"I...I couldn't say. I only ate a meal with them. Night before last." He thought for a minute. "I guess he didn't look very well."

"I thought so. Have to get out and see him. What did you think of the mission?"

That question was easier. "In bad shape." In St. Louis, Scott had heard tales about the Alta California missions. How wealthy they were, how imposing their buildings. This mission didn't measure up. The room he slept in was open to the sky, and he was offered only a few tortillas and a plate of beans. The water was delicious though, cool and clean.

"You think you could repair that mission?" Tilman asked. He didn't appear to be making a joke.

"Huh?"

"Have any carpentry skills?"

"Guess so. Built a house for my aunt once." Another exaggeration. He had helped others dig a cellar and raise the walls. He could use a hammer. Was that what Tilman wanted?

"Interesting," Tilman murmured. "All right then. Start tomorrow. Early," he said.

Scott eased his way down the stairs, leaning against the wall for support. Not even a day in town and he had a job and a place to stay. Oh, if his father could see him now.

He stumbled over the last three steps, landing unsteadily

on his feet, sure that Tilman would open the door any minute and rail about the clatter.

Behind the closed door, a chair scraped the wooden floor. Then, silence.

His father would have already been upon him, throwing punches, shouting, "Wha's wrong with you, boy?" The most accurate answer was, "Nothing," but that would further enrage the man. If Scott told him something favorable, his father hit him; unfavorable, he hit him twice. Or vice versa. No cause to his action, no connection between the statement and the act. Stinging slaps on his shoulder, hard cuffs to the ear, his backside hit with his father's belt, a switch, or when he was older and bigger, a tree limb. Knocked him silly more than once. As often as he saw the blows coming, they always startled him. From some place within him a voice whispered, Why me? Hard as the blows were to take, they were only to his skin, his stomach or face, his muscles, tendons, bones. Allowing himself, a grown man, to be taken unawares showed his true weakness, he thought. Toughen up, close your mind, expect the worst, he told himself. But every time, his father's brutality caught him by surprise.

Scott trudged down the road until he came to the plaza he had passed coming into town the night before. Two men leaned against the church wall. Striped blankets Scott recognized as zarapes covered their bodies; large-brimmed hats shielded their faces from the sun. The men looked at him idly, then turned away and resumed their conversation.

He kept walking. One group of low mud-colored, flat-roofed buildings and then another. A smoldering fire around the perimeter of a field and a few cornstalks told him the newly harvested land would soon be planted again. A vineyard next. Row after row of bushy vines. Men bent double, harvesting plump purple grapes. Fruit in late September—imagine that!

As he gazed at the field, he felt something strike his shoulder. Next to him was an Indian, his body swaying gently from side to side. The man was young, about Scott's age, but shorter by at least a head. His skin was dark; his hair, matted and coarse, fell to his shoulders. His narrow eyes and long nose gave him the look of a fox. Scott smelled liquor on the man's breath.

The man grinned at Scott before he stumbled away.

Scott walked on without giving the man another thought. He attempted to see his journey from beginning to end, but order eluded him. Instead, images tumbled forth like random drops of spray from a river. Each caught the light for a moment, only to drop quickly below the dark surface again.

He recalled pissing in a stream just over the highest mountains of the journey, his pee a bright flash in the sun's last rays. For days before, he had climbed steadily, slowly, until going up seemed like all he would ever do. At the top, he nearly wept. Moved away from the others. A long broad valley started a mile or so below and swept away, a curve of green, farther than he could see. Boulders the size of wagon teams loomed even larger as he and his comrades made their way down the mountainside.

He was part of a scraggly band. Fewer than twenty at the start, the number shrank as the journey wore on, a dozen experienced trappers and eight inexperienced "muscle" who manned the canoes, cooked the meals and put themselves out front when Indians approached. He was the most green of the muscle, so he pulled the worst duties—cleaning beaver pelts, ugly rodents, their death masks dominated by massive front teeth; rowing day after long day, then portaging through stinging nettles wearing a canoe like headgear. Freezing mountain mornings quickly became stinking hot afternoons.

No matter how hard he worked, he never questioned his decision to leave St. Louis. So desperate that he had crossed the threshold of a small cabin one morning and signed up for the expedition his cousin Ned had urged on him. "Sign says they need ten strong men. You don' have to know nuthin' about trappin' beaver," Ned told him, his eyes blinking quickly. "I'm goin'. Why don' you?"

Why don't I? Scott asked himself that night, curled into bed next to his three younger brothers. They'd never take me anyhow. But they did. Ned was too slight for the job, the men saw immediately. Henry Scott, however, was another matter. Big frame, large hands. They took him out back and told him to split a rail as a test, delighted when he did it faster than any of the other young men who'd walked in that morning.

The journey started in the spring of 1843 and was supposed to go as far west as the Yellowstone. The trappers would take their fill of beaver in the high mountain country—in addition to lynx, bobcat, fox and whatever else they could shoot or trap to adjust to the dwindling population and popularity of beaver—and return to St. Louis the following spring, their horses loaded down with precious pelts.

By the time they had traveled up the Missouri and started down the Yellowstone, Scott knew he wasn't going back. He listened to others talk. Three of the quieter ones planned to leave the rest, cross the high mountains and proceed to the Great Salt Lake. No one said exactly what he was going to do there, but it didn't matter. Scott sidled up to the group and ventured, "We'd be stronger as four than three." He said little during the twelve hundred miles they'd crossed together, but he could more than pull his own weight, they agreed.

They sneaked off one night while the rest of the camp slept. For the first time Scott was included in the shared laughter as they speculated on who was going to skin the damn beavers. They knew no one would come after them. They were free men after all. They swaggered around the campfire. The money they'd lose by not returning to St. Louis they'd more than make up in San Francisco or Santa Fe.

Turned out they were younger and more stupid than they realized.

By the time they reached the Great Salt Lake, they were sick of the sight of each other, tired of eating squirrels and rats and whatever fish they could catch. They'd spend a whole morning arguing about the best route. Sometimes they followed a stream for a whole day, sure that it led to a river, only to find themselves perched on a ledge overlooking a deep canyon. Scott usually sat off to one side and listened. The others regarded him as a dumb but amiable beast. They could count on him to fetch firewood or go off into the woods and return with a few birds, a squirrel or marmot—the slingshot had been a handy weapon in finding food for his brothers and sisters when his father was off drinking—a little meat they could share for dinner.

Gabriel, the weakest of the three, had the most difficulty holding his own, whether walking or arguing. He was the quickest to anger. Wasted anger about a soaking rainstorm. Righteous anger when the others wouldn't listen to his entreaties about which way to go. At the Great Salt Lake, he had had enough. He convinced Scott they should take off for the Pacific together. After all, Jedediah Smith had done it the first time twenty years before, and he, like they, had started in St. Louis. Scott knew Jedediah's story and didn't need much urging to keep heading west.

They left in the night, as the four had earlier deserted their companions; this time there was no laughter. Neither professed high knowledge about the route, although Scott's comrade never admitted he couldn't find the way. Scott simply took over figuring out the day's direction, using the sun as a guide.

How he found a route he didn't know. Expected he'd never know. Dumb luck. Not too much luck, when he got down to it. Enough to keep himself from starving. Enough to withstand days without water. His stomach shrank as his body, toughened by months on the trail, moved forward. Before the journey he thought of himself as a big dumb ox. Now he knew himself as a camel, moving forward through sun and heat, one foot in front of the other, expecting nothing, not even hoping for, water.

Luck ran out for his traveling companion. Well into the march across the southern desert, Gabriel fell when his horse faltered on a rock. He landed on his side, his chin pointed to the sky. Scott approached and touched him gingerly.

"Gabriel. You OK?"

The young man groaned and reached out his hand. "Water," he said, the words hardly a breath through his parched lips.

There wasn't any.

The rest of that day Gabriel lay on the sun-scorched ground, moaning occasionally and cussing when he worked up enough energy. He screamed with pain at Scott's attempt to move him a short distance under the bone-white boughs of a smoke tree, its branches twisted, its leaves thin and papery. Scott gave up and sat in the dust by his side, watching him through the day, guarding him from marauding coyotes through the night. His companion's breath grew more and more shallow.

As the sun rose, a man approached. Short and slender, he wore only a breechcloth and no hat over a full head of shoulder-length black hair. His skin was the color of well-tanned hide. Though his ribs showed through his chest, his arms were well muscled. He held a clay pot in front of him. Setting the pot next to Scott's feet, the man turned away. Scott leaned over and inspected the pot's interior. He reached his hand inside; cool water made his fingers tingle. When he looked up again, the Indian had already disappeared from view. Did he blend into the landscape or hide behind a low dune? Was Scott's sense of time so distorted that the Indian was only a spot on the horizon when Scott finally looked for him?

Scott didn't speculate for long. Before he could raise the

pot to his lips, Gabriel sighed. Scott quickly scooped up water in his cupped hands and leaned toward his companion. It was only then he noticed: the man's mouth was slack; his eyes, open wide, unblinking.

He hoped Gabriel was seeing the Pacific.

Scott had been gone only a few minutes when a knock at Tilman's door interrupted his concentration. He forced a smile as Henri Rougemont entered. Slow to allow Mexican hospitality to override his stern Yankee discipline, Tilman had to make a nearly physical effort to put aside his papers and urge the young man to sit down for a visit.

"You are well?" Tilman inquired, trying to still his impatience and look kindly at Rougemont. Although he had lived in the pueblo for over fifteen years, he felt more comfortable with the cool Anglo-Saxons than the warmer Mexicans or French. And then, he had to overcome his antipathy to Rougemont's uncle.

Tilman had befriended the elder Rougemont soon after the Frenchman arrived in the pueblo a few years after Tilman. A shrewd businessman, Rougemont purchased large tracts of land near the river, brought renowned French grape vines around Cape Horn, and in a move that took the mission fathers by surprise, aged wine for a year or more in the French way before offering it for sale. Mission grapes had long provided wine for the pueblo, but Rougemont's wines were far better. A quiet competition ensued. Quality won; Rougemont sent casks of wine north to Monterrey to be consumed by the larger population there, making him a wealthy man.

"My uncle offers you this wine." He offered a bottle to Tilman, who accepted it with a nod. "He thought you might enjoy it with your lunch."

Tilman allowed a silence while he wondered how much

the young man knew about himself and the elder Rougemont. The two men had severed their friendship a few years before when Tilman lost a piece of property to Rougemont in a horse race. Tilman continued to blame the man for exploiting what he considered his one weakness: gambling. But business and courtesy demanded him to be hospitable to the family.

"I've come to inquire when you'd like to begin our portrait sessions," Henri Rougemont asked to break the silence.

"Eh?" Tilman allowed a wrinkle of doubt to crease his forehead.

"I painted the portraits of your wife and daughter as you requested." Rougemont nodded toward the two paintings on the opposite wall. "I can begin any time on yours."

"Of course, very nice, very nice."

"So you would like to sit for me...when?" A recommendation from Tilman could mean portraits of other prominent Californios, up and down the coast.

"Yes, to be certain...of course, that's why you're here," Tilman responded. A little warmth crept into his tone. Only that morning, his wife had pressed him to begin. "Did you know that I've purchased a ranch about twenty miles south?" Tilman said abruptly.

"No, I didn't."

"It's not common knowledge yet," Tilman said, picking an imaginary piece of thread off his pant leg. "I thought you'd want to know that the portraits will hang in our parlor." And you can tell your uncle about the purchase, Tilman finished silently. Twenty-seven thousand acres, a cattle ranch. He was known as the owner of the pueblo's first store; imagine how much more respect he would gain as a ranchero.

"Next Thursday," he offered.

"Good. Very good," Rougement said. "You may want to come to my uncle's home, Don Rodrigo. I've set up a small studio."

Tilman had been looking for a way to heal the breach

with the elder Rougemont. Bad feelings over the loss of a wager reflected poorly on Tilman's character. Besides, his loss cured him forever of his gambling habit. "Thursday morning, yes, at your studio."

"You Henry Scott? My brother said you'd be around this morning." A voice emanated from the store's dim interior.

A man stepped out of the shadows. He wore dark trousers, white shirt sleeves and a cravat. His shoulders, curved around a thin, hollow chest, straightened as he approached. Scott saw a man only a few years older than himself. Slight, almost insubstantial, the man made up for his size with a booming voice.

"Edward Tilman," the man offered, without expression, without welcome.

If Edward looked into his eyes, Scott didn't see it. His own were now fixed firmly on the other man's hand and beneath it, the hard-packed dirt floor.

"Take a look around. I have some work to do." Edward Tilman retreated to the dark corner of the store where he picked up a quill with a flourish, dipped the tip into an ink pot and made a show of being busy.

The store sold more than dry goods, Scott realized as his eyes became accustomed to the dim light. He noticed a variety of merchandise he had seen only when his mother sent him to buy something the family couldn't grow, beg, borrow or do without. The shelves closest to the window held bolts of cloth next to rows of shoes. Beyond these lay household items: spoons, forks, knives, plates, bowls and cups. Covered tins and boxes took up most of the counter in front of the shelves. Nearly all the floor space was given over to saddles, casks and baskets. He stood waiting for Tilman's brother to speak.

After a time, Edward placed his quill on the counter and

approached Scott again. "I'll tell you a little about some of these items," he said. "Tomorrow you'll be on your own. Next to the cloth behind you are the shawls worn by the women in this country, rebozos," he began. "Down there"—he indicated the shelves on the end—"are a few blankets woven at the mission. The cloth used to come from there too. Now we get cloth from Mexico and the United States. Except the silks. They're from China." Edward Tilman spoke so quickly that Scott had a hard time keeping up.

"A great trading port, the village of Los Angeles." He added in his booming voice, "That's why I came here from the East." He pointed to several casks on the floor. "We stock wine and brandy from the pueblo's vineyards. Saddles...," Edward Tilman said, indicating several piled near the store's entrance. "And bridles." He waved his hand toward a row of pegs at the rear of the store. He opened a large box on the counter. "Buttons from England," he said. "In this box"—he lifted the lid—"are knives, from England, Spain and America. And these two are stockings—men's and women's from Massachusetts and Rhode Island."

"Rice here"—Edward removed the cover on one of the casks—"is from China. The gun powder too," he said, uncovering another. "Sugar in this"— he removed the cover from a third cask, directing Scott to look inside—"from the Sandwich Islands."

"Now, hides and tallow. Those are the most important. We buy from the ranchers and trade with the ships for most of this," he indicated, his outstretched arm taking in the store. "You'll learn about hides, how to judge their quality and determine their price, but not yet. I learned quickly. If you do too, you'll be asked to stay. If not, my brother won't want you here."

Scott remained silent, his gaze once again fixed on the floor. Having had to make his way in the world with a drunk for a father, he had learned whom he could trust. Not Edward Tilman, he had already decided.

"For now, when someone wants to talk hides, direct him to my brother's office upstairs," Edward concluded. "Questions?"

Scott shook his head, like the dumb animal he appeared to be. "No." Never before had anyone expected so much from him.

"You don't speak Spanish, do you? Didn't think so. Well, you'll have to learn quickly. There aren't too many people around here who speak English." Edward's lips coiled upward in a smile too large to be real, exposing a gap between his two front teeth.

Scott took his place on the other side of the counter and waited for a customer. He wondered why Tilman had hired him instead of a Mexican.

Edward Tilman had asked his brother the same question the night before, shrugging his shoulders when Don Rodrigo cut him off. "It's my store. I make the decisions."

Edward, a younger half brother, had appeared unexpectedly in the pueblo of Los Angeles a year before. Given to expressing opinions about matters he knew nothing about, he also acted as if he had a right to everything his elder brother owned. Scott had arrived at the right time. Tilman needed someone to run the store while he was occupied with the ranch purchase, and Edward tended Tilman's storehouse at the harbor twenty-five miles south. If Edward failed at this task, as he had at others, Tilman planned to put him on the next boat back to Boston.

The shuffling of papers, the scratch of Tilman's quill from the rear of the store nearly put Scott to sleep. He would have helped if there were anything to do. Seeing nothing, he waited for time to pass. Finally, in late morning, a Mexican woman, trailed by her servant, entered the store. She looked somewhat grand, Scott thought, with a low-cut blouse that exposed her neck and arms, and a full red skirt. Her dark hair was piled on her head beneath a small black hat.

"Buenos días, señora Rubio. A sus órdenes." Edward

Tilman rushed forward to greet the woman before she could approach Scott, who stood behind the counter.

"Buenos días, señor." They exchanged pleasantries in Spanish, smiling and nodding at each other. "I understand an American ship docked a few days ago in the harbor." Finally, she arrived at her point. "Do you have any new cloth?" she asked, still speaking Spanish.

"Climb up to the shelf there," Edward ordered Scott, without bothering to translate the woman's request. "I think those bolts at the top are the ones she wants."

Scott pulled the ladder from the corner and leaned it against the shelves. He climbed slowly, uncertain whether it would hold his weight. On the fourth rung, his weight was too far back. The ladder pulled away from the shelves. Scott hung precariously in midair for a moment, then slowly leaned his weight forward until the ladder settled into place again. Carefully he negotiated the remainder of the rungs, captured the cloth and set it on the counter.

The señora smiled. "Not all days are so exciting, do you agree, Señor Eduardo?"

Edward smiled at her, scowled in Scott's direction and unrolled one bolt after another. None appealed. After she left, Edward climbed the ladder himself to put the cloth back.

"Too big to be any good," he muttered. Scott felt the familiar sting of humiliation.

It was like that for the rest of the day. When Edward asked him to measure out a pound of rice, Scott spilled part of it on the floor. After unrolling several pairs of stockings for a gentleman, he spent a long time matching them again, unable to tell one size from another. Scott pushed the button box across the counter to a young woman and watched it crash to the floor. The young Tilman asked him to figure the cost of three purchases. When Scott's total was incorrect, Edward hastily refigured the numbers. He was grateful that Edward Tilman didn't ask him to read.

When he wasn't berating himself for his clumsiness and stupidity, he was listening to the words Edward spoke to customers. At the end of the day, he could recognize only "buenos días." The words for the commonplace items in the store eluded him as did any notion of how to engage in small talk. To make matters worse, Edward Tilman became more and more critical. Out of the corner of his eye, Scott saw him hunched over his papers; the scratch of quill grew louder and more irritating.

Scott stood behind the counter until the patch of sunlight coming through the open door traced a golden triangle on the dirt floor. He noticed a vine with white-petaled flowers in a clay pot outside the door.

"Mr. Edward," he said. "That plant out there. What is it?"

Edward looked up, surprised to hear the young man's voice. Scott hadn't spoken since early morning, cleaning up his mistakes quietly, his body awkward but willing. "Passion flower. The Mexicans say, 'La pasión del cristo.' You know anything about Catholics?" he asked. "One of the padres at the mission raised these kinds of flowers until he got too old. He used to give us some to sell, my brother said. This is the last one left. Water it once a week. I think my brother likes it. He'd never admit it though."

Scott remained behind the counter and repeated "la pasión del cristo" to himself, adding a few Spanish words to his vocabulary.

"We'll close early today," Edward said, peering at his pocket watch. He knew his brother was visiting a ranch a distance west. "It's after four o'clock, and there's rarely any business for the next hour anyway. You go ahead. I'll show you how to close up tomorrow morning on my way to the harbor." The work day nearly over, he could afford to be benevolent.

Scott didn't need to be told twice. "Good night, Mr. Edward," he called over his shoulder. Without waiting for a reply, he plunged into the road. He rarely ran—a big man and clumsy—but today he did. So many hours spent confined to the store. He had tired of it in the first ten minutes.

As he reached the plaza, he slowed to a walk. The light at this hour, when the Missouri sun would already have cooled, was warm and bright, a golden light that made him forget the day's trials. Like the previous day, he kept walking. Today, he was struck by the differences between St. Louis and the pueblo of Los Angeles. Although he had last seen St. Louis six months before, he had no difficulty recalling its air of purpose, the commerce on the river, in its stores, hotels, slaughterhouses, tanneries, brickyards and bakeries. Factories turned out soaps and candles, bells, pottery, jugs, flatware, jewelry needed for a people that numbered thirty thousand. The area's stone houses and log cabins, constructed in the French style—logs laid vertically instead of horizontally—stood side by side with newer houses of milled lumber, so much needed that the forests south of the city were being rapidly reduced to stumps. The smell and feel of bodies pressing against his on the narrow lanes, competing for space with wagons and carts. In the city, the sounds of animals—horses, pigs—the calls of men, the steamboats' whistles as they left the docks. In the country, the squabbling of his brothers and sisters, his mother's deep sighs, his father's angry bellow. Birds overhead, pheasants in the bushes, the thrum of bees on summer afternoons, the crack of snow-laden branches in the winter.

And the city's prosperity! On afternoons around town, wealthy women wore silk gowns, copied from styles in London and Paris, although his mother, a remnant of the French-speaking founders, wore the cotton cap and kerchief of a poor Creole. Even out in the country where he lived, in Vide Poche, "empty pockets," so named by the locals because of its citizens' poverty, a considerable population occupied the land, tried to farm, often came up empty, but that was their lot, wasn't it? At least what Scott expected.

What was here in the pueblo? A few hundred families. None he had yet seen—not even Tilman—looked as prosperous as St. Louis's grandest. Low, squat houses that seemed to blend in with the dirt around them, flat roofs reinforced with tar that left ugly dark streaks on the walls. Too few horses, sheep and goats to counter an unnerving quiet. Even his mother, little as she had, cultivated a small garden of roses, hollyhocks and violets. Here, there were no flowers, no butterflies. Flies, though, and lots of them, alighting from horseshit piles on the road.

But he had to admit, the light was warm, even comforting, casting the mountain's long shadows onto the plain as day slid into evening. And most important, two thousand miles lay between him and his father.

He soon came to the river, barely remembering his crossing only two evenings before, more dead than alive. Nothing like the Mississippi, a mile wide, a hundred feet deep he'd heard said, and a twelve-day trip to its mouth at New Orleans, even by the fastest steamboat.

To his unfamiliar eyes, this river looked puny. From where he stood, orchards and vineyards at his back, he saw small islands that dotted a shallow river bed. Tall reeds and willows grew on the islands, a variety of birds grazed the river, ducks bobbed their heads into the water where the stream was deep enough to pluck out a fish. There *were* areas that looked to have some depth, but others nursed a trickle of water, barely enough to cover pebbles the size of those beneath his feet, certainly not rocks the size of boulders.

Used to living alongside a river that accommodated a huge volume of water in all seasons, he didn't know that at this time of year the river was as dry as it was likely to get. October was nearly upon them and, with it, the season of rains would begin. The placid stream in front of him could become a raging torrent in a few hours. He was unaware of storms that changed the course of this river every year, sometimes redirecting it only a few feet east or west, other storms so violent the river changed course entirely, entering the Pacific Ocean not at the port in San Pedro Bay directly south of the pueblo, as it did now, but toward the west. He didn't know that the San Gabriel River flowed out of the mountains east of the pueblo and, for the present, emptied into the Río Porciúncula. He was ignorant about the importance of these rivers and all their tributaries and side streams: they watered the vast plain he had crossed to get here; brought water to the pueblo and to the ranchos he hadn't yet seen; irrigated orchards and fields in the few places where the land was cultivated; nourished the cattle whose numbers grew daily; had, in fact, nurtured a thousand generations of Indians before Scott and his kind were ever seen on the land. He wanted to scoff at those who called this anemic stream a river when they had never seen the likes of the Mississippi. Instead, he looked into the river, noticed how clear the water ran—unlike the mud-sludged Mississippi—and found the questions he hadn't known enough to ask.

What was here for him in the pueblo? Refuge, of course, but what else?

He turned his back on the river, surveyed the handful of houses and a cluster of field workers headed off to whatever they knew as home, heard a lone donkey bray, all under the mountains' protective cloak of twilight.

What was here for him?

Infinite space, yes.

Infinite opportunity too?

Scott kicked the dirt with the toe of his boot.

[2]

The road between Tilman's store and the Rougemont vineyard could be traversed in less than quarter of an hour, but on Thursday morning, Tilman was in no hurry. He walked his horse, allowing himself a moment, seldom taken, to enjoy the weather. Following the hot winds and bright sun of the previous few days, cooler temperatures had returned. He knew that cool sunny days would alternate with an overcast few. Rain would fall periodically and unpredictably. Overall he liked the mild fall and winter although he missed the brilliant autumn colors of his Massachusetts boyhood.

Sometimes fog covered the morning landscape, refusing to burn off until late afternoon. Today's weather was fine though. A few clouds high in the sky didn't interfere with his view of the mountains. Under their great brow, a vast plain extended east of the pueblo. He knew that a large part was uninhabitable, too moist from streams that flowed this way and that out of the hills. The Indians had found ways to live in and around the wetlands, but his people never would.

Hoping to avoid the older Rougemont, Tilman cut through the vineyard to reach the artist's studio, a small adobe at the rear of the rancho.

As the young artist hung Tilman's hat on a nail behind the door, Tilman looked around the simple room. Windows to the north and east, their shutters already open, faced onto the wide expanse of fields. A chair was positioned next to the east window. A few feet from the chair, an easel held a blank canvas. A palette lay on a table next to the easel. Tilman noted the palette's array of colors: dark blues, muddy browns, bright yellows and deep reds.

"Please be seated, Don Rodrigo." Rougemont gestured toward the chair. Tilman tried to be patient while the artist gently prodded him into a pose. Rougemont kept up a steady stream of conversation in French-accented Spanish to distract his subject.

"Let's move your head a little...," Rougemont suggested. A light pressure from his hand gently tilted Tilman's impassive face toward the window. "Good, we'll let some light fall on your face...a beautiful day, isn't it?...too bad you missed seeing my uncle...he left early. I think he went down to the port to oversee some casks of brandy he is sending off to San Francisco." Rougemont stepped back. "Yes, that's right. Perfect, Don Rodrigo, I like the set of your jaw. We will make a fine portrait of you, non?"

Tilman refused to reply.

"Now your hands, Don Rodrigo, how shall we pose them? On your lap, yes, on your lap, please clasp them on your lap." The artist took hold of Tilman's hands and attempted to place one on the other. Tilman scowled and squeezed his fingers together, making tight balls of his fists. His good mood had already been replaced by a fever of anxiety. How long was this going to take? Rougemont hadn't even started drawing; at least a quarter of an hour must have passed already.

"A little too tight, n'est-ce pas?" Rougemont said. He demonstrated how he wanted Tilman's hands to look: loose and comfortable in his lap. The artist stared at Tilman's hands, willing them to relax. Tilman ignored him.

"Well, let's get started. We'll work out the rest of the pose later. If you can just look at me..." Rougemont sat down in front of his easel, wiped his brow with a large kerchief and took up a brush.

Uncomfortable under the artist's scrutiny, Tilman glared at the opposite wall.

"Please relax, Don Rodrigo," Rougemont pleaded. Then he offered, "My uncle tells me that wagon trains brought a group of Americans to San Francisco last year. And, of course, I have met the Workman family here in the pueblo. Arrived from Santa Fe two years ago, non? You must be pleased that your countrymen have chosen to settle in Alta California."

Tilman shifted in his chair. The man must be a fool or know nothing about politics, he thought. At least he knows nothing about me.

"Likely to be overrun by these newcomers," Tilman barked, unable to remain silent.

"Please, Don Rodrigo, do not move," Rougemont cautioned, only half-listening to Tilman. "You are not pleased with the company of Americans? I understand you were born on the Atlantic seacoast."

"Yes. But I've been nearly twenty years in this territory. As you know, I married a Mexican woman. I was baptized a Catholic, like other Mexican citizens."

"Ah yes," Rougemont ventured, "a Catholic. As am I." Tilman's expression didn't change, although his brow smoothed a fraction. Drawing the outlines of Tilman's body, the artist noted his subject's arms, head and legs, vigorous for a man in his fifties. Rougemont would describe him in a letter he sent to his family in France as "vital and full of energy." He glanced at Tilman's face. The scowl was deepening.

To distract him, Rougemont said, "Then you know yourself as a Mexican?"

"Yes. Of course. A man can't be two things at once." Tilman sounded very definite on that point. It was true that he spoke Spanish perfectly, and he had learned to be a gracious host in the Mexican style. But he did not consider himself to be a Californio, as did many of his peers; he hadn't been born in Alta California and wasn't a descendant of Mexican settlers.

He was a simple man, he told himself. He went to the

pueblo church when his wife insisted, although his adopted religion placed too much emphasis on ceremony to suit him, born a Congregationalist in the spare Puritan tradition. He had become a Mexican citizen—a requirement for land ownership in Alta California—and taken the name Rodrigo, after the Spanish warrior who vanquished the Moors from Spain.

But he was never able to erase his boyhood completely. If he thought about it—although he rarely allowed himself to dwell—he remembered the sadness he felt as a boy when his sea captain father, fortunes failing, sent him and his brother away. Raised by an uncle in the western Massachusetts town of Deerfield, Tilman didn't see his father, stepmother and siblings again until he returned to Boston as a young man, soon to set sail for the Sandwich Islands.

"Don Rodrigo, please keep your chin tilted up...yes, that's right...thank you for suffering this intrusion on your time. I know you're a busy man. I'm nearly finished with a preliminary sketch...now, you were saying, about American settlement in Alta California..."

Against his better judgment, Tilman declared, "What I'm saying is that immigrants from the United States could make life difficult for those of us here—Mexicans, Californios, Americans, even the French."

Ignoring Rougemont's plea to sit still, he stood up and began to pace the small studio. "Yes, we could be sitting pretty here in Alta California if the politics of the whole thing could be sorted out. The state needs a proper government, not the succession of governors poorly suited for the task that Mexico appoints according to its whim. We need a budget that can support the construction of buildings and roads, instead of requiring the province to support itself through taxes on ships' cargoes."

Rougemont stopped drawing.

"We need to be a state." Tilman's voice rose. "No, not a

state. That won't do. If the Americans come, they could well overwhelm us. Although I fear that they might already be on their way." Tilman sat down once again. Plucking his watch from his vest pocket, Tilman raised his eyebrows in surprise. "Have I been here less than an hour? Seems far longer. How are we doing, Rougemont?"

Not very well, Rougemont would have said if permitted to speak honestly. To paint a proper portrait—one that Tilman would approve and pay for—he would have to find a way to make Tilman relax and present the serene countenance the man usually presented to the world. He settled Tilman back into position, tilted the man's head toward the sunlight now streaming through the window and said, "Are you fond of our wines, Don Rodrigo? Which ones do you prefer?"

But Tilman could not be dissuaded to consider a less serious topic. He ignored Rougemont's question and returned to his previous ruminations. "How are we supposed to do business in a place where the government sends us inferior leaders?"

This time he remained seated, although no less emphatic than before. "Look at our governor, the drunkard Alvarado. Last year, he surrendered to an American commodore, who mistakenly believed the United States and Mexico were at war. American marines and sailors took possession of the Monterey presidio—and thereby the capital. Then—and only then—did the commodore realize that Mexico and the United States were *not* at war, apologized and removed his troops."

Rougemont kept his hand moving across the canvas. At least Don Rodrigo was keeping his chin up and his gaze projected toward the vineyard outside the window. Rougemont drew his subject's receding hairline, his narrow eyes—blue, weren't they—his pointed, clean-shaven chin.

"New governor. General Micheltorena. Fine. A man of culture. We expected good things of him. Instead, he recruited convicts and cholos. They arrived in Los Angeles and got only as far as the Santa Barbara presidio. There, the governor received word that the emergency involving the American commodore was over." He paused a moment for breath. "Then, what did Micheltorena do?"

"Yes?" Rougemont was trying to get the bend of Tilman's elbow just right.

"He turned around and returned to the pueblo." Tilman paid no attention to the artist. "Spent the winter and spring here, only leaving after we protested to the Mexican government about the beatings our citizens were subjected to from Micheltorena's so-called army. Hooligans! Just a few months ago, he and his troops decamped for Monterey, where they are now terrorizing its citizens." He stood as if preparing to pace once again.

"Please, sir. Stay seated," the artist cried out. "Perhaps we should continue this sitting on another day." The artist laid his brush and palette on the table.

"No, no, I promised my wife I'd stay for at least two hours. She will be very annoyed with me if I disappoint her." Tilman looked at his watch again. "I will be silent, I promise you."

A truce reached, he sat down and composed his expression. Tilman knew the artist could read the turmoil on his face and hoped the man would not repeat his worries to anyone. Commerce was a dance in which everyone had to be made happy. It wouldn't do to side with one group or another. Somehow, the issue of Mexican governance had to be settled, if only because Mexico's neglect of Alta California was bad for business.

The morning sun heated the small studio. Flies buzzed past his ear now and then, startling him. Soon he fell deeply into thought, speculating on how his friend Thomas Larkin would want the game to go. The United States consul, Larkin lived in a grand house in Monterey. Tilman planned to visit as soon as he took title to his land. He wanted to use some of Larkin's design in building his own home. They had passed several evenings together chatting about how each had arrived in Alta California and the territory's problems and promise.

Larkin, born in Massachusetts a decade earlier than Tilman, found little to admire about the Mexicans. Although Tilman disagreed, he considered Larkin to be an honorable man. But when he heard that Larkin had communicated the surrender of Monterey to the American commodore, Tilman began to reconsider Larkin's character. Why had Larkin given up the capital so easily? What was Larkin's real purpose in California?

Troubled by Larkin's view of United States expansion but, reluctant to disclose his doubts, he had challenged Larkin cautiously during the consul's summer visit. "True, I can see why the Americans wouldn't want a power like France or Russia on its doorstep," Tilman said, "but you have a lot of wilderness between the United States and Alta California."

"You?" Larkin picked at the pronoun, Tilman remembered. "Who is this *you*? Are you no longer an American?"

Tilman slowly unfolded his legs. "You must know, Mr. Larkin, I have been in this country for nearly half my life. What I know is what I learned here. Is it not that way for you?" he asked, although he knew what the man would answer.

"No. Absolutely not. I could stay here the rest of my life—although I doubt I will—and I still wouldn't consider myself a Mexican."

"Perhaps not, but why not try to understand how Mexicans see the United States?" Tilman had kept his voice steady.

"I think they see us as meddlers, if not thieves," Larkin replied. "They fear we will come in and take their land. You and I know that even if California becomes a territory, or even a state, the Mexicans will be treated fairly."

Tilman's face hadn't recorded his doubts.

"Alta California is the western edge of the continent,"

Larkin had finished. "This land rightfully belongs to us. We're a nation of laws. You can be sure of that."

Tilman knew that if the day came when the Americans took over, and his land were on the block, only a man like Larkin could save it for him. He'd nodded. "More sherry, Mr. Larkin?"

Over the next two weeks, visitors to Tilman's office above the store came and went. Scott heard chairs scraping the floor overhead; sometimes a loud laugh reverberated through the ceiling. Tilman rode out nearly every day—Scott heard him clatter down the stairs, saw him free the reins from the post outside the store, watched him mount—but didn't stop in at the store.

Every few days, Edward rode into town from the harbor. He went into the store and looked around. As soon as his brother left his office, Edward took off in the opposite direction.

With no one to tell him what to do, Scott kept busy. He carefully swept the floor three times a day, dusted the merchandise at least once, and, after the first day of standing sentinel, moved around the store—paced, really—most of the day, straightening a saddle, carefully stacking and restacking the wine kegs, watering the passion flower vine until it died from too much attention. When he couldn't find anything to clean, he picked up the quill and ink pot that Edward had left carelessly on the counter and wrote out columns of figures on a scrap of handbill dropped from a customer's pocket.

As a child his mother had taught him sums, to pass the long evenings when his father was out drinking. "You are the eldest boy; you should know your numbers," she said, tucking a wisp of curly brown hair under her cap. By twilight in the summer and candlelight in the winter, she'd recited numbers in French and English until he could count to one hundred in both languages. By the time her sixth child had been born,

Scott was thirteen, and she was too tired to do anything but sleep as soon as his brothers and sisters had been put to bed. Looking at her by candlelight was too painful for him to bear. Her face was as pale as the china dishes she had long before left behind in her parents' home.

The day that Tilman was about to enter the store for the first time since Scott's arrival, Edward hailed him from the street.

"Don Rodrigo." Edward used the name his brother was called in the pueblo. In Massachusetts, he was known by his Christian birth name, John.

Tilman spun around. "Where have you been? It's an hour past opening. I thought I heard you come in from the harbor late last night." He had tried to give responsibility for store and warehouse to Edward to test his brother, but his brother complained so much, Tilman could see his plan wasn't working.

"I did," Edward said. "Very late. I'm getting weary looking after both your business operations, brother." Edward's voice rose. "Every two days I have to make this trip. And there's been only the one packet sailing to San Francisco last week, so why am I there? By the way, your new man is struggling with the language, you know."

Edward's Spanish was none too good either. Tilman let the matter be.

"He's clumsy—"

"Let's give the young man a chance, shall we? Is there anything Scott is doing well?"

Edward considered the question. "He's getting better at adding up the purchases. He's willing to learn," Edward admitted. "Although teaching him is taking longer than I thought."

Tilman raised his hand. "Basta," he said. He motioned to Edward to pass into the store.

Scott was about to greet Edward when he saw Don Rodrigo. He bent down to pick up a small object, imaginary or real, and straightened, his eyes still focused on the floor. Why was the elder Tilman visiting? Was it to tell him about something he had done wrong? Scott held his breath and waited.

Tilman surveyed the store. The floors were slightly damp. Scott must have arrived early to apply water to keep down the dust. The stock was arrayed more neatly than he recalled. He ran his hand over the counter. Also damp. The man actually cleaned.

"Edward and I think you're doing a good job, Mr. Scott," he said, surprising both his brother and the clerk.

Though Tilman hadn't visited the store until now, he had talked to others. He knew that his employee had showed some dexterity with sums and had picked up some Spanish words and phrases, but he refused to smile at the customers or even look them in the eye. The store was an outing for the pueblo's citizens, Tilman knew. The women came to show off a new dress as much as to buy, the men came to learn of politics in Los Angeles and Monterey, and all came to gossip.

Scott slowly let the breath out of his lungs. He raised his head imperceptibly.

"Edward will continue to split his duties between the port and the store for a while longer," Tilman announced. He ignored Edward's low groan.

"You must make more of an effort to learn Spanish, though," Tilman urged. "Get out around town, listen to conversations, ask questions, socialize. That's how I learned. Don't be timid."

Scott was silent. Tilman's demand sounded as difficult as if he had been told to teach a lizard not to cringe.

"Let's see what you can do with a little more time."

In St. Louis, days had marched forward, never varying much from year to year. Scott's family depended upon him for food when his father was gone on a drunk—a day, a week, longer. To feed them, Scott set small traps for rabbits, learned to use a slingshot to kill a bird, stole chickens from farms upriver when he had to, taught his brothers and sisters to do the same.

Sooner or later, a day always came when a rider passing through stopped at the farm and called out, before riding on, "Your dad's in the back of a saloon on Fourth Street" or "in a whorehouse on Market" or "on the road up to Chocteau's Pond. He says you gotta come for him." Scott always set out immediately, trudged the weary miles into St. Louis, found his father, waited beside him until he was sober, then supported his father's weight as they made their way home. There was not much left of Thomas Scott, the handsome keelboatman his mother had left her wealthy Creole family to marry, but Scott hadn't known him then anyway—knew him only as a drunk who gambled away his earnings from a day or two of labor, sometimes beat his wife and always beat him, his eldest son.

In the pueblo Henry Scott had no one to look out for but himself. If he went out drinking, or "socializing," as Tilman put it, he was sure he would expose himself as the awkward butt-of-all-jokes he was at home. Instead, he arranged straw and sacks as a bed in the storeroom after dinner every night and willed himself to sleep.

Dusk came a little earlier each day. By November, when Scott was confident enough to explore outside the few blocks of settled land that made up the pueblo, night was already closing in. One Sunday, his only day off, he saddled his horse and left the pueblo at daybreak to avoid churchgoers. He passed the Zanja Madre, knowing it now as the source of water that fed the ditches that wound through the pueblo. Only a few miles upstream, the river, hardly robust where it flowed past the settlement, slowed to a trickle. He guided his horse north along the sandy bed, sometimes dodging tules and giant reeds embedded in stagnant pools of water. Thickets of willows along the riverbank stood half bare as winter approached. Dense oak forests flanked the river at intervals. Dry washes angled off to the north. On successive Sundays, he followed those as well, allowing his horse to plod slowly forward at its own pace. The land—bounded by high mountains along the margins, wide, devoid of population, empty of distinguishing features such as a fast-flowing river or an outcropping of rocks—overwhelmed him.

Little by little on his Sunday forays, he began to notice the light. Awareness turned to curiosity. How was it that this light, so muted, so golden, made his heart ache. In St. Louis, a day was sunny or dark. It rained or it didn't. Here, light slanted across the landscape, hinted at mountain canyons hiding in shadowed folds. Light illuminated any vegetation in close range—a tree was more than a shape. It was a collection of separate boughs. The willow thickets were not merely brown. Their wiry branches were gray, the color of the few remaining leaves.

As he traveled farther northwest of the pueblo, he came upon an enormous valley where the earth was drier, the sun hotter. He made his way among miles and miles of yucca and cactus, reminding him of his long ride across the desert and of Gabriel's death. And then, suddenly, the river disappeared in a mountain canyon, leaving Scott to ponder the origin of the water that sustained the town. He thought it was the strangest river he had ever seen.

A month passed before Tilman visited the store again. Even in the dim light of a cloudy November day, the store appeared in as good a trim as it had before. Scott was on his own. Edward had returned to the pueblo only a few times, complaining to his brother about his isolation at the harbor without any mention of Scott.

"I'd like you to stay on here until after the new year," Tilman said. Instinctively, Scott cringed to avoid a blow. His worst fear had come true. Tilman was letting him go. "Soon after that, I will take possession of a rancho south of the pueblo." Tilman went on. "It is large, more than 27,000 acres. I'm going to raise cattle. You could be of some use there."

Scott wondered what he would do on a rancho when all he could do was ride a horse.

Tilman would have disagreed. The businessman didn't expect him to master the skills of horsemanship that the vaqueros—both Indian and Mexican—had developed into an art on the Alta California ranchos. While it was true that young men arrived frequently in the pueblo, many were layabouts, content with jobs they could grab for a day or two before moving on. Scott had already proved he would show up every morning and put in an honest day's work.

"Does that interest you?" Tilman asked.

Scott nodded, picked up a cloth and turned away to dust a counter that didn't need cleaning. Missouri was becoming a dark speck on the continent he could nearly obliterate by closing his eyes.

[3]

Tilman strode into the store one rainy December morning before the first customer had crossed the threshold. The store smelled of tallow, the wool of zarapes and saddle leather. Fresh greens had just been delivered and were sitting in a bucket in the corner. Scott liked early morning in the store but little else. In the short, cool winter days, he had only to see a man stumbling past the open door half-drunk or full hungry to forget how difficult he found his daily captivity and remember that he was getting paid.

As the weeks went by, he had found new ways to keep busy. He swept the floor every time a customer left the store, pulled bolts of cloth down and stacked them neatly again, dusted the counter every moment he wasn't doing something else, rearranged barrels until old customers had to look in new places to find salt, sugar or rice. Tilman had seen business increase in the few months since Scott arrived, pleasing the businessman as much for his good judgment in hiring the unpromising young man as for the additional revenue.

"Close up the store...shouldn't be much happening today," Tilman said. "People don't like going out in the rain. Meet me in five minutes at the barn. You're going with me to the rancho."

Scott entered the stable as Tilman was about to mount his horse. The animal, finely bred, danced and wheeled as the servant placed a tooled-leather saddle on its back and slipped a silver bit between its teeth. Scott waited quietly astride the gray that had brought him to California. The animal had filled out, but there was little life in him, especially when compared to Tilman's prancing filly.

"Vàmonos," Tilman said, and they left the barn's shelter. They passed the plaza where sheets of rain obscured the little church. Scott made out the outlines of the Indian village of Yang-na along the riverbank, its domed shelters a curiosity he had been too timid to investigate. He had glimpsed a sizeable number of Indians clustered around the dwellings from time to time. The number seemed to grow or diminish according to no timetable he was familiar with. He didn't know that Yang-na had become a home to Indians who came from many points across the broad plain. People who at one time would have lived in small villages and met for trading or ceremonies had been forced into the missions when Spain ruled Alta California. They were displaced again when Mexico disbanded the missions nearly a decade before. The village of Yang-na, predating the pueblo by a thousand years, had become a kind of refugee center, a place where Indians could live as they searched for work in the pueblo or on the other ranchos in the vicinity.

Scott, confined to Tilman's store all day and rarely venturing out at night, had little contact with the Indians. The sight of the Indian village, however, reminded him of the Indian who had sidled next to him his first morning in the pueblo. More than once the man's thin, fox-like face had appeared before him, although he had not seen him again.

Riding ahead, Tilman forded the river. Because the clear autumn days had only been broken by light drizzles, the river, even in the morning's downpour, could be crossed with relative ease. Tilman guided his mount skillfully through the rushing water, Scott behind. On the other side, Tilman turned and yelled against the howling wind, "We'll likely have more difficulty on our return. Then you'll really see water," and turned south.

Scott followed. He didn't know how far the ranch was, or how long it would take them to get there. What was the difference anyway? It could take an hour or a day. He knew he could ride as long as the journey took.

The rain beat against his back. He pulled up his collar and tugged his hat down, wishing he were able to fit more of himself inside the worn woolen coat Tilman had given him. Little rivers of water trickled down his neck. He shivered, surprised by the storm's intensity. A climate so moderate didn't seem capable of creating such violence. Wind whipped the trees; rain had already turned the trail to mud. In a short time, Scott was wet to the bone; splashes of mud laced his pants.

"I want to see the ranch before I sign the deed." Tilman yelled to make his voice heard above the wind as Scott pulled even with him. Scott nodded, his eyes on the trail. Nothing seemed alive. His horse walked at a steady pace, its head low, daunted by the storm. Seemingly devoid of human wants or needs, Scott rode without complaint.

For the first time since beginning his journey west, Scott let himself think about the day he left St. Louis. It had been raining that day too. Early March. Cold, way colder than this December day. Scott, awake in the bed he shared with two of his brothers, had tried to remain still, lest he wake the others by moving. His younger sisters, their arms and legs entwined as children's often are, slept in the next bed. Behind the curtain lay the baby next to his mother; he knew she had folded the child into her arms to protect her from her husband's sour breath. Wind had blown through the wooden slats of the old cabin, along with droplets of rain. Scott shivered now at the memory. He'd heard his mother stir, then rise from the bed she shared with his father on the nights he made the distance between tavern and home. She'd settled into a long fit of coughing until, finally, she'd stopped, taken a deep breath and shuffled toward the stove.

Now, a rabbit scuttled across the trail, breaking the animals' strides. Tilman expertly reined in his horse. Scott watched horse and rider move forward with one movement.

In his imagination, he saw his mother at the stove. He remembered a time when he was a young boy—she had fairly danced around the old cabin, slim-waisted and light on her feet. Without his noticing, she had become an old woman, her once wiry body scrawny from malnutrition and overwork. Her parents would not have recognized her, this crone of forty-five. As Scott lay in bed that last morning, he'd smelled the stink of his brothers' bodies and the wood smoke of the new fire. The dampness held a moldy smell he would remember all his life.

He'd gotten out of bed quietly, pulled his pants and shirt over his filthy underwear. If he could escape before his father awoke, he'd avoid a final beating. His mother was already standing at the well in the front yard, a patched cloak covering her head and body.

"Is that you, Henri?" she'd said without turning around. "Help me here, ma petite. The handle has frozen." She spoke English with a French accent; sometimes, a French word slipped in, more often as she grew older.

Without speaking, Scott primed the pump several times until water flowed into the bucket. Finally, he'd said, "Maman, I'm leaving."

"What's that, Henri?" She'd turned and looked up at him, rain following the little eddies that time and worry had threaded across her face.

"I'm leavin', Maman. I have a job. With some trappers going west."

Her eyebrows came together as she stared, puzzled, into his face. "No, son. You...," she began, tears mixing with rain on her face, "can't go away now."

Scott had stood between her and his father, taking the beatings meant for her. He had stood between her and hunger.

Scott looked down at his feet. "Got to, Maman."

And with that he'd walked away, leaving his mother to stare at his back, the pump handle dangling from her hand.

Tilman appeared before him, rain dripping off his hat. "That's the river we're hearing," he yelled, indicating the direction west with a sweep of his hand. For the first time, Scott became aware of the sound of rushing water. "The Porciúncula comes down out of the mountains northwest of the pueblo. Flows to the sea, borders my land on the west. Empties into a bay where ships dock and deposit their cargoes. That's where my brother Edward stays...overseeing my warehouse."

He planned to tell the same story to his daughter when he brought her and his wife to the ranch for the first time, but in that telling, he would emphasize his role. He would remind them of the overland trade between the harbor and pueblo that he had initiated before his daughter was born, yes, before his marriage. He anticipated the admiration he would see in them as they recognized all he had done, all he planned to do. Embarrassed by his silent puffery, he wheeled his horse and rode away again.

Scott, seated firmly on his old gray, was aware of following the river's course southeast for more than an hour. Then, the river turned due south and they with it. Scott lost all track of time. In the driving rain, he couldn't see Tilman ahead. Finally, Tilman returned to announce, "A lot of water here—never dries up, even in summer. Your horse. Can it keep up?" He eyed the nag.

Scott nodded.

"I'll take your word for it. Mind the ground though. A marsh..." His words were lost as he rode ahead. Sure enough, the earth softened into mud. Scott had all he could do to keep his horse going forward. Ahead, Tilman had no trouble guiding his filly through watery pools. Scott had to dig his heels into the animal's side, goading it to advance. He followed Tilman dumbly down the trail.

The rain slowed to a drizzle in midafternoon. The wide plain began to take on rounded contours, but Scott took no notice. Sycamore trees dotted the landscape to the east. Scott looked up to see Tilman some distance beyond. He switched the long reins across his horse's haunches until the animal picked up its pace. Tilman turned as Scott rode up. "We'll cross a river up here. The San Gabriel." He wheeled his filly around and took off at a trot, leaving Scott behind.

Scott was barely able to make out his employer's form atop his horse. He heard the filly neigh. Tilman swore. A moment later, Tilman had crossed the river. As he rode on, Scott followed with more effort. His gray twisted its head from side to side, trying to free itself of the reins Scott held firmly in his hands as water nearly reached its withers. Snorting and wheezing, his horse emerged from the river. Scott could feel the animal's body shivering beneath him. The horse had faithfully carried him over the mountains, across the desert. He felt bad about asking so much of it now.

Tilman rode on but soon paused until Scott caught up. "The Río San Gabriel comes out of the mountains..." He turned around in his saddle, pointed toward the mountains northeast of them. "Joins the Río de Porciúncula here. We'll be on my land shortly. Rancho de Los Ríos, Ranch of the Rivers."

He mumbled the last few words, in case they were heard as prideful. "Do you see how sparse the growth is here?"

Scott, wet and tired, tried to pay attention.

"You'd be surprised if you went a little farther west, to the river." Tilman's voice rose again. "You'd see brambles and thickets, ducks and geese—all manner of wildness and waterfowl. Then, if you were here during a storm, a heavy sustained rainfall, I mean, not the half-day deluge we just endured, you'd see this a different place, I tell you, a different place. A mighty flood. Water covers the plain," he said, gazing into the distance, as if he could see the plain through the wet mist surrounding them, "leaving wide swaths of marsh until days pass and the water seeps into the earth again."

Late in the day, the sun pierced the clouds for a few startling moments, giving Scott a brief window onto the landscape he would come to know fully. Low, rolling hills stretched to the south and east. Unlike the mountains he had crossed on his way to Alta California, no towering trees obscured his view. The hills were covered with small bushes and low ground cover. He saw the West's vast space as something to wonder at instead of fear. Before Scott's gray could take ten steps, the sun ducked behind a cloud again. The day's light faded.

"Hurry, while we still have a little light," Tilman called out. "Over here, young man." Scott guided his animal quickly down a rock-strewn riverbank, barely able to make out Tilman's shape in the shadows.

"Watch out there," Tilman warned. "Your horse can easily trip over a downed tree." Long coils of bare willow branches blocked any remaining light. Scott heard the rush of water. Somewhere beyond the branches lay the river.

He slowed his pace, taking care to avoid the larger rocks. He heard Tilman strike a match. "Follow me," he said. Scott's eyes followed the glow of his employer's cigarette as the man dismounted. He could barely make out the man's form as Tilman tied his horse to a rail in front of a small adobe. Scott did the same.

He looked up as he heard footsteps reverberate across a wooden floor, the creak of a door. He followed Tilman into the house. "The original owner's daughter had this built...don't know why...so close to the river. I'll build my casa grande up there." Tilman nodded toward the top of the embankment.

Without making a fire or offering a meal, he opened a small chest next to the fireplace. He tossed a bed roll to Scott, took one for himself. Scott, his eyes now accustomed to the dark, watched Tilman slip off his coat and shoes and curl himself into his bedroll. Within a moment he was snoring in sleep.

Scott lay down on the opposite side of the room and tried to do the same. He dozed briefly and awoke with a start. He smelled the dampness but no hint of charred wood; the fireplace hadn't been used for a long time. Minutes dragged by. The sound of the river drowned out everything except Scott's thoughts, which meandered back in time to his days in St. Louis. Scott had three brothers. Why was he the only one of them his father beat?

He examined the little he knew: His father had come to St. Louis from Philadelphia around 1810. He could do anything in those days, his mother told him. "First saw your père when he was twenty-six years old. Smelled like the river," she had said, more to herself than to her son. "Musty and wild." He put money aside in those early years of marriage, maman said, managed to keep out of the taverns, knowing they had been his own father's undoing.

Then maman, only sixteen when she married the handsome keelboatman, lost one baby after another. They were either stillborn or died within a year of their births. When Scott was finally born seven years into their marriage, his father's first thought was, "Why him?" This his father told him during a beating when he was seven or, maybe, eight: "That you, the ugliest one of all the babes your mother birthed, survived, proves there is no God."

The year after Henry was born, his brother arrived, a well-formed infant his father named Thomas, after himself. The boy died the next year in a malaria epidemic, sending his father to the taverns for solace. By that time, Thomas Scott had gotten used to failure. In the Depression of 1821, he lost the small plot of land he had managed to buy within the city's limits, dooming the family to move farther downriver. Then, the steamboats came in, and the days of the keelboats were over. "The beasts make the trip upriver from New Orleans in twelve days; keelboats took ninety," his father often complained. Until the day Henry left, his father was drunk most of the time and worked only occasionally, arguing with anyone he could get to listen to him.

Henry was frightened of his father. Hated his father for making him afraid, for beating him, for beating his mother, for the suffering his father had put them through, and for something else he couldn't quite remember. Trying to concentrate on what it was, he fell asleep.

The next morning, Scott found Tilman seated on the veranda step. He was staring into the pale sun that had just breached the mountains, the highest peak covered in snow.

"Here." He pushed a cloth-wrapped rectangle toward Scott. "A few tortillas and some beans. No time for a fire—I want to get an early start," he said.

A few minutes later, Scott was following Tilman on foot through a dense tangle of branches that scratched his face. "I want to show you this river," Tilman said over his shoulder. "Pay attention. We don't want to end up as breakfast for a bear or mountain lion."

The next moment, Scott broke through the brush and found himself on the river's bank. The river was wider than he expected, more than twice as wide as the point where it flowed through the pueblo. A wide, muddy bank flanked a fast-flowing torrent. Splintered logs crashed against each other and butted against rocks, large and small, on their journey to the ocean. Scott peered into the dark water to see silvery fish dart between a network of fallen branches close to shore. Without the buffer of the bare willow thicket, the river sounded a low roar.

The two men stood side by side. Scott was surprised at the river's expanse. Tilman had all he could do to stifle his glee at standing on land that would soon be his. Abruptly, he turned around and made his way back through the underbrush toward their horses, still tethered at the small adobe.

The sky lightened as they emerged from the embankment and made their way onto the plain. Tilman reined in his horse at the top of a low hill. "We're here," he said. His face relaxed into a smile, surprising Scott. Though he followed Tilman's gaze toward the south, the weak winter light and low hanging clouds masked whatever Tilman was looking at with such obvious satisfaction.

"Here is where I will build," Tilman said, more to himself than to Scott. He began to walk his horse in a large square, muttering as he went. "Here will be my casa grande. Two-story. Like Larkin's...better than Larkin's..." He turned his horse around to face the mountains. "I will own all this." He swept his arm across his body, taking in the land and saluting it in one gesture. "I'll raise what will soon be one of the largest herds in Alta California."

Suddenly self-conscious, Tilman cleared his throat. "We're going to ride the rancho's boundary today. We better get started."

He led the way north, retracing the path along the Río de Porciúncula they had taken the previous nightfall. Not far from the site that Tilman intended for his ranch house, Scott noticed a sycamore tree atop a low hill. From a thick, mottled gray trunk, its naked limbs stretched outward like an umbrella. Spindly branches like emaciated fingers flung themselves upward as if reaching for the sky. Scott figured the tree to be over ten feet tall, a stark contrast to the low bushes and grasslands surrounding it. Withered leaves clung to the tree's topmost branches, faded refugees of autumn that in other climates would have stripped the tree entirely. The tree seemed to own the hill, as if it had sat on the land since time began.

They rode along the river trail for a time without speaking. The storm had spent itself. As the morning passed, wisps of clouds slowly disappeared until the plain was topped by a cloudless sky in a blue more intense than the color of the bluebells Scott was accustomed to seeing every spring in St. Louis gardens.

Off to the east, Scott saw only a monotony of marshlands, nowhere that grazing cattle would find food. Tilman had said that much of the water seeped into the earth. Scott supposed his employer understood the land he had purchased.

Ahead, Tilman had stopped and was looking at him. No, not at him, Scott realized as he came abreast of his employer. Tilman was looking south along the trail they had taken that morning. Tilman pressed his left leg into his filly's side, which obliged by turning west toward the river.

"Does that seem like a particularly large clump of willows over there?" he said. "Hard to tell, when the branches are bare. I think we've reached the northern border of the ranch."

Without another word, he turned southeast. Sometime later, Tilman stopped again. He had pulled a piece of parchment from his pants pocket. "This diseño passes for a map around here," Tilman said, as Scott approached. "Want to look?"

Scott took the diseño from his employer. The borders of five ranchos were delineated on the fragile parchment. The diseño marked a few hills and rivers, not much to go on if a man wanted to ensure he was within the borders of his own land.

"The 300,000 acres of land the King of Spain granted to a Spanish soldier about sixty years ago was split into five ranchos. Rancho de Los Rios is one of the largest." Tilman was pleased by his tone. Flat. Betrayed no pride in his good fortune. "Which way do we go from here?" Tilman asked.

"We continue southeast a ways," Scott replied. He had always been good with maps.

Tilman must have agreed, because he set off immediately in the direction Scott indicated.

They ambled along the plain, guiding their horses through pools of water rimmed by wiry pickle grass and tall bushes with sharp pointed tips. Startled by the horses, great white herons lifted off from shallow streams, then flew silently on their broad angel wings.

The marshes reminded Tilman of nothing he remembered from his childhood. Central Massachusetts. Deerfield. In the fertile Pocuntuck Valley. Farmers made prosperous by soil enriched by the Connecticut River. Tall grasses provided milk cattle, sheep, pigs and goats with fodder. Lined the banks of the Deerfield River. Long summer days, the river flowed deep and clear. Tilman had known nothing of the longhorns the Mexicans raised until he came west. Learned to read cattle like a book. Which ones supplied the best hides, the most tallow; which ones were likely to die quickly or fall prey to diseases that killed off a herd. Visiting all the ranchos around the pueblo, buying from all, he had amassed enough knowledge that even the Mexicans, accustomed to their own breeds, looked to him for advice. Now, he'd own the animals instead of buying their hides, guaranteeing him a profit from the cattle trade as well as the hides and tallow he would sell.

A distance from the standing water, they reached a spot where water bubbled up from the earth. Tilman dismounted. He indicated the wall of mountains to the north with a wave of his hand. "A lot of the rain coming off the mountains ends up like this, in underground streams." He crouched down and drank from his cupped hands. "Come on now," he said. "You must be thirsty."

Scott needed no second invitation. He flung himself at the water. The sun was nearly at midpoint. He had drunk only a handful of muddy liquid scooped from the river early that morning.

Tilman pulled a hide bundle tied with twine from his saddlebag. "More beans and tortillas. I don't know about you, but I'm getting a little tired of this fare." The corners of his mouth creased as if he were going to smile.

Scott was surprised at the man's familiarity. "Thanks," he mumbled.

Before Scott finished eating, Tilman took up his reins and began to walk his horse forward, slowly at first, then more quickly, until the filly reached a full gallop. Scott tucked the rest of his lunch into his coat pocket and followed.

He tried to keep his employer in view as they rode south, veering east after Tilman stopped once to pull the diseño out again. The sun was well past midpoint when he saw Tilman stop ahead. As Scott rode closer, he saw Tilman dismount and extend his hand into a shallow stream.

"The San Gabriel," Tilman said.

Scott was confused. "I thought we crossed the San Gabriel yesterday, north of your ranch boundary?" he said, curiosity prompting him to speak.

"You're correct, young man. One and the same," Tilman said, pleased that his man had kept track of the surroundings. "Most of these rivers are shallow; they overspill their banks and carve new channels in years of heavy rains. For now, the San Gabriel splits at the base of the mountain range that rims this plain. One branch feeds into the Porciúncula on my land, as I told you. This branch flows south, becoming only the trickle you see. Within a few miles, it flows into a bay and then the sea."

From the river, they turned southwest, ambling along a creek. Gulls flew overhead, one diving into the creek to pluck out a fish, still wriggling, its silver scales glinting in the sun as the gull clutched it in its beak and flew away. The sun beat down on the plain. Scott dropped behind Tilman again, removed his coat and stowed it beneath his saddle's cantle. He pulled his hat down to shield his eyes. The old horse refused to trot; Scott peered ahead at Tilman, who grew smaller and smaller in the distance. Once in a while, a salt-scented breeze came up.

After about an hour, they reached a clump of cottonwoods on the edge of the stream.

"Rancho Los Alamitos," Tilman said, nodding due south, and turned his horse northwest to avoid trespassing.

Scott followed obediently, his head awash with landmarks, names, bits of information about the land, and most of all rivers, streams, water.

A shallow arc took them back toward the low hills where they had started in early morning. This time, however, they avoided the casa grande's future site and continued riding south. The hills became more prominent until Scott saw Tilman urging his horse up a hill that dwarfed all the others around it. Scott, too, urged his horse up the steep hill, reaching Tilman as his employer looked due south. Toward the west, the sun shone above a haze-obscured horizon.

"Now, we'll have some fun," Tilman said.

The next moment, Tilman was galloping full speed down the hill toward the horizon. The haze deepened to fog as Scott did his best to keep up. They reached the plain, Tilman far ahead. As Scott rode, he heard a boom and crash he would only have described as cannon fire. A regular pattern, the sounds came quickly, one after the other, followed by a short period of quiet that soon erupted again. The farther south they galloped, the louder the sounds became. Scott concentrated on catching up with his employer. He glimpsed Tilman ahead, then looked past him to a wide sand beach. Through the gloom, he spotted low rolling breakers. Beyond those, waves gathered to crash full force onto the shore. The boom of cannon fire, be damned! This was the Pacific!

Scott chuckled. His laughter rolled like the waves, expelled from his large mouth in gulps and gasps and finally in unfettered sound that, he imagined later, could be heard from the decks of approaching ships, if any had been near.

He couldn't remember laughing like this before. Perhaps he never had. There was nothing to laugh about in St. Louis. Here in this landscape composed of endless hills, high mountains, a wide plain and rivers both shallow and deep, there was something more to see—an endless ocean that carried the waves and wind from distant shores. Not even among the tallest trees had he felt so insignificant and so free.

Rain had begun to fall again when Tilman reached the pueblo late the next afternoon. In a hurry to reach his office before nightfall, he had left Scott to find his way upriver to town. Work on the ranch deed awaited him. Dismounting in his barn, he noticed his brother's horse and two others he didn't recognize.

"Good afternoon, Señor Tilman." A colonel wearing the uniform of the Mexican army jumped to attention when Tilman entered his office.

"I brought these gentlemen from the harbor a short while ago." Edward Tilman nodded toward the colonel and a younger lieutenant.

Tilman tried to recall if he had ever seen these men before. The colonel's face was marked by a scar that ran from the outside corner of his left eye to the corner of his mouth, a memorable deformity. The younger man idly shifted his feet until a sharp nod from his superior signaled him to stop.

"They insisted on seeing you," Edward said, nervously. "Colonel Mendoza and Lieutenant—"

"Yes, I saw two unfamiliar horses in the barn." Tilman shook each man's hand, nodded for them to sit down and sauntered back to his desk. Picking up a paper from a tall stack, he looked at it briefly before replacing it.

"I must report to the presidio day after tomorrow." Mendoza let Tilman know he had no time to waste. "In Santa Barbara."

"Of course," Tilman replied, without shifting his gaze from the papers in front of him. After a moment, he came toward them again and sat in a fourth chair his brother had hastily pulled forward. The waning winter sun placed the room in semi-darkness, but no one had seen to the lighting of the lamps. "May I offer you some brandy?" he asked.

"No," Mendoza said. "I've come to discuss a matter of great importance."

Tilman sat, unimpressed. He was used to self-important army officers coming to ask for lodging or a free meal. He always obliged.

Mendoza cleared his throat, drew his eyebrows together and paused. Then, he launched into questions, as if he and Tilman were taking up a familiar topic between them instead of meeting for the first time. "You know that Texas declared itself independent from Mexico?"

"Eight years ago. Of course." Tilman strove to keep his tone neutral. He looked at Mendoza's face. The man's pointed nose and high cheekbones marked him as being of Spanish descent.

"And you know that the American states are at each other's throats about slavery?"

"I wouldn't put it that way," Tilman said, "but I know what you're saying."

"Very interesting. How would you characterize the relationship between the northern and southern states?"

"I don't think you're here to talk about slavery, Señor Mendoza."

The colonel allowed a moment to pass. "In a way, I am, Señor Tilman." He stopped again. A muscle in his cheek worked, activating his scar.

Tilman gave up hope of getting any work done that night. He thought of his wife and daughter waiting dinner on him, how the fire would warm him, how he would enjoy sleeping next to his wife tonight, after his absence. He was known for his patience, however. He didn't hurry the colonel.

Mendoza began with greater vigor. "At some point, your nation—"

"Colonel, remember that I am a Mexican citizen."

"At some point, your nation will fight a war over slavery. We—"

"Who is *we*?" Tilman asked.

"We believe that the United States will start a war with Mexico to make Texas a state."

"Oh?"

"The real design will be to seize all of Mexico's land north of the Rio Grande River."

"Including Alta California?"

"Of course. The whole territory will be opened to slavery, and the United States' borders will reach the Pacific."

"Slavery will never be a part of California." Tilman was aroused despite his efforts to appear dispassionate.

"But you don't dispute the possibility of a United States war with Mexico?"

Tilman could barely see Mendoza's eyes, but he knew the urgency that drove the colonel. His own diatribe at Rougemont's studio, his discussion with Larkin, now this visit from a Mexican army officer: All told him that Alta California's situation was precarious. If the United States launched a war against Mexico, the Californios lacked the numbers—much less the will, he suspected—to defeat them. If California passed into United States' hands, how would he and other landowners fare? The United States government could honor their land deeds. Or would he find himself, in his sixth decade, having to defend everything he had carefully built?

"Let's have some light," Tilman said, in an even tone. He composed himself in the few minutes his brother used to light the office's two oil lamps.

"I think it's time to tell me why you are here, Colonel Mendoza," Tilman said, quietly.

Frustrated at his failure to intimidate Tilman, Mendoza motioned to his adjutant. The man's boots tapped loudly against the floorboards as he left the room. Obeying Tilman's glance, Edward also hurried out, shutting the door behind him.

"I am not only an army officer, Señor Tilman," Mendoza said after the men left. "My lineage goes back to Spain, but I fought on the Mexican side in our war for liberation."

Tilman's bland expression masked his thoughts.

The rain began again, pounding against the building.

"I come here not as an army officer but as one who loves Mexico. From the Yùcatan to Alta California."

"As do I," Tilman said.

"Then we have the same heart," the colonel said. "And you will not be offended by what I am going to say."

Tilman didn't reply.

"If the United States attempts to make California a territory, what will be your part?" Mendoza asked.

Ah, that's what this is all about, Tilman thought. Well, why didn't you come right out and say so? His shirt felt damp against his back. He longed to be home.

"I'm not going to help the United States," Tilman said, telling the man what he wanted to hear. "I am a Mexican citizen."

"And yet you were born and raised in Massachusetts. Your branches may be Mexican, but your trunk was formed in the United States. What does that make you, Señor Tilman?"

"I told you: I am a Mexican citizen." In truth, he couldn't say he would fight for Mexico, nor that he would fight for the United States. He'd have to see which government offered more. That is, if he had a choice. He guessed he would not. He knew that if the United States wanted land, they would get it. A fight might never be necessary. The sheer numbers of Americans who were willing to commit themselves to a new life in the west would determine the future of Alta California.

The lamps flickered, sending the shadow of each man onto the whitewashed wall. Tilman's shoulders rounded. Mendoza's frame, which had crackled with energy at the beginning of the conversation, now went slack. "My family and others in Mexico City urged me to stop here on my way to the Santa Barbara presidio. They want me to convince you to use your influence with Americans like yourself to resist a United States overthrow of the Mexican government in Alta California."

"And how would I do that?"

"That would be up to you. Surely you know your compadres well. You know the arguments you can use to convince them that a future under Mexico holds a brighter promise than one under the United States."

Tilman looked at the army officer's face. Having completed his commission, his scar melted into his cheek. Tilman thought of Alta California's quick succession of governors under Mexico and the recent clashes between army and citizens. On the other hand, he was one of many who were prospering under Mexico's lax rule. A government with a stronger hand might impose laws that would be less favorable.

"I will give your request my sincere consideration, Colonel." For the first time, Tilman's tone became cordial. Best to leave the door open for more confidences between himself and the influential Mexican families Mendoza represented, for the business opportunities they could offer, if nothing more.

Earlier that day, he had felt like a young man, flooded with the excitement of beginning something new, anticipating the rewards that awaited him. Alone after the colonel's departure, Tilman hunched into his chair and stared into space.

[4]

In early February, Scott moved south to join the dozen or so vaqueros already on the land. Although he had avoided becoming an object of derision in the pueblo by staying out of sight, he couldn't do the same on the rancho. He spent day and night with the vaqueros, only half-understanding their directions, their profanities. He tried to learn by observing and imitating— mounted his horse when the others did and rode off toward some distant point following the direction indicated by Felipe, the vaquero in charge. He watched as a vaquero lassoed a steer and waited patiently while foremen from neighboring ranchos delivered cattle, two or three dozen at a time, nearly every day. Scott took his turn at the cooking fire, burning the beans in the iron skillet as the others did. Soon after sunset, he bedded down, like the other vaqueros, under the old sycamore tree on the hilltop that he had noticed on his first visit to the rancho with Tilman.

In an effort to fit in, he twisted his ankle and tried to conceal his limp. He didn't complain when the vaqueros provoked him by stealing his zarape, used for everything from a shirt to a blanket; made him the last to get water from an underground spring; or pushed him forward, making him the one assigned to keep watch all night when a bear was sighted prowling along the river.

If his life was harder than it had been in the pueblo, it was better than St. Louis.

The vaqueros' chatter woke Scott early one morning.

Tilman had told him they'd soon be building a house on the ranch, but no work had begun.

Felipe prodded him in the side with the toe of his boot.

"Wha'?" Scott sat up, barely awake.

"Come with me," Felipe said. The day was drizzly and gray. Water dripped from the tree's bare branches.

Scott pulled on his boots and got to his feet. He walked a short distance behind Felipe, feeling the wet ground beneath the worn soles of his boots. The other vaqueros shuffled behind like a rag-tag parade. Where the horses were tethered a short distance from the sycamore tree, he learned why Felipe had pushed him awake. His old gray lay dead, tied on a now-slack rope to a stake in the ground. The other horses snorted and pulled at their ropes, trying to put distance between the dead animal and themselves.

No time to mourn, and why mourn anyway, the death of a dumb beast that had carried his carcass over the mountains. Loyal, though. Steadfast. Faithful. Scott looked away. When the sun was high, flies would cover its flesh. He'd have to drag it away, but before he did, he'd have to choose another horse.

He had seen the vaqueros' riding skill. Envied these tough, small men. Their agile bodies. The deft use of their legs and hands. The way a vaquero seemed to melt into his horse so that horse and rider moved as one. He could bury a spur into a horse's flank so hard the horse jumped away and ran like hell, then pull the animal up short and pivot sharply to the right. Scott was sure the horse would falter, but the animals knew as much about staying on their feet as the riders knew about staying in the saddle. The horse responded every time, turning or stopping at the rider's will. His horse had barely been able to keep up, and he hadn't minded. He knew he lacked the balance to perform those feats on any horse.

"Joven," Felipe called, beckoning Scott with his outstretched arm.

Scott walked away from the gray, his eyes fixed on the ground. Losing his horse was a blow. Until now, his only advantage came from being different—the sole Anglo—in the small group of mestizo and Indian vaqueros. Word had spread among them that he had worked in the store for Don Rodrigo Tilman. This advantage he was going to lose as soon as the vaqueros saw him on a horse like theirs, one that had known the freedom of plains or pampas and hadn't worn itself out, like the gray, from carrying a large white man over the Rocky Mountains.

"Sí," Scott answered, walking toward Felipe.

"You need a horse?" Felipe asked in Spanish, looking down at Scott from his own, a black mare, whose eyes moved nervously from side to side even as his rider held him steady.

"Yeah."

"Try this one," Felipe said, pulling a horse forward to let Scott see the choice he had made for him. The horse was a piebald, the ugliest of the lot, with the head of a plough horse and the body of a running horse. The beast looked at Scott from one blue and one brown eye, then turned away as if disinterested.

Scott couldn't slink away as he had sometimes been able to do when his father had called, "Boy. Boy, come 'ere." Scott had three brothers, but he knew "boy" meant him when his father was irritated or drunk, which was nearly all the time.

The other vaqueros approached, forming an uneven half circle. The rain had stopped. The sky was turning from black to deep blue, lighting the winter morning's verdant landscape. Scott stopped himself from flinching as a chill ran down his back. He halted while there was still space between himself and Felipe. The man in charge wasn't a bad sort. A few vaqueros showed real cruelty to the horses and cattle. Not Felipe.

"Ride this one," Felipe said.

Later, Scott didn't remember mounting the horse. One moment he was standing, the next he was astride, his legs bent nearly double to fit into the too-short stirrups. The reins were in his hand—how had they gotten there?—and he sat gazing at the ground from a greater distance than from the gray's back. The piebald was nearly two hands taller.

The next moment, he was face down on the sodden earth, a stinging pain on his cheek. He wiped away mud and blood as he got to his feet, too stunned by the fall to feel the wet cold of his shirt and pants.

The men laughed uncontrollably, slapping their thighs, clapping each other's backs. They all spoke at once in Spanish. Scott ignored them.

"OK," he said, because he knew what was demanded of him.

This time Felipe—who hadn't laughed and still hadn't said a word—held the reins near the bit under the piebald's head while Scott mounted. The horse sensed that Felipe was in charge and obeyed his touch.

As Scott mounted, he noticed that the stirrups had been lowered and were now at an angle that allowed him to grip the horse with his thighs. He felt some confidence begin to build. Some. Not much.

He released his hold on the saddle horn and grabbed the reins. The piebald stood still, snorting nervously. Felipe backed away. Scott applied more pressure to the horse's flanks, tensing his muscles from groin to knee, from knee to ankle. Instead of going forward, the horse reared and came down hard, kicking its hind legs skyward. Scott whipped back and then forward, managing to keep his seat.

Without pausing, the horse repeated the maneuver. Scott thought he was ready this time. He stood up in the stirrups, preparing to take the impact with his legs. Instead, he landed hard in the saddle. His ass and balls screamed pain as the horse planted its forefeet on the ground, again kicking its rear hooves toward the sky.

"Oof." Scott's lungs expelled air. Immediately, the horse kicked its hind legs a third time with greater force, doing what it knew would remove the despised presence on its back. Scott hung on to the saddle horn and nearly pitched over the horse's head. He righted himself just in time and sat straight in the saddle, tensing his thighs.

The horse came to earth and stopped. It pawed the ground, snorted furiously. Scott drew in a breath. Without a pause, the piebald took off running for all it was worth, stopped suddenly and shot its hind legs in the air. Scott sailed over its outsized head, landing in a heap five feet away.

He groaned loudly.

This time the men were silent. Scott had stayed on the horse's back for three of the animal's best efforts.

A cooking fire was burning when the men returned to the sycamore tree. An Indian girl bent over the flame. Her bare feet, caked with mud, protruded from under a worn cotton skirt. She clutched a faded rebozo with one hand, stoked the fire with the other. The soft fur of a rabbit pelt cape around her shoulders offered some insulation from the early morning chill.

She didn't look at the men as they stared at her.

Scott drew a little closer. He saw that she was young, younger than him for sure. The rounded cheeks of a young girl, a dark-complexioned version of his sister. Her hand was trembling. Scott looked sideways at his companions, who were now advancing toward the woman.

If they had been horses, they would have tossed their manes and kicked up their hooves, suddenly remembering they were wild.

Scott limped forward, putting his body between the vaqueros and the woman. He was at least a foot taller than the tallest of them and fifty pounds heavier. He could hear the river, high from the recent rain, rush in his ears. Scrub jays twitted overhead. Behind him, the grass rustled—a fox, a quail, a lizard. He paid no attention.

He picked up a dead sycamore branch and drew it across the earth one time from east to west. The stick made a harsh, grating sound and left a deep impression in the earth. The men watched silently. They looked at Scott and beyond him to the woman who was now putting the pot of beans on the fire. Muttering to themselves, they headed back to the tree to wait for breakfast. Scott limped along behind them, wet through and through, shivering. Felipe began to lay out the day's work plan. Scott listened, trying to understand what he was saying. For a moment, the woman was forgotten.

His sister had cried out only once when their father had entered her. Their beds separated only by a curtain, he had heard her. He was seven. Eight at the most. A small boy. Hadn't gotten his growth yet. His father could have swatted him like a fly. Scott had lain next to his younger brother. The boy was asleep and didn't hear anything. Did he?

When Scott looked at the fire again, the Indian woman was gone. She had placed the pan of beans on a rock before she left, a bucket of water next to it. The men rose slowly and headed back to the fire. They ate the beans and washed them down with water from the bucket, each taking several mouthfuls. They used the water that remained to splash on their faces and hair. Each man put on his sombrero, then headed toward his horse.

The sun had just topped the horizon.

They were ready to work.

Where had his mother been? It must have been the time she'd gone to midwife her sister's baby. She couldn't have been in bed with them both. Could she? This horse, this horse, how to mount it. How to stay on its back. His sister, crying out just once. This horse, ugly, its face close to his, demanding that he pay attention.

For the next few days, Scott rose earlier than the others, before winter's bruise of light spread across the sky. He left his zarape on the ground, rose to his feet, quickly, quietly, trying not to rustle the branches above his head. The February mornings were chilly, not St. Louis frigid, but sometimes cold enough to form a cloud of steam as he exhaled. When he reached the horses, he untied the piebald and led it a distance away, through the coyote bush and horseweed. The animal's ears went back, but it followed Scott obediently. Scott threw a blanket on the horse's back and slid the saddle into place. As he cinched the saddle, the piebald brought its left hind leg up and kicked Scott in the thigh. Scott limped out of range. Slowly, the pain subsided.

Once again, Scott approached the animal. He guided the bit into place. This time the horse laid its ears flat back in anger. Scott mounted quickly, foolishly thinking he could take the beast by surprise. The next moment, or the next after that, he was on the ground.

He picked himself up, rolled his head slowly from side to side and mounted the horse again. This went on for ten minutes, thirty minutes, an hour. Each day he stayed on a little longer. The horse had been given to him to ride. He had to show the animal who was boss, or he couldn't do his job. Every day, the horse managed to throw its rider. On the tenth day, Scott succeeded in riding the horse around in a wide circle, then a tighter one before he ended up, as usual, on the ground.

The next day, the animal trembled while Scott slipped blanket and saddle on its back. Its teeth came dangerously close to Scott's ear, but it accepted the bit. Scott swung his leg over the horse's rump and seated himself firmly in the saddle. He waited for the animal to rear up on its hind legs or kick until Scott fell in a heap to the ground. Instead, the horse stood still, as if waiting for Scott to make the first move. Scott walked the animal toward a clump of sage and beyond to another.

He touched the horse's flanks with his spurs.

The animal shot forward in a dead run. As Scott's left foot came out of the stirrup, he slid dangerously to one side. He glimpsed the ground coming up at him. "Dammn-i-t-t-t," he yelled, righting himself. Astride again, he turned the horse toward the sycamore tree. The line of vaqueros in front of him told him they had gathered to see his humiliation. He slid off the horse as soon as he reached them. They turned their backs, disinterested, and walked away. Only then did he realize that this was the first time he had dismounted of his own accord.

Don Rodrigo Tilman stood in the imagined doorway of his casa grande. From the hill where his new house would sit, he could see the distant ocean. He breathed in salt air and the multiple scents he had learned to associate with early spring. In mid-February there was a shift, imperceptible to new arrivals who, like himself more than twenty years before, had come to California from colder latitudes. They expected spring to announce itself with blooming crocuses as they remembered from childhood. But spring in California was early and subtle. That's what he had learned over the years. Barely past Christmas, or so it seemed, sage and wild roses scented the air. Now, in mid-March, the air was a profusion of fragrance. Willow and wild cherry mixed with elderberry, sugarbush and the ever-pungent sage. He shook his shoulders and stiffened his spine, drawing himself to his full sixty-five inches.

He unrolled the sheet of paper he'd been clutching in his fingers and held it out in front of him. A sketch of the casa grande provided by Henri Rougemont. Tilman's portrait was yet to be finished, but the young man had obligingly drawn a plan as Tilman described his dream. Tilman wanted a two-story home in the Monterey style of his friend, Thomas Larkin. More grand than the one-story adobes that Alta California landowners were accustomed to. The sketch revealed a U-shaped building. Across the front on the first floor would be a spacious dining room, the front door, vestibule and parlor. Stairs with hand-carved struts would lead from vestibule to a second-floor master bedroom that he would share with his wife. His daughter would have her own room next to theirs. A wide second-story balcony that angled somewhat southeast would be comfortable and private, overlooking a large garden. Here his family could see the ocean and enjoy the cool breezes.

But that wasn't all. The south wing, one floor only, would house a storeroom, blacksmith's forge, pantry and, on the end farthest from the main house, the foreman's room. The north wing, also one story, would consist of a large room for the vaqueros and more storerooms. Like all casa grandes, the kitchen would be outside under a ramada, near the dining room.

Tilman turned to face north. His back to the sea, he honed in on the space between the rancho's sheltering arms. Here there would be a large open area where horses would be brought to be shod. Vaqueros would leave at sunrise to ride the range and return at dusk for their evening meal. At night, high wooden gates on the west would close to keep him and his family safe.

Business—the buying and selling of cattle, hides and goods—would be conducted within or just outside the gates.

He imagined the area alive with activity, as it was today. Following Tilman's orders, the vaqueros had rounded up the cattle for their boss's inspection. Two hundred head were milling about, lowing loudly and roiling the dust. The vaqueros prodded the animals apart and calmed them by keeping up a soft, steady chatter. When an animal showed signs of growing restive, a vaquero was there to cull it from the herd and move it to the periphery.

"Ay yay! Paco!" Felipe gestured to one of the youngest riders, sending the vaquero off at a gallop to follow a steer that had taken off at a dead run. A dozen or so animals followed, and then thirty. Suddenly, Paco wasn't alone chasing one defiant animal; the whole herd and all the vaqueros were in motion. Horses reared and wheeled. Riders turned their mounts as cattle stampeded in all directions at once. In the melee, Tilman saw Scott on the ugliest horse he had ever seen, a piebald, whose great head looked far too large for its muscular body. For a moment, he forgot how clumsy Scott looked simply walking down the road. In the saddle, Scott looked confident. Except for his large frame, he looked no different than the others.

The next moment Scott was off after a steer, arms pumping, galloping at full speed, trying to close the distance between himself and the wayward animal. Tilman saw Scott pull his horse up short, awkwardly twirl a lasso and throw it toward the animal's head. The rawhide circle fell short of its mark. The steer kept running. Scott caught up and tried again. Tilman narrowed his eyes, trying to see if Scott was successful. He figured he wasn't, because Scott appeared an hour later without the animal in tow. Along the way, though, he had picked up several younger strays, and was policing them, riding close and urging them on in Spanish: "Vaya, vaya, vaya."

It was nearly dark. The vaqueros moved like shadows between their horses and the sycamore tree. Tilman motioned for Scott to follow him a short distance away from the others.

"I've been watching you today. You're not doing a bad job." And then, abruptly: "Do you want to take on the job of mayordomo?"

"Mayordomo?"

"Foreman."

Scott raised his eyes from the hard-packed ground where

the cattle had milled earlier that day, and looked at Tilman face to face for the first time. He noticed the man's skin was the color of lightly tanned leather, evidence of hours spent in the saddle under Alta California's sun.

With the work nearly done for the day, some of the vaqueros lounged against their horses. Scott heard a laugh, then a cough. A chill wind brought a memory of St. Louis when he was nine years old.

"You rotten son-of-a-bitch, you little fart. I'm gonna kill you when I get my hands on you." His father, in a drunken rage, was swinging an axe above his head, chasing Scott down the road. He had hidden in a neighbor's barn that night, shivering from fear and cold while each minute poised—and passed. When he returned home in the morning, his father lay across the kitchen table, snoring loudly, the axe nowhere in sight.

"Well?" Tilman said, brushing dust from his arms and shoulders with quick hard strokes.

"Don Rodrigo..." He knew nothing about the cattle and hide trade or about being in charge of a ranch. His eyes still on Tilman's face, he tried again. "Don Rodrigo...Felipe would make a better choice."

"I've spoken to Felipe. He thinks you are best to fill the job at the present time."

He chose not to reveal the conversation with Felipe he had had early that morning. In rapid Spanish he told Felipe, "I'm going to make Scott mayordomo."

The vaquero pulled back as if struck. Startled by the sharp move, his horse had wheeled in a circle. Felipe reined it in and positioned the animal so that he was face to face with Tilman again. "Why do you choose him as the foreman and not me?" Felipe had demanded.

"He can build my house. He can read and write," Tilman answered. He could have taken a hard line with Felipe, but thought it better to let the man blow off steam. The success of the ranch rested on his choosing the right mayordomo, Tilman knew. That person would be in charge of the ranch day to day—horses, cattle, men, supplies, trade. Felipe could do that job, Tilman was sure, but the man was illiterate. Without being able to read or write, do basic arithmetic, he couldn't conduct or record transactions.

Tilman needed a mayordomo who could manage the business of the ranch and supervise the building of the house at the same time. After many sleepless nights, he had concluded that the job needed two men, one to look after the cattle and vaqueros, the other to look after the house and Indian laborers. He congratulated himself on his unconventional solution.

Felipe was silent. He had confidence in himself as a leader. But while he knew the simple construction of an adobe, he didn't know about the two-story Monterey-style structure it was rumored Don Rodrigo wanted to build. And what Tilman said was true. He didn't know how to read and write. He looked past Tilman toward the horizon and began to plan his next move. He knew of many ranches in Alta California. There was nothing to keep him here.

Don Rodrigo anticipated the man's thoughts. "I'll make you this offer. You will be in charge of the vaqueros and the cattle. Scott will build my house. I will pay you equally."

Felipe was listening.

"You will teach him what to look for in a cattle trade. He will teach you to read and do sums. Nothing difficult," Tilman added, seeing Felipe's jaw tighten. "Just the alphabet and simple numbers."

Felipe took his time before answering. He looked first toward the mountains and then toward the sea, considering Tilman's offer.

"When the house is complete," Tilman concluded, "you will become the mayordomo."

"Yes, I'll do it." He would help Scott; Scott would help

him. Felipe was old enough to know that it didn't always work that way. But he had seen Scott with the horses, the vaqueros and the Indians. All gave the yanqui distance. Scott won over his critics, as he had the piebald horse, with honest, hard work. If Scott continued to act like a man, they would all profit.

[5]

Within a week after Tilman named Scott mayordomo, Indians began to converge on the rancho. First came the Tongvas, descendants of the people original to the plain. They came from Tibahangna, the Indian village near the ranch, then from other villages, north and east. From neighboring ranchos—Rancho San Pedro to the west, Rancho Los Palos Verdes farther west still, and the Rancho Los Feliz, near the pueblo. Luiseños walked from the southern coast; Chumash rode plank canoes from villages around the Mission Santa Barbara. A month later, the numbers of workers grew as Cahuilla arrived from the desert, and Serrano trekked from the mountains northeast of the plain. Felipe had told him they'd be lucky to have fifty workers. Within six weeks, they had more than a hundred.

Scott wasn't aware how fast the tale of his protecting the Tongva girl against the vaqueros had spread. What started as truth—Scott put himself between the vaqueros and the Indian girl—became larger in the retelling. In one version, he severely beat a vaquero who had tried to touch the woman.

"He is a large man," the Indians said, "and no one dares to challenge him." They were disappointed when they saw him the first time—his gait so loose-limbed it seemed as if his arms and legs went in separate directions. He rarely looked at them, hardly looked up from the ground at all, and seldom gave direct orders. As the days passed, they began to interpret his posture as modesty and his actions as trust. Unused to being trusted, they returned the favor with hard work.

Without the Indians' help, he wouldn't be able to build

the casa grande. The little experience he had in building a house—why had he mentioned it to Tilman, and how had Tilman remembered, a tidbit of information during their first meeting—was nailing a few boards together for the wooden frame of his aunt's house when he was twelve. The house was never very steady, after all. It swayed when the wind blew hard. Adobe didn't sway, he was told.

"Adobe crumbles in an earthquake," a vaquero said. "Better to sleep under a tree." The notion that it was safer to sleep outside wasn't lost on Scott, who would be given a room in the ranch house once building was completed. Neither was the vaquero's underlying message: Jealousy. Resentment. Scott paid no attention; he was used to worse.

Felipe delivered another lesson early one morning. "Clay holds sand together. Sand prevents cracking. Straw gives strength." Scott nodded, grateful for the primer on making adobe blocks. A glimmer of hope: He understood every word of Felipe's explanation, all told in Spanish.

Still, Scott didn't know much about adobes; fortunately for him, the Indians had learned from doing similar work on other ranchos. They hauled water from the river, poured it into a large wooden pit. They dug shovelfuls of clay-like soil and tossed it in the water. Some collected sand from the river and carried it, bucket upon bucket, to be mixed into the water and clay. Women tramped on the watery clay and sand, mixing it with straw carted from nearby ranchos. Other women slapped the wet mixture into rectangular forms wider than a hand span and three inches thick, smoothing the tops even with the forms.

The sun beat on the bricks. Two days, three. It was early April; the days were growing longer. Some days, the hot sun shone hour after hour. Scott sweated. The bricks dried.

A carreta arrived one morning, heavily loaded with victuals needed to feed the vaqueros and the Indians. Sacks of beans were piled high, bags of ground cornmeal, onions and late-winter squash filled the cart. An ox pulled the load. Riding alongside was a man on horseback who flicked a lariat against the animal's haunches from time to time. Tilman rode in front of the carreta.

"Some adobes dry? Good. Let's start the house," Tilman called out to Scott.

A surveyor had already visited. Within a few hours, he had laid out the perimeter of the ranch house, marking each of the four corners with a pole, the distance between the poles with rope. Tilman approached the flag at the northeast corner—a vivid red scrap of cloth tied onto a thin, straight tree branch stuck in the ground. He had long since memorized the floor plan, keeping it locked in his desk drawer and pulling it out to study when no one was around. He removed a handkerchief from his pocket and spread it on the ground.

"Bring me a bucket of adobe mud," he ordered.

Scott nodded to the Indians standing by. They knew what he needed and went to fetch it.

Tilman took off his jacket, rolled up his sleeves and knelt on his handkerchief. An Indian gave Scott the bucket, who in turn set it on the ground next to Tilman.

"Now," Tilman muttered. He scooped a handful of mud from the bucket with his bare hand, spread it on the ground and smoothed it with the wooden trowel held out to him. He set an adobe brick on top. Tilman placed the adobes needed for a neat corner, then rose to his feet, wiping his hand on his kerchief. The mud-stained cloth fluttered to the ground.

"You can do the rest," he said. Scott thought his employer was satisfied, although he'd shown no evidence of that. In truth, it was the happiest day of Tilman's life.

The Indians went to work immediately. One man, who had been designated a mason, quickly spread mud on the hard-packed earth. Other men—women and children too—brought bricks and set them next to him. The mason went to work, laying each adobe, joining one to the other with thick, wet clods of mud. He mortared each into place, patiently smoothing the adobe over the brick's top and around the sides. The Indians worked quickly. At the end of the day, the casa grande's dining room had an adobe floor.

Once the house's floor was dry, the masons—more men were drafted for the task in a process the Indians devised with no argument from the still-overwhelmed Scott—began at the northeast corner again, this time laying a thick coat of adobe mortar, then a layer of adobes on top of the foundation. Each new layer of adobes overlapped, locking together, making a wall, then making it stronger.

"The first floor wall for my family's living quarters must be three feet thick," Tilman had told Scott before they started. "It has to support the second story."

What Tilman had ordered emerged as Scott looked on.

The encampment seemed to run itself. From the hours before daybreak, when he heard the first sounds of women building the cooking fire for breakfast, until the last cigarette had been extinguished for the night, twenty people, then forty, then a hundred, then more were in constant motion. Each Indian laborer seemed to know what to do and did it.

Spanish had become a familiar language. Once he knew the words, the syllables were neat and clean. Sí, verdad, hombre. He recognized "el" and "la" as similar to the French "le" and "la" that he had heard in his mother's speech. These words needed the tongue and teeth.

Within a few weeks Scott could speak a little of the Tongva language, the words new but pleasurable. Syllables in the Tongva's language slid easily against each other like a well-made hinge: Ean, bone. Wehe, two. Kwah-ech, food.

Several weeks passed before Scott recognized one of the

adobe-makers. He had glanced at the pit, seeing that the Indians were at work mixing the adobe mud with their feet. He looked a second time, drawing closer. Yes, it was the Indian girl who had cooked for the vaqueros the morning Scott had first ridden the piebald horse, the day he had stood between her and the other men. Today, the weather too warm for the rabbit skin stole she had worn around her shoulders that morning, she wore a loose blouse of Mexican style, her breasts covered with string upon string of shells from her neck to her waist—cowries, conches, limpets, small clamshells. As Scott watched—her bare feet rising and falling rhythmically to mix the clay with straw, the shells swaying, clattering gently against each other—she admonished a small child playing in the mud that had sloshed over the pit's side. He recognized the tenderness in her face as the way his own mother had looked at him.

The boy was her son, he knew at once.

The child obeyed and moved away. For a moment, he was still; the next, he planted himself in the mud again. This time the Indian girl called out sharply, "Koo'ar," and raised her foot, preparing to leave the pit. Scott heard her voice, saw her little feet, mud caked like wet boots around her ankles, glimpsed the curve of her small breasts under her necklaces. He strode forward, took the young woman's hand and helped her from the pit. Just as quickly, he turned and walked away.

The murmur of Indian voices stopped. Few had ever seen a white man offer help in the way Scott had aided the Indian girl, twice now. A few shrugged their shoulders; all returned to work.

Scott retreated to the opposite end of the work yard where he sneaked a glance at the Indian girl from time to time. He had been with women. All whores. The first when he was thirteen. His pa had some money from a hog-butchering job he had just lost. Scott showed up to bring him home while there were still some coins left in his father's pocket. His father would have none of it, was already drunk, likely the reason he was fired.

"You're old enough to be a man," his father had roared. "I had my first woman when I was twelve, a neighbor girl. Let's go."

Scott followed him up the summer-sweltering streets. A long walk, from the western edge of town nearly to the river. Everything smelled of blood and whiskey. Or was that only his pa? Scott followed him into the first saloon they came to. A madam approached. Scott's father shoved his son toward her and said, "Take him, he's yours," and pressed some bills into her hand, laughing so hard he had to sit down.

Scott followed her to the back of the saloon where seven girls—a few as young as Scott, some old enough to be his mother—stood against the wall or sat, their legs akimbo, on straight-backed chairs.

"This one," the madam said, as she pulled the arm of a woman who looked old, at least twenty. The whore took the boy's hand and pulled him into the back room, her jaw set. She unbuttoned his pants. He held his breath. He felt her soft flesh enclose his hard prick. She pushed him away and pulled him toward her, once, twice. With a gasp, he spilled out all over her.

"Hey," she yelled. "This's the only dress I have." She walked away. He wanted to laugh. She looked so funny, her ass pooched out behind her, walking with her legs apart, trying not to wet her dress with his stuff.

After that, Scott waited for another chance. Wanted a little neighbor girl like Pa had had, but what girl would have him? Girls either looked the other way when he got close, or they looked through him as if he weren't there at all.

His father took up a new harangue. "Wet your whistle again?" he'd say, laughing. Nothing was funny that Scott could see. Every once in a while, when he'd worked a job and intended to bring the money home, he went to a whorehouse again, discovered there were lots of them. More than he ever visited. He felt guilty using money maman and the children needed to buy food. The places he could afford stank. He'd heard of disease; men were infected in places like those. He was afraid. He never got a disease and never stopped going the whole time he lived in St. Louis.

California was different. Not many people in the pueblo. If Scott visited a whore, he was sure Tilman would know. Disapprove. He couldn't take a chance. Now, he pinned his hopes on the Indian girl. Not to use like a whore. Something else. Someone important.

After a while, Scott figured out his job: keep order and answer questions. In St. Louis, his size was a liability. His father beat him harder the taller he grew. Boys his own age derided him for being big and slow. Here, his size was an asset. If a Mexican laborer was lolling in the sun, he set to his task as Scott approached. An Indian woman who stood by while the others worked got the same attention. He towered over the mayordomos from other ranchos who came to sell their cattle. With them, his size was his only advantage.

He had his first insight into all he had to learn when he accompanied Tilman on a cattle buy little more than a week after the brick foundation had been laid. Tilman arrived well before midday, his horse at full gallop,

"Let's go," he called to Scott from his saddle. "We have to meet the mayordomo of Rancho San Pedro this morning." The mayordomos of other ranches made the cattle deals. Felipe had the knowledge of cattle, but he didn't hold the title mayordomo. If Tilman was going to own a thousand head by the time his casa grande was due to be finished in late fall, as he wanted, Scott would have to assume the responsibility. With construction of the ranch house begun, it was time that Scott took over.

Scott had started to move toward Tilman as soon as he

saw his boss approaching. Now, he ran—or what passed for running in a man so large and uncoordinated—for his horse.

Willow and cottonwood trees lined the Río Porciúncula's banks; their heavy foliage shaded the shore and hung low over the water. The piebald obeyed the pressure of Scott's knees and entered the river, venturing forward until the river trailed along its belly. The animal's hooves sounded hollow against the rock-strewn river bottom. Upstream, the river swirled around a small island of cattails and tules. Scott guided his horse through a whirlpool where the water reached its breast. Still, the animal retained its footing. In the middle of the river now, the sun shone directly down on him. The animal moved quickly toward the shallows on the opposite shore as Scott removed the kerchief he wore round his neck. The water low, his horse proven trustworthy, Scott dared bend over to dangle the cloth into a rock-rimmed pool. Light flicked the water's surface; beyond his fingertips a school of steelhead trout swam upstream. He swung himself upright and dripped cold water over his face while the animal carried him forward.

Trees shaded the Mississippi River south of St. Louis too, but benefitted only those who walked or rode along its banks. On a warm spring day—although never as warm as this so early in the season—the mile-wide river absorbed the sunlight and threw it back as heat. When Scott was a boy, and his father passed a day sober now and then, Thomas Scott would speak about the river. Though the man's thoughts were as opaque as the waterway, Scott knew by the warmth of his tone, even once, a catch in his throat, that his father loved the Mississippi. Henry Scott's knowledge of the river was limited to the traffic he observed from the dock along the levee. His only experience was a brief trip downriver as part of a steamboat crew, and the disappointment of being deposited on the shore after colliding with one too many workers, passengers and buckets. Scott couldn't have known it then, living so close to his father's violence, but the Mississippi was the great love of Thomas Scott's life; that he couldn't make a living on its waters, his greatest regret.

Tilman disappeared into a willow thicket on the opposite bank, Scott behind him. They rode without speaking through a field of wild mustard taller than their horses, avoiding bogs where the river had outstripped its shallow banks during the rainy season and created marshes that were drying quickly under the hot sun. Scott lost sight of Tilman in a sea of golden flowers, only to see him emerge farther ahead, atop a low hill. When Scott reached the hilltop, he spotted a corral about a mile distant—half a league, he thought, reminding himself of the Spanish equivalent—and the Dominguez family's Rancho San Pedro hacienda beyond.

Fifty or so steers and cows were confined to the small corral that adjoined a larger pen. The mayordomo took one look at Scott—an overgrown boy, he decided at once—and the ugly brute he rode. From then on, he addressed all his comments to "Don Rodrigo Teel-maan," which he enunciated carefully to indicate respect. The three looked on as a vaquero herded the animals, one by one, through a narrow gate from the corral into a larger pen.

"Look at each animal. Don't make a decision until you're sure," Tilman said to Scott, speaking in English to hide the instructions he was giving to his mayordomo. "Watch how the animal moves. If it drops behind the others, it may be ill."

He signaled the Rancho San Pedro mayordomo, who called out to two vaqueros in the corral. The vaqueros lassoed a steer and brought it to the ground, where Tilman bent over and peered into the animal's mouth. Touching the animal's side with the palm of his hand, he continued instructing Scott. "The eyes should be clear, without redness or swelling. The mouth should be free of sores. Look at the animal's hooves. Do you see any injuries? Touch the animal; how it feels under your hand tells you a lot about its health."

Inspections complete, the animals moved around the enclosure, trotting, stopping, reversing direction, bumping into each other. Tilman and the mayordomo walked away from the pens to make the deal. Tall strands of brilliant yellow mustard grass would have hidden the two men from sight if Scott hadn't stood close enough to hear them. Not that hearing helped much. They spoke so fast, Scott lost most of the transaction. At the rancho, Felipe must have adjusted his speech to a newcomer's ears, Scott decided. He had assumed he knew more than he actually did. How many head of cattle was Tilman going to buy? Scott knew they talked about a delivery date, but was it during the coming week or the week after?

As negotiations continued, the men raised their voices. "Forty escudos for the forty head I liked." Scott understood Tilman as he made his offer a second time. He knew Tilman was offering the equivalent of eighty dollars.

"Impossible. They're worth at least twice—"

"Ridiculous," Tilman allowed himself to say before his scowl relaxed into its usual neutral expression, impossible to read. But he softened his words by inclining his head toward the mayordomo, as if he did not mean to offend.

"Not so, Don Rodrigo. Just last week, I was offered seventy-five escudos for fifty head."

"Not any of these fifty head," Tilman argued.

The mayordomo didn't respond. "Sixty escudos for the forty head, Don Rodrigo. That is the price," he said at last.

Tilman tilted his head back, glaring at the cloudless sky. "No," he said abruptly and walked away. His foot was in his stirrup before the mayordomo spoke again.

"Don Rodrigo," the mayordomo called after him. "I know you are a great friend of the Dominguez family. Why don't you like to buy these for a mere fifty-five escudos?"

"Fifty." Tilman would not be moved.

"Fifty-two."

"I would be honored," Tilman said.

Later that day, Tilman paused along the riverbank. "Now you see how it is done. You'll do the same yourself," he said, more of a command than an expression of confidence.

Scott nodded as if he'd remember it all. He dreaded the day he'd have to make these decisions himself.

On a morning in early May, a new cook took over. She burned the morning beans. Thick, acrid smoke surrounding the ramada told the waiting vaqueros that breakfast would be late. There was even a question of whether there'd be food at all, since the carretas with supplies from the pueblo were already two days overdue. The men grumbled. Their stomachs growled and they milled about uncertainly, even after Scott assured them that breakfast would be ready soon. Their dissatisfaction could have turned ugly if Felipe had not intervened. He culled two men he knew to be troublemakers. Under the supervision of a vaquero he trusted, he sent them north to the pueblo to see if the supply carts needed help. Each man received a short length of dried beef as an inducement to keep the peace.

Scott watched them ride away, grateful for Felipe's intervention. At the same time, he was ashamed that he hadn't thought to do it himself. He couldn't blame the vaqueros if they saw Felipe as the foreman.

Felipe walked away after the men left. The vaqueros lounged around the area that would be the courtyard when the north and south wings were completed, passing the time until breakfast by telling stories Scott couldn't understand.

Shortly after noon, long after the men had eaten and left with Felipe to look for strays, a man on horseback approached the rancho.

"I'm the mayordomo of Rancho La Habra," the visitor said from the saddle, indicating a direction northeast with a wave of his hand. "Don Rodrigo Tilman wants to buy some cattle from us." He leaned down and held out a letter for Scott to inspect. "A few men and the cattle should be here by late afternoon. Can you put us up for the night, and we'll do some business in the morning?"

Scott tried to understand what the man had said in rapid Spanish. Peering at the letter, he recognized Tilman's signature and read the short message slowly to himself three times until it made sense. Meanwhile, the man sat astride his horse, waiting in the hot sun.

"Sixty to seventy head?" Scott asked to make certain he had understood what he read.

"Yes."

"You expect them late this afternoon?"

"Yes." The foreman had heard about the yanqui mayordomo. What a foolish boy he appeared to be. What a long time he spent looking at the message. How poorly he pronounced the language. Tilman was known to be a shrewd businessman. This boy could hardly have been Tilman's first choice as his mayordomo.

Scott knew that hospitality was the first rule of ranch life. Strangers were treated like family. But food was in short supply. Each steer represented an investment on Tilman's part. He didn't want to kill one more than Tilman had authorized. Even if beans had been suitable for the evening meal, there wasn't enough for the vaqueros and workers themselves, let alone the visitors.

If the carretas arrived in time, he wouldn't have to face the embarrassment of offering them a meager meal. "Of course. We'll be ready any time you get here," he lied. "How about some water before you return to your men?" His confidence sounded false to his ears, but the stranger drank from the bucket Scott offered and rode away.

By late afternoon, the carretas still hadn't arrived. The three men who had been sent to find them were probably already in the pueblo, drinking at a saloon, Scott decided. That left him with one extra mouth to feed—there were four men from the La Habra ranch—and a shortage of provisions. The hot wind coming from the desert had scoured the land all day, making the vaqueros more short-tempered than usual as they rode in from the hills. Their shouts sounded like jabs. The best riders allowed their horses to crowd slower ones, although the whole plain was open to them. Once again, Felipe intervened.

Pulling Scott aside, he said, "There's enough dried beef for dinner tonight. Slaughter one of the older steers and start cooking it early tomorrow morning. The meat will be tough, but it will give us enough food for two or three days. The carretas should arrive by then."

Scott agreed, ashamed that Felipe had again come up with a solution.

"The order should come from you," Felipe prompted.

"Of course." Scott immediately told a group of vaqueros what to do. The men went to find a steer of the correct age and size. Scott heard them grumbling as they left.

Traveling to a neighboring ranch was a special occasion. The mayordomo employed by an important man like Tilman should have had gossip to share. He should have been able to tell them about ships that had recently docked in the harbor, offered wine and stories that made them all laugh. Instead, they were given an unsatisfying portion of dried beef. Scott apologized for the absence of wine, explaining that the carretas were late in arriving.

"Pobrecito," he heard a visiting vaquero mutter sarcastically under his breath. Poor little one, as if Scott were a child. He felt like one. He had no gossip and no news. The visitors bedded down early, instead of lingering around the fire. Scott tossed and turned, ticking off his faults until he finally drifted into sleep.

Breakfast the next morning was on short rations. Everyone was hungry. Few Indians showed up for work, unusual and unfortunate. The lack of activity reflected poorly on Scott, and he knew it. The wind blew hard from early morning, creating eddies of dust mixed with wild grasses. The sun shone with a ferocity that always accompanied the hot, dry winds. Devil winds, they made men and cattle nervous.

Cattle buying started immediately after breakfast. Scott's men had constructed an enclosure in an open field between the ranch house and the sycamore tree. The La Habra steers and cows had been deposited there the previous afternoon. An adjoining pen, like the one at the Rancho San Pedro, could be used to examine an individual animal. Felipe, who knew everything about cattle, or so it seemed to Scott, had offered to help.

With Felipe at his side, Scott ordered the vaqueros to send the first animal through the gate and accepted it. He looked into the second animal's mouth, judged it free of sores and, nodding to Felipe, accepted the second animal too.

Scott felt his stomach begin to relax. Maybe he had learned more from Tilman than he thought.

The next animal appeared gaunt. It headed reluctantly toward the smaller pen, its tail between its hocks. Felipe inclined his head downward and said nothing. Scott said, "Not this one." He gave the same verdict about the next.

The mayordomo objected, "Señor Scott, what is the matter? We come all this distance, and you refuse half our animals? Is that the way the game is played in the United States? Not here, señor."

Scott didn't understand all the man said, but he recognized the anger in his voice. How was he going to smooth over the matter with the mayordomo, given his limited Spanish. News traveled fast between the ranches. As the mayordomo of a new ranch, especially one owned by the prominent Tilman, he couldn't afford to be seen as overly critical. At the same time, it wouldn't serve him or the ranch if the purchased animals didn't yield good quality hides.

Instead of replying, Scott signaled for another steer. This one passed Felipe's discerning eye. Two hours later, Scott had rejected only eight of the seventy head. Flowers from wild mustard plants, blown about by the winds, carpeted the field. Scott and the La Habra foreman moved to the shade of the tall sycamore tree to talk. Felipe, lacking formal authority, stayed with the cattle after quietly suggesting a price Tilman would accept.

Scott's mouth was dry with anxiety. Counting anything over forty in Spanish gave him particular grief, and he still had difficulty translating American dollars to gold escudos. As he and his counterpart walked toward the sycamore tree, he silently practiced saying the price to himself.

"I can offer you sixty-two escudos," Scott said, half turning to face his counterpart as soon as they reached the tree.

"No," the mayordomo replied. "You know, you got ten longhorns here. They make the best hides."

Scott's father loomed over him, tall and fleshy, his arm raised to strike him. "You sold a pig for a few coins? You don't know nuthin', boy. Nuthin'. I try teachin' you, but you never learn." Nine-year-old Scott wanted to squeal like the piglet he had sold that morning to a neighboring farmer, an effort to scrape a little money together to feed his mother, sisters and brothers. The next moment, the boy was on the ground; his empty stomach gave up nothing but bile.

"Name your price," Scott said.

"Ninety-three."

Scott was too surprised to speak. That was one hundred eighty-six dollars for sixty-two head, a premium price.

Rancho La Habra's mayordomo didn't wait for an answer. He turned his back on Scott and walked toward the herd.

Scott saw Felipe start toward them. The look on his face told Scott that Felipe was surprised a deal had been reached so quickly.

"Wait," Scott called.

The mayordomo stopped, his back to Scott.

At the Rancho San Pedro, Tilman and the foreman had bargained for a time before Tilman had walked away, bluffing, after all. Scott hadn't expected the Rancho La Habra mayordomo to refuse to bargain. "Ninety-three," the mayordomo repeated.

"You're a little good for nothin'," Scott's father yelled as he beat him. "I'm 'shamed of you."

"Ninety-three," Scott echoed miserably. He wanted only for the transaction to be over.

[6]

"Don Rodrigo, please do not move," Henri Rougemont said, respectfully using the formal command. After many months, the man had finally agreed to sit again for him.

Tilman, about to reach for a handkerchief to wipe his brow, drew his hand back. Nearly eight months had passed since he first sat for the artist. The portraits of his wife and daughter still hung in his office, ready to be carted with his own to the ranch. That he had made no effort to see Rougemont had become a sore topic between Tilman and his wife.

Summer's heat turned the small room uncomfortably warm. Tilman felt sweat collect under his arms. His nose itched. The short temper he usually concealed under a cloak of pleasant, noncommittal observation wore thin.

"I don't have time to pose for a portrait," Tilman had tried to explain to his wife. She would have none of it. Tilman thought about the months of labor he had put in between his previous sitting and this one. Everything demanded his attention at once. His brother continued living at the harbor to oversee the unloading of ships' cargoes, storing the goods in Tilman's port warehouse or arranging to have them carted to the pueblo store. Though Edward was proving more reliable than his original lackadaisical attitude indicated, Tilman didn't trust him. He monitored all of Edward's transactions.

Edward's duties at the store continued too, which was a constant source of irritation between the brothers. Scott's replacements—four men who came and left quickly, one after the other—proved far less capable than Scott and less agreeable.

to the customers, in spite of their abilities in Spanish. Tilman let go of the first for insubordination, the second for stealing, the third for laziness, and was considering firing the fourth because the man arrived late every day the previous week, obviously hungover.

And the ranch. Tilman's face relaxed at last. When he had visited two weeks before, he was pleased to see two hundred Indians and Mexicans working on the house. The sun hung, a fiery sphere, over the late afternoon landscape. Workers moved lethargically in the early summer heat. Still, the house was beginning to take shape. All the exterior walls were up, three feet thick on the living quarters, as he had instructed, to support the second story. From a distance, Tilman observed Scott standing near the adobe pit, overseeing the women. He saw Scott offer his hand to a young Indian woman as she stepped out of the pit, a curious gesture that surprised Tilman for a moment until his attention was drawn elsewhere.

An air of calm pervaded the site. The older man didn't know how Scott had done it, but the mayordomo seemed successful in gaining the workers' respect. They didn't move fast, but they did move; there were no laggards.

Tilman knew that Scott wasn't as successful in his cattle trades. The other rancheros had reported on Scott's meager knowledge. "You've got a good worker in Felipe," they laughed, but your mayordomo..."

Saying anything more would have been insulting. Tilman, however, knew he had made the correct decision. He had hired Scott to build the house. The title of mayordomo was something Scott needed to legitimize his status, so foremen from other ranches would trade with him. Tilman hadn't expected Scott to have any knowledge of what made one steer valuable and another worthless. He knew he had lost some money in the deals Scott had already undertaken.

On the other hand, Felipe told him that Scott was

gradually learning. And the documents Scott had drawn up as bills of sale would stand up to scrutiny by other landowners if Tilman was asked. Tilman counted himself lucky that Scott had done no worse.

"Don Rodrigo, you have stayed so still I have been able to make some progress," Rougemont said. "Why don't you rest for a few minutes while I locate the brush I need?" He opened his leather sack of supplies and began to rummage through it.

Tilman's knees ached as he rose, an unpleasant reminder of age. He limped to the window and gazed onto fields alive with neat rows of vines, already in full leaf though it was only early July. A slight breeze cooled him. No matter how long he lived in Alta California, he was amazed each spring when trees went from buds to leaves in a matter of days, and flowers instantly appeared on plants that had been dormant all winter. It happened months earlier than in Massachusetts. He recalled digging in the hard soil near Boston as a very young boy, trying to coax a vegetable garden out of the frozen ground in early spring. Even in summer, he had battled the rocks, removing ones that seemed to rumble up from some mysterious place deep in the earth. No matter how many he removed, there were always more.

Are we to be a part of that bitter land? he thought. A vast continent lay between his birthplace and Alta California, but, traveling by ship as he had done nearly twenty-five years before, he had never seen it. What he could not see he could not imagine, so he visualized Massachusetts' rolling hills and slow-moving rivers, where he should have seen the West's vast expanses of prairies, towering peaks and tumultuous waterways. These images would have explained the Americans' hunger to inhabit the West and the government's determination to help them do it. He thought about the United States only rarely, most often when his assumed ability as a Yankee tradesman gave him prestige with a Russian, French or American captain, but when he did, he recalled long winter months so cold he was sure he'd never get warm. The contrast with the scene he saw from his window—a land so willing to be productive—brought him more pleasure than he would have admitted.

At the time of the Mexican colonel's visit, months before, Tilman had refused to take sides in any looming dispute between Mexico and the United States over Alta California. Now he scowled, unable to see into the future. Would he lose or benefit if California became a territory of the United States?

"Please, Don Rodrigo, would you be so kind as to smooth your brow?" Rougemont said, as Tilman returned to his seat. "Your scowl makes tension in your whole body. Think of pleasant things."

"Pleasant things, you say." Tilman's scowl deepened. "When it comes to politics, there are none. You know, a United States ship captain, who visited last week, tells me that the Congress is preparing to annex the Republic of Texas."

Rougemont held his brush up to the light to inspect its bristles. "I don't hear much gossip. I'm usually here sketching," he said.

"Hardly gossip. Do you know what that means for Alta California?"

The artist peered at the canvas, unsure whether he had correctly captured the angle of his client's shoulder.

"It means that fulfillment of manifest destiny is near. The Americans will gain control of the continent to the Pacific, in one way or another," Tilman said. "A war with Mexico over Texas will inevitably lead to a war with Mexico over California."

"A very bad thing, I'm sure," Rougemont responded, with less vigor than if he were commenting on a poor quality wine.

"You haven't been listening, but what can I expect from an artist? I'll tell you...at this moment, Alvarado and his band in Monterey are plotting Governor Micheltorena's overthrow—how they'll do it, I don't know."

"Ummm, yes, to be sure," Rougemont said. He had sketched out his subject's jacketed torso, but it still didn't look right to him.

"If the United States does attempt to take Alta California, Micheltorena or any other governor sent from Mexico will be of no help."

"None," Rougemont replied politely, his thoughts on how to capture the folds of Tilman's coat. He painted over his attempt and began again.

"That's the problem with these men that Mexico sends us. We pay for their soldiers, but we get nothing in return."

"Nothing." Rougemont scrubbed out his attempt a third time. "Sir, will you straighten your arm just a bit, please? That's a little too much." He put down his brush and approached Tilman. He touched Tilman's sleeve. The man, deep in thought, jumped in surprise.

"Sorry, sir. I didn't mean to startle you." Rougemont adjusted Tilman's lapel, smoothing a fold of fabric away from his collar until it lay flat.

"One thing I'm sure about. The Americans will have easy going, because we are a divided people. At this moment, we need strong and united leadership, and we don't have it."

"To be sure," the artist said.

Tilman stood abruptly. "I have too much to do to spend any more time here today."

Rougemont put down his brush. "But if you can stay another hour, Don Rodrigo, please," he pleaded. "I'll paint quickly, and then I'll need only one or two sittings to finish the portrait."

"Go today, please," Tilman's wife had chided as he left his home in the pueblo early that morning. He did everything possible to cultivate the love of the two people he valued most in the world, his wife and daughter. "Our house will be finished soon. I want these portraits to hang in the parlor. Please, my dear," she had begged, her hand on his arm, her dark eyes fixed on his face.

He sat down again. "One hour, not a minute more," he said.

Too late for his midday meal, Tilman left Rougemont's to make his second visit of the day: the Avila adobe in the center of the pueblo. The silence of a warm summer afternoon was broken by the shouts of children playing in the Zanja Madre. Tilman guided his horse around them. No need to hurry; he didn't want to disturb the Avila family, who were likely taking their siestas. Now blind to the day's beauty—the air still but not humid, the temperature warm but mild— Tilman's earlier ruminations on the land were replaced by anxiety. If he had been dressed in typical Californio style, which allowed more freedom of movement, he would have been quite comfortable. As it was, he wore a dark woolen suit, one of many he insisted on importing from Massachusetts for all but the most festive events. His mood grew increasingly somber as he passed the cemetery next to the pueblo church. Don Francisco Avila was buried there, doubtlessly turned to dust after eleven years under the barren ground. A pious man, Don Francisco had donated the church bells that still rang over the pueblo. But he was gone, after building the much-admired Avila adobe, after fathering three daughters and a son.

Don Rodrigo stood before the adobe now. The home's longest wing ran north to south, parallel to the river, less than a kilometer to the east. A wing at the north end shaped the building to form the letter L. A porch, where Tilman and Avila had often sat to observe the pueblo's business, ran the length of the building. True, by Massachusetts standards, it wasn't much: thick mud walls, a roof of cane poles and grasses covered with tar. But Tilman noted the French doors and window frames that set the house apart from simpler ones in the pueblo. He knew that the furniture inside was covered in silk damask, imported from France, and the rooms were spacious. He tied his horse to a post, then walked around the house to the patio behind instead of climbing the five steps to the front door. He would wait until Januario, Avila's son, awakened from his siesta.

"Don Rodrigo, how good to see you." Januario Avila emerged from the house onto the back patio as Tilman entered the courtyard.

Irritated at wasting his day under Rougemont's scrutiny, Tilman was immediately soothed by Avila's relaxed demeanor. The younger man was twenty-one, but his round face and wide eyes gave him the look of an innocent boy. He was dressed in the style of a Californio, his trousers buttoned up the sides with large copper buttons, a green shirt and crimson sash around his narrow waist.

"Your mother and sisters are well?" Tilman inquired. Best not to come to the point too quickly. Don Francisco had schooled Tilman in the Californios' ways. "Always take time to catch up on news of the family, of the day, the ranchos, business, politics...don't say too much. No one wants to hear a yanqui full of advice." Tilman remembered how Don Francisco looked away when delivering his lessons, so as not to embarrass the younger Tilman. The landowner was known for his manners as much as for the elaborate fandagoes he gave for visiting sea captains, soldiers, dignitaries, compadres.

A garden and vineyard filled Tilman's field of view. He squinted, trying to distinguish where Avila's vineyard ended and Rougemont's land began, but couldn't see any line of demarcation. The day grew hotter as it wound down.

Tilman drank the glass of brandy his host offered and allowed himself to relax.

"I hear your new house is coming along well, Don Rodrigo," commented Januario.

"Quite well," Tilman said.

"And your mayordomo? How is he doing?"

"Ay, you're going to make jokes at my expense, Januario?"

Avila took advantage of the older man's years of friendship with his father. "Well, you have to admit..."

"Nothing," Tilman said. The lines around his eyes creased, the only hint that he took the teasing well. He had seen the young man grow up and attended the naming of his younger sisters. Since Don Fernando's death, Januario had been in charge of the house and the family's ranch, Rancho Las Cienegas. His uncles, landowners themselves, advised him. Still, it would have been a heavy weight for most young men. But Januario learned quickly. Moreover, he made the transition from boy to man without losing his good nature.

"Believe it or not, Januario," Tilman said quietly. "My man is responsible for building the house and is doing a good job of it."

"Of course, Don Rodrigo, I wouldn't expect anything less."

Although he sounded unconvinced, Tilman let the matter drop.

"I came by today to see if you can deliver some tar," Tilman said. As part of the Rancho Las Cienegas, Avila owned the area's largest tar pits, ten miles west. The thick liquid bubbled up from the ground, was collected in baskets by the Indians and carted off to roof a new house, wherever it was being built. By Mexican law, the tar was free to anyone who wanted it, but Tilman needed the services of Januario's workers as well as his own.

"Of course. For your rancho?"

"Yes, I'll need it next month. What will I pay for delivery?" Tilman stopped himself from adding the figure to the mounting toll of rancho construction costs.

"We can talk to our mayordomo at Rancho Las Cienegas. Let's ride over there together in the morning," Januario said. "He'll be able to give you an accurate price."

Tilman glanced at Januario. Perhaps the man was reminding him about the relative value of their respective foremen. But Avila was gazing at the vineyard, appearing to be mesmerized by the profusion of vines that hid the banks of the Río de Porciúncula from view.

"I'll be here at nine then." Tilman wanted only to be gone. The collar of his black wool coat chafed his neck; he felt his earlier irritation return.

"I'm happy to oblige you, Don Rodrigo."

Tilman drank a second glass of brandy, then pushed back his chair. "Oh, I nearly forgot."

"Yes?"

"Let's make it two days from now. I'm meeting my foreman tomorrow at the mission."

"Going to make a purchase of some cattle? I don't think you'll find many that meet your standards."

"Yes, I expect you're right, but I haven't seen the old padre in a long time. I thought I should look in on him too."

"His health isn't good, that's true. Tell him I send my best wishes," the young man called as Tilman left the patio.

The next morning Scott was in the saddle before sunrise. The twenty-mile trip to the mission could take all day, but if his horse alternated between a trot and a walk, he was sure he could reach the mission by noon, when Tilman would surely have arrived.

"Follow the river toward the mountains," Felipe said, as Scott mounted the piebald. "But continue northeast instead of going west toward the pueblo. You'll come to a stream, the arroyo seco. Ride east a ways—you'll see the mission. It's only an hour or so from the pueblo."

As he headed north, the sky above the mountain range lightened to blue-black. Shortly, streaks of red and gold appeared against a pale blue wash, faded to pink and disappeared, leaving a vista of cornflower blue above his head. A cloudless sky, the kind of summer morning Scott had learned to expect on this wide plain. He rode easily in the saddle, a big man on a large horse. The piebald under him, ugly as ever, had turned out to be a good companion, responding to the gentle pressure of his knees, rarely attempting to throw him, even when startled by a rabbit on the lookout for food or a rattlesnake coiled in the sun.

Scott looked east, pulling his hat down to shield his eyes from the glare. The rancho stretched before him; its hills appeared barren, covered by low bushes—the seep willow's small white flowers, the blue-green sagebrush—since the spring's wild mustard had died off. Scott knew the vaqueros were glad to see the end of mustard grass for another year. Often on a spring evening, Scott heard them swearing at the tall stalks for hiding the cattle, making their work of keeping track of the animals more difficult. They weren't seduced, as Scott was, by the sight of the long grass's brilliant display.

He didn't spend much time thinking about the landscape or the vaqueros. Alone, he thought about the Indian girl. For several days, he hadn't seen her at the adobe pit. Not so unusual, he told himself. She had left for days at a time before, returning always to mix clay, straw and water with the other women. Then, the day before, his early morning wanderings around the courtyard before breakfast had taken him to the ramada, where he knelt to pick up a spoon. In itself, an unusual act for a man, a white man, a mayordomo. As he rose to his feet, he raised his head and saw two eyes peering into his, eyes so brown they appeared black, in a narrow face marked by high cheekbones. The Indian girl.

He had been increasingly aware of her presence since the day he had escorted her from the adobe pit some months earlier. He recalled his surprise at seeing her again that day. She was brave—he never considered that she was starving—to return to the rancho after her first encounter with the vaqueros, who would certainly have brought her harm if Scott had not intervened. He kept her in his sight throughout the day, every day, after that. Noticed where she was standing in the pit; how she and a younger girl carried the heavy adobes to the wall under construction; the way she wiped her fingers on her skirt after she finished eating the tortillas the Indians were allotted for breakfast and dinner; when she admonished her son or stopped to play a moment with him—wherever she went, his eyes followed her. At first, he attempted to look away if she saw him looking at her. Later, he gained some nerve and nodded, a gesture she never acknowledged. Still, she was there, and he felt better knowing it.

Looking into her eyes for the first time, he saw fear and curiosity—at least he thought that's what he saw. She had blinked. He dropped the spoon he still held in his hand and strode to the other side of the courtyard—at least, he hoped he had walked fast and not run; his memory was still a jumble—toward the group of vaqueros, men whom he had never before considered a source of safety.

Felipe had raised his eyes from his plate of frijoles and dried beef. "Now you see a benefit of rancho life," he had said. His tone was flat, but his mouth curved up a little at the corners.

Scott had shoveled frijoles into his mouth and chewed loudly.

Now, Scott heard rustling in the cottonwoods and willows to his left. The thickets bordering the river were in full leaf, dense enough to hide a bear or mountain lion. He kept his eye on the bushes as he rode. He had intended to take a shotgun with him but forgot it in his rush to leave. The river beyond the bushes remained an enigma. He had crossed it with Tilman on their way to Rancho San Pedro. He had braved the thickets a few times on long summer evenings to stand along its banks. It puzzled him. It was in no way similar to the Mississippi, the river that had shaped his early life. The Río Porciúncula had shrunk dramatically in volume as the summer wore on. Scott noted it as another lesson about the plain that stretched east from the pueblo: In the dry season, a traveler had to carry his own water or know how to locate the places where water flowed in underground streams.

His horse headed north, as if it knew where it was going; Scott barely noticed the rivers his horse easily crossed: meager tributaries, then the San Gabriel, the riverbed nearly dry where it joined the Río de Porciúncula. The clop of hooves against bare river rocks faded as he returned to thinking about the young Indian woman. When he had first seen her, she had looked solidly built. Either he was mistaken, or she hadn't eaten well since that day. He hadn't noticed until he was close to her the previous morning how her collarbones stood out under her rows of shell necklaces. Her cheeks, which once had a roundness to them, now looked flat. Skin stretched over bones, her eyes wide in surprise, her face gaunt.

He ticked off the things he knew about her.

One, her name was Girl. She may also have had other names, but he recognized enough of the Tongva language to be sure Girl was one of them.

Two, she was about twenty years old. In his first months building the ranch, all the Indians had looked alike to him, and all looked old. From the first day he had seen her, she looked young. Only a few years younger than him.

Three, she had two children. A boy of about three, and a girl of a year or so. The boy was nearly always underfoot, his round belly the only extra flesh he carried on his small body; Scott had seen Girl's daughter only a few times. Where she was when she wasn't with Girl, he didn't know.

Four, she didn't have a husband. She spoke to some of the Indian men but not to one more than another. At least, Scott hoped she didn't have a husband.

Five, he liked knowing she was close. Even in his earliest

days as foreman, when he felt torn by self-doubt, he felt calmer when she was near.

The mountains grew larger as he drew closer but only a little more clear. A fine mist of dust softened the shapes of rock canyons and dissolved the foothills' chaparral to a blur. Scott turned east as Felipe had told him earlier that morning. His horse easily crossed the trickle of water in the arroyo seco. Only a wide streambed filled with boulders told him that winter rains brought torrents of water and rocks down the mountainside. The land on both sides of the stream was lined with cottonwood and scrub oak. As he rode on, he noticed that many of the trees, in what looked to have been a thriving forest, had been reduced to stumps. Small white alder, scrub oak and cottonwood formed young groves where water drained off the mountain. Where water wasn't plentiful, sage and manzanita abounded. Although Scott remembered neither trees nor stumps nor bushes from his earlier journey, he was certain he had taken this trail from the mission into the pueblo nine months earlier.

The sun was only halfway to midpoint, but Scott urged his horse into a gallop. Soon, the mission came into view. As he came closer, it appeared unchanged in any way since his first visit. He suspected that inside the structure's imposing walls, he would see the same deterioration that he had witnessed before—broken tiles, adobe worn down to its bricks, holes in the roof.

Expecting Tilman, Scott was surprised to see a slim young Mexican come toward him from a gate next to the church.

The man met him where the trail joined the mission path. "I am Don Mariano Gutiérrez, at your service," he said. "The mission administrator." He reached up to shake Scott's hand. "You know who I am, don't you?"

Scott, unable to recall if he had ever heard the man's name, remained silent.

"I'm in charge of selling off the mission land, stock, everything."

Something Tilman had said about the mission lands reverting to private ownership some years before sounded familiar.

"Is Don Rodrigo here?" Holding the reins tightly in his fist, he dismounted and followed Gutiérrez back along the path to the mission.

At that moment, Tilman exited the church. Scott recognized the man behind him as the old padre who had offered dinner on his first visit. From a distance, Scott noticed a difference in the old man. His posture was straight, his gait sure. His face was pale but held an eagerness Scott didn't remember.

"Scott," Tilman called. Scott was nearly upon them when he heard his employer say to the padre, "Fiesta at my rancho...January..."

"I should still be here," the padre said, as he pulled open one of the massive mission doors to reenter the chapel.

Scott tied his horse to the rail and followed Tilman and Gutiérrez into the quadrangle, a large space bordered by the mission on one side and a long row of one-story rooms on the other three. Doors opened onto an arcade that functioned as an outdoor hallway: slats of wood created a walkway shaded by a sloped adobe-tile roof. Here, Scott saw the signs of wear he had noticed on his first visit—exposed adobe block walls, where whitewash had all but worn away, rotted timbers that barely supported the arcade. The quadrangle was littered here and there with piles of adobe and fallen timbers. A few Indians lounged on a step outside a door where Scott remembered a kitchen had been on his first visit. This morning, the kitchen door was closed.

Halfway down the center of the quadrangle, the three men paused as an old man slowly swung open the back gate. Indian vaqueros herded a steer into the quadrangle and chased it down. It was not much of a contest; horses and steers looked equally malnourished. Once on the ground, the animal lay passively, its back legs lassoed together, as Tilman looked into its open mouth and frightened eyes.

"You see what good stock we still have at the mission, Don Rodrigo," Gutiérrez said.

"If you have nothing better to show me, I've wasted my time coming out here today," Tilman said, after inspecting the animal. "I know your job is to dispose of mission property, but you're being dishonest if you tell me these animals are worth anything."

Gutiérrez fingered the string tie he wore around his shirt collar.

"Scott, instead of making the poor wretches parade these creatures, get our horses, and we'll ride through the herd they've assembled."

About a hundred animals were awaiting inspection outside the gate. Immediately, he noticed the first sign of the animals' poor health: the low ratio of vaqueros to cattle. Animals that ordinarily needed a pen to confine them barely moved. Their ribs showed through their skin; their eyes gazed listlessly forward. As Tilman and Scott wove through the herd on horseback, the cattle barely stirred.

"Señor Gutiérrez," Tilman soon called out to the administrator. "There's no point in going on. These animals aren't fit to fatten. They'd have to be fed a great deal to gain enough strength even to reach my ranch."

Gutiérrez's eyebrows shot up. "I think you're making a mistake, Don Rodrigo. These animals have to be sold, and they're going to go for a very good price."

"The price would be high indeed if one of them was diseased, as I suspect, and spread illness to the rest of my herd." Tilman would not be bullied. "Let's go," he said to Scott.

They left Gutiérrez in the quadrangle, the animals milling

about outside the gate. Scott followed Tilman to the Río de Porciúncula. Here, there was enough water to send a trickle down the riverbed and feed a few stands of tules in the middle of the river.

"A wasted morning," Tilman said. "I thought Padre José looked a little healthier than I expected though. Did you notice any difference?"

Scott nodded.

Tilman let it go. The man worked more than he talked. He watched as his foreman started down the trail toward the rancho.

[7]

On a day in late summer, Henry Scott stood in the courtyard where Tilman had imagined his ranch at the start of the year. The ranch had been laid out as Tilman ordered, a two-story house for his family, flanked by a north and a south wing laid out on Rougemont's rough floor plan, now a dog-eared paper Scott folded and refolded into his pants pocket. Storeroom, blacksmith's work room, larder, another storeroom and foreman's room on the south; bunk house and a third storeroom on the north. The walls of both wings, constructed of hundreds of adobe blocks, Indian-made and mortared into place, were finished. Avila's men had helped Tilman's laborers lay tar over the tree limbs and tules that covered the roof.

The second floor was also completed on the Tilman family's center wing. Details like an interior staircase and wide second-floor veranda unique to Monterey-style houses would come after the rancho was roofed. Tilman had wanted the ranch to be completed by November in advance of the winter rains. Scott was certain it would be ready on time.

With the walls completed, emphasis shifted from construction site to working ranch. Breakfast was ready before sunrise, prepared in the ramada next to the family's future dining room. Felipe met with the vaqueros in the courtyard every morning after breakfast. He issued instructions quietly, sending the men north, south and east. They mounted their horses and left immediately, silhouetted against the pale morning sky.

At that early hour, the blacksmith was already working in his small room next to the storeroom, ready to shoe a horse before the day began. Later, he would shape iron tools, forge kitchen utensils and make horseshoes. Eight branding irons affixed with Tilman's double T brand hung on the wall behind him, waiting for the first round-up. Through the open door, Scott saw the sparks fly, sending showers of light around the room's dim interior.

Far across the plain rose the mountains. The highest peak was Mt. San Antonio, a triangle with one long steep side that sloped into the lower, more rounded shapes to the east. By now, he was familiar with the land between the Tilman ranch and the distant peaks: miles of low brush, interrupted by a patchwork of streams and marshes.

As the sun rose, Indian workers came up the path and entered the rancho's courtyard. Scott heard them whispering in a quiet cluck of consonants as they approached. Women and men were lank-haired and poorly dressed in patched clothing, too worn even for the vaqueros in camp or the poorest Mexican women in the pueblo. Their vacant stares made even the youngest Indian child look old.

The vaqueros, most of whom had nothing in their pockets from payday to payday, swaggered and swore. The Indians worked silently or exchanged a few words quietly when they spoke at all. Scott was accustomed to seeing poor folk. Surely, his parents and all their neighbors made do on little, sometimes nothing. There was always sound though—the baby's cries, his brothers' taunts, his father's bellows, of course, and his mother's occasional outbursts of temper. Scott noticed that sound was part of only two events in the lives of the Indian workers. One was during mealtimes. The Indian workers received food for their labor. They ate voraciously, using their fingers to scoop beans and tortillas into their mouths, accompanied by lip smacking and weak grunts of approval. Breakfast sounds were enthusiastic; lunch sounds, after hours in the hot sun, less so. They worked until nightfall but received no evening meal.

On nights when the sea was calm, the wind carried sounds from an Indian village Scott knew was a distance south: voices chanting in time to a muted clatter and percussive beat. He didn't remember hearing sounds like these coming from the village at Yang-na, when he lived in the pueblo. At the ranch, he heard them more often during the late summer than he had earlier in the year, or maybe he was just paying more attention as he worried less about his job. The sounds puzzled him. They weren't the drums of Indians he had sometimes heard along the trail west. His curiosity was satisfied one hot summer afternoon when he came upon a cache of shells, bone flutes and sapling branches abandoned in a thicket near the river.

Taking a few to the riverbank, he stood in the sun and examined each one. Shells joined by long plant fibers clattered against each other as he picked up the strings. He held a bone flute to his lips but could tease out only a few whispers. The sapling branches were trimmed to forearm's length and split halfway down the middle. When he hit one against his palm, it gave off a low whish. Many saplings striking at the same time would produce a rhythm. Now he knew the instruments that were creating the sounds. Still, he wasn't satisfied. Was it Girl's village he was hearing? Was she holding the shells, or the saplings? Was she singing?

Soon after Avila's men had laid tar on the rancho's roof, Scott asked Tilman if he could move into the foreman's room. The idea wasn't his. Felipe told Scott what to say; Scott practiced the words until he could utter, "Señor Tilman. I think I could work later at night if I moved into the foreman's room," without fumbling in embarrassment.

It was the first request Scott had made; Tilman honored it by agreeing. Under Felipe's direction, Scott asked an Indian worker to make him a bed and a table. The bed consisted of a rectangle of four corner posts. Interlaced dried cowhide straps held a palette stuffed with straw. The table was four legs with a board laid on top, sanded smooth. Tilman, knowing that Felipe would soon occupy this room, sent down a reed-bottomed chair made in the pueblo.

The first night Scott spent in the foreman's room, he lay awake until dawn. He had never slept in his own bed, let alone his own room. No more than six by eight, the room seemed impossibly large. Through the unshuttered window, he listened for the sound of water flowing in the river. A mockingbird's call ticked off the hours. Scott lay wide-eyed. He was sure he was dreaming. At any moment, he'd find himself in St. Louis again, his mother moving around the cabin before first light, his father swearing loudly in his sleep, a stench of liquor filling the small cabin. As morning dawned, Scott felt his limbs grow heavy. He drifted into sleep, awakening when he heard Felipe giving orders to a vaquero outside his room. Breathing heavily, he swung his legs out of bed and planted his feet on the hard-packed dirt floor.

Once Scott had a residence, the night took on a new shape. After dinner, while it was still light, Felipe sat at the table and worked sums that Scott scratched out for him on scraps of paper. Addition, subtraction, the times tables up to ten. Felipe learned quickly in the hour he devoted to his studies each night. Reading was another matter. Scott showed less talent for reading than for mathematics. Books being afterthoughts not central to life in Alta California, they shared only a worn Bible that Tilman gave them to work from.

And there was the language difference. The Bible was in Spanish, the logical language for Felipe to read. But Scott could read only English, and not much of that. He started by teaching

Felipe the alphabet, learning some Spanish himself as he wrote down each letter and pronounced it for Felipe.

Felipe's mouth creased into a grin as he corrected Scott. "No Aaa, Bee, See." His jaw worked into an exaggerated grin with each letter.

"Sí, en inglés."

"En mi lengua: Ah, Bay, Say."

Once each had mastered the other's alphabet, they moved on.

"En el principio creó Dios los cielos y la tierra," Scott read from the first line of the book of Genesis. The nights were already growing shorter. Soon they'd have to work by candlelight. He repeated the sentence slowly, underscoring the sentence with his dirt-encrusted fingernail.

Felipe stared at the shapes on the page, willing them to make sense.

Scott recalled how he had learned to read. His mother had sat him down, just as he was doing with Felipe. Handbills he had collected in town spilled over the table. She chose one and read, her accent thick with Creole French, "All able-bodied men who want work should report to—Henri, are you listening?" She paused then repeated, "All able-bodied men," underscoring each word with her right forefinger's torn fingernail.

Scott repeated to Felipe, "En el principio creó Dios los cielos y la tierra." He pointed to each word as he pronounced it, as his mother did with him.

Felipe continued to stare at the page.

"Dios," Scott insisted. He stamped the word with his finger for emphasis. "Dios."

Felipe didn't respond.

Scott took the scrap he had scribbled with a sum and wrote, "D-i." "Dee," he pronounced.

Again, no response from Felipe. Scott took up the quill

again, dipped it in the inkpot and wrote, "o-s." "Ohs," he pronounced. He wrote the four letters again. "D-i-o-s."

Before he could say the word, Felipe broke in. "Dee-ohs," he said. "Dee-ohs."

He couldn't stop himself from smiling. He looked at Scott as if to say, "Now you see how smart I am. I can read."

After Felipe left, Scott sat at the table until all light had faded from the sky. He lit a candle and lay down fully clothed on his bed. He thought about the young Indian woman he had protected months before. Girl. He hadn't wanted to think about her when he was sleeping near the vaqueros. Now, he had a roof over his head *and* a job. More than a job—he was a mayordomo.

Alone with his thoughts, he grew bold. He imagined he was the husband of the Indian woman. He would become the father of her children, and they would have more children together. She would not make adobe bricks any more. He would provide for her. He grew hard as he thought of being with her. His hand moved involuntarily to his crotch. He unbuttoned the few buttons that held his pants together, slid his fingers up and down his cock. Her soft rabbit fur cape brushed against him, her legs tightened around his waist. He groaned loudly and stroked his prick with more force. His breaths grew deep and loud.

"Ogod," he moaned. No more whores. This woman would be different. She would please him.

His body shook with relief.

He didn't think about who would marry them and where they would live. He didn't consider that marriages in the pueblo between Europeans and Indians usually matched a European or Mexican man of some age and means with an Indian woman of some status. He told himself he'd be proud to have her live with him at the ranch. It never occurred to him that she might want him to live with her in her village. Or that neither ranch, nor village nor pueblo would accept them, an Indian woman and her yanqui husband, neither with any wealth, and Don Rodrigo Tilman as their only connection to anything substantial in the world.

Felipe was surprised when he saw the bed and table the Indian workers had made for Scott. The furniture, although crude, was better quality than he'd expected. In his opinion, Indians were generally too lazy to put effort into making something that would last. Several weeks after the table and chair were delivered to Scott's room, a small group of Indian men went to work on Tilman's staircase. Indoor staircases were unusual in Mexican houses. It was likely that none of the men had ever seen one before. Early one morning before he rode out with the vaqueros, Felipe noticed Scott standing in the doorway of the ranch house. Curious about how Scott directed the Indians' work, he found an excuse to return a few hours later. He saw Scott standing in the same place as he had earlier, although now he held a board in his hand. Deep in concentration, Scott didn't hear Felipe as he approached.

Five Indian men were gathered in the rancho's small vestibule. They were looking at Scott and one of the older Indians, who were trying to work out the width of each stair and how many stairs they would need to build to reach the second floor. Scott handed the board to the Indian, who used a piece of charcoal to mark the wall where each step would go. He was able to show where five steps would be placed and then couldn't reach any higher. He handed the charcoal to Scott who used the man's estimate to mark the higher steps. With his back to Felipe, the vaquero couldn't hear what Scott said, but he saw the Indian nod.

Scott turned to walk out the door and saw Felipe standing behind him. "Forget something?" Scott asked.

"Sí." Felipe turned toward the storeroom as Scott walked into the courtyard. Felipe had ridden away from the ranch before it dawned on him that Scott knew a few words of the Indians' language. His Spanish was passable too. Never having gone to school, Felipe couldn't tell if Scott was a good teacher, but he had to admit he was learning. He was surprised that a man with so little grace in his body could do so well with his mind.

If Felipe thought there was more to Scott than he had originally observed, the other vaqueros never saw it. Impressed as they were by Scott's determination to break the piebald horse and his ability to do it, they felt uncomfortable with Scott whenever he set out to ride with them. They expressed their satisfaction when Scott moved into his own room.

"Ay, he never drinks with us," was a frequent complaint voiced by a vaquero.

"He doesn't walk right."

"He likes the Indians too much."

"He doesn't piss straight."

The vaqueros found fault with everything Scott did, even into October and November, after they had been working together for nearly a year. To Felipe, the discord made no difference. He knew that part of the reason they resented Scott was that Tilman had appointed Scott the mayordomo. They knew the job should have gone to Felipe.

One autumn evening, Felipe stepped outside Scott's room, his hour of studies done for the day. He saw the moon suspended just above the mountains, a glowing orange deeper than the color of the fruit that would appear soon in the young orchards in the pueblo. For a moment he wanted to return and tell Scott about Tilman's promise to make him foreman after the ranch house was completed. Instead, he bent to pick up a stone. He threw it hard and heard it land in the dust a short distance away. When he straightened up again, the moment had passed.

PART 2 land

[8]

Grandmother told Girl how she was named:

She said: "We were at the sea the day you were born. High waves crashed off the shore and swept up the sand. The sky was gray and overcast. We were used to sun, to warmth at that time of the year, even as the days grew shorter. But that year, it rained more than once during the dry season.

"We were digging in the wet sand. We wanted to bring the small animals, the clams and crabs, home with us. Our brothers had come from the desert to trade—our abalones, clams, seaweed for their yucca fiber. They brought a large party with them, men, women and children. We were in a great hurry to gather as many animals as possible.

"We walked fast along the sand, ignoring the wind that tried to blow us into the waves. We knew the wind. We knew how to make ourselves small but strong in the wind's face.

"Suddenly, I heard a cry. Your mother stumbled against me. I felt drops of water splash against my leg. But it wasn't the sea. It was your mother's water. You were ready to be born.

"I pulled your mother away from the shore. I felt her body tense with pain. I half-carried her to a pile of driftwood and seagrass that had washed onto the sand. Now, I was glad it had rained. Without the rain, there would be no wood on the sand to shield us from the wind. The other women, young and old, gathered around. Were there ten of us? Twenty? I don't remember. It felt as if we were many. Nilit's daughter spread her deerskin cape on the sand. Your mother squatted over it, as we surrounded her.

"'Push when the pain comes,' I said, as my mother had once said to me. "You were your mother's third child. We knew you would come quickly.

"We waited sixty heartbeats. The pain came. She breathed hard. She panted. The veins stood out on her neck. You were pushing against her.

"You retreated. We waited. You charged forward again. You wanted out. She almost fell over, you were so strong. We women held her up. She bore down and pushed. But no.

"'Maybe we should take her back to the village,' Nilit's daughter said.

"'No,' I said, 'We are out of the wind. The baby will come. Then we will all walk back together.'

"Your mother walked around the deerskin, her steps like a captured bird, anxious and tentative. Each time you tried to push out with your big head, your mother breathed harder. You were taking the breath from her, but this was your way. We had arrived just past midday. The sun was now past the middle of the sky, but not much. Really not much. Not so much time had passed. But it seems like a long time when you know your daughter is in pain, when her bigheaded child wants to be born.

"Your mother knew her time. She came back to the center of the deerskin, spread her legs and crouched. 'Mother,' she said, 'My baby is here.'

"And then you rushed out. We saw you did not have such a big head after all. In the blood, your head emerged, just as it should. I caught you as I would have caught a stone, not so big a stone, really a small stone, a precious stone. I saw you were a girl. You, my granddaughter. My daughter's first daughter. I caught you and laughed. The sky grew lighter, the wind became calm. Your mother lay on the deerskin, moaning softly and smiling.

"Nilit's daughter took the stone her husband had sharpened, the one we brought to cut seagrass, and cut the cord that bound you to your mother. I took you in my arms, then put you on your mother's breast.

"'Look, she is hungry,' Nilit's daughter said. 'Look, the little one is eating.'

"You sucked at your mother's breast. The sky filled with seabirds. They called loudly to one another. They celebrated your birth.

"I said, 'We will call her Big Headed Girl.' That is what I said."

[9]

Girl's first memory:

Slowly. Carefully. She picked her way down the steep bank toward the creek. Twisted elderberry branches intertwined with wild rose creepers, white-flowered mulefat and tall yerba mansa stems. Stands of arroyo willow next to leafy willow trees crowded the slope.

Girl toddled ahead on stubby three-year-old legs. Sun barely penetrated the canopy. She squeezed her eyes to peer ahead in the dim light.

Small steps, forward, forward. Reached up to touch the sharp point of a juncus. Too high. Disappointed. Moved toward a tall cottonwood tree. Hillside gave way—or was she just unsteady on her feet? Tumbled down hill. Righted herself in one quick move—always moved quickly, this child. Her mother's voice: "Step here, here."

Down toward the tules and cattails. What secrets did these tall grasses hide? Feet sank into mud. Toes touched cold water.

"Ai-i-i," she yelped, surprised.

Pulled her foot back. Quickly extended it again. Heard Mother laugh.

Another chuckle. Grandmother. Her voice low, she evoked the seldom-used name of the Tongva god. "Chinigchinich, the Creator, protects all this for you."

On another day, Grandmother ground chia seeds to make meal for porridge. Kneeling, she bent over the flat surface of a rock.

She worked her mortar methodically into a hole in the rock that ancestors, long past, had hollowed.

During her moments of rest, she told Girl how the world was made.

She said: "The Sky, Nocuma, created the world, the sea, animals and plants. Nocuma created the first man and woman out of the earth. Their children and their children's children were born. Then came the boy, Wiyoot."

"Wiyoot." Big Headed Girl rolled the name on her tongue.

"He was born at Puvung'na, a village over there"—Grandmother raised her arm toward the east—"and became a great chief. Wiyoot was kind at first, but he grew arrogant and cruel."

She took up her mortar again. Tiny seeds blew this way and that around the pestle's sides until they were crushed by the stone mortar in Grandmother's strong hands. Four-year-old Girl peered into the bowl, said, "I can help."

"Too young."

Girl frowned. "Wiyoot. Where is he?"

"The elders poisoned him. When Wiyoot sickened, the first people could not bear the pain of his death. They became rocks, hills and stars. Their hearts became stars."

"They are up there?" Girl asked. She pointed her small finger toward the sky. "They see everything we do?" Girl asked.

"Everything," Grandmother said. Her hands were quiet in her lap. "Wiyoot died. Time passed. Then, the god Chinigchinich appeared at Puvung'na. He instructed the people from many villages—ours and others—how to live. He separated the chiefs and seers from the rest—only they were allowed to enter the yovaar, where we honor him.

"Chinigchinich, the Creator, set apart the dancers. When they danced as the deer, deer would come, and we could eat. When they danced like the birds, birds would come. The same for ducks and rats and seeds and yucca and—"

"And that's why we have food!" Big Headed Girl reached into the hole in the rock for the seeds.

Grandmother caught her hands just in time. "Yes, we dance. The Creator provides." She covered Girl's small hands with her larger ones. "When he knew we could feed ourselves, Chinigchinich died. Before he died, do you know what he said?" Grandmother asked.

"Yes," said Girl. "No," she said.

"He said he will be watching our villages from his place among the stars. He will help those who obey his teachings and punish those who don't."

"I will be good," Girl said.

[10]

Girl's village lay in a canyon, a half-day's walk upriver from the sea. A spring rose from the earth at one end of the village, offering limitless fresh water. The spring's runoff created a small wetland, home to nesting birds, cattails and tall grasses. Atop the steep hill that rose above the spring, acorns grew with abundance on ancient oak trees. At the base of the hill, below the wetlands, lay the village.

Berries grew along the creek at the other end of the gulch. The creek: Her secret world. Shimmering rattlesnakes—the Creator's allies. White-bellied tree frogs. Steelhead trout—delicious when caught and cooked. Butterflies wearing blue-spotted wings. Fox and deer. Ducks in fancy feathers with their plain wives. Tall birds on legs like sticks. Small birds dressed in red. Everything she needed was there. Everything that interested her. Everything she loved.

On the other side of the stream rose another hill, then another. Girl could walk for a long time along the spine of those hills, but she was a mother with children of her own before she took that journey.

In what was once a thriving village of more than a hundred Tongva, each kiiy, or dwelling, was made of willow poles and tule thatch, large enough to shelter a family or two. High above their heads, a hole in the domed roof let out smoke from the cooking fire and let in the sky. Inside, a child lying on her tule mat, eyes half-closed, sensed the unlimited space above her head and the limitless land she could roam as had all her ancestors.

By the time Girl was born, the population had been reduced by half. Fewer kiiy were built, most were smaller than they once had been. Fewer babies were born, fewer hands wove baskets, ground acorn meal, twisted rabbit pelts into blankets, sharpened arrow points, stripped branches for spears. Hardly enough people to do the work needed to survive. Barely enough.

[11]

Big Headed Girl lay very still. "Stop moving," the four-year-old willed the tules. She hoped they would hide her from the fierce animal scratching the wet earth on the other side of the creek. She squeezed her eyes shut in terror, held her breath.

Two voices whispered in her ear.

"Go back. You shouldn't be here alone. Your mother will be angry at you." This was a voice she knew well.

"Don't be afraid," she heard. "Look closely at everything around you. Remember everything you see."

She opened her eyes. Tules, tugged by the wind, swayed their long arms. River padded its feet lightly against the shore. Mud pushed back against her belly, matching its breath with hers. Light from the fading sun wrapped her in its blanket, warming her against the cool winter breeze. She strained her eyes to see through the thick grasses to the other side of the river. A young doe was pawing the wet ground, trying to unearth a root. Beyond the deer, large red-orange clumps of toyon berries hung from a tree.

"Child," Girl heard her mother call. Startled, the doe raised its head to scan the opposite bank. Girl's bright eyes peered back through the tall grass. In one quick movement, the doe wheeled, then leaped away. Branches snapped beneath its sharp hooves.

"Mama, I'm here," Girl sighed. Her mother stood nearby, looking down at her. She pursed her lips and shook her head slowly from side to side. Girl rose, followed her mother back up the hill to the village, dragging her feet in the moist earth.

[12]

The Tongva's land once stretched from the great ocean to the half circle of mountains on the southern coast: as far north as the village of Topaa'nga, as far south as the southernmost of the three large rivers that split the plain. All was Tongva, all of it. As long as anyone knew the land at all, the Tongva were there.

North of the Tongva lived the Chumash. To the south lived the Acjachemen. To the east, over the mountains, were the Serrano. To the northeast, the Tataviam. Cahuila to the southeast claimed the desert as home. All were people the Tongva traded with and knew.

For many years, the Tongva saw strangers' boats sail along the coast. The sightings of the first few were ignored. Later, when the boats came more often, their arrivals were marked but only as an item of comment. No one expected to see the men who sailed the ships. But eventually they came, wearing robes the color of dust, holding crosses aloft, led by soldiers on horseback. A line of them on trails worn smooth from the comings and goings of people who had always lived there.

The intruders didn't move on as the ships had done. Some stayed behind; more gray-robed men joined them, often accompanied by more soldiers and horses. On land the Tongva knew as home, they constructed a large house "to God," they said. The Mission San Gabriel Arcángel. They raided Tongva villages, separated families. Forced the men and women they captured to live at the mission, work its fields, keep the cattle, tan the hides, press grapes into juice and store it in barrels until it turned to wine. Men, unused to working for others and forced into constant motion, died. They died of beatings, of starvation, of overwork, of disease, of loneliness. Women and children, too, died by the thousands.

The same story was repeated in all twenty-one missions the priests founded, from San Diego to San Francisco, each a day's horseback ride from the next, all with the same ostensible purpose: make the Indians into "gente de razón," a people capable of reason. Many resisted by running away. Some attempted open rebellion. In Big Headed Girl's great-grandmother's time, Toypurina, a Tongva woman, a "seer," persuaded her people to arm themselves with bows and arrows, then appear at the church ready to battle the Spaniards. The plot was discovered. Toypurina, captured, was punished and exiled from her homeland. Forced to convert to the intruders' religion. Died young.

Unceasing repression led to more revolts. In 1824, the year Big Headed Girl was born, the Chumash, along Alta California's central coast, launched the largest revolt. A comet in the night sky signaled: The world was ready for change. Soon after, a priest whipped a young Chumash boy at the Mission Santa Inés in the coastal mountains, setting off the uprising. The Chumash burned all but the church at the Mission Santa Inés in the coastal mountains, and for a month, occupied the church at the Mission La Purísima Concepción to the north and the church at Mission Santa Barbara to the south. Half the Indians were captured; the rest fled into the hills. Spanish soldiers executed eight. News of the revolt spread throughout Alta California. Every Indian and Mexican heard of it.

That revolt was the Indians' last major stand, but they continued to rebel against the invaders. Staging guerilla attacks. Running away, enduring a severe whipping if they were caught. Quietly honoring their god. Singing the songs, making the tools and eating the foods they knew—secretly, at the missions, when they were able. For a few, remaining in their villages. The world changed around them. Wherever they were, mission or pueblo or village, the Tongva, the Chumash, the Tataviam, the Acjachemen, the Cahuilla, all those native to California, hung on and tried to survive.

[13]

Grandmother said: "There was too much rain the year you were five. Some years we saw little rain. In that one, we saw too much. The dark clouds gathered when the sycamore trees began to lose their leaves. Rain soaked us then and barely stopped until wild mustard covered the plain. Some days, the rain started at first light and went on until the middle of the next night. We were tired of rain that year. Many nights we could not light the fire because the wood was too wet."

"Grandmother, why are you telling me this?" Clouds had covered the sun all day, as it often did when the dry season was in its second moon. Grandmother and Girl had walked up the hill to gather acorns from the big trees. From the hilltop, they saw the sun break through and peek back at them through narrow strings of clouds. It wouldn't be long before the weak, small sun hid beneath the ocean, as it did every night. Girl knew she must work fast to keep up with her grandmother and return to the village with acorns before dark.

But grandmother stopped walking before they took even one acorn from the ground. She crouched until her face was close to Girl's.

"You are nearly seven years old. I'm trying to tell you how your brother died, Big Headed Girl, I'm trying to tell you. You are old enough to hear it."

Girl waited.

"He was a beautiful boy," Grandmother said, at last. "His skin was the color of an acorn, and his eyes like little lumps of charcoal. He laughed often. He was a happy child. He made us happy."

Girl turned her head away and looked toward the setting sun.

"Your brother was learning to walk. If it had been the warm season or like most cold ones, he would have walked and fallen and walked again in the mud or dust between our houses. But during that cold, wet winter we stayed inside. Your brother was stubborn. He was less than a whole year but he wanted things his way. If we did not watch him every minute, he went out the door.

"There were many of us inside. We women wove baskets; we fashioned rabbit skins into blankets. The men smoked, grumbled about the weather and the poor hunting. Children played a game of chance, grabbing pairs of walnut shells away from each other. But your brother. He wanted to go outside. Every time we turned our backs, he toddled out the door."

Grandmother sat on the ground and began to rock gently back and forth. The sun had nearly disappeared into the ocean, but Girl kept looking at it.

"The time I'm telling you about happened after four days of rain," Grandmother said. "Baskets of rain. Boatfuls of rain. We were trying to sleep, trying to put the rain out of our minds. I heard a sound I had never heard before. I thought it was a mountain lion, growling low in its chest. I thought it was a bear.

"The sound grew louder. Then, others heard it too. The sound grew very loud. Suddenly, we were swallowed in it. We felt water under us. The water rose. We were all screaming, women grabbing for their children, men shouting, voices one on top of the other, all trying to yell above the water pounding through our house, washing our house away.

"The water poured over us and around us. It took our baskets, skins, tule sleeping mats. Everything was gone. We heard shouts from other houses in the village. Other families came to find us. Rain ran down our faces like tears. We looked around in the dark. Each silently counted husbands, wives, children. All the men were there. All the women. The children. But not Little Brother. He wasn't there.

"We were cold and wet. I was shivering. I tried to draw you close to me, but you cried, 'Where is he? Where is my brother?'

"Your mother took you, your older brother and younger sister. She ran to your aunt's house, the only house still standing. On the edge of the village. I ran around the village. I looked under the piles of tules the flood had made of our houses. I thought he would jump out, yell 'Grandmother,' and laugh. I prayed to Chinigchinich, 'Please let us find Little Brother alive.'

"The ground was wet and slippery. I fell many times. I didn't care. I kept looking. I was wild with fear. Finally, your father came and got me. He said, 'The boy found shelter. Let him be.'

"His voice was steady, yet I knew it wasn't true. He knew it wasn't true. But we gave up looking. It was dark; the rain was still falling hard.

"The next morning, the rain stopped. The whole village was talking about the river; in normal times, it was a walk toward our west. This time, it had traveled farther than any of us had ever seen. No one knew the river was able to drown our village.

"Your father and I began to look for Little Brother again. In the light we could see the damage the flood had done. All around us were trunks of willow and sycamore trees, even limbs from giant oaks and twisted manzanita branches that came down the river from the mountains. Three large boulders crouched on the edge of our village. If they had come any farther, they would have killed us all. A thick layer of mud covered everything, black as the tar that drifts onto the sand from the sea.

"Your father's strength was greater than I had ever seen. He turned over trees much larger than his height, broke heavy branches as if they were twigs. At last, we found Little Brother. On a pile of stones at the bottom of the hill near our village. He lay there as if he were sleeping. His spine was twisted. His small arm was flung over his eyes as if trying to keep out the light."

Grandmother paused. Seeing her cry, Girl remembered the day they found her brother dead and cried too. They sat in the dark until Girl's father came. He led them down the hill to the village. Girl followed behind. She noticed his limp, a childhood injury, more pronounced than usual. Sometimes, her father entertained them all by limping quickly around and around the cooking fires, a crooked smile on his face.

Not this day.

Her tears told him what they had been talking about, but he was silent. He didn't tell Girl to stop crying. He picked Girl up and held her close as he made his way down the hill, Grandmother following. Inside their kiiy, Grandmother tucked Girl against her body. The two wept all night.

[14]

Big Headed Girl was grinding acorns. As a small child, she had been taught how to grind the nubs into meal. Now, she was seven. She stretched her fingers to grasp the round grinding stone with authority. Her knees made moon-shaped impressions in the earth. She worked over the acorns, reducing the nut to a fine flour. Small gusts of late-summer wind teased bits of powder into the air.

Behind her was the dome-shaped house where she lived. Willow boughs covered with tule thatch, a fine big kiiy. Enough room for Girl, her family—Mother, Father, Grandmother, Older Brother, Younger Sister—kin and visitors. Beyond, oak trees covered the hill above the village.

The men were making themselves ready for a late afternoon hunt. They struck their arrow points with a bone tool to make the points fine and sharp. Women and girls scraped deer skins clean. Soon, nights and mornings would feel early winter's chill. Pelts and hides had to be ready to use as blankets, women's skirts or shoulder coverings when the weather turned cold. Usually, the scraper's rasp was overwhelmed by men's loud voices as they boasted and joked with each other. Usually, Girl could barely hear a sound as soft as the rasp. Chipmunks roamed the dust, looking for bits of seeds or nuts they could store for the winter. Their chatter was loud in the quiet afternoon, but Girl, absorbed in her task, ignored them.

The ache in her back and arms said she had been at her work for a long time. She raised her head, surprised the men hadn't yet left for the hunt. Patches of light illuminated the ground. One by one, they faded into the dust. A slight chill in the late afternoon air told her the seasons were changing. Girl sat back on her haunches and looked around. Where were Father and Older Brother? She looked at the women. Where was Mother?

Grandmother stood over her. She was almost as wide as she was tall, a solidly built woman with a long memory. Her hands could heal a bruise. Her critical glance could turn a man's hands to acorn porridge. She took Girl's arm gently and led her past the circle of dwellings toward the creek. She crouched in the dust and motioned to Girl to do the same.

"Your father has gone away, Girl," Grandmother said softly.

Girl stared at her grandmother. "My father?" Her voice rose to a cry as she stood. "And Mother...?"

"She has gone with Older Brother to look for him."

The night before, as she left the world for sleep, she had heard her mother and father arguing in low voices. The sound had troubled her. She had never heard her father speak in anger to her mother.

Her thoughts took her to a moment a few days before. She had walked with her father to the entrance of the yovaar, the village's sacred space where only the chosen were allowed to enter. He sat on the ground opposite her for a moment. "If I were not here, you could find your way home from the creek or the stream or even the river, couldn't you, Big Headed Girl?" he said.

She didn't understand why he would ask her that question. Her tongue went still.

"I know you could."

Now that she thought of it, he had looked at her the same way Grandmother had looked at her all day. As if he wanted to tell her something but at the same time didn't want to tell her at all.

Why hadn't she seen? He was trying to tell her that he was going away.

She had missed another chance that morning. The first sound she heard upon awakening was a raven's call. The Creator's messenger, he always brought bad news. If she had understood his warning, she could have stopped her father from leaving.

"Girl, your father has gone to join our brothers who are fighting the Mexicans." Girl covered her ears with her hands.

"Listen to me." Grandmother took Girl's hands between her own. "We have lost too many. We must send the Mexicans away. We have tried. We must try again, or none of us will remain alive."

Girl screamed. Her body stiffened. She fell back on the hard ground. Her eyes were open, but she saw nothing.

Night came. Girl awoke inside her house. Mother and Grandmother were kneeling beside her, looking into her face.

"'My father," Girl cried. A wolf was chewing at her heart. She lay on her side, a tule mat beneath her, knees drawn up against her chest. She rocked in pain. "My father, my father," she cried.

Firelight flickered through the sides of her dwelling. Families were allowed in the yovaar to mourn their dead. Unable to make her legs hold her upright, Girl shivered under a rabbit skin, alone, as she heard the villagers sing. Men praised her father's goodness and bravery. At last, the villagers sang the mourning songs. She heard the clatter of gourd rattles and the swish of sticks that kept the rhythm. She didn't ask why they were mourning him. He might be alive at that moment, but she knew, as they did also, that he would fall in battle. She would never see him again.

Many days later, Grandmother said: "When I was a young girl, the world was more water than land. We fished in the streams flowing out of the mountains all year. Always enough fish. Water filled our creeks and streams all year. Even at the end of summer, there was always water.

"Water relieved our thirst. It nourished large villages, so many more of us than now. It gave us food and clothing. Deer came down to the streams to drink. They gave their lives. We used their hides to warm us on winter nights. Willow trees grew along the banks. The bark gave us medicine against aches and pains. Tules grew in the creek. Oh, what we did with tules! Our houses, our boats, sleeping mats, women's skirts, long fibers to make fish traps. So many tules. So many more than now.

"What we couldn't get from the rivers, we took from the marshes. Duck and bird eggs, when we raided their nests. Foxes ran silently over the marsh. We caught them, used their pelts for winter covering. Yucca. We ate the blossoms. Used fiber from yucca leaves for sewing. The roots we pounded and used for soap.

"And the oceans, Girl. No Mexicans, no cattle to stop us between our village and the ocean. We followed the river. Ocean spread out its arms and invited us to take the crabs and sea urchins, every kind of sea animal, to eat.

"Everything we hunt and eat, wear and use for shelter needs water. Until I was a young woman, we had enough.

"Yes, the priests and soldiers came. But the land was so big, there was enough for all.

"By the time your mother was born, everything had changed. The Mexicans had made a city along the banks of the river, three, four days' walk from here. More came. They brought cattle to feed on this land. Hundreds of cattle became thousands. The animals stampeded, pounded life-giving seeds deep into the ground. The cattle drank up the water. Streams stopped flowing as swiftly. Underground streams turned to dust. Our spring gives us less water every year, our creek flows like a sleepy old man; it used to be a young hunter.

"The land, the water do not belong to our village, even to

our brothers' villages, alone. They belong to all of us. The intruders never understood. They didn't ask—they took the land and said it belonged to them.

"Our people were lost to the missions. Our water was lost to the newcomers, the pueblo, the ranches. We had nowhere to go. So, we stayed."

[15]

"It's here." The sky was still a deep blue in the east when Big Headed Girl heard the runner's call. The ti'at, the plank canoe that made the passage between island and shore, had been sighted. As quickly as Girl left her kiiy, others were faster. Children ran about underfoot. Achanchah was already fastening a skirt made of cottonwood bark around her waist, slipping strands of shells over her head. Nilit's daughter held her youngest girl between her knees and plaited a twist of shells through the child's hair. Girl squinted into the dark. The men were coming up the embankment from the creek, where they bathed each morning. Wasn't it father leading them? A full cycle of seasons had passed since her father had gone away.

"Mother, Grandmother, Big Brother, Little Sister," Girl called. "Hurry, or we'll be the last."

The sky had paled by the time Girl and her family joined their village and neighbors on the beach. At this time every year, the ti'at made its last voyage of the season across the channel. The island and the mainland were like brother and sister. Every island family had kin on the mainland; every mainland family had kin across the channel. Soon, the warm fall winds and rough seas would make the journey perilous. Families would be separated until the elderberry and wild rose flowered.

Time stalled as they waited. At first, only a pinpoint of light far beyond the breaking waves, the ti'at didn't seem to move at all. From this distance, the work that had gone into making the canoe could not be seen. Tall trees had to be felled, each tree cut into long planks the length of the tree. Vast amounts of ocean tar collected and spread across the wood. To seal the cracks. To make it safe.

Women and men watched wordlessly as the ti'at slowly advanced toward the beach. Even the children were silent. With each stroke, the morning sun sent shards of light glancing off the water-beaded paddles.

Seagulls circled overhead, screaming as they dived and swooped. Wind gusts ruffled the waves. Suddenly, the ti'at was upon them, cutting through the breaking waves as gracefully as a heron in flight in spite of its size. Shouts of joy joined the seabirds' cries. Singers broke out in praise of the ti'at and its paddlers. Big Headed Girl could see the faces of the ten men who pulled back the water with each stroke of their double-bladed paddles.

"Look," Girl yelled. "Grandfather has come. And grandmother. See, she is sitting in the back of the ti'at."

Na'aro, Girl's mother, sighed. Girl felt her mother's trembling hand on her shoulder. The previous year, Girl's father had been gone only a few moons when the ti'at made its last visit before the rains. Ah'kahkah and Ne'sook, father and mother of her father, had not come that time, the first year they were absent from the celebrations, the exchange of goods. On their island home, they had mourned their son. Through the following spring and summer they were absent too.

Na'aro's cousins, Achanchah and Nilit's daughter, ran out to greet the ti'at. They looked back at Na'aro, but she didn't join them. Others did. In a moment the sea was crowded with mainland kin, each wanting to be the first to greet the boat as it neared shore. They dashed into the waves, oblivious of the cold. Their cries competed with the seagulls until the whole world came alive with sound.

Big Headed Girl squirmed out of her mother's grasp to run out with the others. She held Little Sister in her arms. Like Achanchah and Nilit's daughter, she looked back for a moment to see her mother standing alone on the shore. Grandmother had stepped forward and wrapped a rabbit skin cape around her daughter's shoulders. Na'aro stood quietly, her head bowed.

Big Headed Girl turned her attention to the ti'at again. Ah'kahkah and Ne'sook were climbing out of the steep-sided boat. They held onto its smooth rim, then lowered themselves slowly to waiting hands. The next moment, Big Headed Girl was splashing through the waves, holding Little Sister above the surf. Ah'kahkah caught them both in his arms and raised them up into the air.

"Girl, you are so big," he laughed. Girl saw her father's obsidian eyes, her father's wide mouth in her grandfather's wrinkled face. She gasped. Her father had returned an old man.

He had not.

Ah'kahkah lowered her onto the sand, and she walked quietly next to him. Ne'sook held Little Sister's hand. The old ones embraced Older Brother as he ran up to them. Na'aro continued to stand motionless on the sand, looking out to sea. Grandmother had once again melted into the crowd.

Reunited with their families, the villagers walked quickly north along the river path. They knew the sections where willow trees were the thickest, stepped around them easily. Deer, raccoon and muskrat, alerted by villagers' voices, found other places to feed. Kin who had come across the water carried nets full of soapstone—some carved into animal shapes, some in blocks waiting for a carver's knife. Other nets held abalone shells; the colors that lined their concave surfaces glowed iridescent pink, blue, green. The few women among the travelers held baskets filled with abalone meat, fresh and sweet, for the evening's feast.

Ah'kahkah, Ne'sook and Girl's mother soon fell behind the others, but Grandmother reappeared to accompany Girl and Older Brother. They took turns carrying Little Sister on their backs.

"Why do they walk so slowly?" Girl grumbled. She stepped over the root of a cottonwood tree. "They are not ill."

"Shush, Girl," Grandmother said softly. "They carry sorrow's burden. Your father was their eldest son."

Girl didn't tell Grandmother that she remembered her father's face only when she looked at her grandfather. At first, she had seen his features clearly whenever she closed her eyes. Now she had to think for a long time. She feared that someday he would disappear altogether. She tried to remember his words when Older Brother teased her, or Little Sister crawled into her basket of walnut shells, scattered them around.

"Patience," he had counseled. But the sound of his voice had left her too.

Girl and her family skirted the boulders that had marked the village's entrance since the flood. Visitors from other villages filled the space, making the people as numerous as they would have been in Grandmother's time. Ah'kahkah and Ne'sook sank to the ground near Girl's dwelling. Their kin gathered round. They removed items from their nets and spread them out in front of them on reed mats. Soapstone figures of sea otters or foxes emerged from the nets. Soapstone bowls that held the fire's heat. Soft powder scraped from soapstone to pat on babies after their baths. Shells strung on strong plant fibers to encircle necks, wrists, ankles.

Girl traced aimless circles in the earth with a stick. The wolf gnawed at her insides as viciously as the day her father had gone away. Some moments during the year past she heard the sound of a bird or recognized a flower she once liked, but, more often, the wolf possessed her body and mind.

She looked up when Ne'sook called her name. "And for you Big Headed Girl, your own grinding stone, small enough for your young hands."

Girl frowned. Not a gift. A reminder that she would have

to take more responsibility. Would the wolf allow her to become a woman and a mother?

"And a necklace I made for you," Ne'sook continued.

Girl could not overlook the kindness of this gift. She took the necklace from her grandmother's outstretched hand. Small pieces of abalone shell, each a rainbow of colors flashing in the sunlight, had been drilled through the center and threaded with yucca fiber. Ne'sook had remembered how much Girl admired her abalone shell necklace when they last met.

The sound of a high-pitched flute rose in the early afternoon haze. Circles of kinsmen widened out to make room for dancers. Men from distant villages came forward to form a line that moved north then south, east to west, accompanied by the rhythm of clapper sticks and strings of shells. The music grew in volume, then receded like an ocean wave. Ne'sook, Ah'kahkah and Grandmother shook gourds and strings of shells, their eyes steady on the dancers. Na'aro sat with them, but her gaze fastened on the hill's oak trees, as if she expected someone to emerge from the woods and limp down the slope. The children played hide and seek around their parents' shoulders or joined the dancers.

Dancing continued through the afternoon. It would have gone into the night, but hunger took over. Excitement had dulled appetites for hours. Now, it demanded attention. The dancers scattered to gossip outside the tule dwellings of their kinsmen. Netah'is and Tean-re, two warriors, invited the men, villagers and visitors, to smoke with them. Mother roused herself to join women from island and mainland in preparing dinner. Big Headed Girl, with Older Brother, led children new to their village to the spring to collect water. They showed them the path through the buckwheat and the small, dense marsh to the spring.

When they returned, women were already pounding slices of the abalones' tough feet to make them tender before cooking. Cooking stones, heated in the fire, were carefully dropped into baskets. Greens and abalone pieces were added. The rocks quickly heated the stew. Abalone steaks, threaded on green sticks and held over the fire, cooked rapidly.

As mealtime approached, voices rose. Ah'kahkah took up his flute. Sentries, posted around the village to look out for attacks by Mexican soldiers, waited impatiently for others to take their places.

Yah'ro-re had recently completed the boys' ceremony; he was barely twelve years old, tall and thin for his age. This was his first watch. From his post on a hillock beyond the creek, he turned toward the village. He played a few notes on his flute. The abalone stew awaiting him filled his thoughts. He twisted a piece of juncus to repair his sandal. He inspected the sharp thorns of a prickly pear that shared space on the hill with the oak trees and a lone sycamore.

What he didn't do: Notice dust clouds far off to the north.

Hear horses' hooves above the laughter and music.

A bullet struck his heart. Yah'ro-re fell dead without a sound.

Half a dozen Mexican soldiers on horseback jumped the creek, thundered through the village. In a moment, peaceful order was turned upside down. The assault scattered cooking baskets and flattened dwellings. Younger Indians quickly grasped what was happening and took flight. Old ones among the islanders sat dumbfounded. Attacks on them had ceased long ago; mainlanders were easier prey.

On the hillock, a Spanish padre stepped over Yah'ro-re's body where the young man had stood. The young Indian's blood stained the edges of the priest's robe. The padre paid no attention. He squinted to see the scene in front of him more clearly and adjusted his robe with thin, nervous fingers.

In a moment, the soldiers had ridden to the farthest edge of the village. Bridles raked against horses' necks. The horses reared, turned and galloped through again, this time taking a route along the village's east side. Ne'sook screamed and grabbed Little Sister. For one moment, she held her granddaughter in her arms. In the next, a horse galloped over the old woman. Ne'sook fell to the ground as the horse struck her spine. Her quiet "oooph" was expelled with her last breath.

"Aiiii," cried Na'aro. Grabbing the hand of Girl and Older Brother, she ran through the village toward the thick brush along the lower creek. Grandmother reached under Ne'sook's broken body, snatched a sobbing Little Sister into her arms and followed.

The horses wheeled to make another pass through the village. This time the soldiers shot at old women and children. Bullets whined through the air. In all directions, the old fell next to the very young, still clutching a gourd here, a basket there.

In their final sweep, the soldiers dismounted. With pistols drawn, they walked among the broken willow branches that remained of dwellings and the small fires blazing here and there, oblivious to the villagers' cries, the wails of children. The soldiers grabbed the arms of every young man within easy reach. They led the men to the northern edge of the village where the padre waited. In response to a sergeant's whistle, the soldiers' horses galloped through the village for the last time, their hooves crushing anything that hadn't already been destroyed. The padre signed the cross over the heads of the dozen captives, his face serene. His tasks completed, he mounted his horse, rode away.

The youngest soldier wound a leather lariat around the neck of each Indian, roping them together in a line. He looked back at the village. What had been a scene of celebration minutes before was now reduced to chaos. Small fires burned where cooking stones had been neatly laid out. Here and there, tules and willow branches were ablaze. Bodies lay sprawled in the dust. Children called out for their mothers, their fathers, or lay next to a dead parent. The smells of blood, dust, charred meat, burnt branches mixed with clouds of smoke and rose from the village.

[16]

In the days that followed the attack, the quiet Girl had always known became silence, as if the villagers were afraid to speak. There were fewer people to work, to gossip, to tease. The heart had gone out of the village. Fear and bitterness remained behind.

Two full moons rose and waned after the attack. Before the rainy season set in, villagers cut down willows near the creek to form the structures of their domed houses. They layered tules and reeds over the branches as they had always done for shelter. The women wove baskets to replace those crushed by the soldiers. The men stripped branches for fishing and others for arrows to replace those snapped in the attack. Acorns were gathered, seeds sorted—all with new intensity. Even in the bountiful land where the Tongva lived, survival depended on accumulating food stores. When summer's bounty was gone, food they depended on would be scarce until spring.

Singing went on in the evening, even dancing, but all was done in mourning. The soldiers had killed eight men, sixteen women and fourteen children. Twelve of the strongest men had been taken by force from the village. Though some were visitors from neighboring villages or had come from the island, Girl's village lost the greatest number. Fewer men were on hand to hunt, fish and protect the village. Fewer women would be able to add new lives. The children. They were the biggest loss of all.

With stores of food low, the women set off one early morning for the ocean. The sky was gray; the wind blew cold. Girl wanted to go with them.

"I am old enough to help," she argued. Mother and

Grandmother stood before her. Mother looked at a place on the hill over Girl's head and said nothing. Her mind was clearly on something else, as it had been since her husband left. It was Grandmother who responded.

"No. You stay with Little Sister and help the women here. Grind some acorns. That will give you something to do."

Girl did as she was told.

All light had drained from the sky by the time Grandmother and the other women returned. Grandmother set her net on the ground, ran to Girl. As she had done the day her father left, Grandmother took Big Headed Girl aside and crouched next to her.

"Your mother fell into a wave. The wave swallowed her," Grandmother said.

Girl waited for Grandmother to say, "We left her with Nilit's daughter to warm herself by the fire. She will be here soon."

Grandmother went silent. After a moment, the old woman began to croon, very quietly, a mourning song.

[17]

Grandmother kept the details of Na'aro's death to herself. The women who were there that day did the same. If Big Headed Girl asked how her mother died, Grandmother would tell her the truth. She would say:

"The day your mother died, the sea and sky were as gray as the day you were born. We couldn't see where horizon met ocean, but it was colder, much colder. Like that day, we women were at the seashore, collecting crabs, mussels, sea urchins. You and Little Sister and others your age had remained in the village. We women could work faster if we worked alone.

"The salt spray bit into our skin. The shore was soft and damp from the outgoing tide, good for collecting sea animals. The waves rose up like steep hills beyond our reach. I shivered as I looked at them. None of us thought about going into the water that day.

"Maybe your mother did. Who knows what she was thinking? She had lost her son and her husband. Her husband's mother had been murdered in the soldiers' attack on our village. Your mother was strong. Maybe not strong enough.

"The gulls were circling overhead when we were ready to leave that day. I remember. Round and round they wheeled as we looked up at them. An arrow point of pelicans dove into the water; one emerged with a fish struggling to free itself from the bird's pouch. The others flew on.

"We looked toward the island through fog that was making itself thicker minute by minute. I thought the birds, the waves and the island were saying good-bye. One by one we women turned our backs on the sea and hoisted nets full of sea animals over our shoulders. We began to walk back over the moist sand. Quickly. Shivering in the cold.

"A seagull shrieked. I turned around to see the bird that made the loud noise. I saw your mother running toward the water's edge.

"The sea was already at her hips when I cried, 'Na'aro, Na'aro.' She didn't look at me. Instead, she stumbled on until the sea was at her chest.

"Around her neck hung strings of shells. She still wore the rabbit skin cape I had made for her wedding gift.

"My cries made the others turn around. They dropped their nets and screamed as one voice, 'Na'aro, come back.'

"The wave knocked her down. I saw her roll over. The weight of her shells and cape upset her balance.

"She stood up again but only for a moment. She turned in my direction and nodded to me, as if she heard me. Water dripped from her long, black hair.

"I cried, 'Na'aro' again. She collapsed into the next wave.

"I began to run toward the water. The others too. Nilit's daughter caught my arm. She screamed above the wind. 'You can't save her. She is too far out. The waves are too high.'

"I fought her off and ran on. The cold water bit into my feet.

"'The children...without you?' Nilit's daughter shrieked after me. Wind swallowed her words.

"I stopped running.

"Beyond the waves, I saw a black dot. I saw it. I think I saw it.

"Then, it disappeared."

Grandmother would have told all this to Girl if she had asked. Girl never did.

[18]

After her mother walked into the waves, Big Headed Girl, Grandmother, Older Brother and Little Sister moved into her uncle's dwelling. The husband of her mother's youngest sister was a tomyaar, a chief, entitled to live near the yovaar in the middle of the village. Many nights, she heard the murmur of voices coming from the yovaar. Not the sound associated with religious ceremonies, although it was the yovaar where these took place. The elders and wise men were talking late into the night. They smoked their pipes, remembered better times. The soldiers had accomplished their purpose. The village was slowly dying.

Girl did the work expected of her; she was now a young woman of thirteen years. She wove baskets out of reeds and lined some with black tar from the sea, so they could hold water. She ground acorns into meal, next leached the meal to remove the bitter taste. She formed acorn meal cakes with her small hands, cooked the cakes on stones over the fire.

If she had been born in an earlier time, she would be married to a young man from another village. She might already have birthed a child. Now, the numbers of young men had been depleted, taken by the mission, killed while resisting, lost to disease. Marriage was far off. Maybe. Never.

Sometimes, she heard the creek splashing over stones and watched the few children left in the village take small sticks to float down the river. She heard their excited cries when they were quick enough to catch a fish with their hands. When they were a little older, they would throw seed pods from a special bush into the water. The seed pods contained a poison that paralyzed the fish and brought them to the surface, easier to catch.

She forgot she had ever been a child who loved the creek, the willows and mulefat that grew along its banks, the cattails and tules that thrived in the stream. The foxes, frogs and lizards that hid among them. She forgot to laugh, took no delight in anything at all. Even the gnawing pain of the wolf had disappeared. A hollowness took its place.

[19]

The sun began to rise earlier in the morning, set later in the day. The moon hung, translucent, in the pale sky of early evening. Flavors the villagers hadn't tasted in a year were waiting to be gathered. Aphids feeding on cottonwood trees secreted honey to sweeten willow bark tea. Bushes yielded small cherries that were eaten out of hand. Pits were pounded into meal. Lemonade berries added a good-tasting sourness to food. White sage grew in abundance. Dwellings were cleansed with clumps of smoky sage leaves.

Big Headed Girl paid no attention to the advancing season, even on a day when a raven swooped low over the village in the early morning. Others saw it as a sign. She barely noticed the bird. She was helping her aunt prepare the midday meal when a young man entered the village. Men often played wooden flutes as they walked between villages, but this man came silently. He wore trousers and a zarape like the Mexicans, but, unlike the soldiers, he was barefoot. His long hair, bramble-tangled, fell around his face. His chest was barren of shells and his arms wore no tattoos. Only his face was distinctive. With his long nose and narrow eyes, he looked like a fox.

Conversation ceased as the villagers looked at the young man. Girl saw him approach a child. She was close enough to hear him say the name of an elder. The child pointed to the house next to Girl's. The young man straightened his back and advanced.

"Awerin?" The young man addressed an elder who sat outside his kiiy. The old man was shaping a reed for a new pipe and didn't look up. No one had called him that name in many years. "Lightning" was not the name for an old man who could hardly rise from the ground. Erach'po, old man, was his name now.

"Awerin?" This time the old man pursed his toothless mouth and looked up.

"Who are you?" he asked.

"I am Koovahcho." Erach'po took a moment to remember. He leaped up, forgetting his age.

"Come, come," he shouted to his neighbors. Unable to wait until they gathered, he shouted, "This is my grandnephew. His mother and father were taken to the mission many years ago—how old are you, boy?"

"Nineteen," Koovahcho answered. No one had ever looked at him with interest before.

"They were stolen from the village when he was a baby in his mother's arms." He peered at the young man. The wrinkles on Erach'po's face deepened, and he began to wail. "My son, my son, what have they done to you?"

Girl saw Koovahcho sink to his knees. He looks like I feel, she thought. Empty.

For the first time in many years, old Erach'po walked around the village. He stopped at every dwelling to introduce his kin. "My grandnephew will be a big help around here," he bragged.

The men wondered, What does he know of our ways? The women thought, He's so small and thin, what work can he do? The children stared at him. Is he Mexican or Indian? Koovahcho shifted his weight from side to side, kicking up little puffs of dust. Everything was strange—the tule houses where he would sleep, the villagers who crowded around him so closely, the words they spoke. At the mission, he was whipped when he spoke the Tongva language. Even the little Tongva he had learned from other captives was stunted from fear and disuse.

Able to understand only a little of what the villagers were saying, he retreated to the fantasy he had nurtured since childhood when his mother and father died. In this imaginary world, he returned to his father's village, was instantly treated to all the corn and beans he could ever want. He'd sleep on a straw pallet like the mission fathers. His uncles and brothers would make sure he never had to tend the vegetable garden, or slaughter pigs or serve the padres as he had at the mission. He would sit around the fire all day, tell stories or sometimes hunt, as others told him they had done before they had been captured and taken to the Mission San Gabriel. His kin would look at him with respect because of all he knew about mission ways.

Koovahcho's first day in the village at an end, he lay on a reed mat in his granduncle's dwelling. On one side, the feet of his young cousin poked into his ribs. On the other, his aunt and her husband inhaled softly. His granduncle lay perpendicular to Koovahcho's head, snoring loudly. His cousin's baby woke often and howled. Water whispered as it tumbled over creek stones. The sound irritated him. Unable to sleep, he saw only one face in his mind: the girl who lived in the kiiy next to his. He had sneaked looks at her all day. He thought about her skin, the color of fine dust; her hair, woven through with small shells and twine. He brought his thighs together, trying to control his erection. At the mission, young women were guarded day and night until they entered into a Christian marriage. With this girl, it was different. He could almost touch her from where he slept.

The flesh was evil, Padre José had said.

Koovahcho closed his eyes, saw the girl's breasts move under her necklaces. And her legs—they looked so strong!—tucked under her as she worked a basket into shape.

Padre José had preached endlessly about Temptation and Sin.

Koovahcho finally understood what the words meant.

The next morning, Koovahcho was awakened by a sound he knew well—a pair of hands patting tortillas into shape. The sound made him instantly hungry. He raised his head to look around. Sunshine shone through the hut's woven willow branches. His great-uncle and his cousins were still sleeping. He crab-walked out of the kiiy, narrowed his eyes to protect them from the sun glaring back at him. Big Headed Girl was shaping acorn cakes, not tortillas, in front of her dwelling. He stared at her. She concentrated even more fiercely on the cakes, trying to make each one perfect. After a few minutes, Koovahcho approached her.

"I am Koovahcho," he said. His voice, strong and confident, surprised him.

Big Headed Girl did not look up. "I know. I saw you when you entered the village yesterday." She patted a cake into shape. Why was he standing there? Her uncle and brother went immediately to the river to bathe as soon as they awakened. All men did.

"Would you like to know what I did at the mission?"

Girl didn't answer. She finished forming her last cake, then rose to her feet.

"Where are you going?" Koovahcho asked.

"To the spring."

"To bathe?"

"I need water to steam the cakes."

"I'll do it for you."

"No, it's my job," she said, abruptly.

"I'll go with you." He grabbed a basket.

She turned it over. "This basket has no tar. It won't hold water."

"Yes, I know that," he said, dropping his basket and reaching for the one at her feet. "Let's go."

Grandmother emerged from the kiiy. She watched as they went off together. Koovahcho was neither Mexican nor Indian. He had not been initiated, so he was neither man nor boy. He didn't know their people's ways, and whatever he had learned at the mission was not going to be useful here. He was not the husband she wanted for Girl.

Koovahcho stepped carefully down the steep bank toward the creek. He tried to brush away the willows that barred his way, bent back stalks he couldn't move.

"Don't do that," Girl warned.

"Why not?" Koovahcho stumbled as Girl turned back to look at him.

"We use the willows to make our houses. If they're broken, we'll have to walk further to find good ones."

At the creek, Girl tried to take the basket from him. He pulled it out of her reach and splashed into the shallow water. Bending low, he dipped the basket toward the water. Girl didn't know what to make of him. She glanced at the fine hair on his cheeks and chin. He was definitely a man. Why, then, was his behavior so odd? Helping her make acorn cakes and fetching water? These were things that women did. Did he expect her to sharpen arrow points or hunt for rabbits?

Koovahcho saw the lines between her eyes deepen. "Why do you look at me like that?" he asked.

He stood in water up to his ankles. His pants hung loosely from his narrow waist. His zarape was patched in several places. Even from a distance, Girl saw how clumsily it had been mended and supposed he had done it himself, like other womanly tasks. His lank hair fell into his face as he filled the basket. Suddenly, a frog jumped out from the cattails next to his feet. He stumbled backward and fell on his backside into the creek.

Girl laughed. She hadn't laughed in a long time. It felt good to laugh. She couldn't stop. Koovahcho looked embarrassed, then pleased. The girl liked him, he was sure.

She didn't like him, but as the days passed he became part of her life. He was worse off than she. She had her grandmother, brother and sister, the village. The ancestors. Her memories. He knew nothing but the mission. Every morning, they went down to the creek together. She was there the first time he attempted to catch a fish with his bare hands. Another day, he scraped a flat stone to resemble the arrow points he saw other men make. But he grew bored with the task before the stone took on the fine point needed to pierce an animal's flesh. His attention shifted to a wild rose bush. He snapped off a branch. Girl watched as he awkwardly stripped the bark to make an arrow shaft.

"You know the wild rose is a favorite of the Creator, don't you?"

"Yes," he said. He had seen the sacred space in the middle of the village where worship of Chinigchinich took place, but he knew nothing about the Tongva god. "No," he admitted.

"The blackberry too," she said.

He held the stick up for her approval. "Look, that's a good job I did. I'll bind my stone to it and shoot a fox."

Girl laughed out loud. "You cut into the wood too deeply. Not an arrow shaft. Only a crooked stick."

Koovahcho threw his work into the creek, watched it float away.

Girl was with him one afternoon when he shot a rabbit and followed it into the bushes. Although the animal escaped his grasp, he pointed to a blood spot on the ground, pleased that one of his arrows had found a mark. Next time, he told her, he'd make a kill.

"We'll eat it together," he said. "You are thin. You can use some extra meat."

"Hunters never eat what they kill. They offer it to the village to feed us all," she scoffed. "Why don't you know that?"

The question was too big for him to answer.

Unused to the food his kin ate with relish, his stomach pained him for a long time. At first the seeds and nuts, wild greens and—when hunters were lucky—ducks, rabbits and birds made him ill. More than once, he left Erach'po's kiiy in the middle of the night to throw up in the bushes. His feces were so foul that the men made a show of avoiding any area where he might have shat. At the mission, the padres ate beans, corn, and beef and mutton. Indians ate pozole, a thin gruel. This was what he knew. Finally, many days after he arrived at the village, his stomach accepted an acorn cake.

"I ate a whole acorn cake last night," he announced to Girl the following morning. The dew was wet on the ground, signaling the end of the warm months.

"I eat these every day," she replied.

"I know," he said impatiently. "Can't you see? My stomach is becoming Indian?"

Girl turned her face away to hide her smile. He didn't notice; he was staring at her breasts.

The men, old and young, became used to Koovahcho. Sometimes they helped him. Sometimes they ignored him. After a while, they accepted him as they did an ignorant child. Others had returned from the mission and tried to learn or relearn their people's ways, but they soon left to work on a rancho or get drunk in the pueblo. The villagers were surprised he stayed.

The leaves began to fall from the sycamore trees. Squirrels that had grown fat in the warm months scurried frantically to collect food for the colder weather soon to come.

The whitepetaled flowers with yellow centers the size of birds' eggs died away. The last berries were long gone. Much to the villagers' surprise, Koovahcho was still among them. Erach'po had long ago stopped bragging about his great-nephew. But he argued with his granddaughter when she criticized how much food the young man ate, how little he helped. The only good thing about him, she said, was that he didn't smell bad anymore, because Girl had convinced him that men bathed every morning. Erach'po shook his head at his granddaughter's tirades. He knew she was right, but one kinsman never asked another to leave. His daughter knew that too.

Koovahcho was unaware of people's doubts. After a time, he became as used to the village as he had been to the mission. The one difference was Big Headed Girl. There was no beautiful young woman at the mission. Every morning, he would accompany her to the creek. He had learned to step carefully around the willow trees and thread his way among the tules.

"Why aren't you angry at the mission fathers for stealing you from our village?" Big Headed Girl asked on a day when clouds hung in the sky like puffs of smoke.

He said only, "It wasn't so bad."

"Not so bad? They beat you if you didn't work fast enough. Isn't that what you said?" she challenged.

"Yes." Koovahcho reached up, grabbed a willow tree branch and began to strip off the leaves.

"You told me they made you go to church. If you talked about the Tongva god or spoke our language, they whipped you."

"Yes."

"I wouldn't like that," she said, "I wouldn't say, 'It wasn't so bad.'"

"But you're a girl," he teased. "You can't take beatings." She would be angry if he told her he thought the padres' ways were better. At the mission, every hour of the day and night had a plan. He might not like weeding the fields or planting seedlings, but there was always work to be done. Here there were no plans, and he never knew what was expected of him.

The day was cloudy, cool. Wind blew down from the mountains onto the wide plain. Men and women clutched fur skins around their shoulders. Dust blew in their faces as they prepared to eat their evening meal. Koovahcho sat hunched over, sifting sand aimlessly through his fingers. He paid no attention to his young cousins playing a game with sticks or to their mother's complaints. After a time, he moved closer to his great-uncle.

"Erach'po," he said, quietly. "How do I ask a girl to marry me?"

"You want a wife?" Erach'po said loudly. All eyes turned toward him. Koovahcho brought his knees to his chin, trying to make himself as small as possible.

"Please, uncle, lower your voice."

"Yes, yes," Erach'po spoke more quietly. "What do you want to know?"

"How do I ask a girl to marry me?" he repeated.

"Before I married your great-aunt, I lived with my wife's family for a time. I hunted and gave them what I killed. They saw what a good husband I'd make, so they approved the marriage."

Koovahcho said nothing.

"Now it's different. You want to marry Big Headed Girl?"

Koovahcho lowered his head to his knees.

"You'll have to ask her. She has no mother and father. Her grandmother won't stop you. There are so few young men in the village, and we rarely visit with our brothers in other villages. Fewer chances for girls to find husbands. If she wants to marry, she only has to say yes."

With that advice in mind, Koovahcho approached Big Headed Girl the next morning.

"Do you want to marry?" he asked.

"I don't know. I don't think about it much," she said, untruthfully. She often thought about marriage. She had gone through the women's ceremonies three years before. It was time to marry. But whom?

"I mean, do you want to marry me?"

"No."

"No? Why not?"

"You cannot be the father of my children. What would they learn from you?"

Koovahcho walked away down the creek, slapping the water hard with each footstep. In a short while, he returned.

"I've been thinking," he said. "If you marry me, you will teach our children. I will learn from you also. It won't be so bad. I will protect you."

Girl couldn't believe what she was hearing. He could not even protect himself.

Turning away, she raced through the brambles and stands of willow to the top of the hill. There, she remembered her basket, ran down again to retrieve it. Breathless from anger and exertion, she paused to catch her breath as she approached the creek. Koovahcho stood at the creek's edge; he stared, motionless, at the basket in his hands. A doe was looking at him from across the water. Moments passed. Koovahcho turned silently to look at the doe. Calmly, the doe lowered her head, began to drink.

Even the doe knows it has nothing to fear from this man, Girl thought.

"I will marry you," Girl said suddenly. She was fifteen now. It was time.

The Mexicans' world was growing. Someday, there would be no room for Tongva in this land. Maybe she and Koovahcho would be stronger as two than she would be as one.

Ignorant of custom, Koovahcho did not approach Grandmother or Older Brother asking for permission to marry Girl. He relied on Girl to tell them. He did not bring gifts to them. His only acknowledgment that he and Girl would marry was in sitting by her fire each evening, instead of his great-uncle's.

The evening meal became awkward with Koovahcho there. He ate everything that Girl put in front of him, scooping up meal and seeds with his fingers, gnawing on a rabbit's bones, grunting loudly as he approved of each bite. Older Brother had nothing to say to Koovahcho. He ate quickly and joined his companions elsewhere to smoke.

Girl watched her husband-to-be and waited. Hope lay curled within her like a mouse in its burrow while doubt hovered nearby, eager to snatch hope away.

[20]

The sun rested low in the west when Girl and Grandmother climbed the hill above the village. The next day, the first full moon since Koovahcho had asked her, Girl and Koovahcho would marry. The two women sifted through piles of dry oak leaves, their bodies bent over from the waist, in search of acorns they could use for the wedding feast. When Girl looked up at last, a narrow vermillion line at the horizon separated the dark clouds overhead from the ocean below.

The women crouched in silence as the light faded. A cold wind rustled the leaves.

"Should I marry Koovahcho, Grandmother?" Girl said at last.

Grandmother pointed toward the sky. The shifting clouds ringed a clearing overhead. "Look," she said.

Girl followed Grandmother's outstretched arm toward the glittering heavens. She knew that long ago the first beings had left the earth and become the stars, rocks and hills. She could depend on the village for the food her husband could not kill and offer to all, for the dances and songs her husband did not know, for the worship of Chinigchinich he could not make. The ancestors would be watching.

Clouds filled the window in the sky again. Girl could no longer see the stars.

A strong wind blew through the tule thatch covering her dwelling that night. A breeze chilled Girl's cheek with each gust.

Grandmother breathed evenly next to her. On Grandmother's opposite side lay Little Sister, too excited about the wedding to sleep. Older Brother slept next to her uncle near the opening, ready to spring out if a bear or mountain lion wandered into the village. Her uncle's family had shared the dwelling with Girl's family since the day Girl's mother had stepped into the waves. Girl tossed and turned on her mat, unable to sleep.

Soon after sunrise, Nilit's daughter called into Girl's kiiy, "Wake up. We've come to make you ready." She poked her head through the door. Girl was alone, seated on her mat, the furs used as blankets neatly folded in a corner.

"Where is Grandmother?" Achanchah asked, following Nilit's daughter into the dwelling.

"She and Little Sister are bathing in the creek." Girl spoke barely above a whisper.

"And you?" Achanchah teased. "Are you going to your husband smelling of sleep and cooking fires?"

"Does it matter?" Girl said. Any confidence she had felt the night before had faded.

The women had no answer for such a question. Instead, Nilit's daughter began to wind strings of feathers around Girl's waist and ankles.

"You look like your mother the day she married your father," Nilit's daughter said, as she worked.

Achanchah combed Girl's long hair and braided strands around her face, tying each one with a rope of tiny periwinkle shells. Even a slight movement of Girl's head set the shells dancing. She, too, saw Na'aro in Girl's face and body—the prominent cheek bones, small hands and narrow fingers.

Little Sister had made four clamshell necklaces. Shivering from her bath in the cold creek, she slipped them over Girl's head. She sat back on her heels to admire her sister.

Koovahcho's cousin joined them. She carried a small basket of thin sticks and a powder she had mixed from dried blueberries saved since the summer. She darkened the lines of Girl's tattoos until they stood out boldly on Girl's skin.

Grandmother was the last to enter the kiiy. She tied a bark skirt around Girl's waist. Her hands shook as she laid a rabbit skin cape around Girl's shoulders. She had given a cape like this to her daughter on her wedding day. Na'aro was wearing it when she walked into the sea.

Grandmother remembered weddings in her time but did not speak of them. Days of celebrations preceded a morning when the young man came to take his bride home. Dancing and tossing seeds, villagers accompanied the bride and groom to the young man's home.

Little Sister peeked out the door. "They are here," she said.

A moment later, Girl stood outside her dwelling. The clouds that had hung over the village the night before hovered close to the earth. A glance at the tomyaar chiefs and the dancers told her what they thought about her marriage. Their bodies were covered with furs for warmth, but they wore too few of the necklaces, arm bands and feathers always used for a celebration. Girl and Grandmother took their places behind the men. Each family joined the procession as it passed their dwelling, silently, warily, as if each person, from the youngest to the very old, was as uncertain about the wisdom of this marriage as Big Headed Girl.

Slowly, the procession moved toward a kiiy that the villagers had constructed for Girl and Koovahcho. Families of greater importance lived near the yovaar in the center of the village; Girl and Koovahcho's lay on the farthest edge.

As she drew near, Girl saw the wedding bower: a scanty ramada of a few cottonwood branches and willow leaves constructed near the entrance. Koovahcho sat under the ramada, his body thin as a boy's, the only one among them smiling. He didn't know the ramada should be large enough to cover all the villagers with branches in full leaf.

He didn't miss the family, his family, who would have welcomed his wife into their home. What comfort there was would have to come from skins of animals that others in the village had shot or trapped and worked painstakingly into blankets to warm the couple as they slept.

He didn't think it strange that villagers brought food from their own stores. He had no mother or sisters in his kiiy who would light the fire and gather the seeds, no father or brothers who would kill the ducks and rabbits for a wedding feast.

Girl joined Koovahcho under the ramada. Custom called for Girl's father to offer her words of advice as she entered into marriage. But Girl's father had been absent for many seasons. She no longer felt his presence in her life.

Older men and children began to sing quietly, hesitant to break the silence. Women raised their clapper sticks and beat them against their hands, keeping time, moving outward to form a circle. Dancers moved slowly toward the center. Voices grew louder, the dancers' steps more deliberate. The beat, once established, grew stronger. Not all was lost. They could still dance and sing, even if it was to celebrate a marriage that made them all uneasy.

They may have gone on, but rain began to fall. At first, the dancers continued, undeterred. Slowly, the storm gathered power. Wind came up, blew the few remaining leaves off the ramada's willow branches. Rain pelted the earth, cutting furrows in the dust. The dry ground underfoot turned to mud.

Children began to run for cover; the old ones left, then the young and strong. The tomyaars walked away, toward their dwellings near the yovaar. Grandmother stood in the rain, a small figure shaking her shell rattle and singing until Little Sister took her hand. "We must go," she urged.

Grandmother gave in. She bent down, kissed Girl on the cheek. She patted Koovahcho's shoulder. Her hair was wet through to the scalp by the time she let Little Sister pull her away.

The marriage ceremony was over.

Koovahcho was the first to stand. He could not erase the smile that played around his lips. Now he would lie with Big Headed Girl. Girl felt the stirrings of pain she had known in the years after her father died. Only her curiosity kept the wolf at bay. She followed her husband into their new dwelling. She lay down on the grizzly bear skin that Grandmother had given them from her own dowry and waited.

Rain was falling again three months later when Girl announced one night, "I'm going to have a baby." Happiness eluded her at the prospect of birthing a child with an ignorant father in such perilous times.

They had not seen the sun in four days. Women always had work to do when the rains pounded down. There were seeds to be ground into meal, baskets to make or mend, shells to be drilled for new necklaces, dry grasses to be searched for and gathered in the intervals between rain squalls. Koovahcho sat, smoked his pipe. If there had been men in the family or men in his age group who wanted his company, he would have passed the afternoons with them, but since there were neither, he smoked alone. Once in a while, he ventured out halfheartedly with his crooked arrows. He hadn't yet seen a rabbit or shot a bird; he was ever hopeful.

The juncus stem Little Sister was preparing to weave into a basket fell from her hand. Grandmother didn't look up. She had guessed Girl's condition when she noticed the puffiness around Girl's eyes, the unmistakable sign of pregnancy in her family. Koovahcho nodded to show he had heard. He rearranged his legs and sat straighter. He was sure it would be a boy.

"As soon as it stops raining, we will tell the rest of the village," Grandmother said. Her happiness, like her granddaughter's, was tempered with apprehension.

In the days that followed, the village prepared to celebrate Big Headed Girl's coming child. Girl stopped worrying about Koovahcho and all he did not know. Her baby's first movement inside her held the promise of all the births her village had seen. She did not allow herself to think about the future. Instead, she imagined that she and her baby were alone in a small canoe drifting slowly down the creek. Though the wide river ahead might hold dangers, she would keep her baby safe. She hoped it would be a girl.

A full moon shone on the village the night chosen for the celebration, a night so clear the stars shone as bright as owls' eyes in the dark. Fires were laid in the village center near the yovaar, ready to char the skins of birds, ground squirrels, an unfortunate pheasant and a few ducks that had wandered into range the day before. Girl wore the bark skirt from her wedding day, her breasts fuller and her belly a little more round. Koovahcho was still as thin as a reed, his body that of a boy, not a man, which he thought he had become.

The singers formed a circle, began to beat the rhythms that would accompany the dance. Girl danced first. With Grandmother and Little Sister by her side, she planted her feet firmly on the ground, allowed the rattling shells and clapper sticks to guide her steps. Grandmother, her white hair combed smoothly down her back, had taken the same steps as a young woman herself and later with her daughter. When it was his turn, Koovahcho stood alone before the group, his cousins unwilling to accompany him, Erach'po too ill to leave his kiiy. He shuffled uncertainly from side to side, ignorant of where to move his feet.

Voices, even among their small band, became stronger as the hours went on, fortified by fermented berry juice. The warrior Tean-re passed around whiskey he had acquired when he journeyed to the pueblo of Los Angeles to sell his wife's baskets.

Dancers turned, circled, crouched like deer. Stepped carefully as if on leaves in the thickets bordering the creek. A step between a pounce and a prance. Forward and back. Forward and back.

Women circled the men. Moved like ocean waves. Placed one foot apart from the other. Dragged the other foot to meet it. Slowly. Slowly. Shook shell rattles loudly, together. Moved their arms in wide strokes, rowing a ti'at.

Some danced, others sang. Songs of the sea. The rivers. The great wide plain, when it had been traversed by them alone. Sang of their brothers in other villages across the plain. Those who were kin and those they had traded with but now rarely visited. Serrano, Luiseño, Chumash. Sang of them all.

The singers entrusted to bring forth food took their turns. The singer of rabbits, the singer of birds, of seeds, of wild roses. Their songs would please Chinigchinich; he would provide.

Men came forward, one by one. Played their flutes. The sound, clear as a scrub jay's call, fragile as a hummingbird's egg, pierced the night. Woke the antelope, quieted the mountain lions, left the rabbits deep in their underground burrows, undisturbed.

Children joined the dancers until late into the night. One by one, they fell asleep at their mother's breasts or in their arms. Girl lay on a reed mat. She dozed lightly next to Koovahcho, covered by the grizzly bear skin. She opened her eyes as the sky began to pale above the mountains. The blush deepened to an intense pink and spread above the mountains, until it melted into the lavender of a few remaining clouds.

"A good time to deliver a child, the year's warmest days," Grandmother observed.

Big Headed Girl didn't hear her, so intent was she on

birthing her baby. Pain dove its fingers into her belly and then moved on. Koovahcho's cousin returned from the spring. She held a basket of water while Nilit's daughter dribbled the drops over Girl's face, onto her parched lips. Girl stared at the roof of her kiiy, gathering strength.

Koovahcho took up a place at the edge of the creek where he stripped one willow branch after another. He would have welcomed friends at this time. Erach'po had died during the season when leaves began to appear on the sycamore trees. They had never been to each other what Koovahcho had hoped, but Erach'po would have distracted Koovahcho now. Deer didn't visit for their morning drink, nor did birds hunt for seeds in the mud. Often, a particular red-tailed fox joined him in the early morning, but not today.

Koovahcho lowered his head into his hands. He knew nothing. He had befriended no one. He was left to look at the creek, watch its silver splash and wish safe passage for the boy who would soon make him a father.

Girl labored all day, Grandmother at her side. Sun beat down on the dwelling. As shadows lengthened, Grandmother began to worry. She had already chosen a name: Na'aro, her daughter's name. Her daughter's spirit must have wanted to enter the world again. Why did it delay?

Wind came up as the sun fell into the ocean behind the hills. Scents of sage and wild rose were carried by the evening breeze. Long stalks of willow leaves whispered by the creek. The village waited. A new life, even fathered by an odd man like Koovahcho, would be welcomed. The lines on Grandmother's forehead deepened. Her eyes grew tired. She worried about the baby. She worried about Girl. She had been present when an infant emerged dead from its mother's womb, or when blood flowed so hard death took both mother and infant away.

In the time between pains, Girl studied Grandmother. She noticed the deep furrows on the old woman's face and a tremor in her hands. All the months Girl had carried her child, she had not paid much attention to Grandmother or Koovahcho. She had retreated into the warm place where her unborn daughter lived, protected and safe.

The sky turned from blue to black. Koovahcho did not return to light the fire, as a man might do when his wife was giving birth. Achanchah and her daughter, Erach'po's granddaughter, and Esar, the oldest woman in the village, gathered inside the kiiy. Nilit's daughter and Koovahcho's cousin, exhausted, moved aside to let the others help.

Pain took Girl's body more often. With each pain, the women helped Girl up to a crouch. She pushed furiously and panted hard. No infant emerged. They helped her lie down. Another pain—she was up, pushed with all her strength. Sweat collected under Girl's breasts. Dripped from her face and armpits.

Up, then down. Up, then down. The pains came hard and fast. She pushed, breathed, and pushed again. "Soon," Grandmother said, from her place among the others.

Girl's body shook with a pain more violent than all the rest. She screamed.

"Push," the women called in one voice, as they struggled to keep Girl on her feet. The next moment, the infant slid between Girl's legs. Grandmother reached out and caught it, spied the birth cord wrapped around its tiny neck. With one quick move, Grandmother unwrapped the cord. She held the infant upside down by its feet. It was then she noticed the baby's penis, like a little spout between its legs. She sucked in her breath, surprised.

The baby squalled, his face red, his hands balled in tight fists. Nilit's daughter grabbed the baby. Used a soft rabbit skin to wipe him clean. Wrapped him in another skin and tucked him against Girl's breast. He began to suck immediately. Girl smiled.

A son. She had always known.

Fires burned late that night. The flames had nearly died out when word, "The baby has come," spread through the village. Men and women rose slowly to their feet, gently roused the children sleeping near them. Daytime companions—silver lizards, gray squirrels, a family of skunks— slept on as villagers moved like shadows toward Girl's kiiy.

Only coyote looked on as the villagers gathered to welcome the child into the world.

Only frog along the creek bottom called out in the warm night.

Koovahcho slipped into the dwelling moments after his son was born, surprised to see so many women, so much activity. He saw Little Sister pour baskets of water over hot hearth stones. Vapor rose; steam filled the kiiy. Koovahcho sat on the ground, his knees to his chest, close to the entrance.

He watched as Erach'po's granddaughter cut the birth cord. She wrapped the cord and placenta in reeds and gave it to Achanchah, who took them away. She would bury them in secret to prevent anyone from using the birth shroud to bewitch the child. Koovahcho had seen the same protection taken without the padres' knowledge when babies were born at the mission.

While Erach'po's granddaughter bathed the baby in water warmed on the hearth, Nilit's daughter burned a chilicote plant to ash. Mixed the ash with a little animal fat to make a salve. The infant slept as she spread salve on his navel.

With no grandfather to name the baby, Grandmother had called the baby Koo'ar when she saw it was a boy. Soon after, she fell asleep next to Girl. Her mouth open, she snored loudly.

Girl dozed, sweating under furs and skins. She roused briefly when Achanchah placed Koo'ar on her breast again. Her body ached, yes, but she had never felt so happy. She had a son. A son. She looked into his sleeping face. His dark hair was as wet as a newborn fox. His tiny hands were balled on her breast. She bent her neck to kiss his head. Her voice a quaver, she began to sing. She fell asleep before the song was half-finished.

[21]

Girl watched Koo'ar crawl through the dust. His knee scraped a small rock; Girl didn't move when he cried out in pain. Koovahcho poked his head out the entrance of their kiiy. Awkwardly, he pulled Koo'ar toward him, rose to his feet and examined the scratch on his son's knee. Blood had already formed beneath the surface. The next moment the wound opened; his son cried louder.

"Girl," Koovahcho pleaded. "Why don't you take care of our son? How can you sit here and watch him cry? Keep him away from the rocks."

"Why? So he can grow up to be as weak as his father?" Girl said spitefully.

Koovahcho covered the child's bruise with soft sage leaves and held them tightly against the wound until the blood stopped. He rocked the boy in his arms. Koo'ar smiled, began to coo. He reached to pull his father's hair.

"You are just in a bad mood because of the weather," he told Girl. "The padres told us these warm winds blow from the desert beyond the mountains. None of them liked the winds either." He knew that comparing her to the padres would make her even angrier.

He had learned how to get along with his wife. Most often, he ignored everything she said. Sometimes, he struck back. As a hunter he was useless, but when it came to hurling insults, he knew exactly where to aim his arrow. He put Koo'ar down in front of her and walked toward the creek.

For a few minutes, Girl sat sulking, her chin lowered to

her chest. Koo'ar began to throw handfuls of dirt in the air. The wind blew dust into his eyes. Again he cried.

"Oh, Koo'ar," she said. "Stop it." Grabbing the boy, she drew him into her lap. She held his hands. Her anger melted. She murmured tender words and rubbed his soft cheek against hers.

"What's wrong?" Grandmother asked when she approached Girl a few moments later. Girl looked as if she had been chewing sour lemonade berry.

"My husband thinks I'm a bad mother because I don't stop Koo'ar from hurting himself."

"Is he right?"

Grandmother had noticed that Girl often showed a lack of tenderness toward her son.

"I want him to be strong." Girl watched Koo'ar toddle on unsteady legs to a patch of deerweed and empty his bowels nearby. "Yes, I drip cold water on his face. But only so he will know what rain feels like. You know I didn't swaddle him in skins as other women swaddled their babies when cold winds blew. I want him to grow up strong, able to take care of himself."

Girl fetched Koo'ar and laid him on the ground. He kicked his legs playfully while she washed his bottom, then powdered it with soapstone she had ground to a fine, soft silt. "I will fetch more water from the creek," Girl announced.

"I will go," Grandmother said. She sighed as she rose to her knees and, with more effort, to her feet. Holding a water basket in one hand, she trod slowly down the path. Girl watched her go. The old woman was limping and appeared unsteady on her feet.

"Come back. I'll go," Girl called after her.

Grandmother paid no attention. The cottonwood trees were in full bloom, their branches a tangle of new green leaves. She paused to look up at a few green shoots on a cottonwood tree not yet fully leaved. Craning her neck, she took in the sky and saw, at the top of the tree, the bolls that would soon release a cottony fluff into the warm air.

Only then did Grandmother notice how quiet the world had become. The morning, always full of bird calls, was silent. Small animals in the brush had stopped moving. In the silence, she heard the earth scream, the unmistakable high-pitched sound warning those who could hear it that the earth was about to shake. The seven giants on which the earth rested were starting to move. The next moment, the giants rolled over. The ground under Grandmother's feet heaved, then heaved again. She felt a branch of the cottonwood tree rake her face as it fell to the ground. The basket fell from her fingers. Willow stalks that she could have used a moment before to steady herself lay uprooted on the ground.

Her legs buckled. She fell backward. Her hands clutched uselessly at air. As the ground came up to meet her, she saw herself as the child she had once been, wading into the wide river the white men called the Río Porciúncula. The words she sang as a young girl when she tapped the rhythm on her counting sticks came back to her.

He nik ne
he wa na.

She was the bride being carried to her husband's village near the creek. Above the clatter of the villagers' shells on that happy day, she heard the giants roar. Grandmother flailed her arms, reaching, reaching, failing to find anything stable on the heaving landscape, landing at last on the rolling earth. The sharp edge of a rock pierced her head above her ear. Pain blinded her. She cried out.

The violent shaking stopped abruptly. In the quiet that followed, Grandmother tried to think clearly. The earth rested on seven giants.

He nik ne
he wa na.

Na'aro's face. Na'aro's back as she stepped into the waves. When the giants moved, the earth shook.

He nik ne
he wa na.
Hopsi wahna
he wa na.

Big Headed Girl is born! The little boy, Girl's little brother—oh, what was his name?—is dead. Her hand inched toward her head searching for the rock, trying to push it out of the way.

Whoo!

Her fingers found the rock. Why was it so wet? Sticky too.

Hopsi wahna
he wa na.

Why did her head ache so badly? She gagged as undigested porridge came up from her stomach. Her stomach's vile contents spilled out onto the ground.

She scratched her fingers along the ground, struggled to bring her hands to her sides, to press her palms against the earth, to sit up. Small waves lapped onto the creek bank. A rhythmic, soothing sound. She closed her eyes.

Girl stood alone at the door of her kiiy, clutching the screaming Koo'ar to her breast. "Grandmother. Where is she?" Girl cried. Koovahcho ran up from the creek. "Down there. In the trees. Help me. She's hurt," he yelled.

"Tean-re, find Older Brother. Come quickly," Erach'po's granddaughter yelled, running back to the center of the village.

The giants rolled over again. Struggling to stay on her feet, Girl followed Koovahcho down to the creek. She peered ahead through the tangle of branches, saw her husband kneeling next to Grandmother. The old woman lay unconscious in a pool of blood and vomit.

"Grandmother. Grandmother," Girl called as she ran to the old woman's side. Holding Koo'ar tightly to her breast, Girl knelt next to the old woman, her ear close to Grandmother's mouth. Yes, she was still breathing.

She pushed Koo'ar into Koovahcho's arms and took her grandmother's hand.

Three young men ran down the embankment through the trees. Tean-re, the strongest, picked up Grandmother in his arms. Girl followed him to her kiiy. Blood flowed from the wound on Grandmother's head. The old woman opened her eyes, groaned and passed out again.

Koovahcho stood alone with his son in his arms. He knelt next to the blood-stained rock. He blamed himself. If he had stayed a few moments longer, it would have been he, not Grandmother, who would have taken the water basket to the river.

At the kiiy, women were already wilting mule fat leaves on the fire and brewing willow bark tea. If Grandmother opened her eyes again, the tea would ease her pain. Tean-re placed Grandmother on a deerskin and backed away.

Erach'po's granddaughter cleaned the deep, crimson slash above Grandmother's ear. She took the tender mulefat leaves and spread them on the wound. The village seer came. He evoked the Creator in his songs of healing. Girl watched. Grandmother's body stiffened, then relaxed many times through the long afternoon. Sometimes, she moaned. Each time, Girl thought Grandmother would awake.

After sundown, the hot wind stopped blowing. The night cooled. The giant rolled over once, twice, three times more, surprising no one. The damage had already been done. Women went off to sleep; others took their places. Girl sat up watching. Koovahcho came when Koo'ar cried out in hunger, then left again.

Grandmother's body looked smaller inside her old woman's loose skin the next morning. She barely moved. Women bathed her hot flesh in cool water. A tomyaar stood over her, trying to chant her to wake. He walked away, shaking his head.

Koovahcho returned early in the morning to take charge of his son. He should have been off with the men, letting women care for Koo'ar, but nobody thought to tell him. He bathed Koo'ar in the creek, amused him by making faces, finally lay down in a corner of the kiiy to nap with him. Girl only took her son to feed him. She looked past her son's smiling face toward Grandmother's lifeless body and said nothing to her husband.

Long past midnight of the second day, Grandmother called out softly, "Na'aro." If Girl had been sleeping soundly she would not have heard. Older Brother was among the men who joined women sleeping near the fire pit. They were worn out and knew, like the tomyaar chief, there was nothing to be done. Sparks flickered where fire had been.

Girl knelt next to Grandmother. Except for the white hair that covered her shoulders, she looked almost young, her face peaceful, unlined. Her shuttered eyes slanted up at the corners. Girl had never realized before how much her mother resembled her grandmother. Girl felt for Grandmother's hand under the deerskin. The old woman's skin felt cool; her grip, strong.

"Grandmother. You're going to get well, aren't you?"

"Of course, daughter, of course."

"I am Big Headed Girl, your granddaughter," she whispered near the old woman's ear.

"Yes, yes, I know, Na'aro, my daughter."

"I am Big Headed Girl," she whispered again.

Grandmother turned toward her. "Yes, I see you now." She stared directly into her granddaughter's face. Her eyes were clear.

"You can't die, Grandmother. What will I do without you?"

"I had seen only four full cycles of seasons when my mother died," Grandmother said.

"Koovahcho is not like my father or grandfather. He is no help. He cannot protect me."

The old woman looked skyward. She crooned softly to herself. The women around the fire stirred. An owl hooted.

Coyote and her pups paused at the edge of the village, watching. Bobcat, sitting on a distant rock, sniffed the scents that told him morning would come soon. He stretched out his long golden body, deciding whether he was hungry and would hunt before dawn.

Grandmother sang in a shrill child's voice.

He nik ne
he wa na
He nik ni
he wa na.
Hopsi wahna
he wa na.
Hopsi wahna
he wa na.
Whoo!

Again, the song she sang as a child. "Whoo!" Grandmother cried. "Whoo!" she repeated. Her mouth went slack. She stared, unseeing, into the dark.

It was the season of birdsongs, but the mourning doves and sparrow hawks were silent. It was the season of birth, but muskrats retreated to their lodges in the cattails, antelope to higher ground, jackrabbits to their burrows. They ventured out quietly for food; their young squirmed nervously nearby. The waning moon hid itself behind a cloud.

When Grandmother was born, a few Mexican families were camped along the river near the village of Yang'na. At her death, the pueblo of Los Angeles was home to more Mexicans than all the Tongva who lived in villages on the plain.

The burial was over. A tomyaar had blown the eagle bone whistle used only in mourning, a shrill too-familiar sound. Grandmother's body had been placed in the ground. She wore her favorite necklaces. Interred with her body was her best grinding stone alongside villagers' offerings: shells, beads and small clods of earth. Each of her kin had cried out a mourning call that was uniquely his or her own.

Girl sat on a tule mat watching Koo'ar try to pull himself to his feet. She sifted seeds in a basket like the one she had left with Grandmother. The hard dryness slid between her fingers like grains of sand.

She appeared to be absorbed in Koo'ar's movements, so intently did she stare. In fact, she was not seeing him at all. She was thinking of the days ahead without Grandmother as her companion. This day and the next, Koovahcho would be helping to rebuild dwellings disturbed by the shaking earth. But there would come a time when his unskilled hands would make him useless again. He would return to lazing about the kiiy, telling Girl what to do.

She brought Koo'ar inside their dwelling and prepared the fire for the evening meal. Without Grandmother—her chatter, even her silences—Girl felt small under the dome of the kiiy. Little Sister had married a Serrano from the desert soon after Koo'ar's birth. The tomyaars had decided that four of the younger girls should live with Girl and Koovahcho and help with Koo'ar. Now, Girl looked around her dwelling, deciding where she and Koovahcho would sleep, where the little girls would be comfortable.

Koovahcho entered, startling Girl. "We ended early," he lied. In fact, his attention had been drawn to a pair of birds squabbling over twigs for their nests. He moved at a critical time, dislodging a central pole before it was firmly in place. The collapse took down other poles with it; they'd have to start again in the morning. The anger in his cousin's eyes drove him back to his kiiy.

He didn't fool Girl. She knew there was enough light left in the steadily lengthening days to complete the job. Koovahcho must have done something wrong and been sent home. She glanced sideways at her husband but kept silent. Tomorrow, she would make their house ready for the girls. Tonight she only needed to prepare a meal and put Koo'ar to bed. Then, if she could quiet her thoughts, she could sleep.

Girl lay next to Koovahcho. She cradled Koo'ar to her breast, let him suckle until he fell asleep. She closed her eyes. Koovahcho moved closer to her and swung his leg over her hips. The gesture was familiar but infrequent. In the early days of their marriage, it had signaled that Koovahcho wanted her. She had responded then by turning her body to face him, driven by desire, not by reason. As her disappointment with him grew, she responded with less enthusiasm and put more distance between them. She had declined as surely as if she had said, "No." He had accepted by turning away.

This time he persisted.

He reached out his arm to tentatively stroke her belly. The move surprised Girl. The tenderness had the effect he wanted. She was aroused and allowed him to continue. He crouched on top of her, took the baby from her arms. Koo'ar cried out when his father placed him on the ground. Sucking wildly on his fingers, he quickly fell back to sleep.

Girl spread her legs. Koovahcho put himself into her. A quick intake of breath, a low cry. He ejaculated, then fell back on the mat, satisfied. A moment passed. She sat up and swung her open palm at Koovahcho, landing a hard slap on his face.

"Owwww," Koovahcho cried out. She swore and slapped him again. He grabbed her hand. She tried to wrench it away. Not a big man, but a man nevertheless. He held her arm away from him.

"You are nothing," she screamed. "You are not a husband. I hate you. I want you to go."

His cheek stung from Girl's blow. He grabbed a blanket made from otter pelts and crawled across the kiiy from her, as fast as he could. Ignorant of the wrong he had done, he crouched in the darkness until his limbs cramped. Finally, he stretched out and fell asleep.

Anger tasted sour in Girl's mouth. Koovahcho was a fool. She needed a word of kindness, not his lust. He was no good to her, an empty pot, an extra mouth for the village to feed. She was right in telling him to leave. She'd be better off without him.

Slowly, her anger turned to shame. She shouldn't have given in to Koovahcho. Koo'ar wasn't walking yet. Men and women always waited until their child ran about the village before they came together again. That was the custom; she knew and should have told Koovahcho. Ashamed by her need for him, she cried like the child she had been only a few years before.

Koovahcho awakened. Everything was wrong. The world was asleep, but he was awake and his wife was crying. A wail rose from his belly. If the sound had been words, it would have said: What will become of me?

[22]

The dry season settled its customary heat on the plain. Koovahcho left as he arrived—wandering away on an ordinary day, carrying nothing with him. When he didn't return by moonrise, Girl knew he would not return at all. Still, she was awake most of the night, listening. She heard an owl hoot, a rush of wings. Dozed fitfully, awoke to hear a mouse scratch in the brush. Again, the quick beat of wings. When all was silent, Girl slept.

In the morning, Hah-ke-ke, one of the young girls who had come to live with Girl and Koovahcho after Grandmother died, poked her head out from under her blanket. "Where is Koovahcho?"

"Gone," Girl answered. She turned over on her mat.

The news spread quickly. Older Brother stopped Girl on her way to the creek. "Where is he?"

Girl didn't answer. Her days were empty. Without Grandmother. Without Little Sister.

And now, without Koo'ar, whom she had stopped nursing, ceding to custom, when she knew she was pregnant again. Girl reluctantly brought Koo'ar to Nilit's granddaughter—a new mother—throughout the day and night, so she could suckle both her own child and Girl's.

"Where did he go?" Older Brother demanded. He tore wild grapes from a bush and shoved a handful into his mouth.

Girl shrugged. "Koovahcho is a man without a home. Not here. Not anywhere."

"He does not provide for his child." Older Brother spat his contempt.

"Even when he was here, he didn't provide."

She couldn't think of the night of her Grandmother's burial without feeling shame. From then until the day he left, Koovahcho had spent most of his time at the creek. Often a whole day went by without his returning to the village. He took no interest when Koo'ar's babblings became his first words.

Girl shrugged. "He's gone," she said. "He won't come back."

If Grandmother had been there, she would have soothed Girl as she did when Girl was a child, afraid of the bears that hunted for fish along the river. What Girl would have told Grandmother, she could not tell any other person in the village.

Girl didn't complain about Koovahcho's absence. While she cared for Koo'ar. While her womb grew. While she squatted on her tule mat and strained to bring her baby into the world. This time, Grandmother wasn't next to her. This time, Koovahcho didn't wait by the creek. Her baby was born in the middle of winter. Rain poured down around the dwelling, dripped through the tules onto the ground.

Nilit's daughter had left the village to work at a rancho. Erach'po's granddaughter had died soon after Grandmother's funeral—sharp pains in her belly; three days later, she was dead. Little Sister was gone, and Grandmother too. The younger women—Achanchah's daughter and Koovahcho's cousin—helped Girl birth her baby. Only a few years older than Girl, they were uncertain about what to do. The little girls looked on as Girl labored in childbirth, anxiously twisting their hair between their fingers, then enchanted by the tiny infant.

In the absence of a grandmother to name the child,

Girl murmured, "Tach'i." She would have been Ne'a'yah for Koovahcho's mother, but Koovahcho wasn't there to choose.

Nilit's daughter returned to the village at the start of the dry season. She was an old woman, her body no longer up to a long journey. But she had heard of work seven days' walk from the village at Rancho San Rafael, north of the pueblo. Nilit's daughter had never worked for money, but her grandchildren had to eat. Accompanied by one of her sons-in-law, she had gone.

Now, she was back. She had barely sat down to bathe her swollen feet in the creek when her granddaughter told her about Koovahcho's departure and Girl's new baby. Alarmed, she rose, limped up the embankment.

She found Girl returning from the spring, a basket of water in her hands. Girl shaded her eyes from the morning sun. "Nilit's daughter. Is that you?"

"Yes," the woman called out. She walked beside Girl, skirting the deerweed, full with yellow blossoms along the marsh's edge below the spring. Ducks and birds laid their eggs in the spongy shrub during this season.

"You have a daughter?"

"Yes, her name is Tach'i. Three full moons have come and gone since her birth."

"Koovahcho...?"

Girl held out her hand to steady the woman as they stepped around standing water.

Nilit's daughter ignored Girl's help. "I have something to tell you," she said. "One of our people from a village near the mountains worked at the ranch. This person told me about a strange young man he had seen in the pueblo. The young man had a long nose, like a fox. He wore a zarape and trousers, but he wasn't a Mexican. Not so much an Indian either. He spoke Spanish like the mission fathers and had no tattoos. The man was begging in the street, drunk. Soldiers took the man away. To jail. Do you think he is talking about Koovahcho?"

"Koovahcho isn't a bad man. Why would they put him in jail?"

"You know what happens when our men drink. They cause trouble."

Two lines appeared on Girl's smooth forehead. Koovahcho in jail? He had been gone two full seasons. The man might be him.

"What can we do?" Girl asked.

"About Koovahcho? Nothing. But if it is him, I think he will return when they let him go. He has nowhere else."

Nilit's daughter sat down on a rock. Even the short walk to the spring had tired her. "Take the water to your children, Big Headed Girl. I will rest here awhile."

Girl continued toward her dwelling; her thoughts were not on Koovahcho. She was more interested in the rancho the older woman had seen. More and more nights, she went to sleep hungry. As the ranchos grew and multiplied, more cattle were brought to the land. Cattle were ugly beasts, Girl heard villagers say, with long horns more threatening than a buck's and wide, long faces. They attracted bears, which became aggressive. They drank water—so much that everyone could see the difference in the river from year to year. Floods took over the land in the cold season, but the river went dry sooner during the warm months. The earth, always generous, had less to give. Villagers complained that oak trees made fewer acorns. Willows and tules grew less dense. There were fewer fish and deer, small animals, even birds.

If all had been as it once was, men would have danced for the food each was entrusted to bring forth—rabbit, bird, trout, acorn, seed. Their dances would have pleased Chinigchinich; he would have provided. But few were left to dance and sing.

Hunger showed on people's faces. Their bodies looked gaunt, and they were often ill.

Girl remembered Grandmother's words: "Soon our people will have no place on this land. The pueblo and the missions will kill us all."

During the longer days of the warm season, Nilit's daughter sat outside her kiiy, barely moving. On mornings when a cool mist covered the plain, she rested inside. Gradually, the lines on her face relaxed; her feet healed. When the first leaves on the sycamore trees began to fall, she and her son-in-law began their long walk back to Rancho San Rafael.

A few days after Nilit's daughter left, Girl heard Koo'ar cry out. He toddled into the kiiy, tears rolling down his cheeks. His screams woke the sleeping Tach'i from her morning nap. Girl folded her son into her arms. "What's wrong?" she said.

Koo'ar sobbed harder. His straight black hair hung over his face.

Girl patted Tach'i back to sleep and took Koo'ar's hand. Squinting in the bright sunlight, she led him out of the kiiy. A figure stood near the opening. She looked up and saw what had frightened her son—a man, willow-branch thin. Strands of hair caked with dirt fell past his shoulders. Scars marked his shoulders and arms under his ragged shirt. His mouth twisted into a smile.

"Bi' Head' Girllll," he slurred, then toppled onto the ground.

Koo'ar began to cry again. Girl shoved him behind her as she approached the fallen man. He was snoring loudly and smelled of alcohol. She leaned over to peer into his face. Koovahcho. He had left as a young man; he was returning as an old one. No wonder his son hadn't recognized him.

Girl sent Koo'ar off to play with Hah-ke-ke and her

sisters. She watched Koovahcho the entire day—as he lay curled like a snail into its shell; as he stretched out his arms and legs in the dust; as he snorted, snored and muttered in his sleep. What kind of a man was he? she asked herself, as she had many times before.

The sun rode the horizon. Cool winds had begun to blow off the ocean when Koovahcho sat up. He blinked his eyes and stretched his arms above his head.

"Girl," he said. "Are you glad to see me?"

"No."

"I'm your husband. I'm home."

"Why did you leave?" Her words fell from her tongue like the bones of a trout, sharp and brittle.

Koovahcho drew back. "I'll tell you what I've been doing," he said, attempting a tease.

"I don't want to know. I can see. And smell."

Koovahcho changed the subject. "Do we have a boy or a girl?"

"*I* have a girl."

"She is mine as much as yours."

"If you believe that, act like her father."

"That is why I returned," Koovahcho said. He pulled a small bottle from the pocket of his ragged pants, took a long swallow and tossed the bottle into the dust. "That's it. No more. I belong to the village again."

He had no conviction in his voice. Not one of the villagers had come to welcome him. They did not trust him either.

Hah-ke-ke and her sisters returned with Koo'ar after sunset. The girls had told Koo'ar that the man who had frightened him was his father. The little boy toddled toward the seated Koovahcho to get a closer look. When his son approached, Koovahcho reached out his hand. Koo'ar stepped awkwardly over his father's legs to sit in his lap. He pressed his small body against Koovahcho, buried his face in his father's neck.

The night air was warm and smelled of sage. Koovahcho sat next to the fire. The glow reflected on his face. He ignored Tach'i, who slept in Girl's arms.

"You go to sleep. I'll stay here until the fire is out," Koovahcho said at last. His voice was kind.

Girl took her tule mat a distance away from the fire and lay watching him. Koo'ar was sleeping by his side. Every now and then, Koovahcho patted his sleeping son.

Maybe his time away has been good for Koovahcho, Girl thought. Maybe he is ready to be a husband, a father. She thought about what she would say to him the next day.

Girl slipped off to sleep. When she awoke the next morning, Koovahcho was gone.

During the rainy season following Koovahcho's visit, nearly every week a man or woman left the village to work on a rancho, making the same choice as Nilit's daughter. They left their children behind with wives or old women. With fewer men to hunt or fish, the women of the village were more diligent than ever about gathering nuts and seeds. In spite of their ongoing search, they could not find enough to eat. Whenever a man returned to visit his wife and children, the others set upon him, urging him to hunt, so they would have food for a few days. The husband would agree, but even the best hunter could not feed the whole village by himself.

"Girl, how do you feel?" Achanchah's daughter entered Girl's dwelling one morning. At last, the sun had begun to rise earlier, a sign that the rainy season would soon end.

"Better," Girl said, raising her head to cough. She peered at her friend over the edge of her blanket. "Hah-ke-ke has taken the little girls to look for seeds." A cold wind blew through the ragged tule thatch that covered her kiiy. A man's work, the repair of thatch, had gone undone. From time to time, Girl heard pieces of thatch flap until they broke off and blew away.

"Do you have anything to eat?" Achanchah's daughter asked.

"No, but I climbed the hill yesterday," Girl said. "I saw a few acorns on the oak trees. We will have more food soon."

"Where are your children?"

Girl lifted the grizzly skin to show the woman. "Koo'ar ran around all morning coughing. Hard to keep a young child still. We were cold. I set him under the blanket, and he fell asleep."

"Tach'i?"

"She sleeps most of the day and night. When she awakes, she cries. I think she's very hungry." Girl coughed again.

"Like us all."

Minutes passed while each woman considered her troubles. Achanchah's daughter spoke first. "You know that three hills north, a white man moved some cattle onto the land?"

"Yes, Older Brother told me before he left to find work. What do they call this new one?"

"Rancho de Los Rios. My mother is working there."

"I didn't hear."

"She has been gone only a few days. My husband saw her yesterday when he returned from Rancho San Pedro on the other side of the river. My mother says they need a woman who will help her fix breakfast for the vaqueros. Will you go?"

The request was sudden, unexpected. "How do I cook for vaqueros? I know nothing about their food."

"She told Tean-re they eat tortillas, beans. You must boil the beans and make the corn tortillas." Her disgust at such food matched Big Headed Girl's. Neither considered corn and beans fit to eat.

"My mother will show you what to do," Achanchah's daughter assured her.

Mountain lions and foxes were still hunting the next morning when Girl awoke. She listened to the drizzle of raindrops and allowed her eyes to adjust to the dark before she slid out from under her blanket. A peek at Koo'ar, next to Hah-ke-ke on the opposite side of the kiiy, assured her that her son was sleeping soundly. When the infant Tach'i woke, Hah-ke-ke would bring her to Naho't, the wife of Older Brother. Her sister-in-law had agreed to suckle Tach'i along with her own newborn, as Nilit's granddaughter had done for Koo'ar the previous year.

Girl cupped her hand across her mouth to mute a cough. She looked around the kiiy for the clothes Achanchah's daughter had shown her how to wear. The chemise and blouse were still on the ground near the entrance, where Girl had left them the day before.

White women's clothes. How strange they felt.

She slipped the chemise over her naked body, watched it pool in small folds on the ground. "How will I walk?" she muttered. One of the little girls sighed. Girl moved faster.

She drew a loose blouse over the chemise. The wide skirt, faded and worn, came next. The skirt, its waistband far too large for her narrow body, slipped to the ground. With one quick move, she picked up the long sash Achanchah's daughter had given her and wrapped it twice around her waist, holding the skirt in place. She draped the rebozo across her shoulders.

The clatter of shells woke Koo'ar as Girl slipped her necklaces over her head. "Mama," he called out. If she answered, she knew she would not be able to go.

The night's rain had stopped. The air felt moist and heavy. Tean-re came up beside her as she pulled her rabbit cape across her shoulders. If he thought she looked strange wearing the clothes of a white woman, he didn't say. He set off at once. She followed him down the slippery embankment through the willows and rushes to the creek. Near the bottom, she tripped on her skirt, slid on her backside, stopping just short of the water's edge. She grasped onto a bullrush and forced herself to her feet. Tean-re was already halfway up the embankment on the other side.

Rain had swollen the creek. Girl balanced on a rock, gasped at the unfamiliar feel of cold, wet cloth around her ankles. Lifting her skirt above the water with one hand, she used the other to hold her cape and nearly lost her footing. Three more rocks stood between her and the opposite shore. She took a deep breath. Stepping quickly from rock to rock, she left the swift-flowing creek behind. She panted as she climbed up the embankment on the other side.

Silently, Girl followed Tean-re across the spine of the next hill and down again to a narrow gully. Here the stream was shallow; she crossed easily. This was as far as she had ever gone north of the village.

"Hurry," Tean-re hissed over his shoulder. She quickened her pace.

The sky was beginning to lighten as they climbed the second hill. Sycamores and oak trees dotted the landscape. Prickly pear cactus grabbed at her. She had to walk carefully to avoid the sharp spines. She would have knelt to see if the lemonade berry had begun to flower, but Tean-re was walking too fast for her to linger. She ran to keep up. They dropped down into a valley again and began to climb the third hill when Tean-re abruptly stopped.

"Rest here a moment," he said. "We have a long walk now. I will show you where to meet Achanchah. I must go on to Rancho San Pedro on the other side of the river."

"Why can't you stay with me until we see Achanchah?" Girl asked.

"The vaqueros don't want to see Indian men around."

"I hear that many vaqueros are Indians."

"Yes, those who learned to ride horses at the mission. They have no use for men like me, men from the villages." Tean-re started off. "Let's go."

Fewer trees grew on this hill. Gradually, the slope leveled out. Needlegrass, buckwheat and sage carpeted the plain. For a while the low bushes made walking easier. As they neared the river, the terrain became more marsh-like and harder to traverse. Girl used all her strength to lift her feet from the wet, spongy ground. The marsh gave way to pools of standing water, too large to avoid. Girl followed Tean-re around them, costing them more time.

The sky over the mountains was a pale blue when Tean-re stopped. He waited for Girl to catch up to him. "This is as far as I can go," he said. "Look there." He pointed to a sycamore tree in the distance. "Beyond that tree is the river the Mexicans call the Río Porciúncula. You will meet Achanchah above the riverbank. Go there now."

The sun rose as Girl walked on alone. When she moved closer to the tree, she was surprised by its size. It was a very large sycamore, or maybe it seemed so because it stood alone on a rise. From the trunk, mottled gray and brown, its upper branches strained toward the sky; small clumps of wrinkled, brown leaves and spiky seed pods clung to the tallest limbs. The tree's lower branches reached out as if they wanted to touch the world in all directions—the mountains, the ocean, the river, the plain. These branches were gray and bare, but by the end of the rainy season, the tree would make a leafy canopy for anyone resting underneath.

Girl noticed men and horses in the distance. She avoided the tree and headed for the riverbank, as Tean-re had directed. The sun was moving quickly in the sky; she must find Achanchah and start breakfast.

"Achanchah," she called softly. A wall of willows and cottonwoods hid the river from view.

She cried out again, louder, "Achanchah, where are you?" The river's roar drowned out her voice.

Girl ran toward the sycamore tree. The men would soon be there, wanting breakfast. Near the tree, Achanchah had laid out the food and implements that Girl needed. A fire had been laid in a pit surrounded by stones. Across the fire lay a comal. Rounds of dough waited to be shaped into tortillas, as Achanchah's daughter had instructed. Girl picked up a mound and smelled it. An unpleasant odor. Corn, Achanchah's daughter had said. Girl touched the stones; they were warm. Next to the fire lay a large pot. Girl looked into the pot where she saw a mound of beans, ready to be eaten.

She grabbed a poker lying next to the fire and prodded the wood. Sparks rose; the fire blazed hotter. When she looked up again, she saw the vaqueros approaching. A few were Indians like herself; more—she saw by their mustaches—were Mexicans. They stopped for a moment, looking at her. She had never seen these men before, but the way they paused, all together, all at once, the way they held their bodies, the gaze they fixed on her told her what they wanted. One took off his hat to stare at her more freely. The men of her village would never look at her like that, revealing their lust so nakedly.

She gripped the poker so tightly that her knuckles paled. With her other hand, she grabbed the corners of her rabbit skin cape, trying to cover her breasts.

The men began to come toward her.

A man limped forward, his eyes fixed on the ground. The man was Henry Scott. The tallest vaquero didn't reach his shoulders. He was the largest person Girl had ever seen and had the lightest color skin.

Girl feared he was coming for her; she tensed her body, ready to run if he took one more step in her direction.

Instead, Henry Scott stopped midway between Girl and the vaqueros. He turned around slowly to face the men. It was then Girl noticed he held a long branch in his hand. He drew the branch across the dirt from east to west, etching a line into the wet ground. Girl understood the line meant: "Do not cross." So, too, did the vaqueros. Disappointment and anger sounded in the breaths they released through their pursed lips.

The vaquero who had removed his hat stepped forward.

The big man raised his stick.

Another vaquero, one she hadn't noticed earlier, came up behind the men. "Vengan aquí," he yelled at them.

No one moved.

"Vengan aquí," the man yelled again.

"Sí, Felipe, sí." The men did as they were told, a weariness to the oaths they repeated quietly to each other. One by one, they retreated to gather under the sycamore tree. The large man limped after them, the last to leave.

Girl peered into the fire, the poker still held tightly in her hand. When she dared to raise her eyes, she saw the men gathered around their leader under the sycamore tree. She threw down the poker, turned and ran toward the river.

She had been a child the last time she ran this fast. Her bare feet made no sound on the wet ground. She broke through the wall of willows and cottonwoods, ignoring the branches that cut into her arms and legs. She didn't stop until she reached the riverbank. The water raced along, black and turbulent, carrying rocks and large branches in its rush to the sea.

Pausing only a moment, she ran down the muddy shore, following the river's course until she spied a bramble of willows thick enough to hide her. She crawled into the bramble and sat. After a long time, her body stopped shaking. She listened. Was anyone following her? She heard only the rush of water. Praying to the Creator that the willow's tangle of branches would hide her from view, she remained in the thicket all day, all night.

The rain had begun to seep into the earth when Girl made her way home the next day. She crossed the creek carefully, stepping on stones nearly covered by the fast moving flow. Her skirt trailed in the mud as she walked up the embankment and stood for a moment facing the village. Smoke rose from only a few dwellings; no one was about. She noticed how the houses leaned at awkward angles to one another. Until recent years, a summer encampment on the coast would have ended with a return to the village when the previous year's dwellings would be set on fire. The villagers would build new ones before the rains began. Now only the very young and the old were left, none able to make the walk, set up a village near the ocean or build anew when they returned. Well into winter, dwellings had always stood straight and firm on the land. Not this year.

"Older Brother," Girl called at the door of his kiiy. She entered and saw his wife suckling the baby boy that Nah-o't, her sister-in-law, had birthed the week before. Beside her lay Girl's daughter Tach'i, whimpering.

"How are you feeling today?" Girl sat near the hearth. Thin spires of smoke barely warmed her.

Nah-o't looked up. Her hollow cheeks and dark circles below her eyes gave Girl her answer. They watched the baby silently. His infant cheeks puckered as he strained to draw milk from his mother's breast.

"Your brother left at daybreak for the rancho beyond the bay," Nah-o't said at last.

"Good. He found work." Girl stared into the smoke. She didn't tell her sister-in-law what had happened at Rancho de Los Rios. She was ashamed and didn't want to cause more worry. After a few moments, she left with Tach'i.

Her son was playing outside the kiiy when she walked up behind him. He turned and flung his arms around her.

"Mama, mama." He hugged her legs, backing away when he felt the unfamiliar wet cotton next to his face. She knelt in the mud beside him. Inside, the three little girls lay under blankets, shivering. Girl quickly set to work building a fire from a few scraps of wood.

"Where is Hah-ke-ke?" she asked.

"At her mother's. She said she would return soon with food." One of the girls peeked over the blanket of muskrat pelts. "We were hungry."

Girl sat on her knees next to the fire. Her son climbed into her lap. The children drew their blankets closer to the hearth. Girl nursed Tach'i, waited until Hah-ke-ke returned with a small basket of seeds. Then, Girl carefully ground the seeds into a fine meal and combined it with water to make porridge, trying to stretch the little she had into five portions.

"Achanchah's daughter was here. She will come back," Hah-ke-ke said.

The children felt better after eating. They sat in the corner carving twigs for a new set of counting sticks. Her son circled the girls, playfully poking them, sometimes tumbling into their laps.

"Big Headed Girl?" Achanchah's daughter called out as she entered. Girl looked up. She hoped her friend would tell her why her mother hadn't met her at the encampment. "Did you find the vaqueros? Did my mother teach you what to do?"

"I found the vaqueros. Your mother wasn't there."

"Wasn't there? Of course, she was." Girl's words sank in. Her voice rose, "Where could she be?"

"I'm sure she was told to do another job," Girl said, trying to reassure her. She didn't tell Achanchah's daughter that she couldn't see there was anything else to do. She didn't tell her how close she came to being violated.

"Maybe your mother will come home tonight and will tell us all where she was." Girl tried to sound hopeful.

"Will you return in the morning?"

Girl couldn't answer. If she returned, would the vaqueros come after her again? Would the tall one protect her a second time?

"I will talk to your mother before I decide," she said.

That night, the two women waited for Achanchah. Girl held her sleeping daughter, offering her breast whenever the baby stirred. The little girls slept on their mats, Koo'ar snuggled beside them. Both women grew more worried as the hours passed. Achanchah didn't come. Finally, her daughter left the dwelling.

[23]

The moon came round once in the sky after Girl returned from Rancho de Los Rios. The rainy season was over; young green leaves engulfed sycamores, cottonwoods and willows. Acorns and seeds were plentiful. Meat was not. The new season hadn't brought much game to the village; even if it had, few men were around to hunt. Word came that the ranch needed workers to build the casa grande. Girl had to feed her family. Whatever danger she would face, she must leave the village to work.

Seeing that Nah-o't didn't have enough milk for her own child, Girl decided to take Tach'i with her. Koo'ar too. At two-and-more, he was always hungry. Achanchah's daughter asked Girl to take her oldest girl, Tah'hi'ech. Four less stomachs for the village to fill.

Before Girl set off for the rancho, Tean-re brought the news that vaqueros had found human bones scattered along the riverbank. The bones were stripped clean of flesh and marked with a mountain lion's unmistakable, cruel incisors. Pieces of Achanchah's white woman's skirt and shells, which Tean-re picked up in the mud where the bones lay, told him the remains were hers.

The discovery of Achanchah's remains set the village grieving. Soon, Girl's sorrow brought her to the dwelling of Esar, the village's oldest woman, her back rounded into a perpetual curve. She told Esar what had happened the day she went to cook for the vaqueros.

The woman listened and said, "Now you must tell the

others. A man like this, though a rah'nah'wat, a white man, may be a person we can trust."

Some were not so optimistic. They had seen too much evil to trust any white man. Nevertheless, word spread. When they heard that the tall white man who had protected Big Headed Girl had been named chief of the ranch, Indians from the plain and beyond journeyed to Rancho de Los Rios to work. Girl and her children were among them.

A steer roasted over the fire in the ramada, the open-air kitchen at Rancho de Los Rios. Girl's mouth watered. The ramada was on the north side of the field, an area that would soon be enclosed within the rancho's adobe walls. The sun had barely advanced across the cloudless sky, but already nearly a hundred Indians were working. In a large pit on the opposite side of the field, women crushed straw underfoot, mixing it with water and the rancho's clay-like soil to make adobe. Their feet moved rhythmically up and down, ignoring the mud they splashed on themselves, on each other. Nearby, men mounded wet adobe into wooden forms. Already, a line of adobe blocks dried in the sun.

Girl heard the sounds of various languages. Tongva, her language, most often. Chumash from the northern coast. Luiseño from the south. Serrano from the desert. Familiar languages to people who traveled along the plain and beyond to trade. Different enough that Girl could understand only some of the speech of people who were not her own.

She stopped turning the spit long enough to baste the meat with drippings from a long handled wooden spoon. She used all the strength in her slender arms to move the spit a quarter turn. Tach'i lay sleeping in a basket near her feet. Koo'ar toddled underfoot, trying to avoid the women who worked beside his mother beneath the ramada's thatched roof.

"What is he doing, Tah'hi'ech?" Girl said.

"Who?" The little girl yawned. She leaned against the spit, trying to make it move. She had helped Girl with the roasting animal since well before sunrise.

"The white man chief." In her two weeks at the rancho, she had learned the name of the man who had stood between her and the vaqueros: Henry Scott. He was the mayordomo, foreman, of the ranch.

Girl watched Henry Scott circle the field. He paused at the adobe pit. Next, he leaned down and inspected the adobes that were drying in the sun. The first time she had seen him near the sycamore tree, she thought he was the largest man she had ever seen. Observing him every day, she noticed how his shirt and pants hung loosely from his frame. In fact, he wasn't so big as he was tall. Taller than any Indian or vaquero, even Felipe, the chief of the cows—she knew *his* name too. Taller than Don Rodrigo Tilman, the man in the black coat and pants, who had visited a few days before to lay the hacienda's first adobes in the ground.

Girl imagined what Henry Scott would look like if he were a hunter from her village. He might wear a breechcloth; his torso, arms and legs would be naked. If she felt any desire, it disappeared when she imagined the white expanse of his body. His flesh would be the pale color of an old clam shell. When she thought of touching him, her skin prickled with displeasure.

"Ay, ay." Girl heard the shouts of vaqueros as they returned for their midday meal. They arrived in a rush on their horses, each trying to show the others how close they could get to an Indian worker. One Indian jumped out of his way at the last minute and lay sprawled in the dust. The vaqueros laughed as they dismounted. No one dared help the fallen man to his feet.

Girl kept her back to the vaqueros as she had since returning to the rancho. If Scott remembered her, she would feel ashamed. If the vaqueros did, they might come after her. She remained close to the cooking fires. When anyone called out for more food, another woman went, or Girl sent Tah'hi'ech.

"Come with me, Tah'hi'ech," she ordered the young girl, who was squatting in the dust. "We must get water. Don't be afraid."

Trembling, the child followed Girl past a row of low adobe bricks, the start of the rancho's south wall. Across the field, beyond the adobe pit, and a short distance west, lay the river. Neither Tah'hi'ech nor Girl wanted to go. Every time Girl fetched water, she was reminded of the day she spent in the brambles on the river's edge. Tah'hi'ech feared encountering a mountain lion, like the one that had killed her grandmother.

They picked their way through the thick brush to reach the Río Porciúncula. Standing on its banks, deeper memories replaced more recent ones. The river was still a welcoming and familiar place, the same river she had once walked along to reach the ocean, the same water: blue-black in the shade, green sparkle in the sun. She stooped to fill her tin pails—awkward, unfamiliar vessels—and looked across to the other side. Later in the dry season, the river would run slowly; clumps of rushes would grow on sandbars that water now hid from view. Before the white men claimed the land, before they took her people to the mission, tule canoes sailed the waterway, carrying Tongva from village to village.

"Are you ready?" Girl called out to Tah'hi'ech. "Let's go." The girl was sitting on the riverbank, staring into the water. At Girl's voice, she rose to follow Girl through the brush.

Girl tried to keep her pails steady while she slipped through the willows. When she was a child, the god Chinigchinich had seemed larger to her than any man could be. Maybe Henry Scott, ugly though he was, had been sent by the Creator.

The numbers of Indian workers grew each day. The north wall was finished. When more women arrived to work in the ramada, Girl took a new job: She joined others in the adobe pit, mixing adobe for the rancho's south wall.

The sun rose above the eastern mountains, cloaked by an overcast sky. More than a hundred Indians waited for instructions. Big Headed Girl waited with them. Felipe had ridden away with the vaqueros shortly after dawn. Girl squinted into the sun as she looked at Henry Scott, who was standing on the other side of the field. Indian workers had already brought water from the river to wet the mud that would become adobe bricks. All that was needed was for the white chief to give the order to begin the day's work.

The workers didn't look like the people Girl had always known. They were too scrawny to pursue game, too frail to protect themselves against marauding bears, too somber to drink and dance. Many men hung their heads. Some women squatted on their haunches, drawing aimless circles with their fingers in the dust.

"What is he waiting for?" Girl said.

Scott walked slowly toward the adobe pit. The sun was at his back, making it difficult for Girl to see his face.

His gait was more a stumble than a stride.

He walked slowly, without authority. While that puzzled the workers, it also reassured them.

His walk and his face—the neutral expression they could see as he approached—gave them no reason to fear. He didn't have the swagger that even the poorest Mexican showed toward any Indian.

He didn't speak through narrowed lips the words that

foremen on some ranchos used to begin the day, "Empiezas, burros," as if they were animals.

As Henry Scott neared the mud pit, the men stood aside, making their bodies more like branches than twigs. Women rose to their feet.

"Me-ah," he said, in Tongva, his tone no louder than if he were speaking to one person, not a hundred. His voice carried a distance in the damp, still morning. Although the word meant "go" in their language, the Tongva workers understood he didn't know the word for "begin" and moved purposefully into action. Serrano, Luiseño, Chumash followed. At the chief's signal, the men and a few women began to stomp their feet in the adobe pit, mixing the ranch's clay-like soil with straw transported from the Rancho San Pedro. They carried buckets of adobe mud and began to spread it alongside the bricks they had laid the day before. When completed in a day or two, it would make the foundation for the rancho's south wall.

A rope, anchored by wooden pegs, marked the wall that was being built. As long as the rope stayed in place, and the workers edged the bricks against the rope, the wall would be straight. After inspecting the last peg, Scott stood, then glanced at the pit again.

Big Headed Girl turned away. Over the weeks she had been at the ranch, she watched Henry Scott. Today he saw her looking at him, she was sure.

Girl stepped quickly into the pit where she began to tread the mud, straw and water vigorously under her feet. Tach'i, bound in the rebozo across her back, laughed at the sudden motion.

"Koo'ar, stop playing so close to the pit," Girl admonished. "Too many people here— you'll get hurt." He moved away but returned immediately.

"Koo'ar," she said. When he didn't respond, she raised her left foot out of the mud, over the edge of the pit.

Before she could shake her right foot free, Scott was at her side. He extended his hand to her. Without looking at him, she took his hand and set her foot on the ground. She scooped Koo'ar into her arms. She didn't look up again until Scott had moved away.

Silence fell on the field. No white man chief helped an Indian worker, a woman, as this white chief had done, twice.

Girl stared at his back. Now that Henry Scott had touched her, she was sure. He hadn't been sent by the Creator. His touch was as firm as any man's. He didn't walk like a god. Why had he helped her?

After days of long, overcast mornings, a hot wind blew. It dried up the land, caked Girl's skin with dust. Women shuffled in the pit, treading lightly on water and mud, exhausted by the heat. Young girls worked harder, going often to the river to fetch water for thirsty workers. The men who made adobes sat back on their haunches and gazed at the trees that lined the river. Their eyes stung; their faces revealed weariness, hinted at bitterness. A low grumble started among the workers. Usually, they bore their suffering like old wounds. Not today. In the distance, even the big sycamore tree seemed to wilt under the hot sun.

Trouble began before dawn when a new cook burned the beans. Indian workers had to wait for breakfast until food was cooked again. Hungrier than usual, the meal didn't slake their appetites. Sometimes, the white man chief allowed second helpings. Not today.

Word spread that supplies were short. "We won't have enough to eat. That is their way," Girl heard one woman tell another.

"They've gone to the pueblo for more food," the woman hissed. But the first one just shook her head.

The morning advanced. Every so often, a brick maker

turned over a bucket of water needed to get the precise mixture for the adobe blocks. More trips to the river. Anxiety grew with every squeak of a tin pail handle, every dry gust of wind, every growl of a worker's empty stomach.

The Indians ate again when the sun was above their heads. True to what had been whispered about, there wasn't enough food. Big Headed Girl, facing the mountains, noticed a rider approaching from the north. She could just make him out above the tall yellow mustard grass that bloomed every spring. He emerged from the mustard as he neared the rancho. She couldn't see his face, but he sat astride his horse like the mayordomos, the foremen, who had come from other ranchos to sell their cattle. He held his back very straight. If she had known the English word, she would have said he rode with pride. Too much pride.

When the visitor reached the field, Henry Scott went to meet him. Girl watched them, Scott so tall he barely needed to tilt his head back to talk to the mayordomo, who remained on horseback. She saw the white man chief motion to an Indian to bring a bucket of drinking water. The visitor removed the ladle and drank from it in long, slow swallows. Before turning away toward the mountains, he grabbed the ladle again, took a mouthful of water and spat it on the ground, just missing Henry Scott's foot. The gesture told Big Headed Girl that the mayordomo didn't think much of Henry Scott. The white man chief must have known that too. Girl saw his shoulders sag as the visitor rode away.

Late in the afternoon, when the sun was at its hottest, the stranger returned with three others. They drove a small herd of cattle in front of them. Ugly creatures, their mouths lolled open, their tongues hung out, their eyes bulged from their sockets. Most frightening were their horns, which stuck straight out from the sides of their heads like poles before curving toward the sky. Girl knew mountain lions and rattlesnakes, but nothing scared her more than steers.

The next morning, many Indians stayed away. Some worried that food wouldn't be given out, there was so little the day before. Some were deterred by the dry wind and hot sun. If they were living in their villages, they could hide from the sun within their dwellings or next to a shaded riverbank. Here, there was no shelter. Only a large field, all of it exposed.

With fewer people, work proceeded slowly. Big Headed Girl used the time to watch Scott. In the early morning, workers had chopped down three cottonwoods growing along the river. They had split the trunk, then worked them into rails. They added tree branches to build a fenced enclosure between the rancho and the sycamore tree. Girl saw Scott and the stranger climb the fence. A vaquero cut a steer from the herd, drove a cow through a gap in the branches. She watched as Scott kneeled to inspect a cow. Felipe stood close to Scott, leaning closer to talk into Scott's ear from time to time.

Squinting, she could make out how Scott's shoulders slumped toward his chest. His head hung low, then lower.

In midafternoon, the two foremen moved to the shade of the sycamore tree. In the distance, she saw them talking. The next moment, the visitor walked away. She heard Scott yell after him. The mayordomo paused and waited.

Scott yelled louder this time. Though the sound came to her from a distance, Girl could hear its pleading tone. Only then did the visiting mayordomo return to the sycamore tree. The men shook hands—even from a distance, Girl saw how reluctantly Scott put out his hand—and walked toward the rancho. Scott's chin rested on his chest. He looked like his Indian workers. Used up. Beaten. She forgot his skin was pale and ugly. She pitied him.

"The white chief—what do you think of him?" Older Brother asked. He was making his first visit to the pueblo since he had begun work at Rancho Palos Verdes five full moons before. Girl had come home to the village to spend a few days with Koo'ar. His energy had proved too much for her while she worked. She had had to leave him behind weeks before when she last visited the village.

The dry season was in its fifth month. Work on the rancho began soon after dawn and ended with the day's last light. The long hot days offered plenty of time to work; the rancho showed the results. The north and south walls were finished at a height of eight feet. The adobes for the south wall were already in place, three feet thick to support a second story. Don Rodrigo came down from the pueblo often to oversee the planning for his garden, his special project. Already, the blacksmith was spending a day or two every week at the rancho. Girl had peeked into his workroom, saw branding irons, metal pots and dishes hanging from racks or stacked on the floors. When he wasn't making tools or kitchen implements, he was shoeing horses in the courtyard.

"I have a different job," she said to Older Brother. "I don't work in the kitchen very much."

"What do you do?"

"I make adobe."

"You have to carry the heavy blocks?" Older Brother asked.

"Tah'hi'ech helps me. I am paid with a coin."

"The chief pays you? We are paid with our meals." He added, "Sometimes we get a coin," reluctant to admit how seldom that was.

Girl grabbed Koo'ar, who was stripping a branch to make an arrow shaft, and hugged him to her. When he was very young, she had tried to withhold attention to make him strong. Now, she saw so little of him, she couldn't stop herself from touching him. She loved his small, warm body. She loved the questions he asked about the creek and the land. He was a serious child. At three years old, he rarely smiled.

The one question he never asked was, "Where is my father?" Maybe he remembered Koovahcho's visit the year before, was afraid the man would return. Or maybe he remembered and wanted him to return so much, he couldn't speak of him at all.

"Girl, I asked what you think of the white chief," Older Brother said. "Why aren't you answering me?" Big Headed Girl ignored his short temper. His life had changed as much as hers. They both wanted to remain in the village, impossible if they were going to feed their families.

"I don't know." She looked at her son. He had escaped her grasp and was busy with his branch again. She couldn't tell Older Brother that the chief had helped her step out of the adobe pit one day. His gesture had made the others talk. She had not encouraged the white man's interest. He must know she was a married woman.

"He treats us all with fairness," she said. She couldn't tell him that she and Henry Scott seemed to know where the other was at any moment during the day. She didn't want her brother to know how often the white chief stood close to the adobe pit, although he never reached out his hand to her again. She could never tell Older Brother that she felt safe whenever the chief was near. On the mornings she watched him ride away with Felipe or Tilman, the sun seemed to take forever to cross the sky.

"Mo'ng-ah and Havach-me helped him make a staircase for the house," she said, naming two men the age of Older Brother.

"Good," he said. "I've heard they can use a hammer and a saw. I want to learn too." He bit his lip, ashamed that he did the least skilled jobs—clearing brush from the land or unloading carretas. He had been a hunter; now, he was nothing.

After he left, Girl sat in the dust next to her kiiy, the sun a disk of fire above her head. Tach'i toddled up, lay in her lap. Girl freed her breast from her necklaces and offered it to her daughter. She thought about walking to the river, where the willows and cottonwoods would give them shade. A dragonfly buzzed past her ear.

"Hello, Big Headed Girl." Hearing the voice, she whipped around, dislodging her daughter from her breast. Tach'i wailed.

Koovahcho stood a few steps away. A glance told her he was different from the last time. His pants and zarape were clean. He was lean, but not as pitifully thin as before. He wore woven reed sandals on his feet and had learned to walk like other Tongva, silently, without crunching leaves or pebbles underfoot. His approach was so gentle, so quiet, he had even surprised his son.

Koo'ar remained where he was, intent on his arrow shaft for several seconds while his mother and father took each other in. When he looked up to see why his sister was crying, he saw Koovahcho.

"Oh," he yelped as he ran toward his father. Koovahcho stooped, gathered his son into his arms.

"What are *you* doing here?" Girl raised her voice. More than twelve full moons had hung in the sky since his previous visit. When he had arrived drunk and left without saying good-bye.

Villagers began to emerge from their dwellings where they had gone to escape the hot sun. They formed a half circle around Girl and Koovahcho, close enough to watch, far enough away to let them talk in low voices without others hearing what they said.

"I stopped drinking spirits."

"Why would I care?"

The obvious answer, "I'm your husband," wouldn't satisfy. He went on, "I'm living in the home of the priest in the pueblo."

"You're a Christian?" Girl mocked.

"No," he said softly. He came toward Girl and sat beside her. The others moved away. Tach'i began to nurse again. She stroked her mother's arm, looked up into her face. Koo'ar sat between his father's folded legs, solemn as always, content to be near him.

"I took a Mexican woman in the home of the priest. Soon, she will have my child."

Girl felt her throat dry. The sun was too hot. She had sat for too long. What about *her* children? She wanted to scream at him, "You could help in our village. We need every man."

Instead, she asked, "Why have you come?"

"To tell you I am sorry. I don't care for this woman as I do for you, but I will stay with her. She is young and has no one."

His words. The hot sun. Her effort to control her anger. Her vision grew fuzzy. She flattened her palms on the ground to steady herself. Her kiiy seemed to tip sideways. She lowered her head to her lap. Tach'i grabbed her mother's hair and pulled.

"Ouch." Girl breathed hard, raised her head. The world stopped spinning, but nothing looked the same.

Word passed from person to person that Girl's husband had returned. Girl did not tell them why he had come. Koovahcho took Koo'ar down to the creek. He held the little boy's hand. They walked up the bank as the sun was setting. Koovahcho was smiling; Koo'ar, laughing.

Later, the little girls brought water from the river. Hah-ke-ke caught a fish. Her great uncle trapped a snake. Three rabbits were killed. Girl steamed her portions of the meat in baskets over hot rocks. They all shared the food. The sun set; the moon rose large and full. The little girls melted into the darkness, knowing without being told they should sleep at their parents' dwellings that night.

Girl and Koovahcho sat outside the dwelling. Wind came up, rustled the leaves on willows near the creek. Girl heard voices in the dwellings around them, but the sounds were too low to make out the words. She waited for Koovahcho to leave, but he stayed where he was, gently raking his fingers through the hair of his sleeping son.

"I am leaving before sunrise to return to the rancho," Girl said. "You should stay until the afternoon. When you go, embrace Koo'ar. Then go away and never come back. Will you do that?"

"Yes."

Hawk and eagle slept on branches of a tall oak tree on the hill. Girl had seen them at nightfall and wondered what drew them to the same tree.

After some time passed, Koovahcho and Big Headed Girl entered the kiiy with their children. They lay down beside each other on their tule mats. Girl turned toward the wall of the dwelling, cradling her daughter next to her breast. Koovahcho turned in the opposite direction, his legs and arms encircling Koo'ar. Girl and Koovahcho did not touch, but each knew the other was near, even as they dreamed, even as they moved in their sleep, their spines like semi-circles that couldn't make a whole.

"What is the white man chief doing, Tah'hi'ech?" Girl said. She was glad to be working in the kitchen for a few days when she returned from the village. The sun rose early and set late; every day was hotter than the one before. Beneath the ramada, she enjoyed a few hours of shade.

"He is looking at you."

Girl ladled beans into a large earthen bowl. The next time she peeked at him, Henry Scott had moved to the area where a dozen workers were on their hands and knees patting clay into wooden forms to make adobe bricks. She turned her attention to the beans again.

Concentrating on balancing the heavy bean pot over the

bowl, Girl didn't see Scott approach the ramada. He came up quickly in front of her. In his haste, he knocked a spoon on the ground and bent over, intending to pick it up. One minute she was spooning beans into a clay bowl, the next she was staring into Henry Scott's face.

Barely a hawk's wing away from him, she noticed how young he looked. Even as he had helped her from the pit, she had been afraid to look at him. From a distance, his awkward body made him appear older than he was. Now, close to him, she saw a younger man than she expected, only a few years older than she.

Light-colored hair hung from beneath his hat in dirty strings. His face was streaked with sweat. His clothes were dirty too. He stank. His eyes, though, were gray. The gray of a mourning dove. She had never seen a gray-eyed person before. This man, so awkward, so different from her with his pale skin and yellow hair. Looking into his gray eyes, she felt drawn to him.

Scott had never looked at Girl as directly as he did now. The morning he had stepped between her and the vaqueros, his glance had told him that she was solidly built. Either he had been mistaken, or she hadn't eaten well since—her collarbones protruded under her rows of shell necklaces. Even the day he had helped her step from the pit, her cheeks seemed to have a roundness to them. Now, they looked flat, her skin stretched over prominent cheek bones, her eyes wide in surprise, her face gaunt. An unusual face, unlike his mother's, his sisters' or any Mexican woman he had been bold enough to look at in the pueblo. A beautiful face, nonetheless.

Scott left the spoon where it lay. He stumbled to his feet and headed quickly across the courtyard toward the vaqueros, men whose company he never willingly sought.

PART 3 fire

[24]

July, 1833. Padre José stooped over a dead leaf, dew-soaked, on one of his beloved passion flowers. He plucked it off, crumpled it in his fist. The sun, barely clear of the eastern mountains, already tortured him, his sharp nose and sallow cheeks covered by a wide-brimmed hat, his body encased in a heavy woolen robe.

"Dios," he muttered under his breath, more a curse than a plea.

He straightened up slowly. He was thirty-five years old, a middle-aged man made older by years of pain.

Alone in the garden plot, between the San Gabriel Mission's rows of wheat, corn and vegetables, he stared down at the sole beings that claimed his devotion: the delicate, tangled vines bearing his passion flowers, their creamy petals set off by blood red stamens and blue fringe.

In another moment the mission bell would call the mission's Indians to morning prayer.

Only a moment...

The morning sun had been hot like this the day he discovered pleasure. He was ten years old, enrolled at the preparatory school attached to the Cathedral of Toledo in Spain's heartland. He had been a pupil there for three years, a guest of the padres, as they often reminded him. They were cautious with the praise they gave the motherless boy, although he was bright and pious. Every day of his three years there he was sure was his last. They would discover some crime he had perpetrated in innocence, send him away. Day after day, he studied Latin, Spanish and history. He became the youngest of their altar boys and helped the padres in every way he could devise—washing their clothes, scrubbing the patio tiles, bringing fresh flowers to the altar, sometimes stealing a few from the flower vendor to hide under his shirt, then pulling them out to enjoy their fragrance when he was alone.

Christ's love was like a flower, blossoming, a refuge from everything evil. He had reveled in that love during his first few years at the cathedral, had believed that he would know more of it as he advanced in age and wisdom.

Now, Padre José stared into the face of the passion flower, oblivious to the hawks circling overhead, the snakes sleeping at this early hour on the sun-warmed earth beneath the cornstalks.

The summer he—his name was Tomás then, as he had been christened—was ten years old, his father came to take him away.

"The father of your mother has died," his father said. "We're going to Granada to make a new start. Your mother's family will take care of us now that the old man is dead."

Tomás, small for his age, brave only when it came to standing up to smaller boys, clenched his fists at his sides.

"They'll see you boys—especially you, all sweet faced and priest-y—and they'll want to help."

Guilt silenced Tomás. Poverty had been his father's only crime, a poverty of the soul the boy found more difficult to forgive than the squalor in which his family lived. His older brothers—Bartolomeo and Mateo, Tomo and Teo, they were called—were, like his father, strangers to God's love.

Only Jaime, Tomás's youngest brother, seven years old, held promise. Jaime visited Tomás at the cathedral nearly every day, sprinting from the family's one small room on Toledo's steep cliff above the Tagus River, running along the city's cobblestone streets on his spindly legs and large feet. Now, more than two decades later, Padre José could still see him: Jaime nearly as tall as Tomás, though three years younger, his body already hinting at the large man he would someday become.

Their father spent his nights fighting, gambling or whoring. Snored the day away while Tomo and Teo begged for food on the streets or stole from their neighbors. In the midst of this, Jaime thrived. Tomás never understood how, but he thanked the Lord for Jaime's good nature, sneaked food to him from the padres' table and talked to him of his plans as they hid behind the statues of the saints in the great Cathedral of Toledo.

"Soon, I will ask Padre Justicia if you can join me here. I will supervise you," he said, as if he were important. "Padre Justicia is a kind man. He will say yes."

He never had a chance to ask.

The bells of the Mission San Gabriel rang; their sound reverberated in Alta California's vast, empty land. Padre José removed a square of cloth from the pocket of his robe, wiped his face, slipped off his hat and stored it in the lean-to that he had ordered the Indians to build for him long ago. He made his way slowly around the periphery of the vegetable garden, out the gate and through the quadrangle where the mission stood at the opposite end.

As the last Indian moved out of the sun into the dim light within, Padre José approached the chapel door. He paused in the building's shade. They would wait for him—what else could they do?

The Indians shuffled into the church, yawning, their faces streaked with dirt, fingernails broken, feet calloused. Wearing rough cotton tunics and loose pantalones, they gazed down at the hard earthen floor. They did not raise their eyes to see the glorious altar, brought from the capital, its six carved figures—

Saint Frances of Assisi, the Virgin Mary, San Joaquin, Archangel Gabriel, San Antonio de Padua and Santo Domingo—luminous in ornate, gilded dress.

They sank to the floor and prepared to stay. The bravest sneaked glances at the open door, watching the light rise. On a summer day like today, the chapel's thick walls offered protection from the relentless sun. One by one, they dozed off, tacitly agreeing to bear witness as the padre talked to his god. They kept their own, the mighty Chinigchinich, outside the church, safely hidden from their mission lives.

In the sacristy next to the chapel, Padre José began to dress for the Mass. "Boy," he said, as he beckoned to a young Indian in the corner. The Indian took a step forward, in no hurry to comply. "Help me with this," the padre ordered, holding out his alb.

The boy took his time draping the long gown over the padre's worn gray robe. Padre José's predecessor Padre Ignacio had ordered the alb from Mexico City, commenting often about the purity signified by its ivory color and its fine linen texture. Padre José didn't notice either of these attributes.

Another boy, younger and smaller than the first, stepped forward. Across his outstretched arms lay a capacious chasuble, clearly made for a larger man. He stood on tiptoes to slip it over the padre's head.

A third boy approached. His nose was long and straight, his eyes small. He resembled a fox, Padre José had thought when he noticed him years before. The boy—Koovahcho was his name—was getting older, likely approaching his twelfth or thirteenth year. His matted hair fell into his face. "Tell Juan to cut your hair," the padre ordered, naming one of the Indian overseers. "No, I'll tell him," he said, correcting himself, thinking—incorrectly—that the boy knew as few words of Spanish as the padre knew of any Indian language.

"Unclean beings," he muttered, ignorant of the Tongva

custom that sent men, women and children to the river to bathe every morning and to burn down their domed houses when the dwellings became infested with fleas. He was also unaware of Koovahcho's grasp of Spanish.

Koovahcho drew a blue cincture around Padre José's waist and knotted it in front. He moved as quickly as possible. Padre José did not pretend to be his friend. Koovahcho was four years old when his mother and father had died at the mission. Padre José took no interest in the unbaptized; his face registered no emotion when he ordered an Indian to bury Koovahcho's parents without ceremony in unmarked graves.

When Koovahcho was six, Padre José sent the boy to fetch a tool from the orchard. Because he chose the correct tool, the padre sent him on more errands. To secure an able servant, the padre baptized Koovahcho a year later. Singled out and baptized, Koovahcho was insured some extra food now and then, but he never accepted the padre's god.

As Padre José readied for Mass, he glanced from time to time at a mirror in a corner of the room. The mirror allowed him to spy on the assembled Indians, to see if they broke any rules: Did they look around the chapel instead of keeping their eyes focused on the altar or the floor? Were they whispering to each other? Were any of the men trying to attract the attention of any of the young, unmarried females seated together at the rear of the chapel? Or worse, was a woman making eyes at a man? When the padre had arrived at the mission eight years before, the threat of Indian insurrection had made the mission padres vigilant. Although disease and dependency had reduced the threat, the mirror allowed the padre to keep close watch on his charges' more benign misbehavior that could be corrected by the withholding of a meal or a rap across the knuckles with a knotted rope.

Koovahcho placed a stole around the padre's shoulders and stepped away. Padre José, cloaked with the dignity lent by his vestments, entered the chapel from a door behind the altar. He stood facing the altar, his back to those gathered, further set apart from them by a low railing. On the table in front of him lay the artifacts of the Mass: Two large silver candelabra adorned the table's edges; an ornate silver chalice and gilded paten were positioned near the center.

Koovahcho stood in a corner of the chapel, ready with a censer when the padre prompted him to swing the small silver cage full of sweetish smoke around the altar. He watched as the padre prayed aloud, sometimes bowing to the altar. The young Indian couldn't hear the padre's words, didn't understand the Latin language the padre was speaking and wasn't persuaded to become a Christian. The padre had often told him, "Pay attention. Listen. Your knowledge will come as you learn to love God." Koovahcho didn't understand what "loving God" meant. Chinigchinich, the god of his people, saw everything and must be obeyed. He knew this from whispered conversations with his parents and others like himself, a Tongva.

He wasn't aware that Padre José himself didn't love God.

Minutes passed slowly as the padre chanted. Finally, Padre José brought the chalice close to him and poured wine into it. His arms held high, he offered the chalice to the altar of saints. As the priest lifted the chalice, the Indians roused themselves and shook off sleep. They knew their work day would begin soon.

His arms held out in front of him, Padre José offered a wafer to the saints. Koovahcho knew that this part of the ritual was very important. In some way, the wine and wafer had become the blood and body of Jesus Christ. But Koovahcho himself had poured the wine into the chalice and set the wafer on the paten. They were drink and food, not blood and body.

The Mass nearly over, the padre turned to face the Indians for the first time. He approached the carved wooden railing that separated him from the congregation. "May almighty God bless you, the Father"—he signed the cross—"the Son and the Holy

Spirit." The Indians were already rising to their feet, grimacing as they straightened their limbs.

Padre José watched the Indians leave the chapel. He was sure they had gained nothing from their morning prayers.

When he was a young boy, the padre had lived with God inside of him. He believed God had guided him from the streets into the Cathedral of Toledo in his seventh year. Outside, the narrow, winding streets were slick with cold winter rain. Inside, the cathedral glowed. Even on that cloudy day, shards of light danced off the golden altar. He stood in the center of the church and turned slowly around, awed by the choir's carved pillars, the ornate carvings that adorned the choir stalls, the huge stained glass windows above the entrances. He stared. For the first time in his memory, he cried. His sobs echoed in the highest corners of the cathedral soaring overhead.

Padre Justicia, a young priest, approached the boy. He wore the gray robe of the Franciscan order, a rope tied around his waist.

"A wonderful sight, yes?" he said gently.

Tomás nodded, embarrassed to be seen crying, to be noticed at all. His shirt and pants, ragged and wet, clung to his slight body. If his father or brothers Tomo or Teo saw him, they would scorn his emotion. None of them had much use for God. When his father was angry, which was nearly always, he swore at God for taking his wife after she birthed Jaime.

"Your name is...?" Padre Justicia prompted.

"Tomás, padre."

"Come with me," the priest invited.

Tomás followed him into a large chapel. The figure of Christ looked down on him from an enormous cross.

"Do you know who that is, young man?"

"Of course. It is Our Savior, Jesus Christ," Tomás replied, surprised at how easily the words rolled off his tongue.

"You go to Mass often?"

"Not exactly." In fact, he hadn't been inside a church since he was four years old. The priest gazed at Tomás. The dampness of the cathedral and his wet clothes were making the boy shiver.

"Can you come back tomorrow?" the padre asked.

"Yes." Tomás heard the angels burst into song, though maybe it was only the bread and vegetable vendors calling out in the street.

The next morning, Tomás was awakened by a crowing rooster. Tomo and Teo were sleeping soundly. Older than Tomás by five and seven years respectively, their nighttime excursions took them all over the city. Tomás and Jaime had been asleep when their older brothers came in. Their father was nowhere to be seen. Jaime lay curled in the crook of Tomás's arm. The room where they all slept was, as always, in disarray. Cobwebs hung from the low ceiling; empty wine cups were overturned on the table top; grease saturated the window paper. The room smelled of rotten farts and rotting garbage. Tomás swung his legs to the floor without a sound. He left, closing the door quietly behind him.

The Cathedral of Toledo loomed ahead in the pre-dawn light. He stopped in a doorway to look at its one tall, slender tower and the smaller chapels—each the size of a church—clustered around it. As the sky lightened, he saw what he had not noticed the day before. The cathedral reached toward the sky. He was sure that anything spoken in the church was heard directly by God.

What Padre Justicia showed him that day convinced Tomás that he was right.

"Come with me," Padre Justicia greeted Tomás. Sun sent narrow fingers of light onto the silent streets as Tomás followed

Padre Justicia down one block, then two, into the Church of Santo Tomé. The boy looked up at the large arched windows before entering the church. He breathed in the musty smell as he followed the priest down an aisle. A huge painting hung above the altar.

"Do you know the painter El Greco, lad?" asked the priest.

"No, padre."

"An artist of great fame. This is my favorite. 'The Burial of Count Orgaz.' What do you see?"

Tomás gazed up at the painter's work. In the lower half of the painting, two men wearing sumptuous gold garments held the armor-clad body of a bearded man between them. The warrior's eyes were closed. A monk, a priest and many prosperous-looking gentlemen, wearing black robes crowned with tall frilled collars, were gathered round.

Despite the scene's opulence, it was the dark upper portion that claimed Tomás's attention; he moved closer to get a better look. In the cloud-roiled heavens, he saw the Virgin Mary. Christ captured the space at the top center of the canvas. Winged angels and the bodies of men rendered in solemn gray tones told Tomás that the men were dead.

"Can you see a figure in the cloud between the Virgin Mary and the man opposite her?" asked Padre Justicia. "Yes," Tomás replied, his eyes on the painting. Calling up his courage, he asked, "Is Count Orgaz going to heaven?"

"Very good. The body of Count Orgaz is attended in death by Saint Augustine and Saint Stephen, the figures in gold below. And yes, the cloud in which the figure appears is drawn upward between the Virgin Mary and St. John the Baptist, opposite her. The soul of Count Orgaz is ascending to our Lord, Jesus Christ"—he signed the cross—"and to heaven."

Tomás, always hungry, left the church feeling as if he had eaten a full meal. What he had thought was true. His prayers were drawn upward from the church into the heavens, like the soul of Count Orgaz. God would hear his prayers and answer them. Someday God would receive *his* soul too.

[25]

Padre José stood in the chapel until the last Indian had filed out, then returned to the sacristy where the three boys waited. They removed the padre's vestments in the reverse order in which they had dressed him—stole, chasuble, cincture, alb—until Padre José looked like himself again: small and shrunken, a perpetual scowl on his face. Gone was any thought of the Mass he had just performed.

His steps would ordinarily have taken him from the sacristy to the quadrangle. From there, he supervised the daily duties of the Indians. He could also greet any travelers who were traveling to or from the pueblo along the main trail past the mission.

This morning, he lingered in the sacristy. The thoughts stirred by his early morning reflections as he tended his passion flowers—Spain, his family, God—wouldn't be ignored. A familiar pain stabbed at his stomach. He opened a wardrobe door, reaching automatically for two choir copes, one black and one red, that Padre Junipero Serra had ordered from Mexico City only a few years after founding the Mission San Gabriel. The copes were made of heavy damask, obviously of superior workmanship. Padre José fingered the cloth pensively.

When Tomás's father had gone to the Cathedral of Toledo to claim his son for the trip to Granada, ten-year-old Tomás had resisted. "The padres won't let me go," he said. But his father could not be dissuaded. The padres said good-bye to Tomás at the school gates and turned away, shaking their heads. What a good pupil! What a good priest he would have made!

A week later, Tomás, his father and brothers had traveled well into La Mancha, the hot, dry plain that lay between Toledo and Granada. It was a summer day much like this one at the mission; the sun warmed the ground soon after sunrise. With Tomo and Teo's help, his father had overpowered a horse and rider the night before, stolen the man's horse, money, and a flask of whiskey before letting the rider go. The family was sleeping soundly. His brother Jaime— traveling with him was the only happiness in Tomás's journey—lay next to him, his face turned toward him, breathing sweetly through his mouth.

Tomás got up from the dirt to walk toward one of the trees he had noticed on the opposite side of the road. The tree he chose to pee against, a fig tree, resembled a large bush. Its narrow trunk supported unwieldy branches of large-lobed leaves. As his urine soaked the earth, he noticed the tree's fruit, a little pouch, like a man's testicle. Curious, he picked the fruit from the branch, used his thumbnail to slice it open. Under its purple skin lay the flower. Pale violet meat surrounded a mass of delicate tentacles.

He bit into the tentacles gingerly. The sweetness overwhelmed his mouth, brought tears to his eyes, made his ears buzz. He devoured the fruit and threw the empty skin to the ground. Quickly, he grabbed another fruit, brought it to his lips, bit into it. He ate the whole fig, skin and all, threw the stem to the ground and reached for another. Another. And another. Pleasure existed. Sweetness held in the mouth. Delicious on the tongue. Teased out of an ordinary fruit. He was incredulous.

As he ate, he began to question the padres' lessons. Perhaps there was more to life than following—with no deviations—Christ's teachings. More than living by St Francis's example: hard bread and cold rooms. Woolen robes that irritated the skin. The word of God.

Where else might pleasure lie?

He continued to devour the fruit, one fig at a time, faster and faster.

"What have we here?" He looked up to see two soldiers on horseback across the road. They were looking down at his father and brothers. Tomás shrank into the dense leaves of the fig tree. He saw his father sit up slowly, too hung over to make sense of anything. Tomo and Teo were awake too. The three rose to their feet. Only Jaime slept on, a child's sleep, deep and unburdened.

"Good morning," his father said with a nervous laugh. His brothers were silent. Knowing the authorities' brutality, all avoided the local police and ducked around corners when they spied a soldier. "Where are you going?"

"Anywhere," the soldier, fat and unshaven, answered. He held out a flask to Tomas's father. When the old man reached for it, the soldier yanked it away. "Ha, did you see that?" he asked his partner.

"Yes, yes, now let's be on our way, before our regiment catches up with us and strings us up from the tallest branches of a tree." The smaller man looked around. "They wouldn't have much luck with these fig trees though, would they?"

Tomás, hidden by the thick leaves, didn't move.

"This stinking war; what does that bastard Napoleon want of us?" the fat soldier rattled on. "I'll tell you one thing, I'm not going back to get killed. They'll have to kill me first. Hey, you," he turned his attention to Tomás's father. "Got any whiskey?"

"No, sir, no. We finished it last night." This time he giggled.

"What about money?"

"Oh, sir, nothing really. Only a few coins to get me and my sons to Granada." He held up a small pouch.

"Let's have it," the fat soldier ordered. Tomás peeked through the branches. He saw the man take his sword from his scabbard and brandish it above his father's head.

"You can't do that," yelled Teo. At seventeen, he had the broad shoulders of a man but the sense of a boy. He rushed forward to stand between the soldier and his father.

"Who says I can't?" Without another word, he plunged the sword into Teo's heart.

Tomás's cries were drowned in the screaming that followed.

"That's my son. You killed my son," the old man yelled. Kneeling, he cradled Teo's head in his arms. "My son, my boy," he cried.

Tomo, the fifteen-year-old, threw his empty whiskey flask at the soldier, catching him on the side of the head. He rushed the horse, grabbed at the soldier's legs, trying to pull him to the ground. While the horse wheeled, the soldier resisted, swinging his sword. The blade caught Tomo on his neck, carving a long gash. Only then did Tomo falter; blood spurted from his neck in a heavy stream.

For a moment, Tomás took in the scene: His father wringing his hands and crying, Teo lying dead in a pool of blood, Tomo clutching his neck, trying desperately to staunch the flow. Tomo fell to his knees, then to the ground, where he lay motionless, blood flowing freely from his wound.

Jaime, a small whirlwind, rushed past his father. Clambering up toward the saddle, he beat his fist against the soldier's legs. A step behind Jaime, his father struck the soldier with his walking stick. The man grasped the stick and wrenched it away. With his free hand, he reached around, clutched Jaime's shoulder and threw him from the horse. For a moment, Jaime was suspended in midair. Then, Tomás heard the small bones of his brother's neck crack as Jaime hit the dirt. All was silence. A moment passed. With a grunt, the soldier grabbed his short knife from his boot and planted it in Tomás's father's back. The old man crumpled to the ground.

"Such a show," the second soldier said. "Too bad it's wasted."

"Huh? What's that you say?" The fat soldier tucked the money pouch into a leather bag behind his saddle before dismounting. Breathing heavily, he knelt and began to wipe the blood from his sword on a small patch of grass.

Occupied by his task, he didn't notice as the second soldier slid his sword from its scabbard. Bending low in his saddle, he brought his sword down hard against the fat one's neck. He didn't wait to see his partner's head fall cleanly from its body. He thrust his hand into the dead man's bag and grabbed the money pouch, wheeled, and spurred his horse toward the mountains. The dead soldier's horse, riderless, waited only a moment before it followed.

Only then did Tomás run out from behind the tree. "Jaime, Jaime." He knelt over his brother's body. The boy didn't move.

"My brother, my dearest brother," Tomás sobbed. "Oh God, please, a miracle. Please come down from heaven and save my brother." Gently, he turned the boy's face toward his. Jaime's eyes were closed. His mouth was open as it had been when Tomás had left his side, but he was not breathing. Behind him, he heard a rattle in Tomo's throat. The sound reminded Tomás of his mother's last breath, his only memory of the day she delivered Jaime. Tomás turned toward Tomo. The boy shuddered; his shoulders heaved. He lay still.

Tomás sprawled in the dust, sobbing, drawing his body to his hands and knees only to vomit bile and fear and undigested figs over and over until his stomach ached. He lay down again, trying to make sense of what had happened. He had been savoring the sweetness of life when his family was destroyed before his eyes. Worse, he had done nothing to stop the soldiers. He had hidden in the branches of the fig tree when his father and brothers—most of all, Jaime—needed him.

He had prayed to God. God performed miracles. He knew it. He had saved the Israelites by parting the sea. His son had multiplied one loaf of bread and one fish into enough to feed the multitudes. Every day during the Mass, God changed wine and wafer into the blood and body of Christ. If he did all this, what would it have taken to save the life of one small boy?

He lay grieving until shadows painted the mountains a dusky violet. The horse that his father had stolen the night before returned, found figs to eat at the base of the trees. Tomás was roused by the horse's loud smacking. All day, he had wanted to bury his father and brothers but knew he lacked the strength. After the horse ate its fill, Tomás mounted the animal. He rode back toward Toledo, cradling Jaime in his arms.

The late afternoon sun shone hot as the fires of hell. Padre José walked under the grape vines, peering down each row to catch laggards who might be napping in the shade. He knew the Indians' habits well; he had looked after them for eight years. Most ignored him, some endured, a few took to their chores with a show of energy, even on a day like today when no cloud broke the blue expanse of sky. Their task today was this: Fill a bucket with water from the zanja, the irrigation ditch; carry it to a row of grape vines; empty the bucket into the channel they had laboriously dug between the plants earlier in the year and return for more water.

The padre's gaze wandered along the rows toward the mountains, the source of water that made this fertile land yield the mission's bountiful crops.

The zanjas were a boon, the padre had learned early in his mission years. Dug by the Indians at a padre's order soon after the mission's founding, the zanjas delivered water that flowed down from the nearby mountains. Sugar-sweet peaches and plums fell from the orchard's fruit trees; bushels of vegetables—

corn, beans, varieties of squash, peppers, tomatoes—were picked every spring and summer. Abundant irrigated land fed rapidly growing wheat and supplied the water to run the molino that ground it.

Water gave life to nearly fifteen thousand head of mission cattle. Cowhides and fine brandy from the mission's vineyards anchored the mission's economy. In mid-July, the grapes were large and green; a month later they began to ripen; the next month, the grapes were picked and pressed. Their juice fermented in barrels during fall and winter. In spring, the barrels ended up at the ranchos. Some casks would find their way to Alta California's capital in Monterey; the finest brandy was loaded onto ships returning to the Old World.

Such an important part of the mission economy would wither if the padre weren't here to supervise, Padre José was sure.

"You there," he called out to a youth far down the row who was drinking from a bucket. "Don't drink it all. Pour it on the plant."

Koovahcho pretended not to hear. He kept drinking.

"Did you hear me?" Padre José walked toward the boy. Koovahcho dumped the rest of the water on a plant, then sauntered away. The hat he wore low on his brow concealed his identity.

More than a thousand Indians lived at the mission. Padre José and his superior, who had recently returned to Spain, were in charge of them all, aided by half a dozen Mexican soldiers. Many Indians died or ran away. Those Indians who stayed soon understood that Padre José was interested in their souls, not their physical features. He couldn't tell an older man from one of middle age. He grouped all the youths in one class—lazy. The women were either of childbearing age or weren't. He didn't know their ancestors or their thoughts.

Only one question was important to him: Do you accept Christ? If they answered yes, they received a few days instruction in the faith and were baptized. If they indicated no, he'd ask again and again. Eventually, some gave in.

For those who accepted the Lord and worked diligently, rewards came as extra food or a small plot of land they could work themselves. A padre married them; when they died, their souls would rest safely in heaven.

Those who refused baptism—a greater number than those who did not—longed for the day they would return to their villages. Their fathers and mothers may have died, but they dreamed that others would welcome them home.

After prayers that evening, Padre José summoned Koovahcho.

"Where have you been all day?" he asked the boy.

"In the vineyard," Koovahcho said.

"I was there and didn't see you."

"I worked all day," Koovahcho insisted.

Padre José gave up. The boy would never admit his transgressions. "I want a bath. Bring a tub and fill it with water," the padre ordered. "Get others to help you," he called out the open door.

The padre's room was the size of a prisoner's cell and just as spare. His bed was a sliver of straw mattress laid on a web of cowhide strips. The Holy Bible rested on a small table under a narrow window. A candlestand. A half-burned candle. The only adornment was a carved wooden crucifix hung above his bed—two pieces of wood, lashed together by the tough twine of the yucca plant. The clay figure of Christ, a gift from Padre Justicia on the eve of Padre José's departure to the New World, was affixed to the center.

Next to his bed was a rug—the color of mud, woven at the mission. His feet rested on the rug first thing in the morning and last thing at night, the only physical comfort he allowed himself.

Except for a bath, once a week.

He sat on the edge of his bed, waiting. The pain in his stomach, dormant all afternoon, returned.

All those years ago, the horse had carried Tomás across La Mancha's arid landscape for three days. The boy could do nothing but stare ahead down the road, oblivious to the sway and jounce he endured in riding a horse for the first time. Every night, he had slid off the saddle, cradling Jaime in his arms.

"You'll soon be home, Jaime," he assured his brother. "Mother and father will be there to greet you. They will give you meat and sugar candy."

Tomás's lips grazed his brother's cheek; he paid no attention to its chill.

When he reached the Tagus River, he found a moist patch of land within a grove of trees. He held onto the nag's neck with one hand. Holding Jaime's body with the other, he felt his feet touch the earth. He laid Jaime next to a tree and began to dig his brother's grave. The well-watered earth gave way under his hands easily. He dug until he reached dry soil. Jaime's body fit neatly into the shallow grave. Tomás covered his brother with the earth he had set aside in mounds as he dug. When he finished, Tomás added leaves, twigs and a stout limb on top, hiding the burial place from strangers or animals.

The sun had set, the sky had lost nearly all its color when Tomás stood next to the grave at last, his head bowed. He wanted to say some words he had heard Padre Justicia use when burying the dead.

Leaves rustled in the trees overhead as Tomás eulogized, "He was a good boy. He was generous and kind." Tears welled in his eyes. He couldn't go on.

He bowed his head, made the sign of the cross. "In the name of the Father, the Son and the Holy Ghost," he said.

Always before, Christ was near. Here, at Jaime's grave, Tomás felt only grief.

He tried again. "Oh God," he prayed. "Take Jaime to heaven and keep him safe." He felt no presence of God. He was alone. He wasn't certain that Jaime would go to heaven; he could do nothing to help him. He threw himself on Jaime's grave and howled. When he finally stood up again, he left the horse behind to give Jaime company. He turned his steps toward the rock-strewn path and began to climb the hillside toward the city of Toledo.

Five Indians entered, filling the padre's room. Two put down the half barrel they were carrying. The others emptied their water jugs into it. Sighing, the padre rose to his feet and peered into the barrel. He reached in. The water touched his wrist, cool, but not cold. They must have warmed the water over a fire. He nodded his approval.

"More water," he ordered. He stood watch over the tub as the water lost its heat.

Finally, the men returned. Stooping under the weight of their water jugs, they emptied the jugs into the barrel and retreated. Padre José closed the wooden door behind them, slid a timber across to secure it. He moved the rug from bed to barrel, untied his robe and let it fall from his shoulders onto the floor. He was well acquainted with the limitations of his physique—small stature and frail trunk. Muscled arms and legs could have made up for those deficiencies, but he could never forgive his skin color. More dark than light, he would have described himself. Not as dark as an Indian, but darker than a proper Spaniard should be. Somewhat the color of a mestizo. Nothing to be proud of. He was sure his color was his mother's fault. She was a gypsy, the poorest of the poor.

He climbed over the barrel's side and sat down in the

water. The men had brought enough water to cover him to his waist. Thankfully, it still held a little warmth. He pressed his knees to his chest and rocked back and forth in the barrel, slowly forcing the water level higher along his back and stomach.

He sighed. A bath calmed his stomach. The mission's thick adobe walls blocked any sound from human or beast.

Surprised to see the young boy again and so soon, the padres had welcomed Tomás back. He ignored their questions, shrugging politely. Among themselves, they surmised that Tomás had run away. Pleased to have him return, they didn't press him to explain.

"We have our pupil safely with us again," Padre Justicia observed to Padre Alejandro soon after the boy returned.

"The Lord works wonders," Padre Alejandro replied.

Tomás studied hard and sang in the choir as he had done before. He recited the prayers. He never spoke about his time away. No one asked. In the padres' eyes, he hadn't changed. Tomás knew he had. He never stopped grieving for his father and brothers. For Jaime, most of all. He recited the prayers with his lips, not his heart. His life was over, but he had a whole life to live.

Stomach pains became a frequent visitor. Pain tore into him in the middle of the night. His bowels cramped. His stomach bloated. Some days, he begged the padres to be allowed to stay in bed. They rarely let him give in so easily. God's son had died on the cross. Their brother, Padre Junipero Serra, had walked, lame, from Mexico to Alta California. What were stomach aches when compared to that suffering?

"Dyspepsia," the priests' physician diagnosed, after Tomás had endured a year of pain. "Most often we find this ailment in older people who eat too much rich food. You're not sneaking out to buy cakes, are you, boy?"

"No, señor doctor."

Padre Justicia looked on with amusement. The doctor didn't know the boy; that was obvious. Tomás was the padre's best student. The church was his life. The investment the church fathers were making in him would one day produce a young priest who would faithfully carry the word of God. Already, the padres had plans for him. Upon his ordination, they decided he should take the name José, after Joseph, the Lord's father, faithful and obedient. Padre José would go to the New World. So much to do in the Spanish colony of Mexico; so many souls to save!

Beneath Tomás's grief and pain lay a memory that made his losses harder to bear: the succulence of a ripe fig. He brooded about sweet moments he had never known: a sugar cake from an indulgent father, a soft cloak to protect him from winter's chill, the scent of a mother's bosom he could lay his head upon. Resentment grew alongside his grief. His stomach ached. Christ was no comfort. God didn't exist. The cathedral, once filled with light, now seemed as dark as the heavens in El Greco's painting. No one, ever, would welcome him home.

[26]

His mood brighter after his bath, Padre José felt well enough the next morning to eat a little of the eggs and tortillas he ordered the cook to prepare before sunrise. He was reciting the last prayers at Mass when a soldier poked his head through the chapel door. The padre finished the service quickly, then walked outdoors, still in his vestments. The soldier stood close to a wall that cast some shade, shielding himself from the sun.

"I've been sent ahead to tell you to expect Hermano Antonio today or tomorrow," the man said. "We arrived last night at the port."

The padre had been expecting the arrival of a Franciscan to replace the mission's senior padre, Padre Ignacio, who had boarded a ship for Spain six months before. The Franciscans had been told that Mexico was going to make good on the promise it had made when winning independence from Spain in 1821: Mission land would be sold into private hands. The mission fathers could stay, but the missions would have to support themselves with no assistance from Mexico. Padre Ignacio, twenty years older than Padre José, chose to leave as soon as he heard the news.

"Come home to Spain with me. Do you want to see the missions reduced to real estate for opportunistic rancheros?" Padre Ignacio had said one evening before leaving. He and Padre José had finished dinner, were seated across from each other at the heavy wooden table in the dining room. The candles flickered as the winter wind blew through the room's one small window.

The younger priest paused before answering. He thought about what awaited him in Spain. Padre Justicia, whom he considered his only family, was dead. If Padre José returned, he would have to take up residence at a church in some small Spanish town. Bishops and older priests would order him around. Alta California wasn't home, but he knew what to expect at the Mission San Gabriel. He'd remain until someone told him to go.

"No, I don't think so," Padre José had replied. "There's still work to be done with the Indians. If all of us leave, we will forsake our duty to bring Christ to these heathens."

Padre Ignacio had wiped his mouth to conceal the smile at his companion's pious excuse. In the older man's opinion, Padre José lacked the proper balance between the church's Christianizing mission and the need for discipline. Padre Ignacio wasn't opposed to ordering the mission's soldiers to whip a runaway or a recalcitrant Indian who refused to work or gambled too frequently. But Padre José administered these punishments without the counterweight of a joyful respect for the Lord. Hearing Padre José recite, "May almighty God, the Father, and the Son, and the Holy Ghost, bless you," pained Padre Ignacio. The younger man spit out the final words at a brisk clip, like a horse treading a familiar path toward its stable. Any "Amens" from the Indians were silenced by the sound of the sacristy door as it closed behind Padre José, as if he wanted to escape before he heard the Lord receive even the barest acknowledgement.

Having witnessed the Mass in Padre José's hands, Padre Ignacio took over the duties himself as often as possible. When he assigned a Mass to his junior, he never attended. Padre Ignacio's repeated pleas for a Mass with more religious fervor went unheeded.

So, too, did Padre Ignacio's admonition, "You'll never win over these people with physical punishment. It must be balanced by the love you show for God." The younger padre continued to enforce discipline by slapping an Indian across the face or striking a knotted rope against an offender's knuckles. After all, Padre José reasoned, he ordered the beating of an Indian less frequently than some padres, and never with the use of a wicked cat-o'-nine-tails. He had never ordered an Indian to spend time in the stocks. Both practices were taken up by padres at other missions, he knew. Padre Ignacio also knew this, and alternately overlooked or moderated Padre José's failings until an incident the previous year.

A young solider had come to him—voice trembling, hands shaking—reporting a particularly brutal raid on an Indian village. The soldier described a scene of carnage, where the children and old people were killed by horses and gunfire, while Padre José watched—coldly, the soldier shuddered—from a nearby hillock. The ground was strewn with crushed baskets, toppled ollas, soapstone pots and abalone shells, as if the raid interrupted a celebration. This struck the soldier as particularly cruel. At the end of his telling, he sobbed, "Lord, forgive me," until Padre Ignacio laid a hand on his shoulder and promised him salvation.

Like other raids over the last ten or fifteen years, the number of potential converts was small. This one had yielded only about a dozen for the mission, not enough to add significantly to the baptismal rolls or even the number of workers. The raid hardly seemed worth the effort, especially since the padres already knew there was talk that mission lands were going to be sold. Perhaps Mexico would make good on its promise to give every mission Indian a plot of land. Then again, maybe not. But Padre José had gone to the village despite Padre Ignacio's attempts at dissuading him. After hearing the account, the padre began to think seriously of returning to Spain.

Since the older priest's departure, Padre José had been on his own, supervising farming and ranching, responsible for the lives and souls of his Indian charges. His digestive difficulties had become worse; until now he ate only tortillas soaked in goat's milk or a thin corn soup. The morning's eggs had already begun to churn in his stomach.

Late the next afternoon, Brother Antonio arrived at the mission, accompanied by two Mexican soldiers, their backs straight, their uniforms as tidy as if they had just come from the laundress. Brother Antonio sprawled over his saddle's pommel. His sandaled feet protruded at right angles to his horse's flanks. His head bobbed back and forth with every step the animal took. Tolling church bells in the mission's tower marked the end of the work day as the soldiers helped Brother Antonio dismount.

"Good afternoon," Padre José welcomed. The moment he had heard the soldier identify the new man as "hermano," brother, he had inwardly rejoiced. Church authorities in the capital could have dispatched a priest to replace Padre Ignacio. Their choice of a brother, not an ordained priest, told him that he, Padre José, would at last be in charge.

"I was just about to lead evening prayers. Would you like to join me?" he invited the friar.

The man hid his face in his cowl. All the padre could see were the man's gray-green eyes. "No..." He shook his head, unable to finish.

The brother was clearly ill, perhaps the result of the long journey—and young as well, Padre José thought. I'll have to teach him everything. The thought made him tired.

"Please go into the main house then." He softened his tone to convey a kindness he didn't feel. "You'll be given whatever you need. I'll join you after prayers."

Wild roses grew next to the path between the sacristy and the priests' rooms. The thorns of one tore at his robe. The padre paid no attention to them or to the sweet, strong scent of jasmine, always pervasive on spring and summer evenings.

"Ah, you're here," he said, as he opened the dining room door. Brother Antonio set down the glass of water he was raising to his lips. "I thought you might already have gone to bed."

The friar had pulled his cowl over his mouth again, but not before Padre José saw what the young man was hiding. The youth's mouth looked like the work of a punishing God: his upper lip an off-center slash, creased back, revealing the lip's raw underside. The young man was looking at him, the lower half of his face hidden again.

The padre noticed another feature. The young man was light-skinned, several shades lighter than he. The brother must be born of nearly pure Spanish blood, the padre surmised. Such revelations coming all at once—the man's deformity, his doubtless high-born birth—silenced him.

"Good manners to 'ay good nigh'," the friar said into his cowl. He had risen to his feet when the door opened but sat down quickly.

"Yes, yes, it *is* good manners to say good night." Impatience colored the padre's tone. But in the words the brother was able to pronounce in their entirety, the padre recognized the clipped pace and perfect enunciation heard in Spain, where the language was spoken properly. Padre José had wiped out all traces of his own lower class speech while in the seminary.

Confident that Brother Antonio was destined to be his junior, he came straight to the point. "Tell me, brother. What will be your position here?"

Brother Antonio looked down at his clasped hands. "Hel'...hel' you ayve 'oul...of Inyun."

"Speak up, young man. Sent to help me save what of the Indian?"

"'oul...'oul." The brother's voice became softer with each

repetition. He pleaded, barely above a whisper, "I go my room. Long journey."

"Of course, my boy, of course. Just one more thing. How did you come to be here, your...?" He pointed to his own lips.

"Lord gave me hi' love in deformity I learn from," the youth answered, as if he had been coached.

"Yes, well, and...your parents?" Padre José knew he was asking too many questions for politeness. But who was there to criticize? The boy was here to serve.

"From 'pain. Five generation family in Mexico," was the answer, his head bowed, exhibiting no pride in his esteemed heritage.

Padre José had heard enough of the brother's story. He understood: The youth's parents were particular enough to marry others from Spain more often than intermarrying with Mexico's Indians and Africans, accounting for the youth's light skin. They were wealthy enough to keep their afflicted son alive—parents of little means would have no choice but to leave a misfit to die—and buy him a place at the prosperous Mission San Gabriel. Privilege had brought the boy here. This conclusion grated on Padre José. He knew too well that he had come from nothing.

On the other hand, Brother Antonio was well mannered in spite of his affliction. Perhaps he had enough schooling to make him a person the padre could converse with, although he didn't know how he would understand the young man. Besides, what would they talk about and what did it matter? Once Padre Ignacio and Padre José were confident that each could discuss philosophy and church history, they had rarely spoken about these topics again. Their mealtime conversations touched on the day-to-day trials of administering the mission's many enterprises, and, except for Padre José's frequently muttered references to his ill health, seldom strayed to the personal.

"I'll have one of our Indians show you to your room." He couldn't resist adding, "You'll be awakened at sunrise for Mass.

Afterward, I will show you the mission." Brother Antonio nodded into his cowl.

No sense in giving him an easy way, the padre thought. The boy didn't have his parents to watch out for him anymore.

He smiled as Koovahcho silently led Brother Antonio to his room. His stomach was quieter than it had been in weeks.

The next morning, Padre José emerged from morning Mass to see Brother Antonio leaning against the sacristy wall. The brother's head was bowed, perhaps in prayer, perhaps in pain.

"Good morning, 'adre." Brother Antonio lifted his head and covered his mouth with his cowl in one gesture. His voice was nearly inaudible, even in the morning's quiet.

"Yes," was Padre José's reply as he strode toward the dining room, his robe flapping vigorously around his ankles. Reciting the Mass at the start of every day was a duty. Exchanging pleasantries was too much to ask.

The dining table was set with simple pottery plates and bowls. A wrought iron candelabrum rested in the table's center, holding six white candles. Padre José liked the splendid isolation of meals eaten alone. "Everything of wood or clay in this room was made at the mission, except these chairs," he forced himself to say as he sat down at the head of the table. His glance took in the long dining table, eight carved chairs and a carved wooden sideboard. "They came from Mexico."

Koovahcho brought in a small bowl of pozole—a rich mix of boiled barley, beans and meat more substantial than the Indians received—a plate of dried beef, another of watercress, asparagus and cooked squash. He set these in front of Brother Antonio.

"Asparagus grows wild along the river," Padre José offered, his eyes following the plates' journey. For the padre, Koovahcho carried a bowl of goat's milk and a plate of corn tortillas. Padre

José accepted these with a brusque nod. He gave up his pretense of affability. Deprived of meat for another day. Fear that his stomach would burst from pain. Every pleasure denied him.

Voices in the kitchen went silent while Padre José muttered a quick blessing over the meal, then began again as a murmur.

Silently, the padre considered the consequences of straying toward the meat. In the end, he slid the milk and tortillas closer to himself, while Brother Antonio put a few bits of beef and a stalk of asparagus on his own plate.

"That's all?" Padre José asked.

"I nah hungry." Brother Antonio's eyes creased at the corners, hinting at a conciliatory smile without revealing his lips.

"Of course." Padre José dipped a tortilla into the milk and bent over to shove it into his mouth.

The young man watched with interest, then lowered his head to slip a small piece of dried beef between his lips. He chewed slowly. The women in the kitchen began to hum softly.

"Bach?" Brother Antonio asked.

"Yes. A cantata." The padre continued to dip a tortilla in the milk.

"Inyun know id?"

"We have taught them to play musical instruments and to sing," the padre answered. He bit into the milk-soaked tortilla. Liquid dripped down his chin.

"Good."

"Yes. Our Indians are not intelligent like us, the gente de razón, people of reason, but we work diligently to teach them the habits of civilized men."

Padre José abruptly pushed back his chair. "Let's get on with our tour." The next moment, he was out the door headed toward the church, the brother struggling to keep up.

"You saw our magnificent bells upon your approach, of course?" Padre José said.

Brother Antonio hastened to catch up to him. "No. I wa' ill."

The padre hoped the young man's honesty would soon dull. He was far more used to hearing what he wanted than the truth.

"In that case..." Instead of going into the chapel, he led the young man along the trail in front of the mission. Walking briskly, he heard the brother breathe heavily behind him. To the east lay the cactus hedge that bordered a field. To the west, the long, low shelters for Indian bachelors. "Look at this." The padre turned around to face the mission, simultaneously sweeping his arm across his body.

The morning sun illuminated the mountain range behind the mission. Canyons folded and refolded upon each other. Rolling foothills ascended to craggy peaks. Against its imposing backdrop, the mission resembled a fortress, dwarfing the surrounding fields and low buildings. Its high walls were pierced only by a line of narrow windows near the roof. Five grand church bells hung above the mission's arched doors.

Padre José wanted to tell the young brother about the bells—transported from Mexico during the previous century—and about the mission design, "by the same architect who designed Spain's Cathedral de Córdoba," he usually told visitors with pride. But a look at the brother stopped him. Between the cowl drawn down over his head and up over his mouth, only his eyes were visible. They were half-closed.

At that moment, Koovahcho, black hair falling across his eyes, stepped forward with a tray of cups and a pitcher of water. Brother Antonio took the cup Koovahcho offered and, turning away to hide his mouth, downed the water in one gulp. He belched loudly.

Padre José glared at the brother, then led the way back toward the mission. Bypassing the chapel's tall wooden doors, he opened a gate and led Brother Antonio past the chapel and sacristy. From here, Brother Antonio could see a long, contiguous rectangle of adobe buildings surrounding a large dirt field. The field, known as the quadrangle, ran the length of three Spanish galleons, a fact Padre José ordinarily was pleased to tell guests. A narrow sloped roof supported, at intervals, by vertical beams created an exterior corridor that ran the length of each building.

"You recognize where you slept last night, of course," said Padre José as he pointed toward the row of doors on the quadrangle's west side, adjacent to the sacristy. "Those are our rooms."

The quadrangle, empty when Padre José had finished Mass, was now filled. Workers led goats and horses across the yard. Some carried buckets of water and straw brooms.

Brother Antonio paused under the shade of the corridor's roof, watching the activity going on before him. Far down the north arcade, Indian workers were hauling barrel after barrel from a carreta and carrying them into a nearby room. Twenty or thirty women were gathered in several small groups within the quadrangle, too far away for the brother to see what they were doing. Closer to him, women sat in the dust trimming candle wicks with sharpened stones. All wore shapeless cotton shifts; their hair hung long around their faces.

An ox's bellow broke the silence.

"What are you doing?" Padre José called to him, noticing that Brother Antonio had lagged behind. "We don't have time for laziness. Too much to do. You. Indian. Take the brother's arm."

Koovahcho took Brother Antonio's elbow gently and led him down the corridor until they reached the padre.

"Good," said Padre José. "I'll walk more slowly. You keep up."

The brother nodded.

But the padre soon stepped out from under the roof to walk rapidly into the quadrangle. The brother hesitated before stepping into the dust. Heat immediately penetrated the soles of his sandals. Seated in the sun's full glare, the women that Brother Antonio had seen earlier wove deer grass strands into a long coil and sewed the strands together with juncus. A child looked up as the two men passed; the others ignored them.

"Those women are weaving baskets," the padre said, "and those"—indicating a group who were sitting off to the right—"are making bowls from coiled clay. Can you see how they do it?" he asked.

Brother Antonio couldn't answer. All his energy was being used to pay attention to Padre José in spite of a painful headache and a thirst that hadn't been quenched by the water he had drunk so quickly. The padre returned to the north corridor, which was now fully engulfed in sun. Brother Antonio fell behind as the padre quickened his step once more.

Raising his voice, the padre explained, "On this corridor are the carpenter shop, the leather-working and metalsmithing workshops. Also, the candle-making..." To make sure the brother had heard him, Padre José turned around. Koovahcho had disappeared. Brother Antonio was proceeding slowly toward him. The padre couldn't help but notice the brother's pallor. For a moment, he thought about letting the young man return to his room. Instead, he retraced his steps. Reaching Brother Antonio, he tucked his arm through the young man's.

"Now, we can go more quickly," Padre José said, forcing Brother Antonio to accept his pace.

"Here is where the young women sleep," the padre said, indicating a heavily padlocked door. "They are locked in from night until morning." He would have liked to rant on about the promiscuity of the Indian men and women, but he knew the lock protected women from the soldiers and visitors as well as from their own men. Padre Junipero Serra himself had walked to the capital to protest the Spanish soldiers' treatment of Indian women.

Syphilis, which had proliferated with colonization, had vastly reduced the numbers of Indian women and their infant children. Padre José was sure that women still found ways to end a pregnancy or let a newborn die, although he never asked himself why that was done. It would have taken more understanding than he possessed to see the depth of despair that would impel a woman to kill her own child or to view what he termed "promiscuity" as an attitude toward sexual relations different from the one proscribed by the church.

Further along the corridor, the priest peered into an open door. The brother dutifully looked over his superior's shoulder into a room stacked from floor to ceiling with identical sacks.

"Those are filled with wheat and barley. Such rich land we have—we make use of it all to earn our keep." Padre José was at his best now, telling the mission's tale and, by association, his part in creating civilization out of wildness. "We harvest enough wheat for our use and for all the ranchos around. You'll see how busy we are during harvest."

The Indians unloading the carreta were still working. They wrestled the barrels from the cart, then carried them into a second storeroom, sweat dripping down their faces. Half the room was filled with barrels stacked from floor to ceiling; in the other half, cowhides created a thick carpet that reached nearly as high.

"Our cattle are raised at the Rancho San Bernardino, over a day's ride east. Sometimes the hides are sent down here to prepare for sale," Padre José said. "Would you like to see how we turn these cowhides into cash?" Without waiting for an answer, he stepped into the full sun of the quadrangle once again.

The men stopped in front of two long stone vats. Dozens of hides lay submerged in murky water. At the edge of the farthest vat, a dozen Indians pulled the skins slowly from the water. They grunted softly under the weight of the waterlogged hides.

A few steps beyond, Padre José stopped next to another large group of Indians. These men knelt on the hot dirt, using metal scrapers to remove the hair from the animal skins. "Our hides are our biggest source of income," lectured the padre. They paused only long enough for Brother Antonio to glance up and see the distant wall that enclosed the quadrangle on its east side. They had walked only two-thirds of the quadrangle; there was still a third left to be seen.

The padre merely gestured to the far corridor. "More storerooms," he said, to the brother's relief. Wordlessly, Brother Antonio followed the padre across the quadrangle toward the south corridor. In a small room, three Indian women were seated at looms, weaving. They moved their shuttles rhythmically across the warp, while a few young girls sat on the earthen floor, slowly picking bits of leaves and dirt from a sea of fleece.

"They make our blankets, rugs and robes, also the woolen zarapes the men wear during the winter," the padre explained, as he led Brother Antonio into the room. A musty smell of unwashed wool and sour sweat hung in the air. The brother gagged. Padre José ignored him and went on. "We are self-supporting here. Make nearly everything we need and trade our excess for goods—"

A man's cries and the slap of a lash interrupted him. Across the quadrangle, a soldier stood above a kneeling Indian. He wielded a lash across the Indian's bare back. Even from this distance, Brother Antonio saw the man's body shudder with every stroke.

"Wha' happen?" Brother Antonio asked.

"Maybe he was caught stealing." Beatings were daily occurrences; the padre had long ago learned to ignore them. "Unfortunately, we will only be able to administer such punishment until the Mexican government formally takes over the missions. I don't know how we're going to discipline after that...," he said, absently. "What was I saying? Oh yes, we trade our excess produce and goods with the ships you saw at the port."

The Indian's blood mingled with the dust of the quadrangle. Brother Antonio didn't argue with the logic of preventing the Indians from stealing. Still, he looked away.

"Blacksmith shop." Padre José pointed to a door as they continued down the north corridor. "See how engaged the Indians are at their tasks? That is our job—to make them ready to live in the civilized world." He hoped his words would lift his colleague's spirit—or if not his spirits, his heels; the young man had stopped trying to keep up and was leaning heavily on the padre's arm.

Koovahcho stood before them again, holding the tray of cups and water. The priest passed him without a glance. Brother Antonio reached for the cup that Koovahcho held out to him. His arm suspended in midair, he groaned as he sagged against Koovahcho. The Indian struggled to break the brother's fall. Pitcher and cups fell to the ground, sending pottery shards in all directions.

At last, the padre was forced to acknowledge the brother's misery. He looked over his shoulder at the young man, who was clinging to Koovahcho, his eyes closed. The brother's cowl had slid off his head. In the bright light of day, the raw flesh of his torn lips stood out against his pale face. Repulsed, the padre looked away.

"I'm very busy today," Padre José said. "I thought you would enjoy seeing your new home." He was satisfied with his aggrieved tone.

Brother Antonio stayed out of sight the rest of the day. After prayers and a brief supper, Padre José returned to his room.

There would be no comforting bath that night. The sky still held its last light as he untied his robe, hung it on a hook by the door and slipped under his blanket. He ignored the scents of jasmine and sage. Sweetness had been too long beyond his grasp.

God was also out of reach. He had known that for many years, but his visit with Brother Antonio today brought back a memory of the innocence stolen from him when he was ten.

Brother Antonio. How I envy you, Padre José thought. You trust God. I can see it. Your humility. I'm sure you believe every word of the Mass. You love reciting the prayers, each one, like honey in your mouth. Lucky boy.

The rough blanket rubbed against his legs. His throat was parched. The pains in his stomach became more intense. He threw his body from side to side on the narrow bed in a vain attempt to make himself comfortable. He felt shame for keeping the young man outside in the hot sun when he was so obviously exhausted from his journey.

For him to cry out, "God, why hast thou forsaken me?" would have been disingenuous. It was he who had deserted God. Yes, his father and brothers had been killed, and God had done nothing to stop it. Neither, he knew, had he. And yes, there had been the figs. The sweetness of life had always eluded him. Yet, he could have lived with his losses, still have loved God had he had faith. Eventually, he might have found his way back to God. Forgiveness...sweetness may have come in other ways.

Look at Brother Antonio. His deformity didn't interfere with his love of God. To the contrary, it had strengthened his belief.

Padre José remembered the moment that had fixed his course.

He was about to take up his vocation at the Mission San Gabriel. Afflicted with violent seasickness on his journey from Spain to Mexico, he had vowed never to board a ship again. In the capital, he heard that a group of priests and soldiers were leaving soon to replace their counterparts in Alta California's missions and presidios. Ordinarily, men and supplies traveled by sea. But a bishop had been charged with inspecting some of Baja California's missions, now under Dominican authority. The bishop was excited to retrace Padre Junipero Serra's steps when founding the missions of Alta California; he recruited others to make the long walk up the peninsula.

Padre José begged permission to join them. The church fathers had seen how ill Padre José had been when he arrived. He did seem genuinely afraid to board a ship again. His petition to go by land instead of sea was approved.

A month later, Padre José stood alone as the rising sun lit the sky over the Pacific. The travelers were five days into their trek up the Pacific coast of the parched Baja California peninsula. The padre had escaped for a moment of solitude after days of walking from the capital to the coast. He had endured the crossing of the Sea of Cortez to land in the city of Loreto, as Padre Serra had done fifty years before. Gradually the immense sky faded to pink. Huge waves crashed against the shore, sending plumes of spray high into the air. Seabirds swooped, dived, cried out.

The ocean knows nothing of its beauty. Or force. Or magnitude, he thought.

He watched the waves roll toward him, then retreat. Nature didn't care how many good deeds he accomplished, how many Hail Mary's his parishioners offered up to God, even how many sins he committed. Nature didn't care, and God being part of Nature or holding dominion over it—he never knew which was true—didn't care either. God and Nature were oblivious to man's suffering.

Don't expect to find love, goodness or forgiveness, he told himself, as the eye of God itself seemed to gaze down on him from a cloudless sky. It's not there; it doesn't exist.

[27]

"Do not think of yourself more highly than you ought, but rather think of yourself with sober judgment," Padre José intoned.

He resisted the urge to run his finger around the neck of his cope. The early morning sun had already begun to bake the chapel's adobe walls. Ordinarily, the homily he said during Mass consisted only of a quotation from scripture that a neophyte might take to heart and use. A brief passage nearly always related to work, recited in Spanish, although many of the mission's Indians knew only a smattering of Spanish and some none at all.

But this morning, he must talk about pride, not for the Indians' souls but for his own. The night before, the padre's sleep was disturbed by remorse over his poor treatment of the newcomer. Pain bit into his stomach, finally subsiding toward daybreak. He had thought himself better than Brother Antonio, that was certain. There was no one to hear his confession about his sin of pride, only the Indians he daily offended with that pride.

The padre approached the rail that separated the altar from the assembled and glared at the Indians crouched on the floor on the opposite side. They filled the chapel, although Padre José knew that a large number of the mission's thirteen hundred souls were elsewhere, sleeping perhaps or bathing in a zanja, which was prohibited but done anyway. Only a few raised their eyes to meet his.

"Romans Chapter Twelve, Verse Three," he added, for custom's sake. "'Do not think of yourself more highly than you ought' means we are all creatures of God, none of us better or worse than the rest. We must not put ourselves first. God...," he began, searching for a word, "doesn't like it when we do." He raised his voice an octave. "God will punish us."

If Padre Serra had been delivering this homily, he might have removed his vestments and flogged himself. To underscore his belief in the wickedness of pride. To illustrate that he, too, was a man and, therefore, capable of this sin.

Padre José never considered beating himself. He was thinking: Where is Brother Antonio this morning? If he were here, he might recognize an apology of sorts, because, Lord knows, I'm not going to apologize. He looked out at the assembled but didn't see the gray robe that would distinguish Brother Antonio from the others.

At the threat of God's punishment, a few Indians yawned. Flecks of sunlight illuminated the paintings on the wall, each one a depiction of Christ at a station of the cross painted by skilled artisans, all Indian.

Padre José turned his back on the assembled and began reciting the Creed, taking up Latin once more.

"I believe in One God, the Father Almighty, Maker of heaven and earth, and of all things visible and invisible. And in one Lord...," he recited, in a monotone. His mind was occupied with the ending of the passage he had quoted from Romans: "Think of yourself with sober judgment in accordance with the measure of faith God has given you."

Faith was central. Sinners could be forgiven if they had faith. If you had faith, you would be saved. How many times had he said these words to the Indians?

He knew himself to be indifferent to the Word. He lacked fervor. He lacked faith. The evil he had seen when his family was murdered remained foremost in his mind, extinguishing his ability to see goodness in any person he encountered, in himself, most of all.

"He will come again in glory to judge the living and the dead, and his kingdom will have no end." The padre recited the Creed. He looked up at the altar. No help there. Even Mary, Mother of God, was silent. She knew, like Archangel Gabriel and the four saints—Francis, Antony, Joaquin, Domingo—all secure in their altar niches, that his sin could not be forgiven. On Judgment Day, he would face God and be condemned for all eternity to hell.

When he had first arrived at the mission, Padre José learned that much of the afternoon was given over to siesta. Indians avoided the quadrangle during the afternoons. The orchards and fields outside the mission walls were rarely occupied. During those three hours, Indian men gambled away anything they possessed of value or drank any aguardiente they had earned for their work. Women worked at the looms if they needed their own clothing, nursed their babies in quiet corners of the quadrangle, or simply hid themselves away.

Padre José never knew where the Indians spent this time, and it made no difference as long as they were where they should be to work again late in the afternoon. The friars looked the other way if they saw evidence of reasonable drunkenness, or contact—within the boundaries of modesty—between Indian men or women in those afternoon hours. It was the only time that extreme order wasn't imposed on the workers. The only time that a shout could be heard from a gambler who had won a little or lost too much, or a woman's laugh or a child's repeated cries. The only time a human voice above a murmur could be heard that wasn't Padre José's or another friar's.

A morning spent in self-loathing made the padre eager for diversion. Instead of napping, instead of lunch, he was drawn to his usual routine. While the young friar tried to sleep away the effects of travel and homesickness, the padre called for Koovahcho to bring a pitcher of water.

"No," he said, when Koovahcho appeared with the jug in hand. "Put that down. I've changed my mind." He pointed to an earthenware flower pot outside his room. The pot contained a whisper of a vine; several leaves, most of them withered, hung limply from the stalk. "Take that instead. If I need to drink, you can get me water from the zanja."

The wide-brimmed straw hat he wore was cooler than the flat leather one that was ordinarily part of his daily dress. He took no notice of Koovahcho following behind. The boy was only "indio" to him, not "niño" or "hijo" and certainly not "m'hijo," my son. As long as Koovahcho was obedient and could answer the padre's basic questions about the liturgy, Padre José paid no attention to him.

Koovahcho, who wore the loose cotton shirt and pantalones of the mission Indians, had no hat. His skin was not much darker than the friar's and would have benefitted from some protection. During the hottest of days, like the ones in this month, his parents and ancestors would have spent the warm hours on creek bank or river, sheltered from the sun by thick willow, oak and sycamore trees. He had been told this was true, although he had never seen it for himself.

Behind the mission, adjoining its northeast corner, was one of the mission's vast orchards. The twenty-three hundred fruit trees here and, two leagues distant, at Rancho Santa Anita, supplied oranges, peaches, dates, limes, lemons for the pueblo and the area's ranchos.

While the orchard was pleasant on a hot afternoon, Padre José headed instead to the southeast field. He lifted his robe to his ankles as he stepped across the zanja. Everything that grew here owed its life to the water that cascaded down from the mountains in the rainy season and fed the ditches year round.

Next to the vineyard, empty now of workers, began the fields. In spite of the heat at midday, the padre's pace quickened.

"Come along," he yelled back at Koovahcho, who purposely lagged behind. "We have only a few hours." He stepped carefully along the narrow path next to the ditch. Rows of wheat, barley, then peas, lentils and beans spread out before him. The padre panted with the effort of walking under the hot sun but, for once, didn't complain.

He passed the kitchen garden, enclosed by tall stalks of corn to protect the area from the chickens and pigs he could hear at a distance. The garden was neatly sectioned off by vegetables. Corn tassels hung limply. Squash and watermelon ripened on the warm earth in one area. Tomatoes hugged their vines in row upon row of towering plants. Chiles grew long and green or small and red on low bushes.

Padre José noted the level of water in the zanja: low. Water was not as plentiful as it had been when he first arrived at the mission. Each year, there had been less. Thousands of cattle, their herds increasing exponentially every spring at the area's missions and ranchos, depleted a supply all had seen as endless. Soon, the missions would be disbanded. How would the zanjas be used when the mission's orchards and fields were no longer tended? How would the Indians fare if not protected by the missions? How would he?

Beyond the kitchen garden lay the pens holding the mission's pigs, sheep and goats bordered on the east by a row of corn. The corn stalks created a wall that blocked from sight everything beyond it. If a visitor had ventured out that far, he would have turned around, thinking he was at the end of the fields. Even Padre Ignacio had visited only once in Padre José's ten years at the mission. Seeing his younger counterpart engaged in some kind of planting, he dismissed it as a harmless pastime, never visited again.

The padre walked to the hut behind the corn row, the

farthest point within walking distance from the mission. Koovahcho hesitated near the corn stalks. He could hide among the tall stalks to emerge only when the priest called for water. The afternoon would pass slowly. His choice would have been to join the other young men who were gambling with the elders, but having been chosen as the friar's servant so long ago he could hardly remember, he was used to waiting while the padre worked whatever magic he could with his plants.

For the padre, the plants he nurtured here *were* a kind of magic. Passion flowers. The only living things that made him happy. When he was working in the garden he had created to cultivate them, his stomach pains ceased, his anger quieted.

Padre José had first noticed passion flower vines winding up a wall near the main cathedral in the Mexican capital. Taken by their beauty, he visited the spot every day. The passion flower was exceptionally beautiful, like a young maiden dressed in white ruffles. This is what had caught his eye at first, he was sure. He was only nineteen years old and though newly ordained still felt the urges that drove other young men. He glanced at the flower. Entranced by its intricate structure, he looked deeper, into its heart.

It was aptly named. The flower *did* embody the passion of Christ. Its ten petal-like parts were Jesus's disciples, excluding the denier Peter and the traitor Judas. Its five stamens were the wounds Jesus suffered on the cross. The flower's stigmas were knob-shaped—they were the nails holding him to the cross. The blue fringe near the center was his crown of thorns.

My God, why hast thou forsaken me? He could almost hear Christ's anguished cry as he peered into the flower. Here was the answering voice to his own pain. Its physical manifestation. A sign that God existed. God, all-perfect one, had given the world pure evidence of his great sacrifice—his only son—the emblems embodied in the virginal white flower.

When he knew he was going to the Mission San Gabriel,

he secreted the plant's hollow, yellow fruit pod in his robe. In a few days, the pod dried and fell away, leaving small seeds. He found a place for the seeds safe from scrutiny soon after he arrived and planted them in the very spot where he stood today. Now, dozens of passion flowers greeted him. The hut was covered with vines. They trailed up the walls and over the roof. If he didn't keep the door clear, he'd find it impossible to enter.

He ducked into the hut, found a small shovel and began to cultivate the ground at the base of the vines. Several angry bees engaged in pollinating the flowers rose up, threatened him.

"Madre de Dios," he swore under his breath. He ducked back into the hut and found a scrap of lace mantilla. Tied around his hat and under his chin, the lace protected him from the bees. He began to dig out one of the vines.

How had he known what to do with the pods, with the seeds? He had never paid attention to any other plant, not to any fruit or vegetable either, except the fig. And those figs, the ones that had given him so much pleasure, were almost lost to memory, more sacred in what they represented—the discovery of joy before innocence and hope were snatched away—than for their taste or texture or scent.

Even as the ocean waves in Baja California told him of God's indifference, even as he doubted Christ's message every time he conducted a Mass, he tended the garden he had been given, nurtured the miracle of resurrection and prayed—fervently, when his stomach pain would allow him; halfheartedly when the pain was most intense—for the gift of faith.

The digging was exhausting—it must be the hottest day of the year, thought Padre José. Where was the Indian? "Boy," he called. "Bring me some water." He tossed a tin bucket toward the zanja.

Koovahcho picked up the bucket and walked toward the ditch.

The padre transplanted the vine from the pot to the hole

he had dug, careful to keep the root ball as intact as possible. He smoothed the dirt over the roots, his dark fingers patting the earth around the plant. Rising to his feet, he checked the three pots behind him. Yes, the vines were beginning to sprout new leaves. Soon, he'd be able to send them to Tilman's store in the pueblo, along with a cask or two of brandy. Whenever he made one of his rare visits to the pueblo, he made sure Don Rodrigo was taking good care of the passion flower vines; he asked for an account of each buyer. Padre José was so insistent in his demands—"water the pots well," "place them in full sun"—the padre earned the nickname "the passionate padre," certainly a joke, because none of the pueblo's citizens could imagine the padre being passionate about anything except "those damned flowers."

The plant safely in the ground, Padre José walked around the hut and filled a bucket with water from a trough on the other side. It was Koovahcho's job to keep the trough filled. He needed only a few beatings to become as convinced as Padre José of the importance of the task.

An Indian could fill the trough. But only Padre José could water the plants.

A dozen times, he retraced his steps between trough and plants, stooping each time to make sure the water landed in the right place, sighing with the difficulty of standing again. When he had watered every plant around the hut, he wiped his hands on his robe. He glanced upward—the sun had already begun to travel westward to the ocean. The Indian was asleep in the cornfield, a bucket of water he had taken from the zanja next to him. Padre José drank the lukewarm water from the bucket, allowing it to drip down his chin and onto his robe. Too warm to cool him. He untied the mantilla, slid back his hat. Ran his fingers through his thinning hair, moist with sweat. Put the buckets back in the hut and left the Indian sleeping in the dirt. He was in the mission quadrangle before he realized he had forgotten to replace the transplanted vine with a new one, leaving his life devoid of beauty until he could visit the garden again.

The Indians had begun to gather after the midday break when the padre approached the soldiers' quarters on the quadrangle's south corridor. He knocked on the door. Thick oak, it muffled the sound of his knuckles.

"Sergeant, open the door. It is Padre José," he called.

Putting his ear against the door, he heard the shuffling of feet. "Who's there?"

"I told you. Padre José."

"Oh, padre. I was just coming to talk to you."

I doubt that, thought the priest. The soldier stepped outside and closed the door behind him too quickly for the padre to look inside.

Sergeant González was tall, heavyset. A dark stubble grew on his chin. He wore the uniform of the Mexican military: black jacket and trousers. Before the soldier slipped his hat on his head, the padre noticed his unkempt hair and bloodshot eyes. That and the odor of liquor told the padre that once again the soldiers had found an escape from a long afternoon.

González was one of a half-dozen soldiers who guarded the mission, went after runaways and doled out punishment. Spanish soldiers had done this duty when the mission was established during the previous century; Mexicans had taken up the duty since independence. The Mexican soldiers weren't as good at their jobs as the Spaniards had been, but, the padre had to concede, their job was more difficult, especially in recent years. The Mexican governor of Alta California had set up commissions at several missions to oversee secularization, which included the transfer of land to the Indians. Once the Indians heard the rumors, they reacted in various ungrateful ways, the padre believed. Indians left the mission more frequently; there was more drunkenness, even insolence.

A few months before, the soldiers had tried to add to the mission's Indian population by raiding a village next to a creek five leagues to the south. A brutal raid, even to the padre who had long since become inured to the casual violence the soldiers inflicted on the Indians daily at his and Padre Ignacio's bidding. The padre had looked away after the soldiers galloped through the village the first time, then turned his horse toward the mission as soon as he had done his duty: signed the cross over the soldiers and their prisoners.

He still imagined that he heard the cries of women and children. A few times, the cries had seemed so real, he left his bed to peer out his window into the night, expecting to see them on their knees, wailing into the dark.

Remembering that day made the padre's stomach hurt. He squeezed his eyes shut to block out the image of half a dozen soldiers riding back and forth over the Indians' crouched bodies, fires blazing where cooking baskets had rested, an old woman sprawled in the dust where a horse's hooves had broken her back...

He pushed the thoughts aside. Whether for good or ill, the raid was the last one he would see. The Mexican government intended to dissolve the missions. Only the padres who were able to remain would be left to save the Indians' souls. The opportunity to make them gente de razón, men of reason—to teach them carpentry, cooking or anything that would make them useful in civilized society—would be lost.

Sergeant González shifted his weight from one foot to the other. The padre had replaced his own straw hat with his leather one to appear more official. Now, he removed it, wiped his forehead with the back of his hand before he settled it tight against his brow again.

"Tell me," he said, as the two men began to walk along

the corridor. "You talked to the soldiers who escorted Brother Antonio from the port. What did they tell you of Mexico's plan to disband the missions?" Subtlety was as difficult for him as patience.

The kitchen stood apart as an outbuilding near the middle of the south arcade. The padre and brother had almost reached it earlier in the day when the brother's collapse had cut their tour short. Now, the smell of pork roasting over an open fire near the kitchen permeated the air. Padre José noticed the sergeant's step slow, but he did not allow any time for the man to savor the aroma.

"Nothing, padre. I know nothing." The padre had been a thorn in his side the entire year the soldier had lived at the mission. Always asking for help doing this and that...why should he help the man now?

The padre purposely quickened his steps.

"You know, your fate is linked with mine." The padre turned toward the soldier, his voice just above a whisper. "Do you want to be posted somewhere you'll have to...work...I mean, even harder than you do here?"

Sergeant González didn't answer.

"I know there will be a new administrator coming to see the mission," the padre continued. "I've heard word of that already. I don't know when that will be, do you?"

"Of course not, padre. Wouldn't I tell you anything I knew?" His voice rose in horror so real the padre almost believed him.

"Certainly. I know everything you do is in the best interests of the mission." He noticed the medallions González wore on his chest. Saint Adrian, the patron saint of soldiers on one medal. Another bore the image of the Virgin of Guadalupe. The padre had no quarrel with the saints, but the Virgin was another matter. She was Mexico's Virgin Mary, dressed in a blue cloak studded with stars. He had seen the cathedral dedicated to her in the capital. Stars! Everyone knew the Virgin wore a plain dark cloak, as El Greco depicted her in "The Burial of Count Orgaz," the painting the padre had admired as a boy. This Mexican madonna was an imposter invented by the Church to win over the Indians. He snorted his dissatisfaction.

The men walked on without speaking. Behind them, they could hear the clang of the blacksmith's hammer as it struck against his anvil. No cooling breeze wafted through the quadrangle; the corridor's roof seemed to trap the late afternoon heat.

Out of the corner of his eye, Padre José saw the soldier yawn. The padre's steps became slow and deliberate as they passed the rooms along the north corridor of the quadrangle. Only when they had walked the whole length of the corridor did the padre turn back. They approached the kitchen for a second time. Sergeant González removed his hat and wiped his brow slowly as if even this small effort cost too much. The padre stopped. For a moment, he allowed the soldier to appreciate the smell of pork roasting over the fire. He could almost see the soldier's mouth water.

"Perhaps you'd like to join me at dinner tonight." Padre José put forth the invitation with as much good nature as he could summon. "We'll have the delicious pork roast you smell roasting. I saw some ripe squash being taken to the kitchen this morning. We're seeing the last of the peaches—they're at their juiciest. And I'll instruct the women to make a dulce de leche for you. You can take some back to your compadres."

The sergeant glanced from left to right, refusing to meet the padre's eyes. "I did talk a little to the man who brought the young friar here," González confessed at last.

Padre José was silent.

"He told me that General Figueroa was appointed as administrator of the Southern California missions."

"Did he tell you when he would visit?" the priest asked.

"Yes."

"And it is..."

"Very soon. The general arrived in San Diego from Monterey the same day Brother Antonio's ship arrived. The soldier accompanying Governor Figueroa said the governor was going to rest some days at Mission San Diego, then ride directly here."

Padre José's stomach wrenched with a pain so sharp he nearly doubled over. There were ten days, maybe two weeks if he was lucky, to prepare. So much to do. So much to make ready. He wanted to shout, "You stupid man. You'd have left me like a hide drying in the sun if I hadn't tricked you with the promise of a good meal."

"The governor delayed his journey here because of some illness he suffered in Monterey," the sergeant volunteered.

"Thank you, Sergeant González," the padre said. He refused to show the other man how much his words had unsettled him. He was half the distance toward his room before the soldier grasped what had happened.

"And dinner, padre?" the sergeant called out.

"At eight," the padre answered without turning around.

[28]

Fifteen days passed after Sergeant González told Padre José about the governor's impending visit. During those days, the padre began his work well before sunrise and continued late into the warm night, supervising a thousand Indians as they weeded, hoed, swept, dusted, washed, polished and shined every foot of mission holdings: orchards, cattle ranch, Indian dwellings, the church and its surrounding buildings. Soon, the season would turn toward harvest when work would continue at the same pace. Brother Antonio was too young and inexperienced to help. The padre looked ahead to months of labor before he could rest.

Exhausted as he was, sleep eluded him. Most of the year, the mission's adobe walls kept interiors at a constant temperature. But at the height of summer, even the usually temperate adobe walls of his room retained heat. He tossed and turned, barely able to breathe in the stifling air, then dozed off, awakened by nightmares or stomach pain.

With the governor's visit only a few days away, he imagined a variety of outcomes, but they always ended like this: He, Padre José, after giving the best years of his life to the mission, would be replaced by a soldier or, worse, a civilian, who would assume his duties. He would be forced to leave. Padre José now understood the wisdom of Padre Ignacio's exit to Spain. His senior had foreseen a time when there would be no place for him. Padre José berated himself for refusing Padre Ignacio's invitation to join him.

Since he had refused to return to Spain, could he begin his life again in an insignificant parish church in a sleepy Mexican town? His mind recoiled at the thought. He would prefer a church in Alta California, but there'd be others vying for any place a priest was needed. He had not had the sense to cultivate a sponsor; no one would step forward as his champion.

One morning, after a sleepless night, his mind seized upon another plan. I can petition to return to our monastery in Mexico City, he thought. I will live with my brothers and cultivate passion flowers. The soothing images of ruffled petals, knobbed stamens, purple-tinged areolas passed before him. He gave himself up to their beauty. Then, reality intruded. In the monastery, he would have to live according to the vows of humility and brotherhood taken when he was a young man. His days would be ordered by prayer. He would have to observe long periods of silent introspection. His authority, worse yet, his autonomy, would be severely restricted.

Too terrible, too terrible. His mind raced as he paced his dark cell. Window to door and back again. His bare feet beat a quick rhythm on the hard-packed dirt floor. He couldn't take it, he couldn't, but what could he do?

That day a dust cloud far to the south in the early afternoon told Padre José his wait was over. The cloud grew larger as it moved forward, until the riders were almost upon the mission. By that time, the mission's half-dozen soldiers, in their full dress uniforms, were standing at attention where the road past the mission met the path toward its front doors. Nearly all the mission's Indians flanked the road. A thousand men, women and children stood or sat silently in the dust, peering over each other's shoulders and heads to get a look at the Mexican governor. No one of his importance had visited the mission before.

Padre José and Brother Antonio stood side by side outside the mission's doors. Both wore clean robes tied neatly at the waist and leather hats on their heads. As the governor came into view, Padre José wiped his brow in a futile attempt to stop the sweat from dripping into his eyes. He took a deep breath and walked forward into full sun to greet the man who would decide his fate.

Behind Governor Figueroa rode a dozen soldiers, each on a horse bedecked with silver-ornamented bridle and saddle, as fine as the wealthiest landowner could show off at a rodeo or fandango. The governor rode a large black stallion whose livery was a web of intricate tooled designs. Two soldiers rode directly in front of Governor Figueroa; each carried the Mexican flag. Padre José imagined the flag flying from the mission once the land had been split up and sold. In his state of anxiety, Mexico's symbolic eagle devouring a serpent became a presence crushing the mission and all it stood for. He concentrated on moving his feet forward.

The dust settled; the Indians sighed as one. Here was the man who would give them land, their land, at last. One of the neophytes, a man of twenty years and good reputation, awkwardly saluted the governor. Governor Figueroa, surveying the crowd as he waited for Padre José, saw the gesture and smiled, exposing the large, strong teeth of his upper jaw. Another sigh rose from the crowd. Some had heard that the governor was part Indian. Even more reason to hope for fair treatment.

Padre José knew the rumor was a fact. If he thought the official would give away his Indian ancestry in his fashion or manners, he was mistaken. Governor Figueroa wore his uniform easily. It was well-tailored and neatly pressed. Thick through his chest and stomach, he dismounted gracefully. As the padre walked closer, he could see that the man was short, perhaps even shorter than he, although the padre had to admit that Figueroa's erect posture, his girth, and, most of all, his self-confidence, made him appear larger.

Padre José intended to welcome the governor, but the governor made the first overture.

"I'm pleased to meet you, Padre José," he said, clasping

the padre's hand. His smile broadened. In a man with a different disposition, his impressive teeth would have been evidence of sinister intentions. In the governor's genial face, they were reassuring, even comical. His eyes were a different matter. He looked into the padre's eyes with a gaze so penetrating, the padre looked away.

The padre hesitated, already more impressed with the governor than he had imagined. "You must be tired after your ride." He bowed his head courteously.

"Perhaps a bit. I apologize for taking more time than I expected to arrive." He looked away. "A little bout of influenza, perhaps, in Monterey." No further explanation. "Please have someone show my men to their quarters. Let's you and I talk. I am here only today and tomorrow; I want to see everything."

The padre was astounded by how quickly the governor took charge. He struggled to regain his composure.

"This is Brother Antonio," he said. "He has been here only a short time himself." The governor should know that he, Padre José, was most definitely in charge. No need to include the young man in serious conversations.

"Good," Governor Figueroa said. "You should join us," he said to the young friar.

The sun had moved barely any distance across the sky before the men met in the dining room.

"I'll see the orchards and fields today. I'd like to see your workshops too," Governor Figueroa said. He declined the whiskey Koovahcho placed on the table in front of him and reached for a glass of water. "We're fortunate in having light for several hours more, yes?"

Padre José didn't think they were so fortunate. Seeing the governor's energy, he wouldn't have been surprised to accompany him by torch. The governor was past forty years old. Although

Padre José had only just turned thirty-six, he didn't need anyone to tell him that he seemed much older than the man drinking from the French crystal glass.

"I'll have dinner in my room tonight...I have work to do...that is, if you won't think I am being rude..."

"Of course not. Para servirle usted." Padre José used the formal "you" to convey his recognition of the governor's station. Over the years, Padre José had tried to keep his Spanish pure, free of Mexican pronunciation and, unless absolutely necessary, the too frequently used informal vocabulary. He was proud of his manner of speaking—polite, with a little verbal flourish now and then, if he wanted to flatter or impress. In contrast, the governor's Spanish was direct. His smile, generous and genuine, softened his words.

"Tomorrow, after prayers, let us travel to the Rancho San Bernardino and look at the cattle. You have more orchards there also, correct? When we return, we can relax at dinner. Good?"

Padre José had no choice but to respond, "Yes," adding, "of course," when he realized he should demonstrate his acceptance of the governor's plans in a more positive way. Brother Antonio looked on silently, his mouth and chin thrust into his cowl.

A few minutes later, the governor stood under the full sun of the quadrangle. He watched a small group of Indians near the north corridor as they tried to help a blacksmith shoe an uncooperative horse. Heat rose in ripples from the scorched ground. Standing under the roof of the outside corridor, Padre José silently berated Governor Figueroa: Any sensible man of his age and importance would be resting indoors.

The governor moved closer, inserting himself into the group. The Indians paid no attention to him, intent on the drama playing out between the horse and the blacksmith, their arms draped around the stallion's neck and back. Suddenly, the horse reared, knocking the blacksmith to the ground. As the Indians scattered to avoid the animal's flailing hooves, the governor grabbed the horse's halter. He spoke softly and stroked the horse's neck until it was calm. The men returned to their task, the blacksmith fitted the shoe expertly to the horse's hoof, and the governor smiled his approval. He lingered, then spoke to the man who now held the halter.

When he returned to the arcade, Figueroa said, "His people come from Sonora—across the desert, over the mountains." He appeared unaffected by the heat.

"And you are...pleased...to see him?" the padre asked.

"Of course."

The padre couldn't understand his enthusiasm. Just an ordinary Indian, not even a mestizo.

"I spent a happy time in Sonora and Sinaloa as a commandante." They resumed walking.

"How many barrels of wine does the mission produce?" Governor Figueroa asked, without preamble. It was a number the padre knew well, a number he often bragged about, but caught off-guard, the padre's mind went blank. "We have well over one hundred thousand grape vines," he responded, aware that he hadn't answered the governor's question. "We crush our grapes in that lean-to," he said, indicating a tule-covered structure in front of the sacristy. "Would you like to see it?" Before the governor could answer, the padre led him toward the shelter. Inside, three young Indian men were splashing water on the earthen floor, stamping on the dirt until it was packed solid.

"We are preparing the room to receive the grapes we harvest soon. Our women press the grapes here," Padre José explained. "We produce the finest wine in Alta California. Our aguardiente is incomparable." It was a fact; everyone recognized the mission's brandy as the best.

The governor moved on to other subjects as they left the

small structure. "How much tallow do you export?" The governor's tone was even, as if the answer didn't matter. Nevertheless, Padre José felt a sharp pain in his stomach. He *knew* the answer. What *was* it?

"How many hides do you send to the harbor?" Silence followed, as the padre searched for the answer that, if not for his fear of the governor's opinion of him, would have easily come to mind.

Striding down the corridor, the governor kept up his stream of questions. "How many fruit trees do you have?" "How many fanegas of wheat do you harvest?" "Of corn?" "Of beans?"

The padre quickened his step to keep up. He stuttered, he stammered. Sweat ran down his face, flowed freely from his armpits under his woolen robe. Koovahcho followed behind with Brother Antonio. At a glance from the padre, Koovahcho stepped forward to offer water. The governor declined; the padre downed one cup and then another. He noticed an unusual level of activity among the Indians. Those he often had to prod to get to work were toiling with more energy than usual. The beasts, he thought. They are putting on a show for the governor, hoping to win his good will.

The late afternoon wore on; the questions continued.

"How many baptisms do you perform each year?" the governor asked. "What have you seen over the years, more baptisms each year or fewer?"

These were the questions that Padre José feared the most; they struck at the very heart of the mission's reason for existing.

"More or fewer, that's hard to tell," the padre answered. He resented being judged by how many souls he had brought to Christ. And why did he have to cite numbers anyway, when it was all there in the mission records?

"You know we've lost many Indians to disease," he began. "More recently, they have heard rumors of land being offered to them when the missions are disbanded. Some ran away..."

Shadows lengthened over the quadrangle. Stray sunbeams pierced the spaces in the roof tiles. As the day's light dimmed, the general's bright eyes and teeth flashed more prominently. Padre José could think of nothing more to say. How could he tell the governor what it was like to be in charge of a thousand people, most of whom would have left immediately if they had been allowed to, or joined in revolt if they detected weakness?

How could he explain the tools he used to inspire acceptance of the Lord—daily exhortations of the gospel, the pomp of ceremony, the fear of hell, the lash? None seemed reason enough to inspire mass conversions. Sometimes...rarely...an Indian was sincerely convinced by the promise of redemption. More often, a man accepted Christ to please a novia's wishes for better food or shelter, or gave in to a system he knew he couldn't resist.

The governor was silent as he waited for an answer.

"Let's look at the baptismal record," the padre began. He peered at the governor, surprised to see that a change had come over Figueroa's face. The light in his eyes had faded. His jaw was clenched, hiding his marvelous teeth. His military posture had dissolved into a sag.

Padre José wondered if the governor was suffering from the ill health that Sergeant González had hinted at. If so, the padre intended to make the most of it. He led the governor out of the quadrangle into the adjacent field, followed by Brother Antonio. The governor didn't speak as he tried to match the padre's pace across the zanja, past the rows of grape vines heavy with fruit. Before long, Figueroa lagged behind. He barely glanced at the rows of squash and beans. Silently, the governor inspected the animal pens and turned back without noticing the passion flowers that lay beyond the cornstalks.

Figueroa was already in the chapel when Padre José entered at daybreak the next morning. The governor was sitting in a chair that had been set out for him next to the altar rail. He was leaning forward, his arms bent at the elbows, his head cradled in his hands. His posture resembled one of despair rather than of prayer, the padre noted as he crossed the threshold between the sacristy and the chapel. But there was no time to ponder the reason. Padre José was intent on delivering a Mass that would impress his visitor with his devotion. To appear more formidable, he planned to climb the winding staircase next to the rail and deliver his homily from the pulpit above the congregants' heads. This he had not done since Padre Ignacio left. In his desire for perfection, he took over the task of arranging the altar instead of allowing the young Indians to do it as they did every morning.

He ignored the governor while spreading the white lace cloth on top of the altar, placing an ornate silver candelabrum on each end and a large silver chalice in the middle. He poured wine into the chalice, set a plate of wafers next to it. As he gave one last tug at the cloth to pull it straight, he heard the chapel door close. He looked over his shoulder. The room was empty.

Before he could consider why the governor hadn't stayed for Mass, the Indians were filing in, slowly, rubbing their eyes and their backsides, shuffling their feet across the dirt floor to sit or kneel in uneven rows. With the governor gone, there was no need to impress. The padre gave up the idea of ascending the winding staircase and raced through the ritual.

Padre José didn't like what he saw as he left the sacristy. The governor was leaning against the chapel wall, speaking to Brother Antonio. The brother wore his cowl under his chin, exposing the rude split in his upper lip. Koovahcho stood close to the young friar, his head bent forward as if he were listening to the conversation. Impossible, thought the padre. The Indian doesn't speak Spanish.

Resting his weight on a gold-headed cane, Governor Figueroa looked up, smiled at Padre José. It wasn't the smile of yesterday, all teeth and eyes. The governor appeared to have aged overnight. The lines in his face were prominent; his glow of health had disappeared. "Brother Antonio was just telling me about the cattle ranches at San Bernardino and Santa Anita. You have nearly twenty thousand head?" The padre leaned closer to hear the governor, whose voice lacked the confident timbre of the day before.

"Yes, but I don't know how the brother knows this," he said, surprised that the young man's deformity didn't repel the governor. "He's been here only a few weeks."

"Apparently, he was talking to some of the soldiers."

Brother Antonio lowered his eyes before he could see the threatening glance Padre José cast in his direction. He knew immediately that he had been too friendly with the governor to suit the padre, but the damage was done.

"And you've been talking also to the Indian?" the padre inquired, pointing with his chin in Koovahcho's direction. The governor's sympathy with the Indians was obvious. No matter, Padre José couldn't take another day like the one before. He was in a bad temper, and everyone, even the governor, was going to know it.

"Koovahcho?" the governor answered gently. The Indian boy moved imperceptibly toward the governor.

"Koovahcho? Oh, that's his name?"

Again the governor refused to take the bait. "He's a good boy. Could benefit from some education in a trade, don't you think?" His voice still held a note of command.

"I never think about that," Padre José said. "Do you want to get started? If you're leaving tomorrow, we'd best go only to Rancho Santa Anita and leave Rancho San Bernardino for another visit. Most of our cattle are at San Bernardino. We'd have to ride the whole day to get there."

The governor cleared his throat. "You are correct. Brother Antonio tells me that Santa Anita is only two leagues distant...but...I'd...like to remain here at the mission today." He pulled a handkerchief from his pocket but barely brought it to his forehead before replacing it again, sighing. "Let's look at the Indians' housing and...perhaps...inspect the orchards."

Visit only the Indians' barracks and the orchards? There was so much more to see. Hundreds of hectares of fields and orchards were under cultivation at Rancho Santa Anita. A large cattle operation lay at Rancho San Bernardino. This was his kingdom, and he wanted the governor to see it. Besides, he had been diligent in his efforts to put everything in the best possible order for the governor. Was he going to be denied the opportunity to show it off?

Figueroa was silent while he waited for the padre to speak. Brother Antonio looked at the governor and then, at the padre. Even Koovahcho raised his eyes, as if to say, "What are you going to do now?" Slowly it dawned on the padre that Governor Figueroa wasn't telling him the whole story. Figueroa hadn't changed his mind; his will ran counter to his energy. The governor was leaning against the wall again, waiting, as if listening to something inside himself. Padre José could see on his face that the news wasn't good.

"Why don't we eat breakfast before we begin?" The padre took charge. "Our time is not so limited now. We can drink some coffee and make ourselves ready for the day."

The governor, whom the day before had seemed like a young man, all dash and vigor, used his cane to push himself to standing. Leaning on it with one hand, he used the other to reach for the padre's outstretched arm.

Governor Figueroa ate sparingly of the large breakfast set out for him. Tortillas and loaves of bread made of flour ground from the mission's wheat fields. Platters of fruit from the mission's fields and orchards: melons, papayas and mangoes, garnished by wedges of lemons and limes. Bowls of last-of-the-season strawberries. To the padre's delight, a few figs were added, evidence that their harvest had begun. Fried eggs were also part of the meal. The padre flinched when he saw them—fried foods aggravated his stomach. The governor also declined. Bowls of pozole were placed on the table last, as if the simple food were an afterthought. These turned out to be the governor's favorite. He quickly consumed two helpings. Too polite to ask about the padre's breakfast of milk and bread, he sat back in his chair and smoked a cigar while Brother Antonio ate quantities of eggs, fruit and bread. Between mouthfuls, he observed with none of his customary shyness, "A fea' thi' good should no' be wa'ed."

The governor laughed, the first sign of spirit he had shown that day. He drank his coffee slowly while the others finished.

When Padre José began to speak, he surprised himself with a steady voice and a command of facts he could not manage the day before. He picked a few at random. "We make four to six hundred barrels of wine a year," he said, "and two hundred barrels of brandy."

Figueroa pushed back his chair. "Let's see what you have, then."

Minutes later they were gathered around a brandy still that occupied a small hut across the quadrangle from the kitchen. The padre was proud of the burnished copper still, manufactured in New York and shipped around Cape Horn.

"You see, the juice of the grape, after fermentation, is boiled in the still—"

He broke off his sentence, followed the governor's eyes to the arcade post visible through the hut's door. The post was covered with the blooms of a dozen passion flowers. "Beautiful," the governor muttered to himself.

The day before, the governor's attention had unnerved Padre José. Today his lack of it had the same effect. "You mentioned you wanted to see where the Indians lived," he offered.

Leaving the quadrangle, he led the governor toward the Indians' houses, three rows of long, narrow buildings for the bachelors and a few tule-covered dome dwellings for the most fortunate married men and their families. Padre José opened a door to the first building he came to and walked in. The governor followed. Brother Antonio peered over the governor's shoulder.

Straw mats lay in two rows on the dirt floor, twenty along each long wall. Next to each mat was a small cache of each man's personal goods: a few arrowheads, a bow in the making, bundles of yucca ready for twisting into cordage. A few gourd rattles hung here and there on the wall. The long adobe barracks bore no resemblance to the traditional domed dwellings the various Indian groups had built for millennia, but if the governor knew how uncomfortable the men must be in this lodging, he didn't say.

He was out the door by the time the padre turned around to say, "Would you like to see the orchards...or we could ride a bit and see the forests?" As the governor hesitated, the padre became more voluble. "Oaks, sycamores, alder. I've been told that great forests once grew on this spot. Many were cut down to build the mission."

The governor shifted his weight from side to side. "You have been very gracious in showing me the mission. I must return to my room now."

"And lunch?"

"No."

"Dinner?" Padre José asked. He didn't try to conceal the pleading in his tone.

"Yes." The governor's face bore only a hint of the glow his smile had lit the day before.

"Find Sergeant González for me," the padre ordered as soon as the governor's door closed behind him.

"I think he's with the governor's soldiers," Brother Antonio said.

"I don't care where he is. Find him and tell him to see me. Immediately."

A few minutes later, Sergeant González's scowl told Padre José that he hadn't liked being interrupted. The padre didn't care.

"What is wrong with the governor?" the padre demanded. "What do you know that you're not telling me?"

"I don't know what you're talking about, padre," the sergeant answered.

"Oh yes, you do. I know you do." The padre's temper rose. All the work. All the worry. And now the governor appeared to be bored with everything—the mission, the Indians and worse, himself. What was going on?

Sergeant González knew that the padre had reached the limit of his patience. He could not prolong the padre's anxiety, much as he would have liked. "I've heard the soldiers say that the governor is unwell."

"Go on."

"His departure from Monterey was delayed because of illness."

"I know," the padre said impatiently. "When the governor arrived, he said he had been delayed by influenza..."

"It may be more than that. He may be seriously ill. That's what the soldiers said."

"Yes?"

"That's all I know."

The downcast eyes of the Virgin of Guadalupe on the

soldier's medal appeared to meet the padre's glare. She was mocking him. "I doubt it."

"Padre, my hand on the Bible, I swear I know nothing else. Maybe..." The soldier hesitated.

"Maybe what?"

"You ought to send for a doctor?"

"I'll ask the governor," Padre José replied, but never did.

"The piccolos. Please, only the piccolos," Padre José cried over the din of a dozen Indians playing an assortment of strings and woodwinds. The church walls vibrated with one final thump of a barrel drum. Lacking musical knowledge and unable to play any instrument himself, he had performed the Mass without song or music since Padre Ignacio left. The musicians were quite accomplished, even he had to admit. They lent drama and texture to the ritual, but the padre exhibited no interest until now.

In preparing for the governor's visit, he had called on them to rehearse, thinking to have them perform during a Mass. Later, he realized that his conducting skills weren't up to the task. Some simple folk tunes from Spain and Mexico played at dinner would have to do. Three weeks of rehearsals made them proficient again, but they didn't have the padre to thank for it. One of their own had conducted the group while Padre José worked elsewhere. A few days before Governor Figueroa arrived, the padre stepped in as conductor. The result was a disaster. He was unable to keep time properly. His arms jerked so alarmingly up, then down, the musicians called him, "la marioneta," the puppet, behind his back.

He spent the entire afternoon with the musicians, going over the pieces again and again. When he was satisfied at last, he let them go. The sun was a deep orange, low in the sky over the hills of Rancho Palos Verdes. Governor Figueroa had not emerged from his room the entire afternoon. Growing more nervous as the dinner hour approached, the padre wandered into the kitchen. The women stood aside as he lifted the lid on every pot. Tasting was out of the question—his stomach couldn't have withstood the assault. But he added salt here, a bit of chili there, as if he knew something about preparing food. Finally, he nodded his approval and walked to the other end of the quadrangle, where a side of beef had been roasting since dawn. Men were crouched around the fire, their dark faces illuminated by flickering flames; they turned the spit every now and then.

"Ready?" The padre frowned.

The man in charge nodded. "Very soon."

The padre stood watching for several minutes. The sun ducked behind the hills, leaving a faded blue sky stained with pink wisps of clouds. He returned to his room, washed his face in the basin of water that Koovahcho had set out for him, slipped on a fresh robe, then went out the door. He almost collided with the governor, who was passing his room in a slow march to the dining room.

"You rested well, governor?"

Governor Figueroa nodded and shuffled forward, leaning on his cane.

There was nothing the padre could do but follow behind. He couldn't believe that the governor, so youthful yesterday, walked like an old man today. Was it true that he was seriously ill, as González said? No, the governor's behavior must have something to do with his disappointment about the Mission San Gabriel, Padre José was sure.

Four of the governor's soldiers were waiting as the padre and governor approached. They lounged against the arcade supports, ignoring the Indian musicians, who had gathered in the dust beyond the arcade roof. The Indians concentrated on tuning their instruments, their faces solemn as they listened to the sound produced by the first violin. Their long hair tied back with twine, they wore clean muslin shifts over loose cotton trousers.

"The governor..." A soldier alerted the others as he saw Figueroa moving slowly toward them. They came immediately to attention. Brother Antonio appeared with a chair, helped the governor sit down. Sergeant González, a last minute choice made to show respect for the mission's forces, hurried up. He tugged at his shirt collar to settle it in place around his neck.

Padre José stepped forward and raised his arms. Down they came, and the Indians—to his surprise—cooperated. Never had the piccolos played so sweetly, the violins so delicately. The padre relaxed. His wrists and forearms, encased in their woolen sleeves, swept across the musicians as he found it in himself to imitate Padre Ignacio's expertise at conducting. The musicians moved easily from Russian ballad to Italian cantata to lively Mexican rancheras. Even the governor's foot tapped; he applauded with unbounded enthusiasm, as the Indians nodded their heads respectfully. Padre José let his arms fall to his side. He turned toward the governor to bow deeply, but the governor was already going into the dining room.

The padre entered to find the soldiers seated at the table. General Figueroa sat at one end with Brother Antonio on his right. Unable to avoid Padre José's direct glance, the young man murmured an apology to the governor and moved quickly to the opposite end next to the padre.

The meal progressed from soup to beef, mutton and vegetables—a large quantity of squash, potatoes, green beans, corn—to two kinds of flan and four cakes. The mission's best wine was poured freely to all except Padre José, who, as always, ate and drank sparingly. Dessert was complemented by a brandy touted by all the ranchos as being as good as any that came from Spain. The adobe walls looked creamy white, candles shone brightly in their silver candelabra, dinnerware from China gleamed. All was perfect, thought Padre José, all except the governor's expression, which changed little even as he consumed a large quantity of food and wine. It was only when dessert was served that the padre saw a hint of a smile on the governor's wide face. Figueroa turned away from Sergeant González, who had filled the seat next to the governor.

"A wonderful meal. You are a gracious host, padre."

Padre José looked down at his lap, pleased by the attention. His moment of satisfaction was brief.

"Padre, let's you and I talk," the governor said. The others rose quickly to their feet, pushed their chairs back to leave the room, taking the last of the wine and brandy at the governor's suggestion.

"Come, sit here." The governor indicated the place next to him, where Sergeant González had been. Koovahcho took the last plates away and obediently closed the door to the kitchen as he left.

The meal and wine had revived the governor. He managed a subdued smile and cleared his throat. "I'm very pleased by what I see here at Mission San Gabriel."

The padre thought he would expire from happiness, right then, on the spot.

"Everything appears very well cared for; the Indians are obviously industrious. I can see from your careful records that the mission pays for itself out of the tallow and hide trade. Am I correct?"

"Yes...and then some."

"If I had one complaint, I'd say that the Indians are not very content here."

Padre José wanted to protest. How could the governor know the Indians after only one day?

"In any case, the Mexican government is very clear on their intention. They are going to disband the missions," the governor continued.

"The Indians are not ready. They are not yet men of reason," the padre objected.

Governor Figueroa ignored the padre's outburst. "If the decision were mine, I would ask that the Indians receive half the mission land with the stipulation that they could not sell it for a period of time. The remainder of the land should be sold off slowly, over a period of years. In that way, mission revenues could continue to support the province."

"The land is very...valuable." What was the governor saying? What did Figueroa's words mean for him, Padre José?

"Yes, the land is valuable, so who is better to receive it than the people who have made it so? That, after all, is what Spain intended by building the missions. To educate the Indians and make them ready for a Christian life of work and prayer."

"The Mexicans said this too, but never put their words into action," Padre José argued.

"Now is the time," was the reply.

What did it matter who the land belonged to? In any case, there was to be no place for him. The ache in his stomach was joined by a pain in his head. Unable to focus on what the governor was saying, Padre José finally asked the question that was uppermost in his mind. "And what will become of us?" His voice rose, even as he tried to temper his tone.

"The clergy?"

The padre nodded. He scanned the governor's face for some sign that Figueroa knew the full impact of the plan he was advocating.

"I will recommend that you and your fellow padres be invited to stay at the missions. We, all of us, need your help in ministering to our spiritual lives."

Another man may have been pleased to take up his sacred calling without being distracted by temporal matters. But Padre José saw a different future, barren and unsatisfying. He would lose his power over the land and his authority over the Indians.

While he and the governor sat talking, everything he had made of his life was being taken away.

Figueroa sat back in his chair. Any vitality his body held while he spoke had disappeared. He took a last sip of wine and, placing his hands on the table for support, stood up. Padre José also rose. The men stood looking at each other until the padre realized the governor needed his help in walking to his room. He extended his arm. The governor placed his forearm on the padre's. The padre felt the weight of the governor's body and, with it, all the weariness. He opened the door and stepped aside, letting the governor pass into the warm night.

In spite of the presence of over a thousand people within the sound of his voice, the quadrangle was so quiet Padre José could hear a slow waltz played by a lone violin in the distance. Crickets caught in the tiles overhead chirped loudly. Later, when he thought about that night, he recalled crickets frantic to be heard, the sound of a languid violin.

[29]

July, 1844. A bucket in each hand, Padre José stepped carefully across the zanja. At the bottom of the ditch, rocks ordinarily covered by water at this time of the year were dry, dark mounds. His gaze took in the fertile ground, once crowded with wheat, barley, oats, and corridors of corn and beans. Now, the long, wide field was planted with little more than sufficient corn for the Indians who remained at the mission, for Brother Antonio and himself, and for the pigs. Feeding a hundred fifty souls demanded fewer crops than providing for the many hundreds who once lived here.

The bare field presented a dilemma. Without sturdy grape vines or rows of tall cornstalks to grasp onto when he tired, how would he traverse the field's length to tend his flowers. He began his slow walk along the ditch, stopping often to catch his breath.

Carrying the buckets had been Koovahcho's job, he recalled as he walked, surprised that he remembered the Indian's name. Koovahcho. Left six or more years ago. The boy had lived at the mission since infancy. Few Indian villages remained. Where did he go?

Koovahcho had been replaced by another young boy, but he was soon gone, as well. After that, the servants were men too old to leave the mission. They served until they died and were replaced by other old men. A few cooks from the old days had also stayed. Mission San Gabriel had been the queen of the Alta California missions. Not now.

He was almost at the far end of the field. The hut where he kept his tools had long ago lost its thatched roof. Dry remnants of vines clustered at the base of the hut's decaying walls. Padre José set down the buckets, lifted his hat and swept his hand across his brow. His hair, dark a dozen years before, had turned white.

One thing had not changed: the summer sun was as hot as ever. He looked up at the sky. The sun was directly overhead, an expanse of pale blue unmarked by clouds. He ought to be getting back for lunch. Instead, he lowered a bucket into the zanja and poured water onto the single vine bearing passion flowers. For a moment, he felt as thrilled as the first time he noticed their dazzling white petals set off by cornflower-blue-bordered skirts. He stared with longing at the blossom. Pure. Whole.

Setting the bucket down in the dirt, he began his slow walk back to the quadrangle.

Brother Antonio waited beneath the corridor's roof for Padre José. Above his head, the adobe tiles showed numerous gaps. Even if there had been laborers to repair the roof, no tiles were available. The adobe workshop was shuttered long ago. In the winter, rain dripped between the roof tiles. In the summer, the adobe cover, once a barrier to the sun, offered little protection. He surveyed the quadrangle. Holes pockmarked dirt-stained adobe walls. Many rooms had been stripped of their roofs, the wooden beams more useful at one of the new ranchos than at the deteriorating mission. The doors, if they hadn't been stolen for their wood, kept no one out, and there was nothing within them to protect.

"So you're returning to the capital?" Padre José began after the servants had left the room. The dining room still held the table and chairs, but every item of value had been sold. The china went to the owner of Rancho del Verdugo, a gift for his eldest son's bride; the candlesticks, an offering to the church in the pueblo of Los Angeles, where they would see more use. The friars ate on simple pottery every day. Visitors, unless they came to loot or buy, were infrequent.

Brother Antonio swallowed his spoonful of atole. He ate simply, the same meals prepared for the Indians. Padre José ate cornmeal mush with goat's milk at every meal. The brother couldn't remember the last time he had seen the older man eat solid food.

"Ye', two weeks," Brother Antonio replied. Over the years, he had learned to speak up for himself. Indians and soldiers alike had long ago accepted the brother's deformity. He was not apt to speak harshly to the Indians and had never ordered a beating; the Indians tolerated him, unlike Padre José, whom they despised. Brother Antonio possessed a sly sense of humor, which even the least educated soldier appreciated.

"You're sailing south? Do you remember how ill you became on the ocean voyage that brought you here?"

"I do, ye'." Brother Antonio spoke in a gentle, respectful tone.

"And you're choosing to board a ship again?" Nearly twenty years had passed, but the padre could easily recall his own journey from Spain, the blue-green ocean stretching beyond and beyond, each swell and fall aggravating his tender stomach. He never regretted the long trek to Alta California that had saved him from another ocean voyage.

Brother Antonio nodded. When Padre José had walked the twenty-five hundred kilometers between the capital and mission, the effort was considered unusual. Even then, most travelers journeyed to the western coast to board a ship for Alta California. These days, no one traversed the distance by foot.

Padre José had exchanged his long silences for rambling accounts, speaking at length about his early life in Spain and his early days at the mission. Brother Antonio appeared to listen, but his own thoughts were given over to planning whatever needed to be done at the mission that day, or silent ruminations on the meaning of a particular Bible passage. This day, as Padre José told the story of his ocean crossing for the second time that week, Brother Antonio waited until the padre paused for breath.

"You come wi' me," Brother Antonio said, more a question than a command.

"I will go. For certain. I want to wait just a little longer. Perhaps after the first of the year. I'm not quite ready. Not quite." Padre José lifted the bowl to his lips and drank the last drops of goat's milk.

"Nothing for you 'o do here, 'adre," the younger man said.

"Yes, of course there is something for me to do. I must take care of the Indians as I have always done." Padre José drummed his fingers on the table. He had endured years of stomach pain and, more recently, shortness of breath.

His control of the mission had slipped away. Most of the land had been sold to rich men, or they had become rich after taking the land at a low price. The mission's great herd of cattle was reduced to hundreds, all so wasted they didn't yield enough fat to make the mission's candles. The padre well remembered how he was ordered to slaughter cattle for their hides to bring more cash quickly into the missions.

Thinking about all this, he became angry. He wanted someone to blame.

"If Governor Figueroa had lived...," the padre said bitterly. "The men who came after him—all were thieves."

"Governor fine man," Brother Antonio agreed.

They were silent, each absorbed in thinking about the governor's brief stay at the mission a decade before. Padre José remembered a genial man, whose obvious regard for the Indians had influenced his own behavior. After meeting the governor, Padre José was less severe in his punishments, although his customary ill humor led him to threaten violence until his failing health took away his breath and, with it, the force of his words.

Brother Antonio remembered the governor as a man of clear vision. Governor Figueroa had produced a decree that put the missions in private hands, but also affirmed the missions' Indians the rights to land they could acquire over the next decade. If that had come to pass, the terrain might now be dotted with the Indians' small ranches. Villages might have flourished as they did in the days before the Spaniards came. Maybe the Indians would have tilled the land, or hired themselves out to ranchos where they would earn decent wages for work as vaqueros, blacksmiths or in other trades they had learned at the mission.

But the Mexican government had overruled the governor. The Indians never saw any land come to them—the governor's sudden death only two years after his mission visit left them no advocate. Those who left—far more numerous than the ones who stayed—had found their way back to whatever traditional villages remained. Most worked at ranchos, usually cheated out of the little money they earned; or in the pueblo, suffering the same treatment; or went to jail if they indulged in the whiskey they managed to get hold of.

Brother Antonio heard the clang of iron pots. The cooks were making it known they were ready for siesta and were anxious to clean up lunch plates. It was time to move on.

"Leading 'rayer a'nigh'?" he asked.

"Don't I always lead evening prayers?" Padre José snapped. The mission padres had been kept on to conduct religious services even as an administrator rode out from the pueblo a few times a month to sell off land and property and supervise the few commercial activities still going on.

"'ardon, 'adre, bu' you don' look well. 'ay in bed today. Need good heal' for a' day af'er 'morrow." Brother Antonio spoke respectfully, carefully considering every word.

"Good health, yes. Who did you say will be here?"

"Don Rodrigo and hi' foreman. Buy cattle for Don Rodrigo's ranch, Rancho de Lo' Rio'."

"Yes, I remember. The mission administrator will be here too. I must make things ready." Padre José suddenly rose to his feet, then just as quickly sat down again. Elbows on the table, he rested his forehead on his hands, rocked slowly back and forth. His posture was similar to Governor Figueroa's the morning the padre had come upon the governor in the chapel before Mass, but he didn't remember, or if he did, didn't care.

Padre José didn't emerge from his room until the next morning. He knew that Brother Antonio would lead evening prayers for the few Indians who attended, as he had done more and more often in recent years. Acceptance of the true faith was not a requirement any longer. The padres could neither punish those who refused to take Christ as their savior, nor reward those who did. But the church had become a way of life for some of the older Indians, who had learned the rituals when they were young. They were Padre José's flock; they saw him as their Father, their spiritual leader.

At least, that was how he saw himself.

The morning Mass and evening prayers he conducted had become ever more perfunctory as the years passed. Having nothing to give, he had given up, sensing that his time was coming to an end, though he feared knowing whether "his time" was the end of his life at the mission, or simply the end of his life.

If one thing could raise his passions, though, it was the Indians' mix of Catholic practice with whatever they knew of their own beliefs. It was true; he himself found little meaning in the rituals. Nevertheless, they should be respected. They had been transmitted over the generations. Who were the Indians to think they could change the Church?

He was one who would never accept the Virgin of Guadalupe, for example, as some kind of Indian incarnation of the Virgin Mary. Although he lacked faith, he accepted its trappings. The Virgin Mary was an integral part of the story. She was the mother of God. The Virgin of Guadalupe was an interloper, a fiction in the mind of an impoverished Indian some three centuries before, who had reported seeing the Virgin clad in a robe bedecked with stars. She talked to the man, a poor peasant, and left an image of freshly cut roses on the peasant's cloak. How was that possible?

But the Indians of Mexico had their proof of a miracle and accepted the miracles of virgin birth, of transubstantiation, of resurrection. They surrendered their pagan religion to accept Christ.

Even the lowliest Mexican peasant had more faith than he did.

These thoughts accompanied Padre José as he entered the sacristy, slipped a chasuble over his head—no young Indian boys to help him now—and stepped into the chapel. The table was laid out with candlesticks, chalice, censer, paten, bells; Brother Antonio had seen to it. Curiously, on a summer morning, the chapel was unusually cool, even cold. A tremor passed through his body; he looked around to see if anyone noticed. A few dozen Indians silently waited beyond the low rail that separated the altar from the assembled. Brother Antonio sat on a stool in the rear of the sanctuary, his head bowed.

The padre stood in front of the altar, crossed himself. He began to chant the Mass.

"In nomine Patris, et Filii, et Spiritus Sancti," he intoned in Latin, his back to the assembly. In the name of the Father, and of the Son, and of the Holy Spirit. His voice was low; his tone, flat. Even if he had spoken the words in an Indian language, the congregants couldn't have heard him. An Indian child—where had he come from, the padre wondered—handed him the censer. Padre José raised the incense burner, swung it back and forth. Smoke poured out; a sweet, pungent scent pervaded the room.

The orchestra was missing. Where were the violinists? The flautists? He stood silent for a full minute until he recalled that the musicians hadn't played since Governor Figueroa's visit, long ago. All had left as soon as the missions were disbanded.

He continued, "I will go to the altar of God. To God, the joy of my youth." These words always made Padre José uneasy. Today was no exception. God. Joy. What use were those words to him? One must have faith. I do not, he thought. His stomach began to ache.

Out of habit, he continued to chant the prayers, but his mind had taken hold of his shame and wouldn't let go. He felt as low as he ever had. In his misery, the room spun slowly around him. He gripped the altar table to steady himself. Years of doubt, disbelief, hypocrisy. The image of Count Orgaz, in the El Greco painting the padre had first seen when he was a boy, rising into heaven. Mother Mary there to greet him. If justice held, the padre would never go to heaven. Who would be there to meet him in purgatory? Or maybe he would spend eternity in hell. His skin prickled in fearful anticipation of the lake of fire in which he would be cast after death.

The service came to a halt. The Indians were used to Padre José's peculiar pace. They had none to compare him to and forgot the speed with which the padre had dispatched the ritual in earlier days. Brother Antonio considered approaching the altar. But he was not ordained to preside over a Mass. He didn't want to upset Padre José. The assembly waited.

Padre José tried to begin again. He lifted his eyes to survey the figures of the saints on the altar. Archangel Gabriel. He had brought Mary the news: She was pregnant with the Son of God.

San Antonio de Padua. San Joaquin, the father of Mary. Santo Domingo. None gave him comfort.

His eyes fixed upward toward the saints, he felt a presence above. Involuntarily, his hands began to tremble. He was aware of a roaring sound in his ears, as if he were hearing the oncoming rush of a great wave. He craned his neck. What he saw nearly brought him to his knees.

The Virgin of Guadalupe hovered overhead, gazing down at him under modestly lowered lashes. The multitude of stars on her cape's azure field glittered in the chapel's dim light. Her mysterious smile, her corona of gold, her hands folded in prayer—the padre saw her clearly.

He could not believe his eyes. He bowed his head, began to pray feverishly. "O holy Mother of God, do not play tricks on me. I am too old, too ill. If you are some devil, cast in the form of this apparition, begone with you!" He shook his fist, clenched tightly at his side, and stamped his sandaled foot on the ground.

He looked up again.

She had not moved. Her eyes gazed into his as if she knew his torment. Forgave him.

Padre José breathed in a fragrance: incense tinged with roses.

No. He shook his head from side to side; the motion made him dizzy. No. The Virgin of Guadalupe did not exist. She was a fiction. He squeezed his eyes shut and opened them again. He was looking down at the dirt floor he had seen every day for the decade since Padre Ignacio had left. He was aware of the familiar solidness under his feet. He saw the skirt of his chasuble and the hem of the white cloth that covered the altar. He forced himself to breathe slowly, evenly. After a moment, he raised his eyes cautiously upward. Slowly, slowly, he angled his neck back.

The Virgin floated in the air above him, her lips creased upwards faintly at the corners. A thought came to him: Even if he doubted her, she believed in him.

Sighing deeply, he surrendered himself to her.

O beautiful lady, O beautiful soul, you are as lovely as a passion flower, lovelier even because you can return my love. I am weary, and I have waited for you for so long.

Whether he spoke the words aloud or in his mind, he didn't know. The padre realized only then that he *had* been waiting. He had wanted only a sign; none had ever come. Now, as his journey was ending, he had been granted a gift.

If those assembled on the other side of the rail wondered what was happening, Padre José wasn't aware. He stared heavenward toward her image, lost in his love for the Virgin of Guadalupe, the beautiful lady of compassion.

Had she come to welcome him into heaven? Was it his time? But no, he was still breathing. He was gripping the table. He heard someone stir behind him. There were others here too. But he didn't look around. The Virgin's image was fading, and he wanted only to live in her light.

Five minutes passed in silence. Ten. The vision faded. Padre José remained rooted before the altar, his eyes closed. He felt the presence of a mother's uncomplicated love.

Slowly, he resumed the Mass. His voice rang with conviction. He skipped easily through the Bible reading and the homily to recite the Apostle's Creed. "I believe in one God, the Father Almighty, Maker of heaven and earth, and of all things visible and invisible. And in one Lord, Jesus Christ, the Only Begotten Son of God."

Brother Antonio looked up. The padre mumbled his way through the Mass these days. No one who had heard the padre recite the Creed could ever believe that the man cared for what he was saying. Today, the padre's voice was clear, his tone sweet, his manner confident.

Padre José continued, "By whom all things were made. Who for us men and for our salvation came down from heaven." Why were these words so difficult for me to say until today?—he asked himself. It was easy to believe, easy to have faith. Faith came as naturally as breath.

He didn't stop to ponder these matters but continued reciting: "He was also crucified for us, suffered under Pontius Pilate, and was buried..." His throat filled with emotion. He paused, then went on until he reached the end. "I await the resurrection of the dead and the life"—he crossed himself again, this time fervently—"of the world to come. Amen."

At last, he had spoken the truth.

Padre José slept the whole night through, not startled awake as he usually was by animal calls, pain or, more recently, a terrifying shortness of breath. He dreamed he was walking up a hill. The Virgin of Guadalupe floated a short distance in front of him, leading the way. Every so often, she would glance back and reward him with a smile so full of compassion, he groaned aloud in happiness. After a time, she stopped and hovered in the air, enveloped in a soft light emanating from her body. As he gazed at her, the light grew brighter. He was aware of the scent of roses, although none appeared. Slowly, she ascended.

Where she had been, he now saw La Mancha, dry and golden as he had last seen it, forty years before. Wending their way single file down the road were his father, his brothers Teo and Tomo, and his beloved brother Jaime. They were older, to be sure, but they could be none else, his father gray and stoop-shouldered riding astride a well-groomed horse, his brothers Teo and Tomo, heavyset—even seated in their saddles, he could see their bulk—and Jaime, handsome in middle age, a smile, as always, on his face. Where had they been all these years?

Granada, he heard the Virgin say, although her lips didn't move.

How is that possible? I saw the soldiers fell them, one by one.

The halo of light around the Virgin seemed to quiver. No, my dear Tomás. They have been in Granada, have grown older and have acquired some wealth. They are traveling north to Toledo to find you.

But I'm not there. I will miss them, he cried in the wordless conversation he was exchanging with the Virgin.

They will wait, she said.

He watched as they grew smaller and smaller in the distance until they disappeared altogether. "They ride so slowly, as if time meant nothing to them." He spoke aloud, but the Virgin had disappeared. In the space where she had been, the light intensified until, finally, he had to close his eyes. When he opened them again, the first rays of daylight cast a dim square on the opposite wall.

He lay quietly, listening to the mourning doves. Their loud cooing in summers past often signaled the first irritation of his day. This morning, he was transfixed by their voices. His father. Teo. Tomo. Jaime. Waited for him, if not in Spain, then in heaven, because that was surely where they had gone if the Virgin could summon them so easily. He would go there too and join them—someday.

He wanted to share the news with Brother Antonio, with the Indians. He even wanted to tell Don Rodrigo Tilman, whom he would see later that day. But Padre José feared they would think him crazy or, at best, hear his experience as the wandering mind of an old man.

During an early breakfast with Brother Antonio, Padre José grunted with pleasure over his milk and bread. How comforting the milk felt going down his throat, filling his empty belly. He wanted to thank the Indian who had served him.

"You are a good boy," he couldn't resist telling Brother

Antonio. "Thank you for assuming so many of my tasks. I don't know how I will manage when you return to the capital."

The brother's pale face flushed.

The padre's step was firm as he walked into the quadrangle. He felt the sun, pleasantly warm on his face. The mountains—how beautiful they were, their contours emerging from the early morning haze. He refrained from complaining about the weather or his infirmities, as he did every morning.

"I welcome our gues'?" Brother Antonio asked.

"No. I can do that. You said they would be here...when?"

"Midmorning."

"Yes. I'll wait for them in the chapel after Mass. They may arrive early, and I don't want to keep them."

Brother Antonio peered at the old man, his eyebrows drawn together. Padre José had never minded letting people wait for him before; in fact, he appeared to enjoy discomfiting any person he dealt with.

A few moments later, Padre José entered the chapel. As he saw every morning, a few Indians knelt or sat on the hard dirt floor, their eyes downcast. Some nodded their heads in sleep. The padre felt an odd tremor in his stomach as he looked at them—the first stirrings of compassion so unfamiliar to him that he thought his stomach pain, which had abated after the Virgin's visit the day before, had returned.

Brother Antonio slipped in the chapel door as Padre José turned to face the altar.

The padre's voice was thick with emotion as he recited the formal prayer.

"In nomine Patris, et Filii"—he made the sign of the Cross—"et Spiritus Sancti." He continued the opening prayer, pausing at times to let the assembly respond. But, as he had not given them a chance to participate in all the years since Padre Ignacio left, they remained silent.

The padre began the assembly's confession.

"I confess to almighty God and to you." The next words stuck in his throat, but he went on, "My brothers and sisters"—there, I have said it—"that I have sinned exceedingly in thought, word, deed." Yes, that was true.

He struck his breast three times, forcefully, as he had been taught in seminary. "Through my fault, through my fault, through my most grievous fault." Yes, the fault has been my own, not God's, nor God's son.

"And I ask blessed Mary, ever virgin"—the blessed Virgin of Guadalupe, Padre José said to himself.

"All the angels and saints, and you, Father, and you, my brothers and sisters," he proclaimed easily this time. Yes, you Indians *are* my brothers and sisters as we are in Christ together.

"To pray for me to the Lord, our God." Please pray for me, hold me in your prayers, that I may meet my brothers and my father again someday, especially Jaime, oh Jaime, I miss you so.

"May the Almighty God have mercy on you, forgive you your sins and bring you to everlasting life. Amen." As he swung the censer that appeared at his right hand, he glanced overhead, but today the space above him remained empty. This was as it should be and did not disappoint him. The Virgin had revealed herself to him. Her appearance foretold his everlasting life, a life which he had never allowed himself to hope for—eternity spent with the family he had lost. Was God so good? He must be, that he could forgive a man so full of sin as himself.

He completed the Mass with a statement of belief as fervent as the day before and remained standing in front of the altar as the Indians filed out of the chapel. A few looked at him nervously. They too had noticed the change in Padre José's demeanor and were unsure of what it meant.

After carefully removing his vestments, Padre José returned to the chapel. He sat on the stool where Brother Antonio had sat during the Mass. Eyes closed, he saw Jaime as a boy running up to the cathedral toward him, his spindly legs pumping hard against the cobblestone road. The next moment, he felt himself engulfed by the intense blue of the Virgin's cloak and, then, the relief that comes when pain has lifted.

"Padre José?" a voice inquired.

Light flooded the chapel. If the voice had been a woman's, he would have known it was the Virgin's. But it was not. The voice belonged to Don Mariano Gutiérrez, the mission administrator. He and Don Rodrigo Tilman stood in the open door, waiting for Padre José's response.

The padre grasped the administrator's hand firmly.

"Padre José, I am glad to see that you're in better health," the administrator said. His tone revealed that he didn't care at all.

Don Rodrigo Tilman, ever the businessman and the more cordial of the two, took the padre's hand. "You are looking well, Padre. I'm glad to see it."

"Yes, yes, well, when you have faith in the Lord, you can accomplish miracles, true?" Padre José observed.

Although the men shook their heads in agreement, they were puzzled. Neither remembered Padre José referring to the Lord at any time other than during the course of his religious duties.

"How can we be of service today?" Padre José asked.

"I've brought Don Rodrigo to see some...ahh...cattle," the administrator answered. The last time he'd brought a prospective buyer to the mission, the padre had harangued them about the poor health of the herd, insisting that the animals had done far better under Church control. The buyer left without purchasing a single steer.

This time, the priest merely said, "Of course, please proceed."

"We're just going to wait for my foreman. He will be here soon." Tilman slipped his watch out of his waistcoat pocket.

"Would you like some refreshment, gentlemen?"

"No," the administrator said quickly. He didn't want to give the padre a chance to begin a complaint. "In fact, we'll wait outside. We don't want to take any more of your time."

"No bother at all," the padre replied, but Gutiérrez was already leading Tilman out the door.

The foreman was riding up the path toward the mission. "Scott!" Tilman called out to his employee.

Padre José followed them toward the foreman, a large man astride a piebald horse. On other days, he would have remarked derisively on the size of the man, the ugliness of the horse.

Today, he said, "I'll leave you to your business then," and walked back along the path to the mission.

"The work on my ranch is going well. When we finish, we'll celebrate with a fiesta," Tilman called after the padre. "You'll receive an invitation."

"The fiesta. When will it be?" Padre José stopped, turned halfway around.

"Soon after Christmas, January perhaps," Tilman replied.

"Yes, I should still be here," the padre said.

Tilman, in a hurry to see the stock, didn't ask the priest where he was planning to go.

PART 4 sky

[30]

A vaquero's shout woke Don Rodrigo Tilman with a start on a morning in late January 1845. Iron pots clanged in the ramada outside the dining room below. Tilman's wife lay next to him, snoring gently. In the next room his daughter sighed in her sleep. They had moved into the rancho only a week before. Tilman was gratified to see they had adjusted so quickly.

A weak light shone through the curtains, telling Don Rodrigo it was past the time he wanted to rise. He anticipated the week ahead, a series of events he had planned since he first envisioned the rancho. A fiesta. A huge party, part rodeo, part roundup, part gathering of families from all over the southern portion of Alta California. A few from the north, as well. As a courtesy, he had invited Governor Micheltorena. As the governor was now living in the capital, Monterey, Tilman did not expect him to come. He was looking forward to Thomas Larkin's arrival, however. In their previous meetings, Larkin had made clear he favored the United States taking control of Alta California. In fact, as consul to Alta California, he was likely working toward that end. While Tilman was unsure about how well Mexican landowners would fare under United States' laws, Larkin's position clearly made him worth knowing. What's more, Tilman had fashioned his casa grande after Larkin's in Monterey and wanted to show it off.

He dressed quickly, choosing Mexican dress over the tailored American-style suits he was more accustomed to wearing. His wife hardly stirred as he drew a wide-sleeved shirt over his head, stepped into his pantalones—he chose dark woolen ones with buttons down the side in the Mexican fashion—and slipped on a short bolero jacket. He tied a striped sash around his waist but quickly removed it. The jacket and pants made him uncomfortable; the sash made him squirm. He looked at his image in the long wardrobe mirror. He had an upright carriage; his face was marked by a strong jaw and narrow grey eyes. In spite of his short stature, he was a person one did not easily overlook.

He was the richest man in the pueblo. His path had taken him from Massachusetts to central Mexico to Alta California. And now he was a rancher, with holdings as far as one could see. He regarded himself as a plainspoken man, a descendant of Puritan stock, a man who needed few luxuries. But this land...these opportunities...

He turned away from the mirror before seeing an expression of self-satisfaction come over his face.

Tilman splashed water on his cheeks from the basin on the side table and ran a comb through his hair. Leaving the room, he felt a sudden longing to see his garden. Instead of proceeding down the stairs, he opened the balcony door and stepped outside. The balcony was wide and ran the full length of the house, shielding the dining room, entrance and parlor below from the afternoon sun, providing a second-floor view to the ocean. Quietly, he stepped through the door—his daughter's bedroom was opposite—and closed it behind him. The balcony was surrounded by a sturdy rail. As he walked toward it, he was encased in fog.

He peered into the garden below, imagining the flowers he would see in the spring. Hollyhocks. Asters. Violets. His brother had already put the seeds aboard a ship in Boston and also tucked in some tulip bulbs. They were making their way through the Straits of Magellan and would arrive eventually at San Pedro Bay. Some day in early spring—Tilman was still amazed that seeds could be planted in April, March, even February in Alta California's temperate climate—the flowers would bloom. His gardens would be the most beautiful among all the ranchos.

The fog, wet and gray, was so heavy he could barely see the ground, let alone the ocean a few miles away. A child's cry startled him. He leaned over the balcony, searching below to see where it was coming from. He could barely see the figure of an Indian woman next to the cypress tree at the southern edge of the garden. She held a child by the hand and was clutching another to her breast. Before he could shout at her to leave, she was gone, walking quickly toward the ramada. Her feet made no sound against the newly turned earth. He'd have to talk to Scott about that. Indians were not allowed in his garden.

Another sound below. Tilman looked over the balcony again. Scott, his large frame always easily recognizable, entered the garden from the west, paused a moment at the tree where the Indian woman had stood a moment before, then walked purposefully toward the ramada. Curious.

Tilman opened the door to the house and reentered, closing it gently behind him. He descended the staircase. Other than the upstairs balcony, the staircase was the feature he was most proud of. Mexican ranch houses were ordinarily one-story. His was not only two-story, in the Monterey style, but his staircase, like Larkin's, was inside the house. Best, it was extraordinarily well constructed, even more of a showpiece than the consul's.

When he praised Scott for the staircase, the foreman had said, "The credit goes to the Indians. A gift to you," and pointed out the graceful hour glass shape of the struts supporting the balustrade.

"I don't know how they knew to do this," Tilman had commented on the struts, moving on to inspect the ceiling beams in the parlor. Later, he reflected on Scott's language. The man had hardly spoken when they met. Barely a year had passed.

Where did Scott learn his simple eloquence, and why would he credit the Indians? Tilman assumed that most people in charge take credit for themselves. He had shrugged it off that day, but now as he descended the stairs, he thought about it again.

Sometime that day, Tilman knew he would have to take Scott aside and tell the foreman he'd have to move on. Although Scott had neither seen nor signed one, a contract always existed in Tilman's mind. That contract had now expired. He had asked Scott only to build the ranch, which was now complete; he had promised the foreman's job to Felipe. Felipe had been a help to Scott, even as Scott kept up his end of the bargain by teaching Felipe the rudiments of reading and mathematics. The Mexican had been patient. Now, Tilman had to make good on his promise. Though the clumsy American had grown on Tilman, Scott would have to go.

Big Headed Girl had made her way toward the ranch long before daybreak. She held baby Tach'i in a rebozo tied Mexican-fashion around her shoulders, her rabbit cape beneath for warmth. Four-year-old Koo'ar stumbled along beside her, struggling to keep up with his mother.

The river was lower than it had been the previous year at this time. She was still able to walk from rock to rock—on these she held tightly to her son's hand—although it was the middle of the rainy season.

She had trembled a bit as she walked, but not from the cold and fog. In the days between autumn and winter, when work on the house had been most intense, she spent many days at the makeshift Indian camp close to the rancho. One day, she had joined three other women in pulling a cartload of bricks from the brick-making area at the southeast end of the ranch house to the opposite side. The bricks would be used to make the wall that would partially enclose the ranch on the west end.

It was arduous work on a warm October day when the winds blew continuously, hot and dry.

Scott had approached with a bucket of water. Using sign language, he insisted the women rest and drink. As he held out the ladle to Girl, he stared at her face. Girl remembered the silence of the vaqueros as they had looked at her nearly a year before. But this time she wasn't afraid. She knew Scott meant her no harm. Still, she glanced away. Scott gave the ladle to the next woman, the next, and finally left.

Later, the old woman Esar had advised, "You should marry him. He will make a good husband." The observation was made with good intention. Since late summer, when Girl had dropped the spoon and Scott had stooped to pick it up, he had hovered around Girl, trying to help her with whatever task she was doing. Others were bound to notice, and they had.

Girl had said nothing in her defense. She was aware that some Indian women married white men. This was not, she believed, what she wanted for herself.

Even as the rainy season approached and work grew more intense, Scott had continued to spend a few minutes every day near Girl. He inspected the ramada when she worked there, leaning on the spit to turn it for her while she shucked corn for the vaqueros' atole. He took early morning rides along the river, gathered juncus and deer grass for her, leaving bundles at her side when she worked with the other women repairing baskets. Often, he accompanied her and her kin to the river when they fetched water. He stood at the top of the bank, rifle in hand, in case a mountain lion or bear took them by surprise. He stayed only a few minutes by her side at each visit, not enough to detract from his work, but enough time to let her know he was watching out for her.

She knew he wanted her. He had come from over the mountains, she had heard. He belonged to no one.

Her ancestors had lived on this land for as long as there were people. She belonged with a man who came from this land.

Still, he was a good man, and she was grateful for his kindness. Taught to repay kindness with like gestures, she had woven for him a small basket of juncus grass, a token really, too small to store anything in. She gave him a multicolored bit of abalone shell. She didn't look at him when he accepted these gifts. She assumed he knew the gifts came from all the women, not from her alone.

But the day before, when people began to arrive early for the fiesta, he sought her out in the parlor where she was dusting. It was a new job for her, and she needed to concentrate to make sure she did it correctly, dusting each chair and table carefully, restoring anything she moved to its rightful place. Her children were in the village where they had stayed for these last two busy weeks, looked after by one of the older women. She would return to the village that night and bring them back to see the fiesta.

Scott came in quietly. She didn't know he was there until he cleared his throat.

"Niña." He used the Spanish word for Girl, addressing her directly for the first time. "Tomorrow," he said, hurrying on in Spanish before she could turn around, "I'm going to ask you something important. I hope you'll say yes."

She understood only the words "mañana," "importante," "sí." His voice, low and heavy with emotion, told her what his words meant. He was going to ask her to marry him. She let out a cry of alarm, stumbled back into a chair. Scott whipped around. His head hit the low doorway as he hustled his clumsy frame from the room.

Henry Scott's day began before Big Headed Girl awakened in her village. The moon shone through his room's narrow window. A sliver of light on the packed earthen floor was the first thing he saw when he opened his eyes. The night was as still as a wound-down clock. Scott had tossed and turned for hours. Over and over again he considered what he had said to Big Headed Girl the day before, how she had reacted. Thinking about it, his spirits alternately rose, then crashed. On the crash, he decided she had understood what he was saying and was going to reject him. On the rise, he told himself she had not understood what he had said to her, was merely afraid that someone would see her talking to him when she was supposed to be working. Once she knew he meant her no harm—only good!—she would agree to be his wife.

Swinging his legs over the edge of the bed frame, he stood up, deep in thought. He teetered on the precipice of doubt before adopting the happier alternative. How soon could they be married? They would be betrothed in any ritual she desired. When he told Tilman he was taking a wife, his employer would undoubtedly tell him to live in the small house next to the river. It was vacant and needed work, but it was surely livable. Some of Tilman's guests were staying there now, in fact. He would go there, a short walk, on the pretense of checking on them. His duties rarely took him to the casita; he wanted to see if it was as promising a home for his bride as he remembered.

Daylight approached. The moon disappeared, hidden by a heavy fog that rolled in off the ocean. Shivering, Scott stepped into his pants and pulled on his boots. An overcoat Tilman had given him in October, when the weather had turned unusually cold, covered the undershirt of his long johns. He lit a candle on the small table, stepped outside for a moment, peed in the dust, then reentered his room.

Next to the candle lay his ranch account book, open to a blank page. A quill pen and tin inkwell next to it were ready for him to use. Instead, he sat down on the room's only chair, picked up a small basket. Big Headed Girl had woven it for him. He brought it to his nose and inhaled. Fresh juncus. A musty smell. He closed his eyes. He had wanted a woman before but never like this one. Never thought that she herself might smell of juncus, that he could touch the hair that slid down her back in a river of dark strands, that he could see her breasts free from the cover of her blouse and rows of shell necklaces, that her legs might clasp around his back, that she might cry out with pleasure at the feel of him inside her.

A coyote yipped, then yipped again. He opened his eyes, abruptly stood up to open the shutters on his larger window, the one facing west. Morning, white with fog, had come. He shrugged off his overcoat and put on a shirt he could scarcely button, his fingers trembled so. Hat on his head, he blew out the candle and walked out the door into the courtyard. During the day, the area was filled with vaqueros, Indians, carts and horses coming and going. Now, silence. Looking toward the east end of the courtyard, he could barely make out Don Rodrigo Tilman's bedroom window through the thick fog. Faint sounds came from the ramada; maybe Big Headed Girl was already there fixing breakfast, he thought. She would be busy. Reluctantly, he put off seeing her until later in the day.

He turned toward the river, toward the little house. Taking care to avoid getting caught in a tangled wall of willow branches, he walked quickly. The house came into view in minutes. Perched on the bank overlooking the river, it was as he remembered—a small, plain adobe with a narrow veranda. He circled the exterior. Four horses tied to the post outside the house and two carts in the small courtyard told him that several people were sleeping inside. After the fiesta, after the guests had left, there would surely be room for Big Headed Girl, her children and any relatives she wanted to bring with her. He couldn't get as close as he wanted when people were there, but the little house seemed to be in good shape, posts holding the veranda's tiled roof without sagging, shutters on all the windows intact.

Satisfied, he headed back toward the rancho, intending to end up where he had started, next to his room at the west end of the south wing. One moment he was in a thicket, his thoughts on Big Headed Girl, the next he was looking into Tilman's garden at the east end of the property. Abruptly, he stopped. An hour or so after dawn, the sky was lighter, although the fog made seeing difficult. He surveyed the garden, reluctant to enter Tilman's private world. Intending to turn around, he heard a child's cry. It came from the vicinity of the two newly planted cypress trees near the garden's southern border.

Suddenly, he saw Big Headed Girl run into the garden. She was following her crying young son, who stopped next to a cypress. As Scott watched, she grabbed the boy's hand and pulled him toward the ramada. Before he could decide whether to go after them, he looked up to see Tilman standing on his second-floor balcony, looking at Girl. Wanting to deflect any criticism of Girl, Scott ran to the tree and stood a moment. Perhaps he would be blamed for allowing an Indian into Tilman's sanctuary. If that were to happen, he would admit his failure; Tilman would grumble but quickly turn his attention to other matters.

Tilman did not call out to Scott, merely turned around and walked inside his house. Scott waited another moment, then followed Big Headed Girl toward the ramada.

Brother Antonio had left the Mission San Gabriel, as arranged, in October. After his departure, Padre José wandered aimlessly around the mission. Every day included a morning Mass, given to fewer and fewer followers as the old ones died, one by one. He dispensed with evening prayers, instead going to bed immediately after dinner and rising after sunrise. Where the mission had once been an important stop for travelers coming over the mountains or along the coast, now few people visited, finding no comfort in ruined buildings and a padre who was old and "muy enfermo."

After the Virgin of Guadalupe had appeared in his dream, Padre José had lived for another sign. With the fervor of the newly faithful, he looked for her everywhere.

As he recited the Mass.

As he made his way slowly around the arcade every day, just one turn, never more, never less, whether it took an hour or, on days he felt particularly short of breath, two.

Through every sleepless night, as his breathing became more and more labored. He dropped off to sleep with the Virgin's image in his mind's eye and woke with a start, choking for breath.

During infrequent visits to his beloved passion flowers. Dry and withering by September, a few hardy vines revived in a late October rain. The padre had taken the long walk to his private garden before Christmas, hoping that the month of Christ's birth would encourage the Virgin to visit him as he tended his flowers. By the time he had reached them, his energy was spent. He could not lift a shovel or bend to cut a stem. Instead, he had to content himself with gazing at the vines' tendrils. He prayed that spring would bring the vines to flower once again. He longed to see their white petals set off by an azure skirt, much as the Virgin's dress was complemented by her star-filled cloak, the same intense blue as the blossoms' filaments.

Although the Virgin did not visit him again, his belief in God, in Christ, in the miracle of resurrection did not falter. He was sure he would see his family in heaven. In due time, he told himself. If the Virgin occupied fewer of his thoughts as the days passed, it was because the effort he had to expend merely to rise from his bed and move around the mission took all his will.

The morning Padre José set off for Tilman's rancho, he

hadn't thought about the Virgin for several days, preoccupied with worry about whether he could make the trip and return safely. He knew his limitations, had surprised himself by readily accepting Tilman's invitation, delivered by a Mexican vaquero in late November.

"Don Rodrigo Tilman hopes you'll accept his invitation," Tilman's vaquero, polite and well-spoken, had said.

"What is your name, son?" Padre José asked.

"Felipe," the man answered.

Padre José nodded as he read the invitation, nicely scribed on a whole piece of parchment. Tilman had spared no expense, he thought.

"I will be there," the padre said.

"Good. Don Rodrigo will be pleased," the rider said. He turned his horse and was down the road before Padre José could change his mind.

The padre questioned himself the morning of the fiesta as he guided his horse inexpertly along the trail: Why did I decide to do this? Over thirty kilometers lay between the mission and Tilman's ranch, a long journey for an old man. He could barely remember receiving the invitation, let alone his reasons for accepting it. He didn't remember the happiness he had felt as he read the invitation and realized he would, for the first time in many months, be in the company of men like himself. Perhaps not as well educated nor as godly, but literate and white.

There would be a week of revelry with a rodeo to witness. Healthy bulls, expert riders. Maybe a horse race. Immense quantities of food and drink—for others, he told himself. Music and dance in the evenings. How long had it been since he had heard music? Except for a poorly tuned fiddle played by an old Indian, it had been years. Invitations like these had always made Padre José suspicious. Why was he invited? What did his host want? If he went, he felt out of place and always suffered stomach pain afterwards, a result of tasting food he rarely ate. Other padres could get away with questionable behavior. He saw his peers drink themselves ill at these events, sometimes even dance with women. A disgrace.

He had accepted the invitation blindly, not so much trusting in God or even the Virgin of Guadalupe to assure his safety, but as something he must do, barely conscious of his vast loneliness.

[31]

As Scott drew close to the ramada, he saw the results of Tilman's planning. At least twenty women toiled.

Some shucked corn that had been stored for months in a rancho storeroom; one ground the dried corn into meal using a stone mortar in the corner of the ramada.

Others peeled oranges. The golden fruit slid from their fingers into reed baskets.

A young woman used a metal box holding hot coals to press a table cover smooth and flat.

In the rear of the ramada, two cooking fires blazed beneath holes cut into a long tile-covered shelf. A deep copper pot sat over one hole; a large comal over the other. More pots, pans and griddles hung from a metal bar across the back wall.

In spite of the morning's chill, the women's faces were moist with sweat. One of these women was Big Headed Girl. Scott could see the shape of a small child held in the rebozo slung across her back; her son was nowhere to be seen. Soft voices echoed from beneath the ramada's sloped overhang.

Scott's arrival halted conversation. Nineteen pairs of eyes turned toward him. Nineteen pairs of hands stopped chopping, peeling, folding, grinding, picking. Only Big Headed Girl continued at her task: she studied the contents of a large pot of beans as she stirred.

Embarrassed by the attention, Scott stepped back; his mouth sagged open. In the next moment, Tilman came up behind him and grabbed his arm.

"What was the Indian doing in my garden?" he demanded in a low growl.

"I...I...don't know. I...just came here to see." He had seen Tilman angry at others, but Scott had never borne the brunt of that anger himself.

Tilman hesitated. Given this convenient excuse, he briefly considered telling Scott then and there that he should move on—the foreman's job was no longer his. He would be saved the unpleasantness of doing it later that day.

"Find out." Tilman softened his tone. "Let's talk a bit. I want to go over plans for the next few days again with you." Scott nodded. Anything he wanted to say to Girl had already left his mind.

"Is breakfast ready?" Tilman began, as they walked away.

"Yes," Scott answered, although he had been more concerned about Big Headed Girl than about breakfast.

"Good. Some of the men will want to go hunting along the river and may want to eat before they set out. How many of our guests have arrived?"

"Maybe forty, maybe more. Hard to tell. They're spread out all over." When Tilman had first told him to expect more than two hundred people, he was dumbstruck by the number they had to house and feed. But Tilman instructed him how to prepare. With no extra space inside his casa grande for the numbers of guests he anticipated, he ordered bolts of canvas for tents from a Massachusetts mill months before. More recently, he sent vaqueros to cut down trees for tent poles from the mountain forests bordering the plain.

Scott himself had ordered all the victuals under Tilman's instructions. For days, ox-drawn carretas stacked with sugar, flour and salt had arrived; then, boards milled by the pueblo's carpenter to make long tables and benches for mealtimes; later, carts full of dry goods for table coverings. A main occupation at the ranch for the last month had been the making of candles. As Tilman ordered, Scott recruited dozens of Indian women to render the tallow for hundreds of candles into creamy white tapers.

Once the rancho was finished in early December, cart after cart of furniture began to arrive. Tilman was already dividing his time between rancho and pueblo. His new home had to meet his expectations before he would allow his wife and daughter to join him. Only a week before the fiesta, Señora Tilman and their daughter had arrived in a carreta followed by two wagons filled with their clothing, jewelry, the household silver and china. Although uncomfortable riding in the rude carreta over the rock-strewn trail south from the pueblo, his wife and daughter had recovered quickly when they reached the ranch. They didn't notice the stares of the Indians workers; their attention was fixed on the ranch house.

"Ahh, mi esposo, qué maravillosa," Señora Tilman sighed as her husband led her into the house. She laughed like the young woman she had been when they had married. Tilman was gratified by his wife's delight.

More carts of furniture had come during the week as well as barrels of wine and sherry from the pueblo's vineyards, once supplied by the mission. Finally, the squash and potatoes, cornmeal and beans that provided the basis of the week's menu, along with sides of beef, whole sheep, chickens and pigs taken from ranch stock. Two carretas of oranges—nearly the whole crop from the pueblo's orchards—had arrived the day before. Tilman quietly exulted in each shipment, although he didn't allow himself the pleasure of sharing his excitement with anyone, not even his wife.

Tilman and Scott continued walking toward the end of the U formed by the ranch house on the east and the rooms on the north and south. After the fiesta, a wooden gate to enclose the rancho on the west would be constructed from the boards that now served as the guests' dining tables and benches.

The door to the large room where the vaqueros slept was open. They had left long before dawn. Their mission: to round up the steers for the first cattle drive at Rancho de Los Rios.

A large pen had been erected on the north side of the property. Here the cattle branding and rodeo would take place over the next week.

"Good work, yes?" Tilman said, looking at the pen.

Scott heard the pride in his employer's voice. "Yes, sir, very solid," the foreman replied.

"Felipe did a good job of instructing the Indians how to build it," Tilman observed.

"Yes," Scott agreed. He took no credit for Felipe's accomplishment, although he easily could have. Before Felipe had begun building the enclosure, he had asked Scott how he had gotten such good work from the Indian laborers. When Scott shrugged, unable to tell him what he didn't know himself, Felipe observed Scott's actions. He followed the mayordomo's example: give the men basic instructions, let them figure it out for themselves, work with them on anything that caused them difficulty.

"The schedule?" Tilman asked.

Scott recited as his employer had drilled. "Breakfast served at the rancho every day from daybreak to noon. Dinner from two to four. Supper from nine o'clock."

"And there's food and drink anytime anyone wants it?"

Scott nodded.

"And?" Tilman said.

"Every day, cattle branding and rodeo in the morning. Roping contests. Horse races."

"That's all?"

"Felipe knows the details."

Tilman frowned. Scott should be in charge of every action, every event.

Scott continued. "Siesta in the afternoon. Fandango every evening."

"The musicians are here?"

"Ten groups. Bunking in the small storeroom."

"Must be crowded."

"Yeah."

"Pues, let's see our guests' accommodations."

Up a small rise, within view of the ranch house, stood the sycamore tree, limbs dignified in age, branches denuded by the season. Makeshift tents surrounded the tree at widely spaced intervals. Scott squinted. He saw a man emerge from a tent on the far side of the tree and warm his hands over a fire. His children chased each other around the sycamore tree.

"The first of our visitors," Scott observed.

"Expect many more today," Tilman said. "Hope it doesn't rain."

Scott squinted up at the sky. "Maybe the fog will clear this afternoon."

"I hope so. Last year at this time, the floods would have made a fiesta impossible. Hasn't rained too much this year, though."

"No," Scott agreed.

Rain. Enough to soak the ground, keep it moist and spongy, feed the aquifers needed by the growing herds of cattle and increasing numbers of residents. One long summer without rain—so unlike the frequent summer downpours he had known in St. Louis—had taught Scott the importance of water.

Tilman offered Scott a cigarette from a small cache he had rolled the night before. Scott accepted it gratefully, allowed the older man to light it for him. The two men stood, smoking in silence, a small island in the fog. The verdant plain, marked by streams, arroyos and low bushes, was invisible. A few oak trees in the distance looked small, barely visible in the mist. Believing that the mountain range, usually within easy view to the north, was still there was an act of faith.

Tilman's earlier irritation with his mayordomo evaporated. Scott's unspoken confidence told him that the foreman and Felipe had discussed the rodeos. Everything was under control. Once again, he asked himself: Was there a job Scott was fit for at the ranch? Why let a good worker go?

He took another drag on his cigarette. No, he was just being sentimental. Scott could not be demoted and asked to stay. His presence would offend Felipe. Scott wouldn't want to remain there anyway, Tilman told himself.

Long past midday, Padre José was still following the river trail south, barely aware of his surroundings. His body, hunched over his saddle, swayed from side to side with each step his horse took. A vaquero, ranging farther north than Tilman's land in search of strays, spied the padre and rode out to meet him.

"Padre José?" the vaquero asked. Having visited the mission church a few years before, he was surprised to see how much the man had aged.

"Yes." Padre José sat up, alert, in his saddle.

"Are you well?"

"Yes, I am fine," the padre said, impatient with questions as always.

"You are going to Rancho de Los Rios?"

"For the fiesta."

"Straight ahead, padre. The rancho is about three leagues."

The vaquero rode on. Padre José turned around to rummage through his saddlebag until his fingers touched a goatskin bag. He lifted it to his lips. Fresh water trickled down his throat. He coughed several times, wiped his mouth and replaced the bag's cover. He looked toward the heavens. The sky had been turning a pale blue when he left the mission. Here, closer to the coast, the afternoon sun was a small fleck of quartz in a granite sky. Once, he would have seen it as the eye of an uncaring God. Now, it was just the sun struggling to reveal itself in the fog.

His horse ambled on. Padre José didn't think about others who rode this trail or whom he might encounter. His daze was interrupted from time to time only by his rasping cough, occurring more often as the day wore on. The journey from the mission that an ordinary rider could make in a few hours was going to take him the better part of a day.

The cry of a red-tailed hawk soaring overhead roused him. Through a break in the willows lining the shore, he glimpsed a half-dozen dome dwellings that marked a small Indian village about a kilometer from the western bank. No one was about. Was this the village where he had led his last raid a decade before? He sniffed at the wind, smelling the gunpowder the soldiers had discharged that day. He saw dead bodies of Indian men, women and children lying scattered about like broken firewood. The village was a confusion of small fires, split tules, babies wailing.

His horse was moving into the water before he realized that he had unwittingly led the animal away from the river trail toward the Indians' dwellings. No, this was not the village he remembered. That one was on the east side of the river, farther south.

He pulled up on the reins, but the horse moved forward until it had waded into the swift-flowing river. "Stop," he cried and pulled harder on the reins. The horse barely paused. Using all his strength, Padre José tugged again. The horse hesitated. Halted. Let itself be led in a half circle back toward the shore.

The padre breathed heavily as the animal stumbled through naked willow branches until it brought the padre back to the trail. Again, the horse stopped. The padre felt a sharp pain in his chest. The reins dropped from his hand.

The scene at the Indian village played out in his mind again: Mexican soldiers galloping through the village, firing their weapons indiscriminately; old men, women and children falling over, dead. An old woman sprawled in the dirt, her back broken. He saw himself too. Standing on a boulder across a creek, watching it all, his face a mask of rigid complacency.

Why hadn't he stopped the carnage? The raid gave the mission ten or twelve new workers; only a few eventually accepted Christ. How many were left dead in the capture of his prize? And how was he supposed to feel now, a decade later? He searched his mind for answers, but none came.

Little by little, his breathing slowed, the pain diminished. He reached around for the goatskin bag of water, knocking it to the ground before his fingers could grasp it securely. Too weak to retrieve the bag, he urged his horse forward. The animal, obedient again, walked down the trail at its same dogged pace, crossed the San Gabriel River where it joined the Río de Porciúncula.

Padre José exerted the slightest pressure on the reins, his attention drawn inward, concentrating only on the difficulty he had in drawing each breath. His horse moved slowly past swaths of low ground cover, until, finally, the padre glanced up and saw the ranch house ahead.

He was thirsty, his robe spattered with mud. He took off his hat and shook it against his knee with as much force as he could muster. Dust rose from his hat and robe. He rubbed at his face. Dust settled on his hands, collected under his fingernails. The promise of water and warm food drove him forward toward the rancho.

Tilman's most important guest, Thomas Larkin, arrived in midafternoon. By then, the sun had broken through the fog; the sky was a clear, bright blue. For a few hours, temperatures would be mild before they dipped again when the sun went down.

"Hola," Larkin said, as he rode into the courtyard.

"My friend, Mr. Larkin, how good of you to come." Tilman walked quickly forward to greet him. "When did you arrive from Monterey?"

"The packet dropped anchor this morning. I had a little business to do at the harbor, then came directly here." His lips were narrower than Tilman remembered, his pointed chin more prominent. Two Mexican soldiers accompanied him, their boots polished to a high shine.

"Come, my servants have made a bed for you in the parlor. You'll have the room to yourself. You'll be comfortable there." He signaled Scott to take the soldiers to a storeroom being used as a second bunkroom and walked Larkin toward the house. An Indian boy followed with Larkin's bags.

"Quite a spread here," Larkin said, with little enthusiasm.

"We think so." Tilman ignored Larkin's tone. He wasn't going to miss the opportunity to show off his prize to an American.

He led Larkin through the courtyard. Tilman knew that the man couldn't help but be impressed by the tents he must have seen as he rode up, the rows of tables and benches set up for meals with their brightly colored cloths. Everything indicated a large fiesta, as grand as any in Monterey. When Larkin realized how much money Tilman was spending on the week's activities, he would have no doubts that Tilman was a man of importance.

"Are you fond of rodeos and fandangos, Mr. Larkin?" Tilman asked as they passed the shuttered doors of the south wing. No work would take place during the next week, but a blacksmith was on hand in case a horse needed a new shoe, or a vital kitchen implement had to be mended.

"Careful here," Tilman cautioned as they stepped onto the

tiled veranda. Tilman opened the door for his guest and allowed him to enter first.

Shouts echoing from the second floor made Tilman frown. Some of his guests' children must have crept inside to see his daughter while his wife was engaged with other visitors.

"Children," he called. His stern tone left no doubt about what he wanted. Silence followed.

Larkin was already examining the staircase. He ran his hand over the balustrade and traced a strut's edge with his finger. Only then did he follow Tilman into the parlor. Larkin looked around the small room, its bookshelves, brazier, handsome New England furniture. "You've done a good job, Tilman," he said.

But Tilman was already at the top of the stairs. The children escaped down the staircase, each nodding politely to Larkin as they passed.

"Come, Mr. Larkin. I want to show you how nicely we've done the upstairs."

Larkin complied. At Tilman's urging, he peeked into the bedrooms. Tilman opened the door to the balcony. "Let's step outside," he invited.

The day had suddenly come into full sun; it shone in the men's eyes. "You'd see the ocean from here if not for the bank of clouds on the horizon," Tilman offered.

"Yes. A damn beautiful spot, Tilman. Good work. You must be very proud." He walked the length of the balcony and back again, smiling for the first time.

"I am," Tilman admitted. He wondered why he had ever felt the man was cold.

"This house and land will be even more important in the future," Larkin said.

"The future?"

"I'd say that within three years, we'll have independence."

He continued, ignoring Tilman's silence.

"California will become part of the United States.

President Polk's views on expansion are well-known. He'll go after Texas, too, make sure of that." Larkin's enthusiasm grew with every word.

Tilman thought back to the previous year when he had been visited by the Mexican colonel. The man had wanted him to advocate for the Mexican cause in Texas. Tilman had refused to commit himself to either side. He was no closer to declaring his allegiance to either the Mexicans or the Americans today.

"You're sure this will be a good thing for us—I mean, we Americans who are Mexican citizens?" he asked.

"How could it not be? You're an American first, a Mexican second. You'll prosper under an American regime—a well-organized, lawful government."

"Yes," Tilman said politely. He had his doubts. Would landholders and businesspeople get more attention from the United States government than they did from Mexico, and why would that be good for business? It would surely mean more taxes and more laws, if not from distant Washington, then surely from the territorial government.

But look at the colonies and how they had prospered as the United States. Annexation could be a good thing, as Larkin suggested.

Too much to think about now. He let the matter drop.

"Look, you can see the cypress trees. They're not native to this area, but they set off the garden, don't you think?" His attempt at engaging the consul on another topic failed. Tilman saw Larkin fidget with his tie. The two men walked inside and parted, Larkin to make himself comfortable in his new surroundings, Tilman to attend to other guests.

But Tilman could see that he had succeeded in impressing the consul. And Larkin had succeeded in unnerving the landowner. The contest was a draw.

Guests arrived all day: large families, riding up, accepting Tilman's greeting and then, led by Scott or Tilman's brother Edward, settling into their tent sites. The sun grazed the hills of Rancho Palos Verdes to the west by the time Scott was able to take a few minutes to find Big Headed Girl.

Scott looked for her at the ramada but saw only Girl's young son teasing his baby sister. Holding a reed above her head, the boy pulled it away as she raised her arms, laughing. The woman he had come to know as Esar watched the children play. She looked up at Scott.

"The river," she said.

"Thank you." He strode through the courtyard, hoping he wouldn't encounter Tilman. Once he was beyond the rancho's walls, he quickened his pace. This was the time of day when animals—deer, yes, but also mountain lions and bears—converged on the river to drink. Hunters knew that too. The crack of a rifle followed by loud shouts sent him stumbling forward at a trot.

Girl and Tah'hi'ech were at the top of the riverbank. They had stopped to adjust their loads, a bucket of water in each of their hands. Seen from a distance, in their long cotton skirts and rebozos, only their long, straight hair identified them as Indians. Scott slowed to compose himself.

He approached the women, lifting his hat as he had seen Mexican men greet female acquaintances, and fell into step beside them. His offer to carry their buckets would be refused, he was sure, as it had been many times before. He could still hear the sound of men yelling; they had shot a deer, he supposed.

Without speaking, they skirted the edge of the temporary encampments around the sycamore tree, where the voices of men, women and children added to the din. Scott hoped he would not be stopped by anyone who needed his help. But the three were beneath the notice of the guests. Scott breathed in the smell of wood smoke from the camp's fires set here and there.

Laughter rose from one family or another, as they anticipated the week's revels.

As they neared the rancho, Scott clenched and unclenched his jaw. He looked down at the top of Girl's head, noticing her smooth black hair, how it lay against her back and shoulders. He stopped and whispered, "Kah-vo-che," Girl. She had never heard her name pronounced by a white man. He had to say it twice before she looked up at him, surprised.

"Meet me at moonrise. Here." He drew an X with his boot heel in the dirt. They were outside the wall beyond his room, the last room on the south wing.

Girl was silent. He wasn't sure she understood. "Here," he repeated. "Here, when..." He pointed to the sky and slowly raised his outstretched arms until his fingertips met overhead.

Girl's eyebrows drew together. Then, she laughed, comprehending his sign for "rising moon." She looked at the X. Her laugh ended in a gasp. She turned away from Scott and quickened her step. Water sloshed over the rim of her buckets. Tah'hi'ech ran after her.

Girl berated herself as she stumbled past the north wing of the rancho toward the ramada. She'd thought Scott would be occupied the whole day and night. She hadn't expected to see him when she emerged from the trees.

She walked faster, putting more distance between her and Scott, in case he followed her.

"Tomorrow," he had said yesterday when he approached her in the parlor. Tomorrow was here. And now she knew the time and place. The X at moonrise.

She dropped her buckets on the ramada's hard-packed earth. Again, water splashed over the sides. Esar looked up, surprised. Usually, Girl was careful about water, about wasting any supplies. Girl picked up a long-handled spoon and stirred the beans so vigorously that liquid splashed over the pot's edge into the fire. She thought about Scott standing with his arms raised overhead. He looked so strange. For a moment, she had been proud that she understood his sign for moonrise. She had laughed. The sound escaped before she could stop it.

How would Scott understand her laugh? she asked herself. She stirred the beans more slowly. Would he think she was going to meet him, as he wanted?

And would she?

Scott turned the corner into the courtyard where he nearly collided with Padre José, who was leaning on Edward Tilman's arm.

"Padre," he said. "Cómo está usted?"

The question was asked in politeness. When he looked at the man, he didn't need an answer. He had last seen the padre in late summer. In the months since, the padre had suffered a steep decline. A fine dust covered his face and robe; his eyes were half-closed. Tilman's brother was half-supporting, half-carrying him. The padre didn't look as if he was able to stand on his own. He breathed with difficulty, moaning softly with each step.

Padre José looked up at Scott. It was clear the padre didn't remember him.

"I'm Henry Scott, Don Rodrigo's foreman," Scott said. The padre showed no sign of recognition whatsoever.

"Scott, take the padre to the casita near the river. We've put the clergy together there." Edward's customary officious tone meant Scott had to comply.

The courtyard was empty. Soon, it would fill with vaqueros and musicians. Supper for the guests was still hours away, but these men ate early to be ready for the evening. "Shall we go on, padre?" Scott asked.

"Eh?" Padre José said. He looked up at Scott, uncomprehending for a moment. "Yes. Go on." He tripped on a rock as he hobbled forward. Scott caught him before he fell.

"Take my arm, padre," Scott said. He spoke Spanish with some fluency, though with an accent many found difficult to understand.

Together the two men slowly walked back toward the entrance. Scott wondered how the padre would be able to walk the half mile through field and underbrush to the little house. After only a few steps, the man was straining to breathe.

"Don't know. Don't know."

Scott leaned over to hear him. "Don't know what, padre?"

Again, silence. Then, "If. I can. Go. Farther."

A few steps beyond the adobe wall, the padre crumpled against Scott and fell to his knees. He clutched at his chest, fingers pale around the fabric of his robe.

Scott looked around. In spite of all the people in the vicinity—family, guests, vaqueros, musicians—no one came. He picked up the padre in his arms—the man weighed next to nothing—and carried him back into the courtyard. He hesitated. The padre was barely breathing. Scott pushed open the door to his room and gently laid the padre on his bed.

[32]

Who is breathing so hard? the padre wondered. He opened his eyes.

A large man was sitting on a chair next to his bed. No, it was not his bed. He looked around the room and saw the windows...his room had only one window, this one had two. The table...why was there a book on the table, a pen, an inkwell? The trunk in the corner...he didn't need a trunk to store his extra robe.

"Padre, how do you feel?" the man asked.

"Who are...you?" The padre spoke slowly, careful to enunciate each syllable. Every word took effort.

"Henry Scott. The foreman. You were leaning on my arm. You collapsed," Scott answered.

The padre looked at the window over Scott's shoulder. The sky, shortly before sunset, was a clear, deep blue. Warm blue, the blue of his beloved passion flowers. Their dainty skirts lifted slightly, swaying to and fro as if they were involved in a dance.

Faded blue, the blue of the sky in La Mancha, the first time he had tasted pleasure.

"Yes, I remember." Suddenly he wanted to be outside this room; more than anything, he wanted to be surrounded by blue.

He tried to sit up but fell back again, clutching his chest. This time his eyes closed and didn't open.

Minutes passed. Scott waited. Every so often the padre expelled a shallow breath. Scott turned to look out the window. The sky was an intense blue. Soon the blue would pale and then deepen to black. The moon would rise. Big Headed Girl would join him; they would plan their life together.

He looked down at the padre, who clearly needed help. He must find a doctor, or a priest. Someone with more knowledge than he. His chair scraped the hard earth as he stood up.

The padre's eyes flew open. "Where are you going?" he wheezed.

"To find help," Scott said.

"There is no help. Stay with me. Stay with me," the padre pleaded. He grabbed wildly at Scott's arm. His hand grazed Scott's shirt, then fell to his side again. His eyelids drooped shut.

Scott slumped back in his chair. Suddenly, the door opened and Tilman stepped into the room. "I've been looking for you," he said. He followed Scott's eyes to the bed on which the padre lay, still as death.

Tilman reached for the padre's wrist and held it. "Faint pulse. I think. Not for long, I expect. Too bad."

Musicians in the courtyard began to strum their guitars. Lively music meant to entice the guests to dance.

"The fandango is beginning?" Scott asked.

"Too early. No, they're warming up. Playing for each other while they eat supper."

"Oh." Scott was at a loss for words. "Can you find a doctor?"

"My wife knows something about doctoring. I'll tell her to stop by with my brother. I think the man would get more benefit from a priest though."

"Yes." A man who had given his life to God deserved to have last rites.

"I'll tell one of the padres." Tilman beckoned Scott to the corner of the room, away from the bed. "You didn't know the padre well, correct?"

"No, I didn't," Scott answered. "Met him only once, last summer at the mission."

"In that case, I'm going to go ahead with the reason I came to talk to you. Been wanting to tell you all day, but couldn't find the time."

Scott hardly heard him. He looked over Tilman's shoulder at the padre's face. It wore a serene expression. Scott had seen death before. Aunts, uncles, cousins, his trail companion. All had looked fearful.

"Are you listening?"

"Yes." He wasn't.

"Well," Tilman cleared his throat. "You've done a fine job here. Fine job."

"Good," Scott said automatically.

"I have to tell you though..."

Another group of musicians began to play, then another. Enclosed between the rancho's walls, the sound grew so loud, Scott could barely hear his employer.

Tilman raised his voice. "You've built the house, and that's why I engaged you. I mean, it was understood that you were the foreman of the ranch only during construction," Tilman said. Scott had never been aware of that understanding. Nevertheless, his attention was focused on Padre José.

Thinking he saw the padre move, Scott took a step toward him, putting himself closer to Tilman. Tilman stepped back.

"It's time for Felipe to take over," Tilman continued.

No, the padre's eyes were still closed. Scott could see the faint rise and fall of his chest.

"Did you hear me?" Tilman asked.

"What?"

"Felipe will take over. You'll have to go."

"What?" Something was wrong. A man was dying. What had Tilman said? He shook his head as if to clear his mind.

"I won't repeat myself." Tilman's temper flared. He had

done what needed to be done and now wanted only to leave. "Stay with the padre. I'll pay you for this week and give you something extra besides. Felipe doesn't have to move in until the guests have left at the end of the week."

Tilman clapped Scott on the shoulder. "I'll send my wife and a priest," he said as he left the room.

Padre José heard the murmuring of the two men as the buzzing of bees: annoying, distracting but nothing he could do anything about. His eyes closed, he concentrated on the color he had seen through the window.

Azure sky became sapphire ocean—a welcoming calm, not the cold blue-green of the angry sea he remembered. He felt himself rocked gently to and fro by the currents.

Overhead, the sky was an equally intense blue.

And who was that? Could it be...could it...?

He smelled the sweet perfume of roses. He held his breath. The blue of her cloak. The Virgin of Guadalupe was near.

His mother's face, drained of color, appeared before his closed eyes. He saw her as she had looked after she died, lying on their only bed, engulfed by the blood of childbirth, her long black hair drawn back from her stricken face. Her pale face wore a bluish tint, a contrast to the dark hand she held at her breast.

The image faded. Now, he saw a line of Indians, who stood, facing him, their backs to the river, which flowed an impenetrable blue-black. A line so long it stretched from ocean to mountains. Every one of them, men, women and children stared at him, reproach in their dark eyes.

Where was the Virgin? Where were his father, Tomo and Teo? Where was Jaime? Still, the blue persisted.

He tried to turn his face toward the window, toward the blue, but he could not.

The light dimmed. After a time, it went out.

Engrossed in her kitchen tasks, absorbed by thoughts of Scott—meet him...don't meet him...marry him...don't marry him—Girl hadn't noticed night coming on, the last streaks of color in the sky. She stepped outside the ramada. Not yet moonrise. There was still time to decide.

She felt a hand on her arm. She whirled around and found herself face to face with Koovahcho. Instinctively, she looked around for her children. Koo'ar was chattering to Esar in a corner of the ramada. Tah'hi'ech was bringing baby Tach'i toward her; the young girl stopped when she saw Koovahcho. Indian servers ran past the couple holding empty platters and bowls; others rushed from the ramada with full plates. Even feeding the musicians and vaqueros needed the efforts of many people.

Girl looked at her husband. "Why did you come here? Where are your woman and child?" She spit the words out, surprised by her anger. In the months since she had seen him, she told herself he had gone back to drinking, was dead, had left his new woman as he had left her— and each time forced him out of her mind. She would never see him again. What was the use of thinking about him?

But Koovahcho didn't look as if he had been drinking. His long hair was clean. He wore pants and a zarape, both spotless though worn. She looked at his hand on her arm. His fingers were long and tapered. She didn't remember ever looking at his hands.

"Where is your *woman*?" Girl repeated.

"She is dead. The birth of our child..."

"Girl." Achanchah's daughter called to her. "We need your help." She placed a platter in Girl's hands. "Fill this with meat."

Girl saw Koo'ar watching her. She hadn't noticed before how much he resembled Koovahcho. Same foxlike nose. Same narrow eyes. He was looking at Koovahcho. Only six moons had rounded since he had seen his father. Perhaps the child remembered him, Girl thought.

"I must work," Girl said, firmly.

"I will wait."

"No."

He took the platter from Achanchah's daughter's hands, began to heap it with slices of meat.

Just like him, Girl thought. He never knows what is women's work and what is men's. But she went back to her task, peeling oranges, arranging the golden segments on a platter.

Needing no one to tell him, Koovahcho removed trays of flan from a grill over a low fire. He set them on a rock outside the ramada to cool.

Koo'ar began to cry. Without speaking, Koovahcho took Girl's place arranging the oranges. She stepped aside to put the baby to her breast.

A long table needed to be moved. Koovahcho wiped the orange juice from his hands and helped three men move the table to one side.

"Come. We must bring a wine cask from the carreta," said one of the men. Koovahcho left with them. The baby was asleep when he returned. Koo'ar was curled up on the ground, also asleep, near the fire.

"The moon is full and bright," Koovahcho told Girl after he and the other men set down the wine cask.

Girl suddenly remembered: the X at moonrise.

"Where is the moon?" she asked.

"In the sky. Where would you expect it to be?" Koovahcho said. The conversation reminded Girl of how they had argued when they first met.

"Tell me, where is it in the sky? Has it just risen? Is it high in the sky?"

"Let's step outside and look. Please," he added, as she opened her mouth to refuse.

She followed him out from under the ramada's roof.

They walked behind the kitchen where the moon was easy to see. A glowing white disk, suspended above the branches of the old sycamore tree. Moonlight illuminated the plain. Girl could make out the shapes of the distant mountains. She knew that toward the west flowed the great river. She knew the names of all the birds and animals that slept or hunted beneath the moon. All the grasses that grew on the plain, all the plants that would flower in the wet season and the dry. She breathed in the salt smell of moist sea air. If she listened hard, if the night were still, she would hear waves crash against the shore.

"Girl," Koovahcho said. "I want you to come with me."

"Now I know you are out of your mind. Why would I do that?" Girl's voice was full of scorn, but she felt less sure than she sounded.

"I have a child, a little boy...," Koovahcho said.

"Oh? So you want me to raise your child?"

Koovahcho persisted. "I work at the pueblo church. I live there. You and the children could live with me. It is humble, but the padre is kind."

"What do you do at the church?" Girl was curious about who would hire this man.

"I work in the kitchen. I serve the padre. Sometimes, I fix things that are broken in the church."

"What do you know about a kitchen? Besides, that's women's work."

"I served the padre at San Gabriel Mission."

"You did?" Girl turned toward him. "I never knew that."

"I was ashamed to tell you."

The music coming from the courtyard filled the air: the whine of violins against a thrum of guitars.

Koovahcho stepped forward and back as he had seen at a fandango in the pueblo.

"What are you doing?" Girl asked.

"I am dancing," he replied.

"You're an Indian," she hissed.

Koovahcho stopped moving. "I was wrong. I left you and our children. I will not leave you again."

Girl adjusted the rebozo around her shoulders. Her daughter sighed in her sleep. For a moment, the music stopped. Off to the east, Girl heard an owl screech. A fast flutter of wings. Her body felt light as if she, too, were poised for flight.

"If you say no, I will go away," Koovahcho said. "I promise I will not return."

One day—it felt like long ago—Koovahcho had asked her to marry him. She had nearly refused but at the last instant had changed her mind.

Scott sat beside the padre, adrift. The padre had died with only Scott to attend him. No friend to hold his hand. No priest to give him last rites.

And Tilman had told Scott to leave, the end of his life at the ranch.

Music rose and fell outside his door. Children's high-pitched calls sounded amid loud voices, raucous laughter.

Maybe Tilman's visit had been part of his state of mind as the padre died. Maybe he had imagined Tilman in his room, and the man had not been there at all.

He turned and looked through the window. The moon was well above the horizon.

Scott placed his fingers lightly on the padre's eyelids and closed the man's eyes. The body was already getting cold. Assuring himself he could leave now, he opened the door.

In front of him lay a scene he knew would please Don Rodrigo Tilman.

The dancing had begun. Women in low-cut gowns, lace mantillas in their hair, danced with men wearing short-jacketed suits, the wool as fine as Tilman's. Their bright cumberbunds flashed as they raised their arms to twirl a partner or lean over as they two-stepped along.

Looking past the guests to the east end of the courtyard, Scott saw Tilman, his arm on Felipe's shoulder. They were talking to Thomas Larkin. There was no doubt. What he had heard Tilman say was real.

He pulled his hat lower on his head, strode out of the courtyard at its west end. Beyond the rancho's wall was the X he had marked for Big Headed Girl a few hours before. Resting on his haunches, he peered down at the figure. The mark was untouched. No one had stood there. No one had disturbed the dirt around it. The lines were as clear as when he had scratched them into the earth.

He stood. The moon had cleared the tallest branches of the sycamore tree. A full moon, startlingly white in a cold black sky.

He walked toward the tree.

Through the low grass.

Between the temporary settlements of the party guests.

He rested his hand against the tree. The lower branches grazed his head. From this angle, he couldn't see the moon and didn't look for it.

Acknowledgements

Although I, like all writers, am responsible for the words on the page, a book is a collective effort. I want to gratefully acknowledge all the people who helped bring *When Water Was Everywhere* to print.

My deepest thanks go to my writing group: our inspirational, learned teacher, the writer Holly Prado Northup, and fellow writers—Marie Pal-Brown, Cecilia Woloch, Kathy Lazarus, Toni Fuhrman, Joan Isaacson, Marlene Saile, Rae Wilken, Mary Ann McFadden, Jill Singer, Pamela Shandel, Toke Hoppenbrouwers and Linda Berg—for their invaluable critique every week.

Research help came from sources all around the Los Angeles area and beyond. Closest to my Long Beach home were Steve Iverson, historical curator for the City of Long Beach, whom I thank for his hours of patience with my questions about Rancho Los Cerritos, and Ellen Calomiris, the rancho's executive director, for overseeing informative programs on local history. Larry Rich, Sustainability Coordinator for the City of Long Beach, gave freely from his rich grasp of local history and geography. I learned about native plants from Meaghan O'Neill, Long Beach Nature Center naturalist, and from visiting the Nature Center many times. I found the speaker series organized by Claudia Jurmain at Rancho Los Alamitos to be both instructive and inspiring. My thanks to her and to Pamela Seager, the executive director of Rancho Los Alamitos.

Thank you also to Glen Creason, map librarian for the Los Angeles Public Library, and to Alan Jutzi, Chief Curator of Rare Books, and his assistant, Anita Weaver, at the Huntington Library. Additional thanks to the St. Louis Historical Society, which helped me locate books about 19th century St. Louis.

I owe a great debt of gratitude to Cindy Alvitre, Tongva tribal elder and director of the Ti'at Society, for accompanying me on this journey from the beginning, reading two drafts of the manuscript and giving generously of her time and knowledge. Thank you to Richard Heller for sharing his knowledge of horses and riders; Neil MacMinn and John Velasquez for their fruitful discussions of Catholicism; to Natalie Richardson, speech therapist, for her guidance on Brother Antonio's impairment; to Joe Linton for information about the Los Angeles River; to Michael J. Hart, for his artistic maps of the Mission San Gabriel and its water sources; and to Lewis MacAdams, founder and director of Friends of the Los Angeles River (FoLAR), whose work awakened me to a vision of the river's past and future.

I consulted several hundred original and secondary sources in my research. Among the most helpful were *The First Angelinos* by William McCauley; *Chinigchinich*, Father Boscana's text annotated by J.P. Harrington; *St. Louis: An Informal History of the City and its People, 1764-1865*; and *Thrown Among Strangers* by Douglas Monroy.

Holly Prado Northup, Frances Woods and Toni Fuhrman edited the book at different stages, offering valuable suggestions. Glenna Morrison became my indispensable go-to person for website development, the publication process and much more. Thanks to Lagoon House Press for their encouragement and support. Finally, thank you to my husband, who obligingly became my research assistant, all-around information expert, technical support and sometime-driver. I'm grateful that he shares my introvert's love for spending whole days sitting in front of a computer.

To my children and grandchildren and all my friends, thank you for giving me the experiences and diversions I needed to keep going on this long project.

Barbara Crane
January 2016

CPSIA information can be obtained
at www.ICGtesting.com
Printed in the USA
LVOW08s2328300417
532800LV00001B/275/P

9 780997 260908